TALES OF THE
SHADOWMEN
Volume 13: Sang Froid

TALES OF THE
SHADOWMEN

Volume 13: Sang Froid

edited by
Jean-Marc & Randy Lofficier

stories by
**Jason Scott Aiken, Matthew Baugh, Adam Mudman Bezecny,
Nicholas Boving, Nathan Cabaniss, Matthew Dennion, Brian
Gallagher, Martin Gately, Travis Hiltz, Paul Hugli, Rick Lai,
Nigel Malcolm, Christofer Nigro, John Peel, Frank Schildiner,
Sam Shook, Michel Stéphan, David L. Vineyard**
and **Jared Welch**

translations by
Jean-Marc & Randy lofficier

cover by
Michel Borderie

A Black Coat Press Book

ISBN 978-1-61227-578-9. First Printing. December 2016. Published by Black Coat Press, an imprint of Hollywood Comics.com, LLC, P.O. Box 17270, Encino, CA 91416. All rights reserved. Except for review purposes, no part of this book may be reproduced or transmitted in any form or by any means, electronic or mechanical, including photocopying, recording or by any information storage and retrieval system, without permission in writing from the publisher. The stories and characters depicted in this anthology are entirely fictional. Printed in the United States of America.

Table of Contents

We open this volume with an exotic tale harking back to the days when Deepest Africa could always be relied upon to provide lush backdrops filled with strange cities and forgotten races. Jason Scott Aiken makes good use of characters and set pieces created by H. Rider Haggard (some of them updated by Philip José Farmer), many of which will be easily identified by our faithful readers. They may not recognize, however, the Queen of Kisimbasimba, the so-called "enchanted city" that is the location of Eugene Hennebert's eponymous 1885 novel published two years ago by Black Coat Press (ISBN 978-1-61227-345-7)...

Jason Scott Aiken: *Galazi in the Enchanted City*

*The twenty-sixth day of uMasingana,
in the one-thousand-eight-hundred-thirty-sixth year of the Amaboona,
The Plateau of Nyonngo, Central Africa*

It had been many moons since Galazi the Wolf had ventured out of the haunted forest on the slope of Ghost Mountain. The king of the ghost-wolves had never traveled so far north before, but, in this instance, he had little choice. For he was hunting killers.

Three members of his spectral wolf pack had been butchered, their remains left to rot on the outskirts of the forest, which wasn't far from the village of the People of the Axe, of which his wolf-brother Umsloplogaas was chief.

A part of Galazi wished he had delayed his pursuit and sought out his brother's aid. But from the condition of the butchers' spoor, they already had a significant lead on him. Hence, the Wolf made haste out of the haunted forest and set off in pursuit, traveling light, wearing his black wolf-skin with streaks of grey near the head and flanks, and carrying his iron-shod war club, the Watcher of the Fords.

Now, after many days of tracking, Galazi had finally located his prey on a vast plateau. The Moon hung high in the cloudless sky, illuminating the three men huddled around a fire. They were seated beneath the only tree in sight, a large baobab with a thick trunk and wide canopy.

The black warriors were broad of hip, with heavily muscled torsos and thin legs. They wore their hair flat and draped themselves in the skins of leopards. Galazi gritted his teeth as he noticed the trio also donned wolf-skin capes, for he was certain of their source. The Wolf recognized the men as members of the Orma people and concluded they must be some type of scouting party. They appeared to be making camp for the evening, and it was Galazi's intent that they wouldn't see the next morning.

Knowing the lack of cover on the plateau would nullify a stealth approach,

Galazi opted to openly challenge the Ormas, for the king of the ghost-wolves was a mighty warrior. The Wolf had the same blood coursing through his veins as the mighty Chaka, the late king of the Zulu people, as well as the current monarch Dingaan. For Siguyana, Galazi's grandfather, was a younger brother of Senzangacona, the father of Chaka and Dingaan.

The Wolf casually approached the Orma's campfire, raised the Watcher of the Fords above his head and roared:

"Butchers! Killers! Galazi the Wolf has come to avenge his kin! Take up your weapons and die!"

Startled, the Ormas hastened to their feet. All three warriors were dressed for battle. From a shorter distance, Galazi now noticed their bodies were smeared with blue, white, and red paint, and they were wearing green pigeon feathers in their hair. Each man was armed with a short handled assegai in his right hand, and wore an elliptical-shaped buckler made of buffalo hide on his left forearm.

The largest among them, their commander, paused for a moment and studied the Wolf with a set of penetrating eyes before responding roughly in Galazi's native Zulu tongue:

"A dog seems to have wandered far from his home. Do you truly blame us for killing and eating those mongrels in the forest? Tell me, how many beasts have you slain and feasted upon while you hunted us, dog?"

Galazi's grip tightened on his war club. "Enough to survive; however those wolves you butchered weren't truly beasts. They were once men! More than that, I considered them kin!"

The king of the ghost-wolves howled and bounded toward the commander, aiming to bring the Watcher down on his skull. The burly warrior would have surely died at that moment if it hadn't been for his comrades converging on him, raising their bucklers to block the Wolf's strike.

The scout on Galazi's left flank stabbed at him with his assegai, but the Wolf side-stepped the thrust and spun clockwise, bringing around the Watcher and crushing the side of the man's skull. A torrent of blood and brains splashed on the two remaining Ormas.

Galazi roared in triumph and raised his war club over his head once more, attempting to bludgeon the skull of the scout on his right, but his blow was checked by the warrior's buckler at the last moment.

The Wolf noticed the commander cocking back his assegai for a thrust and had just enough time to launch a kick at the big man's right thigh. The Wolf's calloused heel dug deep into the flesh and caused the quadriceps muscle to spasm then contract, sending the commander to the ground.

While the Wolf was distracted, the remaining scout rammed his buckler into Galazi's face, dazing him. The Orma then attempted to skewer him in the stomach with his assegai, but Galazi recovered just in time to parry the oncoming blow with his war club. The Watcher of the Fords not only parried it, but broke the sharp ace of spades-shaped tip of the short stabbing spear cleanly off.

Galazi knew the scout was now easy prey and began to ferociously hammer on his buckler with the Watcher. Alternating between powerful overhead and side swings, Galazi quickly wore the scout down enough that he caused the man to make a grave error in the positioning of his shield. Galazi brought the Watcher over his head causing the scout to block high, then the Wolf brought the weapon back and attacked from below instead, delivering an uppercut-like swing. The iron-shod war club struck the scout squarely on the chin, launching his head back so hard and fast his neck snapped. He was dead before his body hit the grass.

Galazi felt the air shift behind him just in time to lean forward so the leader's assegai thrust scraped his back rather than impaling him. But the Wolf was now wounded and grew even more infuriated. The Orma leader was still favoring the leg that Galazi had attacked earlier and, like all wolves who spot wounded prey, Galazi bore his fangs and attacked. The king of the ghost-wolves howled and unleashed a flurry of blows on the shield of the giant Orma. The commander was a mighty foe, proving himself stronger than the other men, as he was able to check Galazi's blows far easier than his subordinates.

It wasn't the strength of the Orma commander that gave out that night, it was his buckler, which Galazi split in half with a thunderous stroke. The Watcher went clean through the commander's shield and crushed the shards of his nasal bones back into his brain, slaying him.

Galazi roared and lifted his club to the heavens:

"Victory! Sleep well, my brothers! I have avenged you!"

After defeating three formidable opponents and sustaining a light injury, Galazi deemed the Orma's camp was a suitable place to rest for the night. He helped himself to some ointments for the cut on his back as well as gourds of fresh water. The Wolf didn't dare to eat their meat, not wanting to possibly ingest the remnants of his own kin.

It was while crouching by the flames of the campfire that Galazi managed his first good look at the trunk of the enormous baobab tree and the objects surrounding it.

Flanking the massive trunk were severed heads, scalps, and skulls, white as ivory, displayed on long spear shafts sunk into the earth. However, it was the strange carvings on the trunk that truly captured Galazi's attention. The images depicted three beings: Loubari, the devil, Mgoussa, the evil spirit, and Mousammmouria, the hobgoblin. They were known to the local tribes as the demons of Lake Tanganyika. Galazi, being an outsider, had no knowledge of their names, but he was certain they were not to be trifled with. He decided it would be best to start his journey home, back to the Ghost Mountain and away from the domain of this unsettling trinity.

Just as Galazi finished this thought, a strange whirring sound began to carry across the plateau, growing increasingly louder. He turned his attention to the northern horizon and could just barely make out figures scurrying about in the darkness. He grabbed the Watcher of the Fords and had snatched up a gourd to dose the fire with water, when the noise ceased. The next thing he knew, his head felt like it was on fire and blood was streaming into his eyes. He clutched his skull and fell to the ground. Through his crimson-stained vision, he could make out a group of armed men approaching him before he lost consciousnesses.

Galazi couldn't be certain of how long he lay on the wooden stretcher, as he continuously drifted in and out of consciousness. Each time the Wolf awoke, he only had a few seconds to gain his bearings before he passed out again. One thing was quite clear, though: he was fastened to the stretcher and unable to move his limbs.

Galazi eventually gained a better understanding of who his captors were, not by looking at them, but by listening. The Wolf was unable to understand their speech, but he could tell by the timbre of their voices that these weren't men who captured him, but women. He gritted his teeth and tightened his fists in rage, for Galazi greatly mistrusted the opposite sex. It had been a woman who poisoned and murdered his father in the *kraal* of the Halakazi, and it was another woman by the name of Zinita, who currently poisoned the heart of his brother Umslopogaas.

From his brief glances at these fierce women, Galazi could tell they were no ordinary maidens. Their bodies were composed of lean, powerful-looking muscle and they wore no elaborate decorations, only loincloths and garments of antelope hide on their torsos. Stoic looks seemed to be permanently carved on their chiseled faces. They numbered around twenty, each of them carrying long iron-tipped spears and round iron-shod bucklers.

The Wolf took note of a leather sling looped through the loincloth of the warrior maiden immediately to his left and realized the cause of his current condition. His skull began to throb at this revelation and he drifted away into unconsciousness once again.

The next time Galazi opened his eyes, it seemed at least a full day had passed. The Sun was beginning its descent and he could make out a massive walled structure in the distance. A large body of choppy green water was visible behind it. The Wolf had never seen a fortress as vast or as spectacular as this. With its towering walls, it had no equal in Swaziland or Zululand.

Unless his sharp eyes were deceiving him, a pair of weathered stone lions stood sentinel atop its high gate. A sudden roar from the direction of the fortress seemed to confirm this. Then the cries of other animals echoed across the plateau. The calls of wolves, leopards, and elephants all seemed to be emanating from the fortress as well. Galazi's already clouded mind became overwhelmed with this additional stimuli and he lost consciousness once more.

The next time Galazi awakened it was to a sight almost beyond his comprehension. The Moon was shining its light on tall stone buildings spread out in all directions.

The Wolf was able to deduce from the high walls along the city's perimeter that he was within the large structure he had seen from the plateau. The same animal sounds filled the air, but they were accompanied by other beasts as well, some of which Galazi wasn't able to identify. He also discerned the buzzing of bees coming from behind him, but was unable to turn in that direction.

Galazi put his chin to his chest and strained to look ahead of him. The women were taking him toward a large, triangular-shaped structure. Resting at the building's peak was a grey stone sphere with a colossal one-winged woman standing atop of it. She was missing her arms, but the rest of her body was still intact and very lovely. The moonlight shone across the beautiful marble woman in a way that filled even Galazi's breast with awe. However, he had no intention of entering such a strange place and strained against the bonds holding him. The butt of a spear thrust into his chin knocked him unconscious before he could make even a hint of progress.

A cold torrent of water to the face caused Galazi to awaken. He was lying on a cold stone floor and his hands were tied behind his back. Directly in front of him was a young black-skinned woman resting comfortably on a piece of furniture with four short curved posts at its corners, with knobs at their ends. Her face was pleasant, and her body was lean and supple. She was outfitted in decorative royal trappings.

Flanking her were fifty male warriors with red hawk feathers in their hair. Each of them was a superbly muscled physical specimen. They brandished iron hand-axes and the same iron-shod bucklers as the female warrior maidens. These well-built men didn't dress very masculine, though. They dressed as women, wearing skirts and elaborate ornaments on their bodies.

At the young woman's feet were five male lions. The huge beasts were lounging about and licking their paws. Three were of the usual tawny color, but there was also a black and golden one. The golden one never took his eyes off Galazi.

The maiden adjusted her position on the couch and spoke in perfect Zulu:

"Greetings, Galazi the Wolf. Welcome to Kisimbasimba, my family's summer retreat."

Galazi scoffed, "Save your greetings, girl! Return my belongings and release me!"

"I'm afraid I can't do that, Wolf. A special adviser of mine has need of you."

"What does a young maid like yourself need with an adviser? Where is your chief? Let me speak with your father! Or am I mistaken and you're no maiden? If so, I'll speak to your husband at once!"

The maiden leaned forward and Galazi noted a cold look fall across her beautiful face. "It is indeed a maiden you look upon, Wolf, but no ordinary one. I am Queen Touloumia of Mkinyaga! You've already been felled by my soldiers on the Plateau of Nyonngo, and now your gaze falls on my bodyguards and pets. Given this display, I trust you'll be on your best behavior until the time comes for you to meet Nomma."

"Nomma? I imagine he's the adviser you speak of?"

"*She* is one of my advisers, yes. But Nomma isn't ready to see you yet. Now, since I've already taken the liberty of having the wounds on your back and head treated, may I interest you in something to eat or drink?"

"So you can poison me? Girl, you must think me a fool! Enough of this, I demand you return what is mine and allow me to leave this place! If not, you'll pay greatly for it later!"

Queen Touloumia rose to her feet and approached Galazi. She grasped him by the throat and he felt the strength of her long fingers penetrate into his flesh. "Your threats mean nothing to me, Wolf. Nomma has informed me you're a prodigious fighter and are of the same bloodline as the mighty Zulu kings, but the empire of my ancestors would make Zululand look like a mere *kraal* in comparison. Long ago, my nation's capital of Akribanza, was just one of a hundred cities in the vast empire of Kôr. My predecessors carved out a domain that spanned the entire continent itself! Your people can't even conquer the white men who seek to settle in the south!"

Queen Touloumia pushed Galazi away and released her stiff grip. "Take him below and place him in a cell for the evening. He can see Nomma on an empty stomach tomorrow morning."

Two of her bodyguards grabbed Galazi beneath his armpits and led him away. The Wolf did his best to fight back, kicking and baring his teeth at them, but a blow to the back of his head put an end to such resistance.

When Galazi awoke the next morning, he was face down in the damp dirt of his cell. Once again the sounds of animals filled his ears.

He rose to his feet, his hands still bound behind him, and walked to the iron bars to get a better understanding of his surroundings. Galazi realized he was in some sort of subterranean cavern system, similar to the stronghold of the Halakazi people that his father had taken him to as a boy. The Wolf was only able to view a small portion of it through the bars, but it was apparent by the steady stream of wildlife passing by, that the underground tunnels must be quite large. Lions, wolves, black ostriches, and other beasts all eyed Galazi as they passed his cell.

After what seemed like hours to the Wolf, several of Queen Touloumia's strapping bodyguards came and retrieved him. Galazi didn't resist this time; he wanted to be in the best condition possible when he met this Nomma and couldn't afford another blow to the head. He allowed the guards to guide him through the systems of caverns and tunnels as he calmly observed his surroundings. This included the detailed bas-reliefs on the cavern walls.

One image in particular caught Galazi's attention. It depicted a seated man holding a knife in his right hand with a bow resting on his lap. He was also wearing a circular medallion. A war drum was positioned on the ground to the man's left and at his feet were a dog and a goat. To the man's right was a lion sticking out its tongue.

Touloumia's bodyguards pushed Galazi forward before he could make further inspection of the image and continued guiding him through the catacombs. They took him through several grottoes where the wildlife drank and feasted at leisure. It soon became clear to the Wolf that the people of Kisimbasimba, the beasts, and the subterranean caverns, all existed in harmony with one and other.

When the guards arrived at a dead end, they forced Galazi to halt. Their leader approached the adjoining wall, pressed his hand into a hollow and twisted it. Galazi heard strange clicking and grinding sounds, and then the rock wall in front of him slid upward, revealing another grotto. At first, it seemed no different than the others, but when the Wolf looked to the center he realized this was no ordinary place.

While the majority of the cavern was composed of ordinary stone, the clear rocks surrounding the green pool of water in its center were quite different. These stones had the appearance of crystals and curved slightly up and out of the floor, creating a large natural basin for the subterranean waters to rest in. Galazi stared at the smooth, glittering stones in awe, but when his eyes fell on her, the Wolf felt only dread.

Nomma was seated between two torches at the opposite edge of the pool, her legs submerged in the green water out of Galazi's sight. The woman's appearance made the hair on the Wolf's neck bristle. Her skin was of a dark green hue and scale-like in texture. The only garments she wore to cover her obese body were a large bronze brassiere and loincloth. There wasn't a hair visible on either her body or head. The Wolf was unable to view her face, as it was wrapped in moist cloth bandages, leaving only her yellow eyes and wide mouth visible. Galazi noticed three red slits running horizontally on both sides of her neck.

Nomma moved her lower body side to side, causing the waters to ripple. She smiled at Galazi, showing a mouth full of sharp teeth akin to a tigerfish. She spoke in Galazi's native Zulu tongue, but in a strange accent:

"Ah, he is a buck indeed! The waters didn't lie! Yes, the blood of the Grey-Eyed Wanderer is evident in this one." Nomma paused and began peering around the grotto. "Where is the queen?" she demanded.

"I'm here, Mistress of the Waters. My apologies for the delay."

Galazi turned to see Queen Touloumia entering the hidden grotto. Rather than her royal trappings of the previous evening, she was now garbed in the same martial attire as the warrior maidens wore. In her right hand was a long ceremonial staff wrapped tightly in white cloth. Shuffling behind the queen was an elderly white-bearded man carrying in his arms Galazi's black wolf-skin and the Watcher.

"No need to apologize. I was just getting acquainted with the Wolf. Speaking of which, there's no need for him to be bound any longer." Nomma flexed the stubby fingers on her right hand and the cords fastening Galazi's wrists slackened and fell to the floor.

The Wolf made use of this opportunity to lunge at the old man holding the Watcher. Seeing this, Nomma quickly reached out with her right arm. Galazi came within a foot of reclaiming his weapon before stopping suddenly.

Nomma made a fist and pulled it back toward her voluminous body. Galazi's right hand fell to his side unexpectedly, then he turned and walked to the water's edge against his own volition. Touloumia circled around the crystal basin and joined Nomma on the opposite side, a mischievous grin fell across the queen's fair face.

Touloumia laughed and spoke:

"Now you see the power of Nomma, Mistress of the Waters, Wolf. Don't feel inadequate, for she possesses powers of another world. All of the prophecies she's made since her coming nine moons past have borne fruit. Including your arrival beneath the great tree on the plateau. By her aid, the empire of Kôr will rise once more!"

"I care not for other worlds or empires, girl. Release me from your witch's thrall at once! I must return home to my pack!"

Before Touloumia could respond, Nomma interjected, "Oh I'm afraid we can't allow you to leave, Wolf. It's true that you're a fine buck, but as far as our long-term plans go, you're merely bait for the bull."

"Cease your riddles, witch! Speak plainly for my patience is lost!" roared Galazi.

"Very well. In order for the empire of Kôr to thrive once again, it will need not only a strong queen, but a virile king as well. Yes, a tree must have strong roots, Wolf. You would make a fine mate for Touloumia, but there is one other who would be better yet. Oh yes, the blood of the Grey-Eyed Wanderer flows through him most strongly, as it does in Touloumia. You know him well. He wields the iron-headed axe Inkosikaas, the iron Chieftainess, also known as Groan-Maker. The man himself is known by many names including Woodpecker and Bulalio the Slaughterer."

Galazi sucked in his breath through his clenched teeth. "You know of my brother Umslopogaas?"

Nomma nodded. "I know all, Wolf."

"Then you should know he'll never journey this far north. He's chief of the People of the Axe and has no reason to leave the village."

"Oh, he has reasons. Three reasons to be precise. I'm looking at one as we

14

speak."

"Never! I refuse to play any part in this, witch."

"You have no choice. Touloumia will send an emissary south to the village of the People of the Axe, bearing your wolf-skin and club." Nomma turned to the young queen, "Make sure it's someone expendable. For your future husband will no doubt peck a hole in the messenger's forehead with Groan-Maker once the message has been delivered." Nomma then turned her attention back to Galazi. "You know your brother better than anyone. Once the Slaughterer knows you're in danger, he'll come north to save you. As soon as Bulalio bears witness to Touloumia's youthful beauty, learns of the lands she holds, and hears the promise of ruling an empire that dwarfs even the Zulu, he'll marry her without question. You know it to be true. I've seen it clearly in the waters myself. Perhaps it's time you saw the power of the waters too, Wolf. Gaze upon them and witness what the blood of the Grey-Eyed Wanderer is capable of."

The witch opened her right hand and lowered her palm toward the floor, causing Galazi's gaze to fall on the green waters below.

Galazi peered into the green waters of the crystal basin, but saw nothing. A moment passed before the Wolf noticed the surface becoming cloudy. He fixed his keen eyes on the center of the large pool where an image was forming.

A blistering sun shined overhead. On a rocky mountainside, a muscled bronze-skinned youth was breaking the back of a large black leopard over his knee. Galazi couldn't help but notice the rage on the young man's contorted face before the image disappeared and another replaced it.

In what appeared to be an underground tunnel system, a bronze-skinned swordsman battled several soldiers wearing armor emblazoned with yellow suns. His sword was most unusual. Its blade was slightly curved and came to a blunt, flat end rather than a point. A laughing bearded giant wielding a double-headed axe was flying through the air behind the swordsman to join the fray. It was clear to Galazi that the swordsman and the giant were kin. Once again the water became cloudy and the image changed.

Another bronze-skinned young man, who bore quite the resemblance to the swordsman, held a black iron-shod scepter high in the air, while a one-eyed white-skinned dwarf looked on proudly. The scepter had a large white figure resting atop its round sphere. The eye-catching ornament appeared to be the same winged woman the Wolf saw depicted earlier on the roof of the temple but in a complete state. Galazi took a second look at the scepter and a surge of familiarity raced through his mind. But the waters changed before he could study it further.

The next image depicted a stone city on the shores of a blue lake. Galazi recognized it as Kisimbasimba but in much earlier days, for there were no high walls hiding it from the view. Approaching the city from across the great plateau was a bronze-skinned man dressed in nothing but a loincloth. He wore an iron knife on his right hip and a medallion around his neck. The man had a bow in his hand and a quiver of arrows on his back. At his sides were a lion and a dog. Behind them were countless other animals including goats, ostriches, elephants, wolves, leopards, rhinoceroses, and additional lions. The image faded before Galazi could catalog all of the animals, but he recognized the stranger as the same person depicted in the bas-relief he studied while traveling through the caverns.

The next image was that of a tall, grim white man in some sort of tomb. He was dressed all in black save for the green sash tied about his waist. The hawk-faced man wielded a wooden staff that came to a sharp point on its end and sported a cat-head decorating its top. Strange symbols were carved into its surface. He was locked in combat with a shapeless crimson horror. Galazi shuddered at the sight of it, and this time, was glad to see the image change so swiftly.

The new picture was a familiar sight. It showed Galazi wielding the Watcher of the Fords fighting back to back with Umslopogaas wielding Groan-Maker. They were battling the sons of Jikiza the Unconquered, who was chief of the People of the Axe and wielded the iron-headed axe before Umslopogaas slew him. Galazi remembered this night well for he and Umslopogaas were victorious against the ten challengers. As a smile began to form on Galazi's face, the scene faded.

At the center of the new image was a bearded bronzed-giant with wild hair, who looked a great deal like the giant in the earlier image, wielding a short-hafted axe and a round shield. Flying through the air above the colossal warrior was a grizzled-haired black man, gaunt and grey with age. The older man had a dent in his forehead near his left temple. Galazi took note of the weapon in the hands of this seasoned warrior and unless he was mistaken, the long-hafted iron-headed axe that was sweeping down toward the back of the giant's skull was none other than Inkosikaas. The image changed before Galazi could study the old warrior further and confirm his suspicions regarding his identity.

The next scene depicted a subterranean temple. A black-skinned warrior wielded the same strange type of sword as the bronze-skinned swordsman had in the earlier image. Fighting by his side was a grey-haired white man using an iron-headed hand axe and a robed bronze-skinned giant with close-cropped hair using only his bare hands. The three were battling a group of hairy beastly looking creatures near a giant glistening crystalline stalk. Just as Galazi's mind began making the connection between the strange plant and the crystal basin, the image faded.

Galazi continued staring at the green water, but no further images appeared on its surface. His head rose involuntarily and he locked eyes with Nomma once again.

"Now that you've seen the secrets the water holds of past and future, what do you say, Wolf?" queried Nomma conceitedly.

"Do you think this is the first time I've seen sorcery at work, witch? Had black wizardry frightened me, I wouldn't have survived my first trek up Ghost Mountain into the lap of the stone Witch. I'm not impressed. Take your magic and choke on it."

Nomma shot out her hand toward Galazi and he felt his throat constrict. It was a horrible feeling, choking, yet being unable to move his body. Nomma's long tongue flickered out of her mouth as she laughed at his expense.

"Maybe it would be better to slay him now, Touloumia. I'm sure the Slaughterer would marry you even if his brother were dead when he arrived. I have ways of making sure of it. Something tells me the Wolf will prove to be a nuisance."

Queen Touloumia stepped directly behind Nomma and nodded her head in agreement. "I believe you've made your most accurate prediction yet!" The maiden suddenly plunged the pointed end of her long staff into the lower back of Nomma. The witch arched backwards and let out an inhuman cry.

Galazi felt the grip on his throat slacken, and then his entire body was free of the witch's power.

Touloumia's elderly attendant approached the crystal basin and raised the war club in the air. The shadow of the Watcher fell across the skull of Nomma.

"Wolf! Assist the queen!" The old man tossed the Watcher to Galazi.

The Wolf snatched the iron-shod war club out of the air with two hands and then turned his gaze on Nomma. The witch's lower body had now emerged from the water, but instead of legs she had a long serpent-like tail with two yellow fins at its end. She blindly thrashed it about behind her attempting to swat Touloumia, who was still tightly gripping the staff impaled in Nomma's backside. Galazi knew this was his moment to strike.

Rather than circling the green water, the Wolf bounded over it like a buck, raising the Watcher of the Fords above his head. Nomma turned her gaze on him during his descent, but she was too late. Galazi brought the Watcher down on her skull so hard the witch's head exploded in a shower of yellow and green fluids.

Nomma's body fell to the floor and continued to spasm, but Touloumia put an end to it with one final thrust of her long staff. The queen twisted her weapon for good measure, then withdrew it. Almost instantly, the green waters in the pool turned to blue.

Touloumia took a step back, cautiously eyed the Wolf and spoke, "Well done, Galazi. The kingdom of Mkinyaga owes you a great debt. I couldn't have defeated this creature without you or your war club."

Galazi's face was stone. "I don't understand, girl. Just last night you were in league with this witch from another world. Why turn on her now when you seemed on the verge of achieving your goal?"

Touloumia was silent for a moment, then began unwrapping the cloth wrapped around her staff, revealing a cat's head. "It was a dream I had. Last night, I tossed and turned in my bed chamber, unable to rest. After many hours, I finally went to sleep. My dream began most pleasantly. I was wading in the blue waters of Lake Tanganyika, behind Kisimbasimba. The sun was shining overhead and the waters were calm. Then day turned to night. The brightest star in the sky grew even brighter and began hurtling down towards me. I tried to run, but I was frozen in place. The metal star splashed down in the center of the lake causing a great explosion on the water's surface. The waters turned green and restless.

"A dark mist formed in the shallows where I waded. Three men emerged from the haze and surrounded me. One was the handsomest man I've ever seen. His only imperfection were two goat horns protruding from his forehead. His voice was sweet and soothing. 'You meddle in matters beyond your understanding, young queen. It's time you put an end to such recklessness.'

"The second man was little more than a shadow, but he spoke to me as well. The pitch of his voice continually changed. 'Yes, you need to stop this wishful thinking before it's too late. That witch's promises are empty.'

"The third had the most hideous face I've ever seen. I could hardly even look upon it without shuddering. Not only that, but his voice was overwhelming. It was the very sound of thunder! 'Yes, you must stop her before it's too late! But you can't do it alone. You'll need help. This particular serpent must be defeated at both ends.'

"The three disappeared back into the mist and the vapor swirled and increased in thickness, transforming into a red fog that soon engulfed the entire lake. I turned toward Kisimbasimba and was appalled at the sight unfolding before me. Flooding out of the grottoes and into the green waters were large, black-scaled abominations. Some had legs, others had tails and fins. They were all armed and muscled like bulls.

"The red fog cleared, and it was daylight once again. When I turned to gaze at the shore behind me, I saw a long staff with a cat's head top piercing into the green water and sand. The staff was impaling the lower portion of a scaly creature that had the traits of both snake and fish. The wooden staff practically glowed in the sunlight. Then a large black wolf whose head and flanks were streaked with grey emerged from the brush and brought his fangs down on the head of the creature. As the beast devoured its prey, the waters shifted from green to blue before my eyes.

"When I awoke, the staff was in bed with me. I knew I had to hide it from Nomma's gaze, so I concealed its true form when I came to the hidden grotto this morning. I knew you would aid me against Nomma once your war club was returned, Galazi, and together we have defeated her! Now she and her spawn will never rule the waters of Lake Tanganyika or anywhere else for that matter. My lions will see to it that no trace of this foul creature remains."

Galazi stood in silence for a moment and thought back to the three unsettling likenesses carved into the great baobab tree on the plateau. The girl's description of the three beings was very reminiscent of those strange faces.

"I'm glad you finally saw through the witch's lies, girl. Even if it took sorcerous means to do so. Now, show me the quickest way to the surface so I can take my leave of this place."

Queen Touloumia seemed taken aback by his declaration. "It's true Nomma spoke lies, but some good can still come out of this. Let your brother the Slaughterer rule over his little village in the south. Stay here and rule Mkinyaga by my side as king, Galazi!"

Galazi roughly tore the black wolf-skin out of the elderly man's grasp and donned it over his brow and shoulders. He turned his back on Queen Touloumia and stalked toward the exit. "I'm already a king, foolish girl! King of the people black and grey who dwell in the lap of the stone Witch on Ghost Mountain! King of the ghost-wolves!"

Matthew Baugh has always liked to mix up genres and this proclivity has never been better illustrated than with this rollicking romp of a story which happily blends criminal masterminds from Old Europe, ruthless rogues from the Wild Wild West and indomitable Martial Artists from the Far East...

Matthew Baugh: *A Dollar's Worth of Fists*

Arizona Territory, 1879

"Excellency," Regis said, bowing, "your first guest has arrived."

Gio nodded and glanced around the room. The Louis XV furniture and Turkish carpet dressed up the chamber considerably, but they couldn't hide what it was: a large natural chamber in an abandoned silver mine. He'd heard that the Colonel appreciated a dramatic flair. He hoped it was true.

"Show him in."

Regis ducked out and reappeared a moment later to usher in a pair of well-dressed men. The first was slim and elegantly attired in a black suit with a Continental cut. Even without the pendant, which Gio knew to be the fabled Scapulary of Mercy, he would have been unmistakable. His bearing, his charisma, and the almost palpable aura of malice that surrounded him could only belong to Colonel Bozzo-Corona. The man with him looked uncomfortable in formal servant's clothes. He was huge and conveyed a sense of bear-like strength.

"My dear Colonel, welcome!"

Gio shook his guest's hand and was impressed by the strength of his grip. He was well aware of the man's reputation for great and subtle intelligence, but not the physicality he now sensed. He gestured the Colonel to a seat at the conference table that dominated the center of the chamber.

"May I offer you a drink?" he asked. "I'm sure after your long trip…"

The Colonel dismissed the offer with a wave of his hand as he sat.

"Straight to business, then?"

"That I am here should tell you that you have my support in this venture… at least conditionally," the Colonel replied.

"I don't wish to seem ungrateful, but may I ask your conditions?"

"We must see if I approve of your ally."

"I assure you, Monsieur Ming is—"

"I am well aware of the celestial gentleman's reputation," the Colonel interrupted. "Indeed, we have had minor dealings in the past. But I have never taken his measure, face to face."

"I'm certain it will go well."

"I hope so." The Colonel's smile was pure, cold malice. "You ranked high in the Camorra in this country before your misadventure. If you were to fail again, I should need to *cut the branch*."

In spite of himself, Gio felt a chill run up his spine. The phrase "cut the branch" was a code within the Black Coats and its subordinate organizations, like the Camorra and the Mafia, for execution. He chided himself. Yes, the Colonel was frightening, and powerful, but he was only a man. He glanced at the huge servant standing quietly near the wall.

He is only a man, he repeated mentally. *And, perhaps a foolish man at that, to trust his safety to this muscle-bound oaf.*

"You don't approve of the Marchef," the Colonel said.

Gio felt another chill, stronger this time. How had the man known what he was thinking?

"He looks impressively strong," he said.

"But…?"

Gio smiled to cover his embarrassment. "In my experience, skill will win out over strength in every case. My man, Regis, for example, is not so large, but is very skilled in *la savate*."

"You think your man could defeat the Marchef?" The Colonel seemed amused by the prospect.

"Louis Vigneron defeated Arpin the Terrible with *la savate*," Gio said. "The wrestler was at least as big as your Marchef, but it took only a few kicks for Vigneron to knock him out."

"What do you think, Marchef?" the Colonel said. "Could you defeat that street Apache?"

The big man snorted.

"Regis is not a Parisian street thug," Gio said. "He is Québécois. He has the skills of Europe and the toughness of this wild continent."

"You admire the combative arts, it seems."

"All my life I have studied them," Gio replied. "When Europe had nothing more to teach me, I hired the finest kung-fu instructors in China. The skills I have learned make me the master of any western fighter."

"Perhaps you are the one who should have a bout with the Marchef."

The Colonel's tone stung Gio's ego. For a moment he considered taking the man up on his challenge. It would be a pleasure to prove himself against the man's pet brute. He dismissed that thought, though. It wouldn't do to embarrass his potential patron.

"Perhaps, when our business is done," he replied, smiling.

Regis appeared at the doorway and bowed.

"Monsieur Ming is here, Excellency."

Gio nodded and the servant ushered in five men. Four wore black, Chinese style blouses and trousers. Their features were concealed by elaborately hideous demon masks. The last was quite tall, Chinese, totally bald and bareheaded, and wore the long black gown of a Confucian scholar. Gio raised his hands—one in a fist, the other covering it—and bowed. Monsieur Ming nodded in response, though the gestured seemed more courteous than the Colonel's had. The Asian's eyes locked with the Colonel's and the two men regarded each other for several tense, silent moments. It seemed to Gio as if there was a literal battle of wills taking place. Then—as if by mutual consent—the men turned their eyes to him.

"I see that you have recruited a number of my countrymen to your cause," Ming said.

"I have, honored sir," Gio replied. "Some of the tongs of this country have proven very amenable. My best fighters come from the *Fùchóu lóngsān hé huì* and the *Hēi xiēzi sān hé huì*."

"You are to be congratulated for reconciling them." Ming smiled indulgently at the Colonel. "The tongs our friend mentions are bitter enemies. The Avenging Dragons function as an arm of the Ch'ing government and the Black Scorpions are one of many societies founded to eradicate the Ch'ings."

The Colonel's expression didn't change, but Gio thought the room felt colder. He decided to interrupt, lest the moment turn hostile.

"There are several *bu how doy* in San Francisco whose services I covet," he said. "Unfortunately, the master of the Wing Kongs will not grant me audience. If you could commend me to him…"

"I regret to say I cannot," Ming replied. "That one is a relic of the past and does not understand my glorious plans. Or, should I say, *our* glorious plans?"

"This is the heart of the project," Gio said as they entered the great chamber. He had been in the natural cavern hundreds of times but the size of it—and what it contained—still impressed him. A massive airship, two hundred meters long, lay at anchor a dozen feet above the cavern floor. The muzzles of two cannon and half a dozen Gatling guns projected from portals in the gondola. Metal caps sealed a number of fissures in the cavern floor and hoses ran from them to the great gas bag. Several score of workers, almost all Chinese, moved around the cavern, tending to the vessel. A dozen *bu how doy*, in their distinctive black clothes and round-peaked hats. They wore fierce expressions and each carried a pair of hatchets in his sash. The Avenging Dragons wore golden sashes and the Black Scorpions wore black.

"This was once the Yellow Horse silver mine," he continued. "It was worked by three brothers in the Black Scorpions. They didn't find silver—at least, not enough to mention—but they did discover the world's richest source of hydrogen gas."

As he spoke, Gio's voice rose in pitch to a comical chirp, as might be made by the diminutive *zana* in his grandmother's folk tales.

"Your voice…" Ming trailed off as his words came out with a similar squeak. The Colonel chuckled, though even this was reduced to an infantile titter.

"Fascinating," Ming said. "A side-effect of the hydrogen?"

"Just so," Gio replied. "We have not been able to contain all the gas. At this level it is perfectly safe, though it has this…awkward side-effect."

"*Perfectly safe?*" the Colonel chirped. "My understanding is that this gas is highly flammable."

"You are correct, Colonel," Gio said. "Any flame in this space would be disastrous. There is no smoking or cooking allowed in the cavern, and our light comes from flameless chemical lanterns of Monsieur Ming's design. Also, my men are forbidden to carry firearms. Fortunately, they are so skilled in kung-fu that security is no problem."

"Your 'hatchet men' are literally limited to hatchets?" The Colonel seemed amused. "A poetic solution—though I would have armed them with air guns."

Gio felt a wave of embarrassment. He had never considered anything like that.

"The airship is a marvel," Ming said, the hydrogen making his normally impressive voice absurd. "Who designed it?"

"A man who calls himself Robur," the Colonel replied, in the same undignified voice. "My organization managed to acquire the plans from him several years ago when he was residing in France. I have heard rumors that he has developed even more advanced craft, but he disappeared before I could seize the plans for those as well."

"No matter," Gio said. "He has already given us the ultimate weapon. With your support, I will build a fleet of these. The armies of the United States and Mexico will be powerless to stop us. I will create my own country from these western territories and its resources shall be at your disposal, my most generous patrons!"

"I do not wish to cast aspersions on such a grand plan," Ming said, "but it occurs to me that you have built your mighty warship inside a mine. How do you plan to get it out?"

"Simplicity itself, my dear Monsieur Ming," Gio said. He moved to a nearby section of the cavern wall where a heavy lever was mounted. Taking a firm grasp, he pulled the lever down. The action was accompanied by a loud rattle of chains and clashing of gears. Sunlight flooded the chamber as a giant section of roof slid to one side.

"I usually keep the ceiling closed to avoid losing any more of the hydrogen than is necessary, but now I open it for the ship's maiden voyage." He took a deep breath and his voice resumed its usual baritone. "As you can hear, the gas disperses quickly once the hatch is opened."

"Most impressive," the Colonel said. "Will this be only a flight, or will you also be testing the craft's martial capabilities?"

"You anticipate me, Colonel. My agents tell me that there is a troop of cavalry on patrol some thirty miles from here. With my ship, we should be able to reach them in under two hours, then you shall see what she can do. In addition to her guns, she carried two powerful gelignite bombs."

"That sounds most effective," Ming said.

"Then let us…" Gio broke off as Regis came trotting up.

"Forgive me, excellency, but we have captured several intruders."

Gio frowned. The timing of this was embarrassing.

"Lock them in a cell," he snapped. "I shall interrogate them when—"

"If you would bring them here, I would like to interrogate them now," Ming interrupted.

Gio nearly glared at the man but managed to restrain himself. It was inevitable that Ming and the Colonel do things like this to assert their dominance. As much as that undermined him as leader, there was no avoiding it. He needed their financial backing…for the time being, at least.

"Very well. Regis, bring them here."

Regis gave a signal and four hatchet men came forward leading a pair of prisoners. The men each wore a set of manacles on their hands. One was a handsome brown-haired young man, dressed like a ranch hand; the other was a huge, bearded mound of muscle who rivaled the Marchef in size. He wore overalls over a torn set of long-johns and looked as if he hadn't bathed since the end of the Civil War.

"Who are you?" Gio demanded.

The younger man grinned defiantly.

"I'm Jesse James and this big fella's my baby brother, Frank."

"*Cochon!*" Regis' right foot shot up in a blindingly fast kick that caught the cowboy in the solar plexus. He dropped to his knees, struggling to breathe. Regis planted an equally solid kick into the big man's midsection. The giant grunted and glowered at him but otherwise gave no indication he had felt the blow.

"You had better start with the young man," the Colonel said. "His 'Baby Brother' will take a long time to break."

"Perhaps not." Gio drew a long, Chinese-style dagger from his coat. Seizing the younger man's hair he pulled his head back and held the blade to his exposed throat.

"Answer my questions or I'll kill him."

Baby Brother's scowl deepened. "What do you want to know?"

"You're here to stop me, aren't you?"

"Sure."

"Just the two of you?"

"Yeah."

Gio pressed the point of his dagger against the cowboy's throat until a thin trickle of blood began to flow.

"You're sure about that?"

"We…there are a couple of others."

"Who?"

The giant's shoulders sagged and he dropped his eyes and muttered something inaudible.

"What's that?"

Baby Brother mumbled something Gio could *almost* make out but didn't raise his head.

Gio rose and brought his face close to the giant's.

"Say it again, fool, and this time, make sure I can understand it."

"The men helping us…"

Baby Brother lunged, his broad forehead slamming into Gio's nose and creating an intense explosion of pain. With a cry, he staggered back.

The guards had their own knives out and held to the big man's throat. Gio raised his hand to his face and the blinding stab of pain as he touched his nose confirmed it was broken. Surprisingly, it was not bleeding. That would have been one indignity too many.

"Kill them both," he said.

"Wait!"

He turned to the workers who had gathered to watch. Two men stepped out of the crowd. The one who had spoken was tall and lean, his well-worn clothes fit him like a scarecrow's but his movements were fluid and sure. He appeared to be only part Chinese. The other man was shorter and fully Asian. To Gio—who prided himself on his ability to distinguish nationality based on facial features—the man looked Japanese. The *bu how doy* moved to surround them.

"Who are you?" Gio demanded. "Agents of the Chinese government? Of the Americans?"

"We serve no government," the taller man said in a gentle voice. He nodded at the brown-haired cowboy. "This man is named Jed Puma. He learned of your plan and gathered us to stop you."

"The four of you?"

"Not the four of us alone. Tashi and I have spent many days alongside your workers. They are good men, who want nothing to do with your plans of conquest and death. They will build your flying machines no longer."

"You think these…these peasants will defy me? Their kind is too soft. They only know obedience and death."

"Is not water the softest and most submissive of all things? Yet, does not water carve channels through the hardest rock."

"You have read Lao Tse, it seems," Gio said peering at the man. Moving closer he caught one of his wrists. Pulling back the sleeve, Gio revealed a brand in the shape of a tiger on his forearm. He repeated the process, revealing a branded dragon on the other forearm. An awed murmur swept through the gathered Chinese.

"What is the significance of this?" the Colonel asked.

"He is a Shaolin priest," Monsieur Ming replied. "One of the most skillful fighters of my country. I realize, as a westerner, the idea of a warrior priest must be strange to you."

"Not so strange. I should tell you of the Brothers of Mercy someday."

"I am no warrior," the Shaolin said. His voice held a note of disdain. "I am only a man, like these other men. We have no wish to fight, but we will serve you no longer."

"You think you have a choice?" Gio said.

"You are powerless to make us do anything." The Japanese—Tashi, Gio supposed—stepped forward with the confidence of a samurai and crossed his arms.

"We shall see."

Gio dropped into a fighting stance but the Colonel placed a restraining hand on his arm.

"Indulge me. I believe this would be a splendid test of your idea that skill will always overcome strength." He nodded to the Marchef, who stepped forward.

Gio hesitated, then nodded. Much as he didn't like the man interfering in his fight, it was to his advantage. If the Marchef won, the spirit of the Chinese workers might be broken. On the other hand, if Tashi won, it would be a huge blow to the Colonel's prestige. Then, he could redeem himself by defeating the Japanese himself.

The Marchef and Tashi regarded each other for a several moments while the crowd shifted to give them room to fight. The Marchef moved first, throwing a powerful punch that would have been devastating had it landed. Amazingly, Tashi caught the big man's wrist and turned into his body. An instant later the Marchef sailed over the little man's shoulder to land on the ground.

"Leading with his right," Gio observed. "Always a mistake."

The Marchef, obviously uninjured, sprang to his feet. This time, he lowered and charged at Tashi, arms spread wide. The little man made no attempt to dodge. At the last moment, he twisted his body, put his arm around the Marchef's body and threw him neatly over his hip.

"This is the genius of Oriental combat, Colonel," Gio said. "The Japanese cannot hope to match your man's power and momentum, so he redirects it against him. The Marchef is overcome by his own strength."

The Colonel didn't reply; he was totally focused on the match. His attitude, Gio thought, was not that of a man afraid his champion might lose. He seemed more like a general planning a new stratagem.

The fight continued this way for the next ten minutes. The Marchef became more cautious, but each attack was met with a skilled evasion and, often as not, ended with him hitting the ground. Still, Gio was impressed; most fighters the Marchef's size would have been winded by now, but he showed no sign of fatigue; nor any hint of anger or frustration. Gio's estimation of the man and the level of danger he represented rose significantly.

Then it happened. Apparently confident in his ability to do anything to his opponent, Tashi stabbed his hand, fingers stiffened like a spearpoint, into the Marchef's windpipe. The blow had no apparent effect, but gave the Marchef a chance to grab the smaller man. He lifted Tashi over his head, then brought him down across his knee with a terrible impact.

"Tashi!" Jed Puma shouted as the little man fell to the ground and lay still. "You bastard! You killed my teacher! I'll kill you!" He tried to rise but the hatchet men held him down.

The Shaolin stepped forward and knelt by Tashi. He lifted the small man and gave him to several of the Chinese workers, who reverently passed him back through the throng. The priest turned to face the Marchef.

"Resistance is useless," the Colonel said. "Will you return to work?"

"No," the Shaolin replied.

"Marchef, kill this one also."

The huge man clenched his fists but Gio brushed past him. It might not be wise to do so, he thought, but the Colonel had pricked his pride.

"These are my men, Colonel. I will deal with their disobedience by showing them my kung-fu is stronger than that of this...priest."

He dropped into the deep, wide stance of the tiger style and extended his left arm, fingers hooked like claws. The priest responded with a crane stance, front leg barely touching the ground and fingers bunched together to form a "beak."

Before they could clash, Jed Puma raised his voice.

"Brothers, it's written that, 'the superior man holds justice of the highest importance.' Let us fight for justice!"

The hatchet men holding him moved to strike Puma but, shockingly, Ming's Shin Tan warriors moved in and dropped the guards with a few well-placed blows. They pulled off their demon masks revealing three Asians and a man in another mask—this one a close fitting hood of silver that left only his mouth, nose, and eyes visible. The other three, who looked like a Chinese, a Siamese, and a Korean began fighting the guards while the masked man took a hatchet and broke the chains on Jed and Baby Brother's manacles. The workers surged forward to fight the hatchet men and the chamber became pandemonium.

"Ming, what is this?" the Colonel shouted.

"Treachery! Somehow these men replaced my Shin Tan!"

Gio saw the Marchef and Regis move to attack the false Shin Tan, then the Shaolin struck at him and he had to shift all his attention to his own fight. He blocked the first attack and launched a series of kicks and powerful clawing strikes. The Shaolin faded back, evading the attacks and scoring with several 'pecking' hand strikes. These didn't seriously hurt Gio but they infuriated him, causing him to attack more recklessly. This proved a mistake as the priest

27

dropped into the lower stance of the snake style. He spun his body, lashing out a leg, and swept Gio's legs from under him.

Gio landed well and easily kipped back to his feet. He didn't resume his attack instantly, but took a moment to scan the fights around him. Regis and the Siamese were engaged in a battle of kicks and knees in which they seemed evenly-matched. The Marchef had also found a good opponent in Baby Brother, though their fight was artless. The huge men were pounding each other with blow after blow and making no attempt at defense. It would be a matter of who wore down first. The others he didn't see but had the general sense that the fight was not going well for his hatchet men.

He launched an eagle talon kick, which the priest countered with a praying mantis block. They went back and forth for a moment, then the Shaolin shifted styles again to mimic the dragon. He seemed almost to float on the breeze, effortlessly evading Gio's attacks. A leaping kick to the chest spilled Gio to the ground and he scrambled backward on his hands and feet to get out of range.

There was no denying the priest's skill. Gio had lost all hope of winning a fair fight; so, he would stop fighting fair. Springing to his feet, he drew his daggers and sent one speeding for the Shaolin's chest. With the fluid grace of the dragon, the priest caught the weapon, then tossed it away. Gio felt his stomach drop. Even with the advantage of a weapon, how could he hope to match the Shaolin's almost magical skill?

The answer came in the form of a burly Black Scorpion, who grabbed the priest from behind. It would take even this man a moment to free himself, but by then, Gio's blade would be sheathed in his heart. He lunged but was brought up short as someone grabbed his tunic from behind and slammed him to the ground.

Gio rose, knife still in hand, to find himself face to face with a grim Jed Puma.

"You'd best hope your man didn't kill Tashi," the cowboy said.

"You can ask him, as soon as I send you to the same heathen hell." Gio slashed with the knife. Puma caught his wrist and twisted it, throwing him. Gio lost the knife, but rolled through the fall and was back on his feet in an instant. He threw a round kick, which Puma dodged, and followed with a spinning heel kick, which caught the cowboy in the shoulder. Jed's arm went limp and Gio smiled.

Off to the side, the silver-masked man delivered a leaping kick with both feet that brought down two of the hatchet men. While they were stunned, he grabbed their heads and slammed them together. As the men fell, the masked man's eyes widened.

"Sammy, Tiger, Joe!" he yelled. "The *jefés* are getting away."

He caught a glimpse of Ming and the Colonel hurrying up the gangplank to the airship. How had things gone this bad so quickly? He knew that, in their place, he would be doing as his erstwhile allies were doing, but it didn't matter. If he survived this, he would have his vengeance on both of them.

Jed Puma brought him back to the present with a kick to the belly.

Puma followed up with a chopping blow with his good hand. His injury made the move awkward. Gio was able to catch his wrist and throw him to the ground. He reached for the cowboy's throat, intending to drive his thumb into a fatal pressure point. Jed used his good arm and legs to fend off the attack, but was not in a good position to kick. He wrapped one leg around the side of Gio's neck in a futile gesture.

Too late, Gio realized it was not just awkward struggling. Jed's other leg locked around the first, trapping his neck in a triangle of muscle and bone. He couldn't breathe, and his fading vision told him that the blood flow to his head had also been cut off. He stopped his attack and tried to break the choke, but Puma's legs were too strong; his leverage too great. As his consciousness dimmed, he caught a series of images: The Siamese had trapped Regis' head in a two handed grip and was driving merciless knee strikes into his chest. The Chinese was using a kung-fu style that resembled a monkey's movements to fight off two hatchet men. The Korean parried a hatchet with a chop of his hand, shattering the handle.

As the great airship rose out of the cavern, a small figure—he thought it was Tashi—slid down a guy rope and dropped the last twenty-five feet to the mine floor. It was the last thing Gio saw.

"Where's Joe?"

"He and El Caballero Enmascarado de Plata follow after the airship on horseback."

"Tashi, you can just call him the Caballero, or Silver Mask, or something. You don't have to spit out that mouthful."

"I find Spanish a very beautiful language."

"D'you think they'll catch them in time?"

"It is unimportant. I have taken care of the matter."

"What do you mean by that?"

"Look; he is waking."

Gio opened his eyes and the disembodied voices took on the forms of Jed Puma, Tashi, and the Shaolin. Puma's injured arm was in a sling, one of Tashi's legs was splinted, and the priest bore a number of small bruises and scrapes. Gio was sitting in an uncomfortable position, his back propped against a gnarled osage orange tree. When he tried to shift position, he found himself lashed to the plant with a rope.

"You're a pretty fair hand with fighting," Puma said. "That kick caught me off-guard."

"You were lucky," Gio said. He was pleased to find that his voice was strong enough to sound menacing, though it was the only thing he was happy about.

"Keep tellin' yourself that," the cowboy said with a grin.

"Your Japanese—I saw the Marchef break his back."

"'My Japanese?' Mister, slavery's been illegal in this country nigh on fifteen years now. Tashi's my teacher and my friend."

"Fine—but how did he survive?"

"If I only knew a few Chinese fighting tricks, like you, I would have been broken in two," Tashi said. "However, I am skilled at Japanese bujitsu, and more than able to adjust to such a clumsy attack."

Gio glanced at the Shaolin, hoping Tashi's Chauvinist comment had angered him, but the man seemed perfectly serene. Gio noticed that there was a little play in his bonds. If he could get to his belt and the knife concealed there...

"I have to admit," Gio said, "your men have an interesting array of skills."

Puma grinned again. "Don't they, though? Tiger is a muai Thai fighter, Caballero mixes wrestling with some high flying moves from a Brazilian style called capoeira, Joe does kung fu, and Sammy... Well, Sammy's Chinese, but he was born and raised in Korea where an Okinawan fella' taught him something called shuri-te, though he's got his own name for it. Calls it kara-te."

"That will never catch on," Tashi said with a snort.

"The Colonel and Monsieur Ming have escaped you." Gio's fingers touched the hilt of the concealed knife at the small of his back and pulled it free.

"Oh, we been keeping an eye on them," Puma said. He picked up a spyglass from its resting place on a nearby rock. "The rest of our little posse is after them."

He looked through the glass and frowned. Gio followed his gaze to see the airship, which was now only a speck against the horizon.

"What is it?" Tashi asked.

"They've turned around," Puma replied. "They're heading back this way and descending, fast."

"Hah!" Gio felt a twin surge of exultation as his sharp blade parted the rope and he realized what was happening. "They're turning back on your friends. They're going to slaughter then with the Gatling guns."

As his captors all turned toward the distant events, Gio slipped free of his bonds. The fools hadn't searched him well at all, he thought as he drew his Derringer from its sheath on his calf.

In the distance the speck blazed with light and began to fall to earth.

"I told you I had taken care of it," Tashi said.

"What did you do?" The Shaolin sounded horrified.

"I lit a fire when I sneaked on board. I'm surprised it took this long."

"So, you win after all," Gio said.

The three turned toward him and froze.

"Ah, this?" Gio lifted the gun and smiled. "A trick I picked up from an old enemy. I don't have enough bullets for all of you, but I will kill anyone who tries to keep me from escaping."

"There's nowhere for you to run," Puma said.

"Let me worry about that. Just don't try to stop me." Gun leveled at the men, he backed into the mine entrance.

"Do not go in there," the Shaolin said.

"He's right!" Puma added. "You don't understand—"

Ignoring them, Gio ducked into the shaft.

The mine was clear of workers, a stroke of luck for him. The chemical lights still glowed, so Gio had no trouble finding his way. He shook his head, regretting the loss of Ming's inventive genius. He supposed that, if anyone could find a way to survive an airship going down in flames, it would be him. The Colonel also had a reputation for escaping certain death, though Gio didn't see how even such men could survive that conflagration.

He reached the central chamber and noticed that his enemies had closed the ceiling for some reason. No matter; he wasn't going to fly out, only take his escape tunnel to the hidden stable where his horse waited.

As he crossed the great room, Gio felt light-headed. Reaching the far side, he steadied himself against the wall.

"They won't catch me!" He was surprised when his voice came out in a squeaky, child-like pitch. Looking around he realized that all the hydrogen valves had been opened all the way. The chamber was filling with the buoyant gas. He also saw bundles of dynamite laid out around the cavern at regular intervals.

"Fools!" he chirped. "You may destroy this lair, but you will not stop me."

He thought he saw a shadow move to his right and turned, Derringer at the ready.

"Who's there? Is that you, Puma? Show yourself!"

There was no reply and he wondered if it had been his imagination. He was getting dizzy and found it hard to focus his thoughts.

"You fools," he shouted in his cartoonish falsetto. "I will be emperor of these lands! It is my destiny!"

He thought he say another shadow flicker. Quick as a striking viper, he pivoted in that direction and fired twice.

Puma and the Shaolin heard the shots and ducked away from the mine entrance a split second before a blast of blue flame erupted from it. It lasted only a moment before it burned out, leaving a faint trace of moisture on the ground.

"Perhaps he survived," the priest said.

There was a tremendous roar that shook the earth as the dynamite went off. It was followed by a blast of dust from the hole and the sound of falling rock that lasted for several moments.

"I'm thinkin' he didn't," Puma said when the noise subsided.

In this tale, which spotlights Harry Dickson, the so-called "American Sherlock Holmes," Adam "Mudman" Bezecny delves into the Mysteries of New York and its shadows-shrouded back alleys that are home to fantastic characters, merciless criminals and mad scientists. Back in his native homeland for once, Dickson and his fantastic new client face a startling conspiracy with worldwide ramifications...

Adam Mudman Bezecny: *Harry's Homecoming*

New York City, 1933

When Harry Dickson got off the plane, the gears in his head were already turning at full speed. Had young Tom Wills been there, he would have seen the gleam in his mentor's eye, and grown excited despite the fact that it was a regular sight for him. Tom couldn't disguise his excitement any more than Dickson could hide when he was deep in thought. Keeping his mind on the various ideas he was mentally amalgamating, the detective sometimes worried that he kept Tom around specifically to fan his ego, which critics accused him of having— after all, there was a reason why he had taken up quarters in Baker Street. And Tom was indeed his most ardent "fan." But that thought merely made him miss 221B, and Tom's presence, especially since there was important business to take care of in town.

He had received an invitation to a conference of detectives and adventurers from the Americas—someone named Donald Carrick had signed it. Dickson had never heard of Carrick before, and most of the names on the guest list were just as obscure. He had hoped to see his friend Ardan mentioned, but no such luck. Still, the event might prove to have some value. Tom had had other engagements—he'd received a letter of his own from someone answering to the name of Tinker, who was hosting a parallel conference for the assistants and biographers of many European sleuths. Dickson couldn't help but be proud. The boy had great talents, and he really did want to make him into a respectable investigator of his own caliber. Now that he was gone, Dickson had no one to talk to— and so he was simply tumbling the same facts through his head.

The front page article of the paper he'd gotten on the plane had talked about an attempt on the life of Dr. Alfred Carroll, an outspoken critic of narcotics—chiefly marijuana. This had taken place after the doctor had publicly linked the local Grisson Gang to the semi-famous Burma Roberts case. Apparently, the Roberts girl had been given marijuana at a party sponsored by the Gang, and when the drug began to affect her health and push her into a life of crime, they had assisted her in the kidnapping of her own niece.

Dickson still had the paper tucked under his arm, just above his single suit-case. Already, he could see the shining towers of his once native home. He'd been meaning to return for some time now, to live up to his sobriquet as the "American Sherlock Holmes." The 1930s were proving to be a wild time in the United States, and he had to admit he wanted in on this wildness. Still, he still had many obligations in Europe, which had been wild since forever. For Harry Dickson, as for many others, New York represented adventure. He couldn't wait to start.

He was nearly outside the airport when someone bumped into him.

When the detective whirled to confront the guilty party, he was shocked to discover the age of the interloper. He was an old man, though it was clear he'd once been stocky. He still looked strong as a bull, but now shriveled with age. His clothes were too big for him, and there were atrophy marks on his exposed arms. His face was beardless, and he barely had any hair left at all. Dickson was able to tell he was probably nearly ninety—if not a hundred, or over.

"Pardon me, monsieur," the old man said, grinning. "I just wanted to know if I could borrow that paper. I've been keeping up on the Grisson Gang story."

Dickson wanted to keep the story for himself, so he silently waited as the elderly fellow skimmed the article. Despite a meager appearance—his clothes looked as old as their wearer—the old man was a quick reader. Not thirty seconds had passed before the paper was handed back to Dickson.

"*Merci beaucoup.*"

"There is an unusual accent to your voice, my friend," Dickson said then. "Obviously French, yet with some outside influence. Perhaps you have some Basque in you?" After a brief second the investigator grinned. "No, your expression says I'm wrong. I think you must have spent a number of years in Flanders, but come from a small French village like, say, Litan. Also, I have only heard that particular Flemish trace in your voice once before—and it does meld so intriguingly with the bumpkin-French—and that was when I was passing through a small town by the name of Quiquendone a few years ago, doing research on a forty-odd year old case involving a scientist who could make plants grow to titanic size, and drive men and women out of their minds. His name was Doctor Ox. That's your name, isn't it?"

"I am impressed. Few these have heard of Litan, my place of birth, but perhaps fewer still have heard of Quiquendone. You are Harry Dickson, the so-called 'American Sherlock Holmes.' I certainly hope that wasn't a title you chose for yourself."

"I believe it was assigned by the media of some country or another," the detective replied.

"Well, if you can live to even a quarter-portion of Holmes' name, monsieur Dickson, perhaps I will have to borrow a moment of your time. You see, my interest in the Grisson Gang is a professional matter. One of tremendous and absolute urgency, at that. I..."

The detective cut him off. "I'm here on business of my own, Doctor. While encountering a man of your reputation is a rare privilege, I must admit I'm not interested in taking a case from a man whose legend is that of an impressive criminal record."

"My most recent crime occurred in 1881, when I exposed the son of the famed Captain Hatteras to a hallucinogenic gas of my own devising. I created and tested it to prove my ultimate theory: that humanity is not special in the universe, being only a composite of various chemicals. Over the last fifty years, I have seen that science has rallied to my side. In any case, the statute of limitations has long expired."

"I can only take your word, doctor, and I don't trust it."

"Age has neutered me. I never meant to hurt anyone, and now, truly, I can't. In any case, Monsieur Dickson, I have learned that, at my age, one can master the skills that you detectives boast about. I can see from your face that the business that draws you here is not of immediate concern. You would have a few days, or even a week, during which you could assist me with my misadventure."

Dickson was silent. He had to admit that his thoughts about Tom had moved to the realization that his absence meant boredom. In truth, he arrived early with the hopes of picking up something to write home about...

Doctor Ox's persistence had convinced him. He could take a leap of faith—such leaps were the fuel of his career.

"When do we start?" he asked.

"Immediately, Monsieur Dickson!"

Doctor Ox had a car parked nearby, and he proved to be a skilled driver. Considering his age and ambition, Dickson realized the old man relished the idea of an automobile. Like many scientists, and indeed, many *mad* scientists, he doubtlessly lived in the future, and craved the technology from eras yet to come. To live for so long in the 19th century only to be given one of these vehicles would be like manna from Heaven.

Dickson wondered if Doctor Ox had ever met his old nemesis, Professor Flax—such a possibility seemed likely. He harbored the belief that the criminal tendencies of such men canceled any progressive traits they night have had, but he accepted that some of them probably contributed *some* good things to the world.

Doctor Ox was wasting no time in presenting the details of his case, knowing that a detective thrived off of them. Dickson sat with his arms folded across his chest, wearing his best neutral, professional face. However, he felt as if he was letting off some faint excitement, and he suspected that the uncanny doctor was able to feel that he was not as detached as he had initially seemed.

"Today's article is the last piece of the puzzle," Doctor Ox elucidated. "The Grisson Gang is planning on using my greatest invention commercially."

"That's a statement that requires more context, doctor," the detective replied. "Your greatest product appears to have been a growth hormone combined with a psychosis-inducing drug."

"Those were just some youthful experiments—I had no idea what I was doing. You know how it is when you're forty." And he snickered. "The plant expansion probably had to do with some herakleophorbia I casually mixed in. Of course, it wasn't called herakleophorbia then, and when it was 'invented,' I wasn't given any of the credit..."

"While I do thrive on details, doctor, I sense you are derailing yourself."

"Too right. Well, throughout my life, I've been curious about the potential of a drug that induces madness. I wondered if perhaps I could make the derangement I put upon Quiquendone a pleasurable experience. I knew of opium, of course, and hashish as well. But I wanted to create whimsical fantasies beyond either of them, via a substance as undetectable as the gas I used in Flanders. I became something of an expert in the drug world, and Georges Hatteras was my first test subject. With the aid of a catalyst potion, I gave him a wonderful dream, where he met Lindenbrock and Nemo alike, all through my hypnotic direction. But I still wasn't satisfied.

"My studies took me to Africa, where I learned of the miraculous *taduki*. It's supposed to induce visions of one's previous incarnations, but in my experience, that is merely superstitious nonsense. I spent three years of my life fighting an addiction to *taduki*, which I gained after just two experiments with it. Eventually, however, I found that I could synthesize the active diethylamide within *taduki*, the active substance that creates hallucinations. In a drink, pill, or gas, I could create a drug that unhinged the mind, but in a pleasurable way.

"Have you heard of the Assassins, Dickson? Of course you have. They are said these days to be, or have been, servants of the Si-Fan. In some of the old stories, anyway, the Assassins took their name from the word *hashishin*, etymologically related to the word hashish. The leader of the Assassins would use hashish, as well as romantic company, to bend the minds of his servants to his will. If I became the master of the ultimate pleasure-drug, I could create an army of criminals that would lay down their lives to me...of a size rivaling those of Moriarty...or even Quartz!"

Dickson raised a skeptical—and confused—eyebrow.

"So I'm assisting a criminal enterprise, then?"

"Ha! I said I *could* create such an army, Dickson—but only if I was interested in such a thing."

"You mean to say you're not?"

"It would only be criminal if possession of it became criminal. In my old age, I have decided to serve a noble goal, albeit a hedonistic one. I want to spread pleasure to the world."

"You would become a common drug-dealer, then, doctor?"

Doctor Ox spat. "During my *taduki* years, I was virtually enslaved by a wicked dealer named Malaglou. I curse him and his whole family. I do not peddle dope, monsieur. I offer freedom."

"Something that can also be used as a weapon does not open the path to freedom."

"Are you some sort of sage, now, Dickson? Do you fancy yourself a philosopher? Let us cease talking now. I still have a standing in the chemistry field, even if it's mostly through infamy—and that gave me a contact at a certain Chicago dessert corporation whose executive, named Pelton or something similar, employed some contacts in the criminal underworld. We're meeting one of them here in this alley. He is a Chinese-American called Ichabod Chang."

Dickson again raised an eyebrow. He never thought he'd hear a name like that. Doctor Ox parked on the street, and already Dickson's eyes could make out a hunched figure standing in the dingy darkness.

The doctor ambled quickly towards this man. Chang's face was rough and serious—to some people who had paranoid suspicions about non-whites, it might be intimidating, but Dickson knew better. Chang had faced the pain of that paranoia his entire life, and that was what had hardened him. Ultimately, the detective did not want to speculate further on this man's life, as that, in his mind, would be to make him a spectacle. Too often, the Chinese people of America had been made into such by the nation's white—made into things to gape at, rather than human beings.

For now, Doctor Ox was talking.

"Good evening, Chang. Thank you for meeting with me this evening."

"Well, we are all brothers, doctor, and you are in need. And it says in Deuteronomy 15:11: 'You shall open wide your hand to your brother, to the needy and the poor, in your land.'"

"Er, yes." The doctor turned back to face Dickson. "Chang is something of a Bible scholar."

"Of course," Dickson said simply.

"Not merely a scholar—a library," said Chang. "I have memorized the Gospel. In any case, I know that you seek insight into tracking something of value to you, doctor, but I am here only to pass you on to the one who has the answer. There is an associate of mine, one of my favorite celebrities whom I also correspond with. Her name is O. Ming Lee. Visit the circus in town, and you will find her."

Doctor Ox turned to face Dickson. "That circus is at Central Park, and today is its final day! It will be simplicity itself to locate this Lee girl, and from there, we will recover my formula!"

The detective saw a look in the doctor's eyes that he had seen before—the sort of desperation that wracks an addict. He wondered if this was the hunger of *taduki*. He had been in Africa before, and heard stories of those who languished under the addiction of the legendary drug, and he had no reason to doubt Ox's own story of falling under its power. Evidently, the doctor had not been able to work out the addictive properties of his creation, and so there was another dimension to his desire to reclaim it.

"Then drive on, doctor," the detective replied. He had the sensation of being on thin ice.

They got back in the car, and soon they were on their way to the circus. Already, night was falling upon them, and the spotlights were coming up under the distant big top.

Harry Dickson rarely used the expression "pick your jaw up off the floor," either verbally or in his head. However, both he and Doctor Ox needed to pick their jaws up at this point. Even though their discussion with O. Ming Lee had been going on now for several minutes, the woman herself was a source of constant surprise. She had been quick to introduce herself under her stage name: "Legga, the Spider-Woman." She had obtained this moniker because she had no less than six arms and four legs. Calling her a spider was a simplification—because she had ten limbs, she was more like a squid. She was clad in a red dress featuring a pattern derived from the Western conception of the Asian aesthetic—the only modification that had been made to it was that there were four extra holes on the torso, to accommodate her arms.

"Chang is a correspondent of mine, it's true," Lee was saying. "He is not the first of my friends to get mixed up in criminal business. He serves the executive Pelton because the man was a friend of his father's." She paused then. "I'm not sure I want to talk about my *second* friend, who was pulled to the underworld. If I can call still him a friend."

"This second man... he was your lover, Ms. Lee?" Dickson asked gently. His face was relaxed, his eyebrows faintly tilted upward.

"Yes. Don Maxwell was his name. He was Ichabod's half-brother—Ichabod's father was named Dong Chang, and he had an affair with a New Yorker with the surname Maxwell before he settled down and married. Ms. Maxwell gave birth to a boy named Don, a corruption of Dong."

"I see."

"I'm surprised that Don Maxwell's name doesn't strike a bell in you, Detective Dickson. To me, you seem like someone who might have once had an interest in vaudeville."

"Not worth my time, Ms. Lee—though I do enjoy the theater now and then."

"I would imagine. In any case, Maxwell always said such great things," Lee said bitterly. "He said he'd deserved to be on the same bill as Rice, and he would bring vaudeville back with his impressions. I tried to tell him that a traveling circus is no way to bring vaudeville back, but he insisted. His idea was that after he resurrected his type of theater, he could leave the circus behind and be a star. But he kept jumping at those assistant jobs with scientists. Thorkel, and someone named Vornoff, were some of the names. Got to pay the bills some-how—that dough isn't going to come from a carny wage."

"Those scientists—what was the...?"

"The last one, the one he saw before he disappeared? His name is Doctor Meirschultz, and it's him who has found his way into the leadership of the Grisson Gang."

Once again, the woman with ten limbs had stunned the two men.

"Don started working for Meirschultz later last year, and unlike his past jobs, he stuck with it for awhile. He always explained it to me that he liked to milk a few months' pay from his employers before quickly getting out. That's because a lot of the men he worked with would end up using him for experiments. The last thing he ever said to me—in a letter, because Meirschultz refused to let him leave—was that, yes, Meirschultz was behind the gangs. That letter came over six months ago, and I feel like his nightmare about experimentation finally came true."

"Thank you for yielding that information so easily, Ms. Lee," Dickson said. "Where is Meirschultz's lab? We'll depart at once, and see if we can learn what happened to Don."

"You should take me with you," Lee said suddenly. "I can help you get inside. Sometimes, Meirschultz keeps his quarters protected. He took on some guards when I kept trying to contact Don."

Doctor Ox grunted. "I have no objections," he said then. He had a weird grin and wild eyes as he spoke. "But you must let me study your anatomy at some point! You are a marvel of the potential of the human body."

Lee didn't seem to see a scientific intent in the doctor, and slapped him across the face with just two of her arms.

Soon they stood outside of a worn-down building that was apparently the home of Doctor Meirschultz. On the way, Dickson asked O. Ming Lee: "What did Meirschultz study, exactly?"

"According to Don, he had an interest in raising the dead," the Chinese girl replied simply.

"Ah!" Doctor Ox declared then, with enthusiasm. "A time-honored tradition."

"If you want to call it that," the so-called Spider-Woman said. "Meirschultz seems to believe that bringing all the world's dead back to life would somehow improve things."

Dickson observed that Doctor Ox seemed to take bemusement in the prospect of a fellow scientist bringing the dead out of their graves. Having just recently met none other than the supposed "Heir of Dracula" himself, he was not amused. Lord, were they all as mad as Flax? Indeed, he really was starting to see that bit of his old foe's soul in Doctor Ox—hopefully not literally.

"Like I said, Meirschultz has security," Lee said. "Someday soon, he probably won't be able to afford their services. But I have a plan for dealing with them. Doctor Ox, your professional credentials will help. The main push behind this trick, though, is going to involve people being scared of a lady like myself."

"I understand," Dickson said. Doctor Ox remained in the dark, not having the patience for deduction that Dickson did, but he figured he would know what was going on soon enough.

They exited the car, and Dickson lead the scientist forward. The doctor observed that Lee stayed behind. As they approached the door, Dickson recognized the guards as the typical American pinstripe-and-fedora gangsters—no doubt they were part of the Grisson Gang.

Dickson halted and waited for Doctor Ox to catch up to him, then whispered in the old man's ear: "Say to them exactly what I tell you to say."

The formerly-stout scientist approached the guards.

"Stop! Put 'em up!" barked one of the thugs.

"I am Doctor Ox. Doctor Meirschultz invited me to come here."

"Doctor. Meirschultz wouldn't invite no one. Man's a damn shut-in."

"No, you don't understand," Dickson said then. "Didn't he tell you we were sent to stop the, er, monster, that he created from escaping?"

"Th' *what* now?"

If he hadn't gotten prior warning, even a hardened man like Dickson would have to run in panic from the sight of the Human Spider. Evidently her act incorporated the deed of charging at crowds screaming monstrously, as she was good at it. The detective knew his setup had definitely helped produce the reaction he'd wanted in the guards, and he couldn't hide a proud grin as, shrieking in terror, the men stopping them immediately bolted into the dead of night. They were so fast that he couldn't tell exactly where they'd run off to—it didn't matter, at least for now.

"Cowards," hissed Doctor Ox. "I hear their leader, Slim Grisson himself, is what you Americans would call a momma's boy. His mother is the true master of the Gang."

Dickson said nothing. He noticed that O. Ming Lee was crying. He had become aware that she must have held some degree of shame for her appearance, and so their tactic was at her expense. He stepped towards her, and gently set his hand on her red-garbed shoulder—a shoulder from which three arms emerged. He figured that would be enough.

At once, she stopped crying, and turned to face Dickson. Without fear she set one on her hands on his shoulder in turn. "Thank you, Mr. Dickson."

"It's no trouble. Thank you for the assistance. Will you be joining us in ending this? Your company would make bearable the disappointment I'm about to get over the simplicity of this case."

"I can't. I have my act in the morning. In any case, I really shouldn't see Don, no matter what state he's in. I'm afraid that I've moved on with my life, and whatever he and I had is over."

Dickson nodded, and she began to move back to the road. "I'll catch a cab," she said over her shoulder.

He was pleased to see that in that glance, she was smiling.

"Marvelous," he mused, once she was out of sight.

"You are perhaps smitten, detective?" Doctor Ox said.

"In a purely aromantic and asexual way, doctor. I am fascinated, as you were, in her appearance, but I saw the person within as well. It's amazing how the human spirit always stays the same, no matter what the body looks like."

"Enough poems, Dickson. Let's get inside and get Meirschultz's hands off my work."

Doctor Ox pushed his frail frame against the lab's door, and summoned the heavy strength of his youth and namesake. To Dickson's surprise, the door yielded, breaking off its hinges—he caught it, to prevent it from smashing to the ground and giving away their presence.

Inside the building, there was only silence, and darkness. It didn't look like anyone was home.

Past an entrance parlor was simply a large chamber that represented, presumably, Doctor Meirschultz's lab proper. To Dickson, it seemed almost like the stereotype of a lab, with beakers, test tubes, and flasks scattered almost absent-mindedly atop endless seas of incomprehensible papers. In his eyes these were all clues, or pieces of evidence that could send Meirschultz to jail before he *did* find the secret of bringing corpses back to life.

Already Doctor Ox was standing near one of the counters, inspecting a syringe.

"'Super-adrenaline,'" the scientist read off the needle's label. "A euphemistic name if ever I heard one." He squinted, and Dickson observed with him that the formula for this substance was written below.

"Good God," the doctor gasped. "This is my drug! My psychosis-formula! He did steal it, that plagiarist basta—"

"Quiet, doctor," Dickson whispered. "We really shouldn't be caught here. Especially if Meirschultz is insistent on experimenting with human subjects..."

"Human subjects indeed!" a boisterous voice called out.

Suddenly, the lights were on in the lab, and Harry Dickson realized that even his dedication to observation had not quite taken in just how many dark corners the room had had. In one of these corners, their enemies had been waiting. The man who had bellowed at them, who crept from the darkness, had to have been Meirschultz. In a lot of ways, he was a match for the old photographs Dickson had seen of Doctor Ox. He was broad and strong-looking, but unlike Ox, he had an enormous Santa Claus-like beard, and thick circle-lens spectacles.

"You can vell imagine I vill use human subjects," the loud man said. "You have finally caught up with me, Ox. You are old and past your prime. Your vork, as primitive as it is, will be the token vith vhich I buy my way into greatness. It has already served me vell—in exchange for keeping my lab safe and obtaining chemicals for me, the Grisson Gang has applied a diluted version of your formula to their street product, their marijuana, to increase its potency. That was my promise to them: they would take the formula to become rich financially, so that I may become rich scientifically!"

Doctor Ox snorted. "What a tawdry use, but I expect nothing less from a group of imbecile mobsters. In any case, you're mad, Meirschultz, and that means something coming from the 'Terror of Quiquendone.' Even I can't rationalize why giving a hallucinogen to street criminals will help you resurrect the dead!"

"You have not paid attention to my vording, Ox. I will use your vork to *buy* the secret of life from someone who has better contacts than I."

Harry Dickson observed that Meirschultz was not alone. Hunched behind him was a thin pale man whose eyes and hair were even wilder than the scientist's. This must have been the ill-fated Don Maxwell. He looked like he had seen some of the worst atrocities imaginable. Ignoring Maxwell, Dickson said: "Who's this partner, then, Meirschultz? Who wants to use Ox's formula in exchange for the secret?"

"There is no point, Harry Dickson, in disguising my presence." There was a new voice in the room now, but the speaker didn't emerge from any shadow. He was just suddenly and simply there. "I am an emissary of Doctor Meirschultz's 'seller.'"

Dressed in a business suit was a stout Chinese man—his face was naturally round, made even rounder by a faint chubbiness. He had prominent eyebrows, and Dickson couldn't determine his age. He had a hateful look to him which was different from the hardness of Ichabod Chang. It was a willful hardness, rooted entirely in the glee of destroying human life.

"I am Li Shoon," the burly man said simply.

"Li Shoon?" Dickson murmured then. "I've heard of a Li Shoon Yen, a name which provokes a weird fear in the criminals who speak it."

"You are mistaken, and you suffer from a confusion of the ranks," Li Shoon interrupted. "The name is Li *Chang* Yen. It is a crime in itself to compare someone like me to him—he is the Master, and I am meant to die for him."

"And who is Li Chang Yen, then?"

"I will not yield that information easily, but perhaps the good Doctor Ox will know of him in one of his many, many names, his numberless faces. Consider a case from the Paris news bulletins of the hunchbacked crime-lord from a few decades back... Dickson, you'd be too young to remember."

Doctor Ox seemed to pale at Shoon's reference, but Dickson remained unimpressed.

"If you won't name your employer, then perhaps you'll identify yourself," the detective said.

"Sixteen years ago, I fought a minor investigator of some note, a 'gentlemen adventurer' named Donald Carrick. He called himself the Human Hound, and he killed my good servant, Weng-yu," Shoon explained. "Even you, Ox, would consider him arrogant, and Dickson resembles the Great Detective himself next to Carrick's foolhardiness. I allowed Carrick to think he'd killed me, but this was only a ruse so that I could wipe him from the world."

"So you sent the invitation that called me to America," Dickson said. "Carrick is dead, because you caught him off-guard by faking your death. And you used his name to forge a lure for me."

"But of course, Mr. Dickson. That I may obtain Ox's psychedelic and kill one of the men on Li Chang Yen's list of potential threats in one fell swoop is too good an offer to pass up. All I have to do is tell Dr. Meirschultz where to find a man named Legendre..."

"Again," Doctor Ox cried. "What use is there in you and your Master using and abusing my formula?"

"It's just possible, Doctor Ox, that your creation can be used to control the minds of those who imbibe it. Thus far, the Master has had many substances that can bind a man's will to his, like the Black Lotus, but he is always interested in obtaining more. It is a wise criminal who has diversity in his arsenal, and there are none wiser than my Master."

"There's more desperation than wisdom in that, you realize," Dickson said. "Or, at least, there's greed, which is rooted in desperation. And he's especially desperate if he is forced to resort to sending secret-leaking agents like you out. It's an unwise criminal who reveals the identity of his employer."

"How dare you?" There was no change in the enemy agent's face—he was perpetually filled with wrath. Doctor Ox was staring at Meirschultz, who was cringing just as Maxwell was, giant beads of sweat pouring down his aged face.

"I dare pretty easily, Li Shoon," Dickson shot back. "You realize that once I get out of this, I can begin tracking down your master!"

"You will not get away, though even if you did, you would not stop the Master. Greater men than you have tried for more than twenty years, and they have all failed to date. Now, if you excuse me, I would like to try to demonstrate, for the benefit the scientists in the room, a chemical marvel of my own—I call it the Lachesis venom, named of course for the Greek Fate. It's most efficient at cutting one's thread of life, and it is beyond even the Master's own toxins..."

Meirschultz cringed, and Dickson theorized that Li Shoon had taken pains to demonstrate his poison's effects before the burly scientist's eyes. The detective turned to look at what his foe's manner of dispensing his hidden weapon. But he never did see if it was a powder, a fluid, or a gas—to his regret. An ability to recognize that poison, he realized later, would have been a good skill to have. But suddenly his vision began to become clouded, as if his eyes had grown rheumy. Light blurred and attained a weird glow. It took him a little time to notice that Li Shoon seemed to be having the same issues with his vision. At once, Dickson's mind was flooded with a confusion akin to and yet searingly stronger than alcohol intoxication. The logic centers of his mind were still active—perhaps overly so. His brain was quickly flooded with weird fantasies and theories. And now the blurred light was breaking, and turning into shapes...

"Tom?"

The young man was standing there. But hadn't he gone with—with Sexton Blake's helper?

"Tom, how are you here? I thought you were in England... m-meeting with..."

"Monsieur Dickson, you are raving without reason," Doctor Ox said then. Immediately, to Dickson, the vision of Tom vanished, and he shook his head in genuine bewilderment. "You'll recall that, when I experimented on Quiquendone, my drug, rudimentary as it was at the time, could be dispersed without odor, color, or taste. Five minutes ago, I crushed a vial of it in my fist."

Dickson exhaled sharply, an act that shook him to his bones. "O-of course, doctor." It was hard for him to believe that this was not the sensation of death—that Li Shoon hadn't managed to unleash his toxin.

The remaining events were a blur to Harry Dickson when he later tried to recollect them.

Li Shoon was reeling, seemingly having had a poorer response to the drug than anyone else. Dickson didn't remember what Meirschultz and Maxwell were up to... though he had the lasting impression that Maxwell was screaming. Doctor Ox's words were turning into mush once they passed through his ears. Before he could do anything, the scientist was at Li Shoon's side, having smashed a flask. He drove the twinkling shards of glass into his belly, and crimson flowers poured from the wound, and danced wildly in the air.

As he died, Li Shoon spoke...

"Li Chang Yen—no matter what name he takes—always gets revenge. He will already know what has transpired here, and who was involved..."

Dickson remembered that *verbatim*. It was hard not to, especially because of what that statement triggered.

He passed out, having no choice in the matter. He had been the closest to Ox when the doctor had broken his vial, after all. But his mind started the act of unraveling the details behind Li Shoon's scheme—and he thought of his Master. The name he mentioned hadn't made sense at the time, but Ox's drug was making the sum of Dickson's memory merge into a single concentrated moment. He remembered now the hunchback called Hanoi Shan—and that name, "Shan," stretched and twisted like verbal putty until it became "Satan." And that name, in its ballet, turned around so it was backwards, instead being "Natas"...

43

And then, Maxwell's scream was gone. The lab was gone, along with everyone in it. A quick turn of the head revealed he was on the lab's lawn. He was now staring up into the night sky, which he realized was bizarrely clear for New York.

He stood up, then, the grass feeling disturbingly wet in his fingers. Without looking back, he dashed down to the road. Doctor Ox's car was gone, confirming his suspicion that the scientist had reclaimed his drug and fled back to the underworld. That left the detective without transportation, but he could stand the walk back. The exercise would help him clear his mind.

The next day, he returned to London.

There was no point in doing otherwise. Donald Carrick's invitation was a fake, and so there was no conference here. Dickson was glad to see New York again, but he had now spent so much of his life in Europe. He would have to make another homecoming soon—but Baker Street beckoned him, and he could never resist.

It was only when he sat alone in 221B that he remembered that *He* was supposed to live in London. He wouldn't be worthy of living here, though, if he wasn't willing to put his life on the line. He couldn't buckle to fear of Li Chang Yen, even though he now had a guess at what varieties of death the owner of that name could supply.

It wasn't long before Tom Wills came back home.

"Tom!" Dickson was glad he could greet his apprentice in the flesh, and overjoyed that he wasn't just a shade made by drugs.

"Good to see you, Guv!" Tom replied. And the elder detective stood so they could shake hands.

They exchanged pleasantries—Tom couldn't hold back the experiences he'd had with his host. It was better that way. The young man had had a much more cheerful experience than he, and Dickson didn't feel like overshadowing that with the implications of his adventure.

Tom was wrapping things up. "...and so that's what I found out about albinism. But before I took off, Guv..." And Dickson's ears perked up. "Tinker got a little obsessed with a story he read in the paper. I couldn't make heads or tails of it, Guv. It was about the murder of some circus freak or another..."

"Freak? What do you mean, Tom?"

"Some sort of spider-lady, Guv," Tom said then. "A Chinese bird named O. Ming Lee."

Harry Dickson felt a chill run through his entire body. He was suddenly struck with a deep sadness at Lee's death—while also feeling revulsion at the evil they'd come close to, which had caught up with her. He knew for sure not all of them would escape that presence, and he wondered if the world would ever hear from Doctor Ox again.

"O. Ming Lee was a wonderful person, Tom," he sighed.

"You knew her?!"

"Yes, I... I'll get to it." He was having rare difficulty with his speech. "I doubt the world will ever again see a Spider-Woman."

"God willing, Guv!"

Dickson forgave him for saying that. He hadn't met her.

And he hadn't seen her cry.

We haven't had a medieval crossover in Tales of the Shadowmen *since Sharan Newman's "The Beast Without" (Volume 7), which starred her own Catherine Levendeur with Bisclavret, a proto-werewolf from one of the Lais of Marie de France. Nicholas Boving follows in Sharan's footsteps with a highly entertaining tale that brings together one of Sir Walter Scott's greatest heroes, characters from the 1985 movie* Ladyhawke, *and Renaud the Montauban, the hero of numerous* Chansons de Geste *of the 12th and 13th centuries. Technically speaking, Renaud and his cousins were operating four centuries earlier in the days of Charlemagne, but what are four centuries between knights?*

Nicholas Boving: *The Aquila Curse*

"Have you heard of Ladyhawke?"

A blast of cold, damp air came down the chimney, blowing smoke out into the already thick miasma of the wayside inn, and threatening to lift its leaky thatched roof.

One of the two men sat before the miserable blaze, waved smoke away and looked curiously at the other.

"Friend, we have sat before this pitiful excuse of a fire for the past hour or more, have eyed each other with some suspicion, and not said a word until now. I am Wilfred of Ivanhoe, how do they call you, and who or what is this Ladyhawke?"

The other man, tall and well-built, dark visage burned by weather and the hot sun of Palestine, with a dark beard showing streaks of grey, smiled and extended a work-worn hand.

"I am Renaud de Montauban. Well, met Sir Wilfred." He leaned his elbows on the rough table. "But, before the story of Ladyhawke, let us see if this miserable establishment can produce some kind of a meal that would not make a pig vomit."

He lifted his voice and called for the landlord in a tone that allowed for no argument. The man, a fat, greasy-looking character with a cast in one eye and greed in the other, sidled over.

Their meal ordered, Montauban gave the man a kick and told him he had half an hour to produce it or he would be the worse for the delay. Then he held out his hands to the blaze and gave Ivanhoe an inquiring look.

"How long were you in the Holy Land?"

Ivanhoe smiled. "Is it that obvious? Then the answer is too long."

Montauban nodded. "And found it a den of thieves with only their fortunes in mind, with the saving of Jerusalem from the Moslems but an afterthought."

Ivanhoe drank from his beaker. "In truth, I found their leaders to be more honorable men than the so-called Christian knights."

"And so you return doubtless to your inheritance," Montauban chuckled.

Ivanhoe shook his head. "That I do not, for it was lost to me some years ago."

"That which is lost may be regained."

"Then I must regain a father with whom I am out of favor."

The Frenchman took a pull at his mulled wine and wiped his ragged moustache. "Families are ever at each other's throats, but a bended knee and an apology may forge reconciliation." He glanced at Ivanhoe. "Unless your knee is too stiff."

Ivanhoe shook his head. "No man but a fool would be so stubborn. But to return to my question, who is this Ladyhawke you speak of, and why should I be interested?"

"A much wronged woman; wronged by an evil man professing to be a man of God. As to why, well, I take you for an honorable man who might care to right a great wrong. I also take you for a man to whom adventure is no stranger, or else why would you have gone to the Holy Land."

Ivanhoe took another draught from his tankard. He said nothing, but the look in his eye betrayed his interest, and to his mind anything was probably better than facing his father in England if there was a way to avoid it for a while.

Their meal came, an earthen bowl of *potage:* a mixture of stewed root vegetables with occasional lumps of indistinguishable meat among them that might have been rabbit or indeed rat. But the smell was appetizing and both men were hungry enough not to care.

Montauban tore a chunk from the platter of bread and cheese that accompanied it, dipped the bread in the stew and thrust it in his mouth. As he chewed he shrugged, "I have eaten worse." He picked up a spoon and jabbed it at Ivanhoe, "Eat, good Sir. I warrant the Holy Land gave you an appetite for most fare." He dipped his spoon into the bowl. "For myself I found some of it to be over spiced, but then, beggars could not be choosers and I was among the beggars at that time."

Finally the bowl was emptied. Montauban wiped at chunk of bread around the rim to get the last drops, ate it, and belched. He drank from his tankard, shouted at the inn keeper for more, and sat back.

"The bishop of Aquila is a venal, evil son of Satan, whose rightful place is on the left hand of the Devil. He will no doubt spend eternity in the fires of Hell, but that fate will be of his own making.

"Some years back he became enamored of a lady, one Isabeau d'Anjou, a woman of great beauty and poise, and goodness. He importuned her, demanded that she returned his advances, and, when she did not, as she was herself enamored of a knight, an upright soldier by the name of Etienne de Navarre, he enacted a final stroke of villainous revenge, summoned the powers to which it seemed he had sold his soul, instead of those of Our Lord, and flung a curse upon the pair of them."

Despite his small belief in such things, for he was a hardened soldier and a practical man, Ivanhoe nevertheless was unable to contain his curiosity. He leaned forward, willing Montauban to continue, but the Frenchman knew that a good story should be drawn out to give the greatest enjoyment.

At that moment, the inn keeper reappeared with the tankards of mulled wine, and Montauban told him he wished to reserve a corner of the room for a private bed chamber.

The inn keeper looked doubtful as the inn was full, but the sight of silver suddenly made all things possible.

"Do you not also wish a place to sleep?" Montauban asked Ivanhoe.

The Englishman shook his head. "I am indeed a fine example of a poor knight, and in any case, I planned to sleep where my horse is stabled, as it would grieve me greatly should I wake to find him stolen in the night."

As Ivanhoe breakfasted poorly on cold, overdone mutton, stale bread and sour ale, Montauban came in; rubbing is hands against the cold. He was followed by a man to whom he bore a resemblance, soon to be explained in that he was his younger cousin. Montauban introduced him as Maugis, and hinted with what appeared a strange mixture of embarrassment and pride, that he had a well-deserved reputation as a wise man. Ivanhoe greeted him cautiously, as the term had darker connotations and implied sorcery, though whether of the black or the white variety was seldom distinguished. He decided to give the man the benefit of the doubt, seeing that the villain of their coming adventure had been described as a son of Satan.

He moved along the rough bench and pushed the remains of his breakfast towards them.

"At what time do we start?" he asked Montauban.

The Frenchman took a pull at the ale jug and made a face of displeasure. "*Sacrédieu!* Even the ale is undrinkable in this pig sty." He wiped his beard. "The sooner the better, Sir Wilfred. It would be well to be clear of this pass before the weather clamps down again; and the plain below is hot and dry at this time. Tomorrow we shall feed on grapes and wine made by those that understand the manner of its making."

From where the trail opened onto the wide valley, it seemed the distance would go on forever until it vanished into a haze and mountains the color of wild violets.

Towards the sunrise, the ground rose in steps with a twisting road splitting it like a crawling snake, until it reached a walled town dominated by an inevitable dome and belfry dedicated to a god who had no doubt long deserted the place. This, Montauban explained, was the fiefdom and see of the bishop of Aquila, he of the evil reputation.

Towards the sunrise and further down the valley, accessible only by a winding and easily defended track, rose the ramparts of a castle in sad need of repair, but to Ivanhoe's trained eye it had been masterfully situated.

He twisted in his saddle. "Which way, Sir Renaud?"

It was the cousin Maugis who answered. "The bishop's lair, and without stealth. It is best in some cases to let your enemy know you are coming."

"Then he has time to prepare," Ivanhoe said.

"Then he has time to be afraid, because he never knows when the strike will happen."

Ivanhoe stroked his beard. "He does not sound like a man who is easily afraid of anything, even God."

Montauban sneered. "Like all bullies he fears attack. He surrounds himself by those of a like mind, but he pays them little enough and the country here is too poor to provide pickings from raids."

"So, they may desert him in his hour of need."

Ivanhoe glanced up at the sky. The sun was past its height. "We must hurry if we are to reach Aquila before night. I doubt they will open the gates once closed."

Maugis clicked his tongue and moved his horse forward. "If we meet this bishop, better to leave the talking to me, at first, as he will recognize me for what I can perhaps do, and that will unsettle him."

A while later as they began the climb to the town gates, Ivanhoe asked, "This man is indeed a master of the black arts?"

"Enough to have put this curse upon two lovers," Maugis replied.

"Repeat it, if you please. It seems a little beyond my understanding, and perhaps belief."

Montbauban smiled. "And yet, here you are, Sir Wilfred."

Ivanhoe smiled back, but with little humur. "Indeed I am. But please tell the story once more."

Maugis cleared his throat. "The woman, Isabeau, is cursed to fly as a hawk during the daylight hours, while Navarre, her lover, is likewise condemned, but to take the form of a wolf during the hours of night. Thus, as you may understand, they may never again meet in their true forms."

"Is there no way to break this foul curse?" Ivanhoe asked.

"There is always a way," Maugis replied. "There is the way of the story, and then, perhaps, there is another way, which we shall discover if necessary."

Ivanhoe thought he did not like the sound of the second way, but then he found little sympathy for the bishop. "And the way of the legend is?"

"The curse may only be broken if both Isabeau and Navarre can face the Bishop together in their human forms."

"Presumably the bishop could be made to remove the curse."

Maugis nodded, "That is another way. But he is a stubborn and evil man."

Ivanhoe grunted. "My sword is stubborn also. Perhaps he will prefer to keep his head."

The sun had almost set when they reached the gates. At first it seemed the keepers were reluctant to let them in, but Montauban was persuasive and Ivanhoe tapped the pommel of his sword in a meaningful way. The moment they had passed through, the gates shut behind with a meaningful thud that clearly said no others would pass that way until dawn.

Ivanhoe eased himself down from his saddle and stretched. "The thought of reaching England and my father begins to look good, for I am weary of eternal riding."

"Even though you and he have this... disagreement?"

"Even so. Now, let us find an inn, food and wine." He raised an eyebrow, "Unless you wish to confront the bishop immediately."

Maugis shook his head and he too dismounted. "I shall send word so that he can have the night to ponder the meaning of our coming here."

An elderly man in a tattered monks robe sat warming his hands at a meager fire. He held a mug of cheap wine as he appeared to seek some answer from the flickering flames. He turned as a door opened, sending in a blast of cold night air along with a young man who closed the door quickly behind him.

"He is here," the young man said.

The monk, whose name was Imperius, replied without turning, "Who is here, Philippe?"

"The one who can save her: they one called Maugis."

"He is alone?"

Philippe scurried to the fire and also held out his hands to its faint warmth. "No. There are two others; knights, though of the poorer kind. From the look, they are recently returned from the Holy Land."

Imperius shrugged, "There are many such; as many as a dog has fleas. Do these men have names?"

Philippe reached out and took the mug. He drank from it and passed it back. "The one is called Renaud de Montauban."

Imperius started. "Devil take it. He is the cousin of this Maugis. There is something afoot. And the other?"

"An Englishman, a Saxon named Ivanhoe."

The monk shrugged again. "Him, I do not know. Do they travel together by design or by chance?"

Philippe shook his head. "That, I cannot tell, but they arrived just before the gates were shut. The guards were persuaded to let them in." He chuckled, "Their arguments were of an edged kind. This is to do with the lady?"

Imperius grunted, "Why else would such come to an accursed place like Aquila?"

Philippe squatted down before the fire. "It is my dearest wish that the bishop shall start on the road to hell."

Imperius gave another grunt, tinged with anger. "He is already on his way." He jabbed a forefinger at the rush-covered floor. "A man such as he can only go in one direction; and that is to Hell."

Outside the gates where the forest began, a beautiful fair-haired woman pulled up her hood and drew her cloak more firmly around her shoulders against the night chill. She reached down to stroke the rough fur of a black-coated wolf.

"I have heard that a strong wizard arrived at the gates last evening. He is with his cousin, an honorable knight, and another."

The wolf gave a low whine as if it understood. The woman replied, "It is possible he will have the powers to overcome this curse." She dropped to her knees and cried in anguish. "Dear God, will this never end? Will we never be free to love again?"

Inside the town walls in luxurious apartments, the Bishop of Aquila, woke from a bad dream and pushed his current mistress away. He got up and padded on bare feet to the window overlooking the main square. There was a full moon shining, coloring everything with a ghostly blue light. He shivered, and recalled the legend that to shiver without reason was to presage someone walking across your grave.

The bishop frowned as fragments of the dream came back showing the flight of a hawk and the lope of a black wolf, then a sudden switch to a bright light that almost blinded him.

His gaze was for irresistibly drawn to a table on which he maintained his private correspondence. There was a note on it, scribbled hastily on a scrap of parchment. At first, he had dismissed it as nonsense sent by an enemy to unsettle his mind, but now: after the dream?

The unknown shiver hardened to a cold clutch of fear in his bowels. He turned and strode to the door of his bed chamber, tore it open and opened his mouth to call for his captain of the guard. But something stopped him: perhaps reason, as he had no idea from where the note had come, and also he remembered his own dark powers. So he closed the door softly and returned to bed. Nothing could be achieved in the darkness, and in the meantime, the shadowy, opulent charms of his mistress beckoned.

The town of Aquila slept under the watchful eye of the moon, unaware that a great drama was about to be played. Good men, good wives, young, old, beggars and thieves; all slept. The wolf and the woman walked through the shadow of the trees, but for some reason she could not have explained, the woman felt a shaft of hope in her breast. The wolf, being a wolf, knew nothing, only that it had a longing and a hunger that was not satisfied by meat, or the chase.

Renaud de Montauban cut a thick slice of mutton from the cold leg. Mutton, bread and thin beer seemed to be standard fare along the road they had taken. He bit a chunk from it and chewed, hard. He looked across at Ivanhoe. "I'll bet that your father's table is better than this."

Ivanhoe shrugged. "It has been some years, but if my memory does not betray me, then yes, good sir, it was a table fit for a man who called himself by the title earl, and looked up all those on his lands as family." He reached for the cold leg and also cut a slice. "Still, a man must be thankful when the alternative is nothing." He smiled at Maugis, "What say you?"

"That the bishop's men will be combing Aquila for whoever sent him the message."

Montauban laughed. "What did you say, cousin?"

Maugis poured a little beer into a mug and drank. "That fate marched at his heels, and he would do well to look behind."

"Some might have said that was over bold and gave him too much warning."

Maugis disagreed, "No cousin, he needs the fear of God put into his miserable soul."

"I doubt that will do it," Ivanhoe said.

"No, good sir, but it will start his devilish mind working. He will, as you say, be searching high and low."

"And he will find us. Aquila is not a large town."

Maugis smiled. "Then we shall lead him a chase, and in doing so, he will trip and fall, for in his anxious haste to find us, he will not be looking where he puts his feet."

Even as he spoke, there was the sound of shouting and boots kicking at doors. At first some way off, it rapidly neared the inn. Montauban snatched the mutton, bread and cheese, wrapped them in a scarf and stood up. "Time to be out of here, good sirs. It would seem the bishop's men have their orders." He tossed a few coins on the table by way of payment.

Sometime later, the three clattered out of the town gates, having made it just before they were reclosed on the bishop's orders to prevent escape. Their exit had not been achieved without some sword play, but the keepers were not all that anxious to face knights wielding swords they patently knew how to use with effect. They left behind a couple of broken heads and much swearing.

As the knights cantered down the trail leading to the valley, the bishop's guard crowded the gate re-opening, orders were shouted, and men ran for horses.

Ivanhoe laughed. After more than several months of dull travel, he felt his blood stirring at the prospect of action and adventure. The slow return from the Holy Land had not been without its dangers, as the roads were much frequented by robbers, but his soul craved action, and it looked as if Maugis' note had provided the spur.

"Will the good bishop be among them?" he shouted.

Montauban laughed, "Leading from the rear if I know anything."

"Do we have a plan?"

Again Montauban laughed, "What do we need of a plan? Whatever plan there is must be to kill the bishop so the curse may be lifted."

Maugis cut in sharply, "No, cousin. Our plan is to cut the bishop from the herd and lead him to the castle." He pointed to the imposing ruin on the far side of the valley. "That is our goal. It is only there that the bishop can meet his fate. Should he die elsewhere, and not at the right time, the curse will not be reversed and the lady and her knight would be doomed for eternity, or the grave."

Ivanhoe touched his spurs to his horse's flank, "The castle it is. Still, I do not think you are without a plan."

Maugis also whipped up his horse, "Time enough for that. The hounds must follow we three foxes. We must cast red herrings and false trails. Let them see us here, and then there, until they are confused and split. Then we shall cut out the bishop like the good sheep dogs we are."

As they reached the meager river that ran winding along the valley floor, the path split. The major spur ran out along the river, the right hand spur led to the castle, while the left hand spur doubled back into the forest that covered the eastern side of the valley.

"I shall take the straight way to the castle," Maugis said. "Good cousin, take the left as you are a great woodsman and will lead them into utter confusion; after that, cut across the valley and come at us from the north." He turned to Ivanhoe, "And you, Sir Wilfred, follow the river until beyond that dark outcrop shaped like a dragon's back, then climb the slope and return to come down onto the castle from high ground."

Montauban laughed, "Not only a great sorcerer, but also a tactician." He reached across and slapped his cousin's shoulder. "With you, how can we not prevail? The bishop's brood may outnumber us, but they are doomed without knowing it."

Ivanhoe clicked his tongue at his horse. "As soldiers, we may prevail, but the bishop is a sorcerer, and one it seems of some strength."

Maugis moved away, and called back over his shoulder, "Then we shall see whose strength is the greatest." He went a little further and stopped. "Remember the hawk and the wolf; they are your friends."

As he spoke, there was a shout from the head of the valley and a group of horsemen appeared, among them, well guarded, was a red-cloaked figure. The bishop might be with his men, but he was not in the van.

Montauban sneered his contempt, tugged his horse's rein, and swung to the east, making no attempt to hide his progress, and in fact waiting till he heard the distant shouts of the bishop's men before breaking towards the tree-covered eastern slope.

Maugis, likewise, did not cover his movements as he took the narrow, rocky path that led to the ruined castle.

Ivanhoe proceeded down the valley at a leisurely pace, making no more speed than an innocent rider on a journey to what lay beyond.

The bishop's band, a dozen or so horses, the noonday sun glinting on steel, broke into a gallop, throwing up a cloud of dust that hung behind them on the still air.

From just inside the fringe of trees, Montauban watched as the horsemen reached the fork in the track. They reined in, milling around, no doubt deciding the best course of action, and fully aware that by splitting their force to follow all three, they therefore weakened themselves.

After a few minutes, the bishop pointed at the castle, and, with four men, began up the track to the castle. Four others swung to follow Montauban, while the remained, apparently thinking they had the easier and hence more enjoyable part of it, set off at a canter down the road after Ivanhoe.

Ivanhoe reached the dragon-shaped spur of rock and swung behind it, urging his horse up the hill so that he would have a view of those following him. As he arrived at his vantage point, he was startled by a voice, grabbed his sword haft and turned to face whatever enemy might be.

What he saw was a mounted and armored man, who held his hand in a sign of peace. It took only a moment for him to realize he was facing one part of the bishop's vengeful curse. He relaxed.

"I am Wilfred of Ivanhoe," he said.

The knight nodded, "And I am Etienne de Navarre, and indeed one part of that foul deed. I can guess your reason for being here, and thank you from the bottom of my heart, as would my lady if she could."

Ivanhoe pointed as a speck materialized from the air and dived at the bishop's red clock, missing him by inches, and swooping upwards toward the ruined battlements. Over the still morning air came the distinctive cry of a hawk.

"It seems your lady is intent on entering the fray."

A look of great hurt and sorrow crossed the knight's handsome face, then hardened to anger. "Would that we could both carry a sword at the same time, for my lady is a fearsome fighter."

Ivanhoe said softly, "Let us do what we came for, good sir."

Navarre nodded, "Then three swords will be better than two. "We three can make a meal of the bishop's men, as they are simply hired mercenaries and have no heart for the work. Whereas we... or, at least, I, have much heart stoked by a terrible anger and thirst for revenge."

Ivanhoe pointed back down the track, "And what of those?"

The small band of the bishop's men deployed to follow and no doubt deal with Ivanhoe, were at best a half mile back.

"Shall I lead them on, while you ambush them from the rear? There are only four of them."

Navarre shrugged. It was plain his mind was on more important things, but he saw the sense. There had been a great clatter of crows and pigeons from the forest on the far side of the valley, evidence to a soldier's senses that hot work had been going on, and then a horse burst from the fringe of trees, a rider swaying in the saddle.

He smiled, "It hardly seems worth the effort."

"But will force the bishop to attack from one point only."

Navarre nodded, "Go then, Sir Knight, a few hundred paces. You will know when to turn about."

Renaud de Montauban watched as the first horseman entered the trees, riding much too fast in his opinion. Generally a horse and trees are a poor combination, especially when some of those trees have low-hanging branches. He smiled grimly. If he was to be the fox, he would make sure some of the hounds had bloodied noses. He swung his horse from the shelter of thick-growing scrub and, making no effort to conceal himself, started up the hill.

There was the expected shout followed by the thud of horse's hooves on the leafy ground. De Montauban spurred his horse just a little, enough to gain ground, then veered sharply into a patch of deep shade, jumped from the horse, taking a long leather thong from over the saddle pommel, and ran back a few yards. There, he grasped the end of a branch that hung low and tempting, quickly tied one end of the thong to and paid out till he could attach the other end to the saddle with a quick release knot.

He waited, but not for long, until the first of his pursuers appeared, goading his mount at a reckless pace. The rider, one hand on the reins and one clutching an unsheathed sword, had no chance.

Montauban released the knot. The branch, held as taught as a bended bow, lashed back with the force of a kicking mule, catching the rider directly across the chest. The man was plucked from the saddle as if by a giant invisible hand, twisted through the air like a tumbler as he gave a great shout of shock, and rammed into the trunk of a tree behind. He fell to the ground and lay still. Montauban knew it was the stillness of death. It took only a few moments of precious time to relieve the dead man of a crossbow and quiver of bolts, and then he leaped back into the saddle and hurried up the hill, looking for a vantage point for his next attack.

It was late when Imperius stretched and yawned. "Breakfast," he said, to no one in particular.

The Mouse, Philippe, was sitting at the rough table. He held out a platter of bread and cheese and pointed to a jug of wine. Imperius shook his head.

"Bread and cheese I will have, but wine is the instigator of this great evil, for it had me in its seductive grasp and I spoke when I should have been silent."

Philippe shrugged as Imperius broke bread from the stale loaf and cut a slice of cheese with his knife. They ate in silence until finally the monk wiped his hands on his front and stood up.

"Come, Philippe," he said. "It maybe that I can undo some of what my weakness caused. Think you that you can get us out of this town under the eyes of the bishop's men?"

Philippe nodded. "What was done once can be done again."

Imperius frowned. The thought of scrambling through the sewers of Aquila was something he did not view with enthusiasm. He picked up his heavy staff and sighed. "Hey ho. Needs must when the Devil drives. Lead the way."

Maugis reached the top of the path to the castle and paused. What he saw pleased him: his plan was coming to fruition. At that moment the hawk flew close by and settled on the dry branch of a small dead tree. Maugis nodded his approval, for he knew the bishop would not be able to resist following, and far below the red cloak proved his point.

"Patience, lady," he murmured. "Soon your agony will be over and that Devil's spawn dead."

And with that he continued to climb until he reached the rickety bridge across the dry moat. He crossed himself and set foot on the precarious structure. The bridge swayed alarmingly, but he, and moments later he was on the other side and scrambling up the broken and tumbled stones that had been the outer wall.

Once inside the walls, Maugis set about learning the layout, for he had a plan in mind that involved his cousin and the English knight, to which company he had now added Captain Etienne de Navarre: for if the lady hawk was near, he reasoned her lover would not be far. To be sure, the bishop had a dozen or more men at his command, but they had no mission but to obey orders and probably little stomach for a fight, whereas Navarre, Ivanhoe and his brother were seasoned warriors and had right and a strong purpose on their side.

He looked at the hawk, still perched on the branch, and pointed down the slope to the bishop and his men. The hawk screeched and flapped its wings in obvious understanding. He would be warned, and had no need to keep watch.

Then he quartered the rock-strewn grounds, looking for a place to make his plan come to fruition. High above the sun was past its zenith: there was time to spare, in fact almost too much. The bishop would need to be kept at bay until the sun began to lower behind the mountains to the west, and that would be several hours.

Renaud de Montauban leaped from the saddle, secured his horse and ran crouching to the edge of the jumbled escarpment of rocks. He had a perfect view of the only possible route his pursuers could take. He put his foot in the stirrup of the crossbow, pulled the string back until it caught in the firing nut and placed a quarrel in the slot, just as the second rider appeared, saw the dead man and made to saw his horse's head around to get out of perceived harm's way.

Montauban fired. The bow string twanged. A split second later, there was a thud and a yell of shock and pain as the bolt hit the man squarely between his shoulders. The horse bolted, with its rider, already near to death, his arms locked around the saddle's front plate.

There was a shout of alarm from whoever followed, and then the crash of hooves through small stones and fallen branches.

Montauban waited, another arrow notched and ready, but the din subsided. It seemed two riders had taken the route up hill and were probably headed back to the town with an improbable story of being attacked by a huge force, or even a powerful wizard.

The other horse, its dead or dying rider still attached, had taken the path of less resistance and was heading down hill, and, in the way of horses when spooked, had no other thought than the safety of its stable.

Montauban sat back on his heels, the warm afternoon sun filtering through branches. He was well satisfied.

Imperius and Philippe slogged along the dusty path towards the valley bottom, when a horse burst out of the trees. The monk grabbed the young man's arm and made to drag him off the path, when something about the way the rider sat stopped him.

"Ho," he said, "Something is amiss. Perhaps luck turns out way for a change." Nevertheless he took precautions and squatted behind the poor protection of some bushes.

As the horse approached them, the old monk sprang out of cover, whirling his staff and shouting. The horse, already spooked, neighed with shock, skidded to a stop and reared. The rider fell off, hit the ground with a thud and remained still. Imperius approached cautiously and poked him with his staff. He looked at Philippe.

"It seems we have gained ourselves a horse and some weapons. God is good to us. Maybe he has forgiven some of my past transgressions."

Philippe wasn't so sure about that, but he untied the man's sword belt, and unfastened the crossbow and quiver from his back. He held them up. "Do you know how to use these things, brother?"

Imperius shrugged, "In my youth I had some small skill."

Philippe gentled the frightened horse. "At least we may ride." He squinted up at the sun, "The afternoon approaches and something tells me we would do well to be inside the castle walls before it the sun sets."

"If we can get past the bishop and his men."

Philippe's expression hardened. "He had the means and intent for hanging me, now perhaps we can lessen the number and give ourselves and the others the advantage."

"You are a vengeful young man, "the monk said, pointing at the bow. "A crossbow bolt is a fearsome thing."

Philippe was unimpressed. "No more so than a rope."

Ivanhoe rode on until he came to a point where the path threaded through a thin stand of trees. Out of sight of the bishop's men he halted and turned, and then like a thunderbolt he charged out of cover, his horse's hooves drumming on the hard-packed ground.

His followers reigned in. The sudden turn of events seemed to unnerve them. But then they got back their courage as they outnumbered the enemy four to one, and started towards Ivanhoe at a fast trot; which transformed into a canter as courage increased.

Behind them, Etienne de Navarre also burst out of hiding, shouting a war cry as he unsheathed his sword, whirling it above his head so the blade gleamed in the sunlight.

The effect of what had been a leisurely pursuit with an apparent obvious outcome, transforming into a two sided attack was nearly laughable: in fact Ivanhoe did laugh as he also unsheathed his sword and spurred his horse even harder.

The bishop's men were not battle-hardened soldiers, but Ivanhoe and Navarre were, and the odds of two to one had little impression on then: such odds were acceptable, and they had faced the Saracens in the Holy Land.

The fight was short. The bishop's men were lost and confused, with little of the trained soldier to keep them steady. Two of them were wounded and unhorsed in the first crash as both knights hit them at the same moment. The other two made as if they would fight, but the moment the knights turned their attention on them they rammed spurs into their mounts and fled back up the track towards the town and safety.

Navarre and Ivanhoe watched their cloud of dust. There was no point in following, and the bishop, if he lived, would have harsh words for them and harsher punishments.

"So what is Maugis' plan?" Navarre asked, wiping sweat from his brow.

Ivanhoe shrugged. "I know nothing except that he is up at the castle and told Montauban and me to join him." He frowned, "How did you know his name?"

Navarre gave a sigh. "You know of the curse. Maugis is a sorcerer and may have the means of lifting it."

Ivanhoe touched his spurs to his horse and took the slope so that they could approach the castle from high ground. There was no debating an unknown outcome, and he felt Navarre would perhaps keep the knowledge to himself until ready.

Maugis gave a grunt of satisfaction as he found what he was looking for. Sorcerer he might be, but he believed in insurance and had no way of knowing how powerful the bishop was.

It was a flagstone. He stood, looking at it, thinking. If he could ... then his cousin and the other could keep the bishop's attention while he focused his powers ... Maugis chuckled. The plan could work. He frowned: the plan had to work, or why else had they travelled so far?

There was a shout from below. Maugis went to the parapet and looked down. The scarlet cape of the bishop stood out like a target. The problem was the guards were no more than two or three bow shots away. He needed the immediate arrival of Ivanhoe and Montauban.

He started to move half a dozen chunks of broken blocks towards the edge. They would have to suffice because he had no weapon other than a knife.

Then he saw two small figures struggling up the slope from the track through the valley. One of them seemed to point at the castle. But who were they: friends or foemen, and there was a body lying on the track. It was mysterious. He shrugged and with a heave pushed one of the blocks over the parapet. It crashed far below, leapt into the air and bounded down the slope, gathering smaller stones as it went. He heard a shout of alarm and rolled the next block to the edge in readiness.

Imperius coughed, waved his hand in front of his face, and spat a gob of dusty muck. He struggled to his feet and leaned against the tree that had in all probability saved his life. He could see nothing but the cloud of dust that had followed the thunder of the avalanche.

"Philippe!" He shouted again, and again, to be finally rewarded with a croak from near his feet. He looked down and saw the Mouse, also struggling to his feet."

"What in God's name was that?"

Imperius wiped his face. "Maybe God visiting retribution on the bishop. In any case, it was an avalanche."

Philippe coughed. "The slope is not enough for such."

"Then there is someone in the castle who started it."

"Hopefully the bishop is stoned to death, though such a quick release is more than he deserves."

The monk hitched up his robe. "Let us find out."

They climbed a few yards until they emerged from the dust cloud, to be greeted by the sight of the bishop standing, apparently unharmed, and two of his men. Another two lay unmoving, felled like trees.

Philippe swore. "The Devil looks after his own."

The monk stopped, panting. "We must even the score somehow."

Philippe unhitched the crossbow. "Do you know how to use one of these?"

Imperius nodded, "In my youth I was a fair shot, at butts you understand, not men."

Philippe pointed. "That red cloak makes a fair target."

Imperius shook his head, "Not until the curse is lifted, and then I will gladly use him as such." He paused catching his breath. "Come, he is not the only one standing. Alone the devil's spawn may become afraid."

The care with which the monk and the mouse climbed the slope was unnecessary: the bishop and his last two men had their attention wholly on the castle. Still, they got within bow shot with ease and snugged themselves behind a small spur of rock. Without a word Philippe handed the monk the crossbow and quiver. Imperius took them almost reluctantly. "It has been a long time." He started to draw back the string until it caught in the nut and quoted, "Thou shalt not kill."

Philippe snort derision, "And eye for an eye perhaps?" Imperius fitted a bolt to the bow and rested it on the rock.

There was a twang as the string snapped back, followed a couple of seconds later by a shout of shock and agony. One of the bishops men whirled, tried vainly to pluck the bolt from his back where it sprouted like an obscene growth; and then fell and lay still. The monk murmured, "It seems my old skill has not completely deserted me, drunken old fool that I am."

"Indeed, it was a good shot," Philippe answered.

"Maybe God's hand directed mine."

"The other one?" Philippe asked mildly.

Again the monk shook his head, "With a hand to reach out to, he may carry on: alone he may turn tail and flee."

Maugis looked up from his task as he heard the click of horse's hooves on rock. He waved, "Well met, sirs." He got to his feet stiffly and held up his knife. "Not the best use for a blade, but needs must, it is said. I had not thought to see you just yet, Navarre."

"Where my lady is, in whatever form, there will I be also." As he said it, the hawk planed across from the tree and landed on the parapet near him. He reached out and touched her.

Maugis was pleased at the display, but there was little time for sentimentality. "Come," he said. "I need your strong arms to set the final piece in my trap."

The sun had moved another hand's breadth across the sky and was nearing the western mountains by the time the great flagstone had been carefully reset and balanced and all signs of disturbance erased. Maugis sat back on his heels and wiped sweat from his brow. "It is good," he said.

"I had thought magical thunderbolts at the very least," Ivanhoe said.

"Stories for dreamers, Sir Knight," Maugis replied. He tapped his forehead. "Real magic is done within the mind: as is believed, so shall it be."

"I doubt the lady and Navarre would agree."

"And yet, it is so. Without the power of the mind, their transformations could not happen." Maugis brushed his hands on his jerkin. "Once the mind is dead..." He spread his hands. "As you shall see."

A deep voice came from behind them, "I see nothing, cousin. You say the bishop's curse can be lifted: but what of the bell, book and candle? Where are the magic potions, the sacred pentagram?" Montauban got off his horse.

Maugis smiled, "I see the bishop's men greatly depleted in numbers, thanks to you knights, and it seems two men climbing the slope towards us."

"Then we outnumber him," Ivanhoe said, "He is beaten. Hah! If he had ten times us he would still be beaten."

Maugis shook his head, "Until he is dead by chance at sunset, we have achieved nothing. Timing is of the essence, Sir Knight. We must lure or chase the bishop to this spot."

Montauban grunted, "No doubt cousin you have a plan for that?"

Maugis waggled his hand. "It maybe that something draws near to fruition."

Ivanhoe frowned, "By chance?"

"The stone, the trap," Maugis said. "Lord save us, Sir Knight, are you so dense?"

"If a trap, then it cannot be by chance."

"It will be chance to him," Montauban said, his voice grim and harsh.

The bishop looked with disbelief at his remaining man. What had seemed easy, a mere exercise in gathering some recalcitrants and administering punishment in the form of a rope, was about to turn into a rout. For a moment he debated the wisdom of retreat to fight another day, but his reputation would suffer irreparably, and that was not to be borne.

He snarled an order at the man hovering anxiously nearby, telling him to gather the horses and wait, then he savagely spurred his own mount and lashed it to mount the rock-strewn slope to the bridge. The bishop was consumed by anger, and with anger his last vestige of fear left, to be replaced by an ache for vengeance. Those who opposed him would pay until they screamed for the merciful release of death.

He forced the reluctant horse to cross the swaying bridge, dislodging a few slats that fell into the dry moat below, and then he was on the ramp that led to the castle courtyard and the way up to the parapet.

The horse's hooves echoed harshly as he went under the long-disused drawbridge, and then lingering sunlight touch him as he cross the open ground. At the far end another ramp led up: he charged at it, careless of who might be waiting, only knowing that he had a great thirst that could only be slaked with blood.

He burst into the sunlight at the top of the castle to be shocked by what he saw. Not the lone sorcerer, but the cousin and the English knight. The odds were long, even with his powers. And then a hawk's screech made him turn quickly, and he was confronted with Etienne de Navarre. The hawk and the wolf were there to greet him. He snarled a challenge.

"So many against one? Have you no courage, any of you?"

Maugis took a step towards him. "The Devil against two lovers? Are you so consumed by greed and lust?"

It was no place to fight on horseback. The rooftop was small and bounded only by low parapets. The bishop leaped from his horse and drew his sword. A second later he had swung at the hawk, intending a death blow, but his sword was blocked with a stinging clash by Navarre.

"Now he fights women, and birds." Navarre's voice held massive contempt.

Ivanhoe and Montauban got slowly from their mounts and drew their swords. They waited for Maugis' words. There was a plan, there was a needful outcome, and it was to him they turned for instructions.

Maugis pointed to right and left. It was all the knights needed to know. They spread out, with Maugis in the centre, funneling the bishop towards the parapet. There was menace in their mien, a certainty that would have made any other run for safety. But the bishop had courage when roused, and he had his sorcery to rely on.

What he had not reckoned with was to have his attention split three ways. He swung his sword, eyes darting from one to the other of the knights while he summoned his force.

Montauban and Ivanhoe made no attack, they simply advanced. Meanwhile, Maugis drew in a great breath as he too summoned his inner force though doubting it was enough to defeat the bishop on its own.

As the deadly scene played out, the sun touched the top of the mountains and a dark shadow began to creep across the castle roof. Navarre tensed. The hawk cried out.

The bishop threw out his left hand, pointing, the forefinger quivering. Maugis stopped as if struck, then breathed deep again and said in a low voice, "Is that all the great bishop can do? It seems we have little to fear." But the bolt of energy had hit hard and his knees weakened. He took a pace forward and crossed his forearms a she spoke some words that neither knight understood. The bishop snarled and made to strike again, but Ivanhoe took two great strides, intent on finishing the matter despite what Maugis had warned.

The bishop shot his hand out again, pointing at the English knight. Ivanhoe stopped as if struck by a battle mace and dropped to one knee. Maugis shouted, "Obey my orders, Sir Knight, or die."

Ivanhoe got slowly to his feet, gripped his sword more firmly and nodded his compliance.

Slowly the bishop was forced back, edging at snail's pace towards the parapet and the trap prepared for him. And the look in his eyes changed from anger to a hint of fear. The sorcerer alone he could have bested, but with the knights dividing his attention, the full power of his magic was diminished.

Long shadows raced across the valley floor and up the far side, turning the woods into a realm of mystery and danger. He glanced up at the western mountains and a feral snarl came from his throat.

He took another step backwards and stood on the prepared flagstone. It wobbled, slid to one side and he lost his balance.

He twisted, fear stitched across his twisted mouth, tried to grab at something, anything, for support. There was nothing.

Ivanhoe, Maugis and Montauban stood, still, watching as the bishop, red cloak fluttering on the evening breeze, desperately tried to back away from the parapet; but his momentum was too much.

With arms flailing like windmills, he tried to regain his balance, and finally with a despairing shout of terror, he was gone.

At that second, the sun, a molten copper fingernail, vanished behind the mountains with a flash of green.

Ivanhoe, Montauban and Maugis slowly turned to where Etienne de Navarre was gently and carefully handing a beautiful, fair haired woman down from the parapet. For a moment, they looked at each other as if in disbelief, and then they were in each other's arms, and what followed was no business of the knights and the sorcerer who had made it possible. They turned to gaze out across the darkened valley.

"You are indeed a great sorcerer," Montauban murmured to his cousin.

Maugis gave a secret smile. "A wise man perhaps who uses what was already there."

"The Devil has by now reclaimed one of his own," Ivanhoe added.

There was a cough from behind them. They turned as one to see Navarre and the Lady Isabeau. Isabeau's eyes were filled with tears as she went to first Maugis to kiss him on the cheek, and then to the others.

"We owe you our lives and all hopes of happiness," she said, her voice husky with emotion. Navarre came to her side. "My sword is forever yours, Sirs, and with that my life."

Montauban shook his head, "Think no more of war: think only of life and the love you have for each other. That will be enough reward for any of us."

"Then let us give thanks," Isabeau said. She knelt, facing the east, and the knights and the sorcerer knelt at her side, the knights with their swords reversed to symbolize the cross.

The chill spring had evolved into hot summer, but the first leaves were falling as Ivanhoe walked his tired horse slowly along a forest path not far from the English city of Nottingham. It had been a long and arduous journey, not without dangers, not least of which was the sea crossing from France. His thoughts were on his father, Cedric the Saxon, and his eyes were turned inward to imaginings of what kind of greeting he might get.

Moments later his horse shied and he found himself surrounded by a ragtag mob of countrymen armed with staves and some longbows. There was one behind a fallen tree who aimed his arrow at Ivanhoe's heart.

"Good Sir Knight, allow us to have your purse and we will send you on your way."

Ivanhoe leaned his forearms on his saddle bow and laughed. "Poor pickings. Rather it is you who should give me money for I have not enough for my next meal."

The man stepped over the tree and lowered his bow. "A good horse, a sword and leather clothes: these speak of a man with money."

Ivanhoe shook his head. "You should apply to my father for alms if you are so desperate."

"Not desperate—although there is a price on our heads and a rope waiting if caught—but also free. We do as we please and answer to no man." He frowned. "You father? Who is your father?"

Ivanhoe sat back. "Cedric the Saxon. And who might you be?"

The man took a couple of steps forward, and then his bearded face broke into a smile. "The Good Lord save us. Can it be ...?" He reached up to take the horse's bridle. "Ivanhoe? Are you Wilfred of Ivanhoe?"

Ivanhoe reached down to clasp the outstretched hand. "And you are Robin of Locksley unless I miss my mark. What is a man like you doing skulking in the forest?"

"Staying out of the hangman's reach, feasting on the king's deer, robbing from the rich and giving to those less fortunate." He shrugged, but there was purpose in the brown eyes. "Doing as we please."

"Which King?" Ivanhoe asked.

Locksley spat. "No king but the usurper who sits on the throne. But our true king is Richard." He turned to his men and raised his fist in salute. "God save the king. Long live the Lionheart." He glanced up at Ivanhoe. "Come to our camp, Sir Wilfred, we will fill that belly and give you ale enough to slake a giant's thirst."

Ivanhoe gathered his reins and shook his head. "It cannot be, Robin. First, I have to make peace with my father. After that... who knows?"

Nathan's story is an informal follow-up (or, chronologically speaking a prequel) to our own "The Sincerest Form of Flattery" published in Volume 7, in which Diabolik met the modern green-masked Fantômas from the trilogy of films made in the 1960s by André Hunebelle, starring Louis de Funès and Jean Marais. To this explosive cocktail, Nathan added superspy OSS 177, created by Jean Bruce in 1949 (James Bond only began in 1953). In the books, despite his name (Hubert Bonisseur de la Bath), OSS 117 is an American citizen from Louisiana, who, after working for the OSS, goes on to work for the CIA. In two recent film adaptations by Michel Hazanavicius, starring Jean Dujardin, while remaining in period, the character was "frenchicized" and now works for French Intelligence. It is that version of OSS 117 whom we meet in...

Nathan Cabaniss: *From Paris with Hate*

November 5, 1964, 08:30:18 AM CEST +0200 UTC

The shadowed figure laced his gloved fingers together, cracking his knuckles and bringing the bustle of the room to a near-complete stop. Their eyes shifted uneasily to the makeshift throne where he sat, but none of them lingered for too long, eager to stay busy, or at the very least appear that way. The master was growing impatient, and none amongst them wanted the blame laid at their feet for furthering his wait. So they taped down cables to the floor, made sure the lights were in the correct position, tested the mikes to ensure the sound quality was up to snuff... anything to keep the eyes hiding in the silhouette upon the throne from singling them out from the sea of black jumpsuits.

"We have the signal," said one sitting behind a control panel, turning to look the director in the eye for further instruction. The director nodded, and the room was instantly silent. The camera whirred to life, and the director raised his hand, starting the count-down at five. He lowered his last digit, and pointed to the sinister figure sitting upon the throne. The lights went up, revealing it for the first time. Clad all in black, the most shocking thing was the creature's face: it had the general shape of a human head, but was utterly alien, with its wide-set eyes and nubbins of ears on each side. Completely hairless, the head was colored an unsettling pale green. A slit opened where the mouth should be, grinning as the thing spoke in a deep voice, smooth as silk.

"Hello, Paris. It's your old friend, Fantomas..."

November 5, 1964, 09:02:06 AM CEST +0200 UTC

"My problem, 117, is that a super-criminal who should be either dead or in a nursing home by now is broadcasting images of the Garde des Sceaux on his knees, bound-and-gagged and dressed as *Liberty Leading the People*, promising to kill him within three days unless he receives three million in three separate currencies..."

Hubert Bonisseur de la Bath, codename OSS 117, sat across from Armand Lesignac, his boss, trying his best to keep a straight face. It's not that he didn't care, or wouldn't do everything in his power to save the French Minister of Justice when it came right down to it, but... The man's image was now flashing across every major news station in the world, bound and gagged and dressed as *Liberty Leading the People*, his exposed right breast quite possibly larger than fair Marianne's. Certainly hairier, at any rate.

"Are you listening, Hubert?"

"Of course, Monsieur," 117 said. "Garde des Sceaux on TV, going to be killed in three days unless paid three million in three separate currencies. So... a bit of a pickle," he said innocently, hoping a little levity would take the edge off the room.

"Quite," Lesignac replied, not at all amused. "Obviously we're prepared to pay, if it comes to that, but it's not going to come to that."

"It doesn't matter either way. He's going to kill him no matter what, or turn right around and do something even worse."

"We shouldn't expect a man proclaiming to be Fantomas to do anything less."

"Do you think it's really him? He hasn't been seen in what...? Decades now? The man would have to be positively ancient."

"If he ever was a man in the first place," Lesignac said, resigned. "Who knows? Perhaps it's a relative... Lupin supposedly has a grandson running around Tokyo. Whether it's the original, a relative or just some thug with an eye for grandeur, all I care about are the threats he makes. And I have good reason to believe them. He's already put one of your fellow Americans into a body cast."

"Who?"

"077."

"Malloy, eh? He always was a bit... thick." Hubert leaned back into his chair, pulling his leg up across his lap. "Well, what's the plan?"

Lesignac smoothed his mustache and took his time in responding. Never a good sign.

"You're not going to like it, Hubert..."

"Oh, come on," 117 said. "We've got less than three days to save a French official dressed up like a tart from being executed live on television. How could it get any worse?"

November 5, 1964, 09:32:18 PM CEST +0200 UTC

It got considerably worse.

117 tried his best not to pace in front of the ice sculpture of mating flamingoes, but it was hard. At least, he had finally gotten Clouseau on task, establishing a perimeter and making sure his men kept their eyes open all around them; not even twenty minutes ago, the fool was attempting to serenade the gala with his violin. 117 would have rather staged the event without him, but Clouseau's history made him the ideal candidate. No one else in the world had more experience in dealing with the Pink Panther diamond and the dangerous types it attracted. It was an awful lot of trouble staging the gala at the last minute, but you can't trap any mice without the cheese. Then again, the more appropriate metaphor would be using the mice themselves to trap the cats.

He dully made his way through the crowd, watching each and every one of their faces carefully as he passed. The gala had been in full swing for over thirty minutes now, and there was no sign of any of the cats just yet. Of course, all of his targets were supposed masters of disguise, and he could have very likely already seen them a dozen times over. Still, there were no outward signs that anything was immediately wrong.

Out of the corner of his eye, 117 caught a glimpse of something glittering on the balcony. It was a girl, a blonde carefully perched against the handrail all by herself, watching the Parisian skyline. Curious, 117 stepped out on the balcony for a better look. She wore a mini-skirt that cut off right at the top of her thighs. It was made entirely of small, chrome discs sewn together in rows, their gaps revealing hints of bronzed skin beneath. Her golden hair was pulled tightly into a bun that sat atop her head, and large, hooped earrings dangled at her jawline. All in all, she was quite the vision—an angel in a miniskirt.

This bears further investigation, 117 thought. He casually saddled alongside her, resting his elbow on the handrail next to hers. She ignored his presence thoroughly.

"What's a nice girl like you doing out here all alone?"

She didn't bother to turn, keeping her gaze fixed on the horizon. "That's funny. I hear a strange buzzing. Must be a fly."

"Don't be that way. I just want to talk, is all. You look lonely out here by yourself…"

"When a beautiful girl is by herself, it is entirely because she wishes to be. Shoo, fly."

"We flies aren't so bad, you know. Victims of terrible rumors and hearsay."

This produced a smile. Finally, he was making progress. "Ah, not so cold after all, are we? May I at least have the pleasure of your name?"

"You may not."

"It's rather quite an easy thing, as far as requests go. Here, I'll show you: I'm Hubert Bonisseur de la Bath."

She stifled a giggle. "You're going to have to do something about that. Quite a mouthful."

"I could show you firsthand," 117 said with a smirk.

She finally deigned him worthy of a look, if only from the corner of her eye. After giving him a quick once-over, she returned her gaze to the horizon. "Quite bold of you, Monsieur."

"Contrary to popular opinion, we flies are bold little creatures. Who else would dare fly up to one such as you, with the threat of being swatted down all but inevitable?"

She smiled in spite of herself, looking down to the floor. "Can't," she said.

"Can't what?"

"My name. Eva Kant."

117 tensed beneath his expensive suit; just as he suspected. At least now he knew one of the cats had taken the bait.

"You are amusing, I'll give you that, but I'm afraid it will still get you no-where," she said, fingering her hooped earrings. "Now shoo, little fly, before my lover catches you talking to me."

"Perhaps I want to talk with him…"

117 jumped at the feel of a cold metal blade against his inner thigh. He felt the warmth of another body behind him, as if it had materialized out of thin air. A voice slipped in from the shadows, as deep and smooth as the would-be Fantomas when he made his televised demands earlier. The voice had the quali-ty of silk sheets being dragged across a bare thigh, or a dark, red wine being poured into an elegant glass: "My knife is pressed against your femoral artery. One slip, and you'll bleed out in minutes. What do you want with Mademoiselle Kant?"

"I was actually seeking the both of you," 117 said, taking care to keep eve-ry one of his muscles from twitching. Eva Kant remained where she stood, un-fazed; an elegant ice sculpture in her own right.

"It's clear this whole Pink Panther gala is a ruse to draw me out. The real question is: why?"

"Not just you," 117 said, a bead of sweat rolling down his temple. "I have need of you and other… like-minded individuals."

"Is that so… You're SDECE, right? What does French Intelligence want with me?"

"It's this Fantomas business," Eva Kant said, unprovoked. She finally turned away from the handrail, and circled around 117. "They want to assemble a special team, of sorts—composed of master-criminals, thieves and other such highly-skilled individuals. They seek to use our particular talents in the hopes of capturing this new Fantomas and his gang." She lifted her hand to 117's face, and traced her finger down his jaw-line. She stopped at his chin, pulling his face to meet eyes as green and clear as marbles fashioned from pure emerald. "Cor-rect?"

"A mind every bit as exceptional as the exquisite form that holds it," 117 said with a smile. The blade pressed harder against his thigh. 117 wiped the smile from his face.

"That really your plan?" the deep voice from behind said. "Pathetic. What do I care if some fat, foreign dignitary is killed?"

"We wouldn't engage your services for free. I'm prepared to make you an offer…"

"What do you possibly have to offer me? If there's something I want, then I take it. Mademoiselle Kant and I go wherever we please, whenever we please."

"Ah, but it would be so much easier without having to look over your shoulder all the time, yes? I can make your Interpol file disappear. Clean slate, for the both of you. That, and a handsome reward for the trouble…"

There was a long silence. As quickly as it had appeared, the blade slipped away from 117's inner thigh. He spun around carefully, just in time to see Eva Kant rest her hand against a shoulder made of shadow. The shadow stepped forward, powerful muscles beneath black leather—a panther in the guise of a man. He was dressed in black from head to toe, aside from the window on the face housing a pair of eyes. A black hand wrapped itself around the girl's waist, and she leaned into him ever so slightly. The connection between them was natural, easy. Unshakable.

Diabolik raised an eyebrow, and a chill crept down 117's spine.

"Who else are you planning to recruit?"

117 shrugged. "Whoever bothered showing up tonight. Best we could do on short notice."

Another long silence paused, and Diabolik took the moment to break his gaze from 117. He looked to Eva Kant, who merely nodded. "All right," he said. "But I want one thing very clear: I don't take orders. Not from you. Not from anyone."

"Fair enough, although we must all work together if we want to be successful."

"Should be easy, if it's just the three of us. Teamwork comes naturally to Mademoiselle Kant and I," Diabolik said, sheathing his knife on his belt.

Just then, an alarm sounded off on the floor above. All three turned toward the sound. Clouseau ran around like a madman inside, screaming his head off and gathering together his men. Someone had tripped the alarm upstairs.

"It would appear our ranks have grown," Eva Kant said.

November 5, 1964, 10:22:27 PM CEST +0200 UTC

117 entered the interrogation room to find the man they called Kriminal sitting in handcuffs. The dull halogen bulb lighting the room from above did no favors for his costume, the outline of a black skeleton carved across a fiery yel-

low catsuit. His skull-shaped mask sat on the table next to him, revealing his true face—a blonde, blandly handsome Aryan ideal.

Kriminal kept his eyes locked on 117 as he sat in the chair across from him, regarding him with a bemused superiority.

"Anthony Logan," 117 said, undoing the clasp to a manila envelope, "a.k.a. Kriminal, costumed thief and killer. Pleasure to make your acquaintance."

"I could kill you now, you know," Kriminal said, smiling. "Police cuffs were the first locks I ever learned to pick."

"Is that right? Then why haven't you done that already, Mr. Super-criminal?"

"Guess I wanna see where this is all going. Something fishy about that whole gala. Felt like a set-up."

"And yet still you came."

"It's the Pink Panther, mate. Can't ignore something like that making a public appearance." Kriminal leaned back in his seat, shaking his head. "You bloody spooks are all the same, with your little elaborate schemes and devices. If you needed my help, all you had to do was pick up the phone…"

"You're smart enough to have figured the gala for a ruse. You smart enough to savvy the reason why?"

"Fantomas, yeah? Best television I seen in years. You Frenchies should just have the original painting redone. Nothing else can hope to compare now." He paused, looking to the floor. "So, what, you putting together a collection of monsters in the hopes you can take on the biggest one of all?"

"We have no clue where to even begin looking. I've got a little over forty-eight hours to find where Fantomas is keeping the Minister of Justice. I already have a small team. Was hoping to rope you in, as well."

"And what's the offer on the table?"

"All record of you will be wiped clean from every database in the world, and we can offer financial recompense, as well."

Kriminal smiled in a way that made 117 very uncomfortable. "Listen here, I'll be straight with you, right? I could give a rat's ass about your little government officials. France could drop right into the face of the ocean and it wouldn't bother me a hair. Be a shame to lose a beauty like Paris, but the world ain't exactly short a' beautiful cities, know what I mean? And if this new Fantomas really is the Golden Oldie himself? I gotta be honest with you: I'm a great admirer of his work."

"You are more than welcome to turn us down, of course, but know this: I have already had it arranged with your own government for you to spend the rest of your natural life in a high-security 'Village,' where they send all the little secrets and mistakes they'd rather forget. Such as yourself." 117 did his best to speak with a level voice. Super-criminals didn't scare easily, so the best way to get to them was deliver the facts as briskly and straightforward as possible.

"And you may be thinking you can escape before all of that will ever occur, but just know that this station is currently surrounded by heavily-armed special forces, all of whom have orders to kill you on sight. As I said before, the choice is entirely yours."

Kriminal sighed. He was seemingly unfazed. "That bird you were talking to on the balcony, she was quite a bit of all right. She part of this little 'team' you got, then?"

"She is, but I'm afraid she's spoken for."

"Those do make for the best in bed." Kriminal shifted in his seat, weighing his options. Was the chance at stealing a rival criminal's girlfriend really going to be the deciding factor here? 117 wanted desperately to slouch back in the uncomfortable interrogation room chair and rub the growing ache at his temples. There was no way any of this was going to work. The chief was a fool to suggest it, and 117 an even bigger fool to agree in carrying it out. Trusting a gang of super-criminals to track down the location of what was very likely the *original* super-criminal? It was beyond absurd. 117 was thinking more and more that, if given the chance, he would just kill the Minister himself so they could all be done with it.

Kriminal finally looked up, his contemplations at an end. "When do we start?" he said with a smile.

November 6, 1964, 07:57:40 AM CEST +0200 UTC

The wheels of the Jaguar E-Type squealed, burning rubber on the asphalt.

Eva Kant flicked the rear-view mirror, saw two Citroën DS' roaring towards her. She flicked the mirror downwards again, checking her lipstick, before returning her eyes to the road. She slammed down the accelerator, barreling ahead of her pursuers, and turned the wheel sharply to the left. The Jag slid into a narrow alley just wide enough to hold it, and she brought the vehicle to a full stop with a screech of the brakes.

A figure leapt down from the roof above, taking his place in the passenger's seat. It was an older man with a graying beard and an eye-patch, dressed in a ratty, tweed suit.

"I take it the reconnaissance was a success?" she asked, with an upturned eyebrow.

"Getting the invitation to Fantomas' hideout, yes," the man said, reaching up to his earlobes. With a yank, he pulled off his entire face, revealing the black mask of Diabolik underneath. "Remaining undetected... not so much."

A stream of bullets pelted the glossy black rear of the Jaguar. The Citroëns squealed their way into the narrow alley, spitting hot lead from hidden machine gun compartments beneath the headlights. Eva Kant put the car into gear, and sped along the alley towards a street through the opening at the other end.

The Jag shot out on the street, Eva Kant's hand steady on the wheel. The Citroëns blasted out after them, knocking over tables and chairs and sending café patrons scurrying in all directions.

"Pesky little things," Kant said, reaching into her purse. She produced a small Walther pistol.

"You carry a gun now?" Diabolik yelled over the roar of the engine.

"Of course. I'm a secret agent," she replied, shifting her rear-end to the open window. "Take the wheel."

Diabolik scrambled to the driver's side, gripping the steering wheel hard after a brief moment of zig-zagging. Now sitting in the open window, Eva Kant took aim with the Walther. She squeezed off three shots. The third one hit, catching the front tire of the lead Citroën. It turned sharply, the opposite side lifting from the ground. The vehicle spun into barrel-roll, turning end over end before going up in a blur of fire and black smoke.

"This really isn't our style," Diabolik yelled. He had now shifted himself into the driver's seat, keeping the Jaguar purring as it raced ahead. "Are we absolutely sure this is the best use of our time?"

"I don't know. I find all this spy business quite fun," Eva Kant replied. "Plus, I don't like this new Fantomas. Gives off bad vibes…"

The second Citroën wheeled around the wreckage of the first, continuing its pursuit. Eva Kant took aim once more, but the Citroën wisely steered to the other side of the Jag. Frowning, she twisted back into the car, straddling Diabolik in the driver's seat.

Diabolik raised an eyebrow. "Hold that thought," she said with a smirk, weaving to the passenger's side. She leaned out the window. A stream of machine gun fire brought her back inside.

"All I'm saying is, what business is any of this to us?" Diabolik spun the wheel to wedge their pursuer into a nearby pallet of fruit cartons, but the Citroën braked, narrowly avoiding being clipped. "We serve no one but ourselves, and that's precisely why we've lasted as long as we have…"

"Be that as it may, we can't stand on the sidelines forever." Eva Kant darted her head and shoulder out the passenger window, pulled her trigger twice. Two spider-webs burst into the Citroën's windshield. The silhouette behind the wheel crumpled, and the Citroën swerved wildly in the street before crashing into a parked car.

Eva Kant leaned back into the passenger's seat, and caught her breath. "We may not need the world, but perhaps, from time to time, the world needs us. After all, if we want to keep leeching off the establishment, we must ensure there is still an establishment to leech from in the first place. Plus, there's no reason we can't find a way to benefit ourselves in this little endeavor in do-goodery…"

Diabolik didn't respond, but gave a slight nod. If he wasn't completely convinced, he was satisfied enough with her reasoning for now.

Sirens wailed closer to their location. Diabolik glanced in the rear-view mirror, and saw the trail of destruction left in their wake. "Hubert won't like this," he said, speeding them away from the scene.

November 6, 1964, 08:32:12 AM CEST +0200 UTC

"I just don't understand why those two get to go off on their own, while I get a babysitter…"

"We needed to split up. Diabolik and Mademoiselle Kant are used to working together, so that leaves you with me. Simple math."

117 didn't want to imply that he trusted the other two a hair more than Kriminal. It wasn't much more, but there was nothing in either of their files that ever suggested they had harmed innocents, so at least there was that. Kriminal, however… The Englishman was little more than a violent thug, willing to maim, torture or kill anything unfortunate enough to get in his way. 117 wanted to keep him on a tight leash, without tipping his hand to even being on the leash in the first place.

"Well, all right then, we're here. Now what?"

"This is the place?" 117 asked. It was a rather humble establishment, a restaurant so small it was barely noticeable when standing directly in front of it.

"It's not exactly hopping with activity at this hour, but if you want the up-and-up on the criminal world in Paris, this is the place to be."

"The plan, then, is to get into character," 117 said.

Kriminal nodded, and took off his trench-coat to reveal his flaming skeleton tights beneath. He produced his skull-faced mask and pulled it over his head.

"Just remember to pull your punches, yes?"

"Now, Huey," Kriminal said, climbing up towards the roof, "how could I ever live with myself if I hurt you?"

He really is the most reprehensible man, thought 117, before shaking his head and entering the restaurant.

November 6, 1964, 08:45:56 AM CEST +0200 UTC

117 exited the establishment through the front door. Or, to be more precise, was thrown through it.

The doorman, a hulking bruiser nearly twice his size, gave him a few choice words as he gathered himself up from the street, before promptly slamming the door behind him. 117 rubbed at his jaw, tasting blood in his mouth. Kriminal held nothing back when he took his shot. 117 should've known that the thug would relish the opportunity to belt him. He didn't like it, but the clock was ticking, and the best way for a criminal to earn another's trust is to point out The Man in their midst. He rolled his neck as he walked down the street, loosening up the stiffness from the blow. The car was parked a few alleys down. 117 got in and waited.

Several minutes passed. Kriminal should have gotten what they needed by now. There was no telling what the thug was getting up to when 117 wasn't around. He'd have to watch Kriminal carefully throughout the remainder of the mission. *Mission*, 117 thought, and laughed at the word. It was a joke. A twisted ruse at his expense. It was then 117 realized that he was almost certainly doomed to fail. The SDECE had ultimate deniability; if the mission was unsuccessful, his chief would wash his hands of it and leave 117 to take the lion's share of the blame. The whole thing was an international incident in the making, and the type of plan that no one would look kindly on... unless it proved to be successful after the fact.

A thud shook 117 from his thoughts, almost out from his very skin. Kriminal crouched on the hood of the car. He slithered off, and slid into the passenger's seat.

"Are you trying to give me a heart attack?"

"Live in eternal hope," Kriminal said, taking off his mask.

"What took you so long?"

"Took a sight more convincing, that one. Whole place was spooked after you came in and did your whole spiel."

"Did you at least get what we were after?"

Kriminal pulled an envelope from the linings in his costume. "Happy to report Phase One's a success, Guv'nor. That's the type of jargon you all use, yeah?"

117 rolled his eyes, and put the car into gear.

November 6, 1964, 07:30:25 PM CEST +0200 UTC

"You weren't supposed to destroy a whole city street!"

"Oh, calm down, Hubert. No one other than the deserving parties were harmed."

Eva Kant sipped her tea as if it was nothing. Diabolik and Kriminal sat behind her, sharpening their knives like they were in some sort of competition. The heater coughed and sputtered in the corner of the room, barely keeping the abandoned warehouse-turned-agency shelter warm from the cold. 117 felt like a ringleader whose circus had left him far behind.

"That's not the point," 117 said, trying his best to hold on to his composure.

"We successfully retrieved the invitation," Eva Kant said. "I thought that was the *entire* point..."

117 sighed. "Just give it here."

Eva Kant shrugged, retrieving the invite from her slender, black purse. 117 opened the envelope Kriminal had provided earlier, pulling out a card with holes punched in elaborate patterns. He placed the invite on the table in the center of the room, a simple missive printed in gold lettering on an elaborate cardstock.

"*Exotic work opportunities*," 117 said, reading the gold print of the invite. "Meaningless to all but the few who have the key…"

117 laid the perforated key card over the invitation, the cut-out spaces highlighting separate letters. He wrote them down on a different sheet of paper.

"All of that just to get a garble of letters?" Kriminal said.

"Not when you swap them out for their corresponding number," he said, flipping the key card over. There was a wheel inscribed beneath the perforations, a circle of characters over another of numbers. 117 traded his written-down letters for their respective number on the wheel. "Just as I suspected. Coordinates."

"Awfully clever," Ms. Kant said, setting her tea down and unrolling a map on the table. All four gathered around as they charted the exact location.

"The French Alps," 117 said. "Why not? Because where else would Fantomas conduct his business? Certainly not anywhere sensible."

"It's a base hidden *within* the mountain," Diabolik piped in. "Count on it."

"Whatever it is, we're hitting it in six hours. I want you all outfitted with the armorer immediately."

"Unnecessary. All I'll need is this baby right here," Kriminal said, flashing his knife.

"You'll need a damn sight more than that. I've already got our equipment picked out."

"A kill that can't be done with a knife is a kill I have no interest in…" Kriminal retorted.

"How original," Diabolik said, twirling his own knife in his hands. "Running around in a mask, knifing people. Wonder where you got that from?"

"Ask your girlfriend," Kriminal said, eyeing Eva Kant. "You ever tire out of eyebrows there, girl, and I'll show you what a real man's like…"

She remained unimpressed. "If you should find one such specimen, then please do send him my way."

"I think a test is in order," Diabolik said, holding his knife out in front of him. "Maybe we should cut open the third-rate knockoff to see if he's the genuine article, or merely filled with straw."

Kriminal smiled, raised his own knife. "Third-rate knockoff, eh? I don't know how long you been doin' this, mate, but I wrote the book on knifework…"

"Enough, the both of you!" 117 broke out. "You're all third-rate knockoffs! You, Satanik, Killing… Each one more uninspired that the last. Each one owing a debt to the original, which is the entire reason you're here in the first place!"

Diabolik and Kriminal cooled, each man sliding his knife back into his respective belt.

117 took a deep breath, and paused a minute to cool himself. "Now, you've got six hours before the bird's in the air. I suggest you all get some rest before then."

117 left the room, leaving Kriminal and Diabolik to glare at each other. Eva Kant picked up her cup, and resumed drinking her tea.

November 7, 1964, 02:24:46 AM CEST +0200 UTC

"Target in five!" the pilot shouted, and 117 and his team took their positions.

The cargo plane's interior was bitter cold, but that was nothing compared to what was coming. 117 put on his helmet for the dive, bracing himself for the worst.

"This a bad time to bow out and be taken in by the authorities?" Kriminal called out over the roar of the engines.

"You never know," 117 snapped back. "If the rest of us are lucky, you won't live out the jump."

Kriminal laughed, and put on his helmet. Eva Kant and Diabolik filed suit, affixing the goggles and breathing masks around their faces and strapping them tightly in place. 117 closed his eyes, and went over the details in his mind for the twelfth time. Jump, pull the chute before the ambient light was swept away from the low angle of the Earth... Ski three hundred meters down to the fortress' entrance at the mountain's base. The rest of the plan 117 didn't know, because he didn't have one after that. They would be flying blind, as there was no time to scout the area and make further preparations. Fantomas could have anywhere from twenty to a hundred men at his beck and call, and no telling what manner of defense set up around the perimeter. They would have to make the rest up as they went, but as long as they were careful--as long as they were quiet--the mission had a hair's breadth of being a success.

The docking bay opened, and the whoosh of cold air was enough to bite through the layers of thick polypropylene knit mesh. The French Alps sprawled beneath them, ghostly white lumps beneath the glow of the moon and stars.

No time to think about it. 117 stepped forward, and felt gravity pull him downward.

November 7, 1964, 02:49:33 AM CEST +0200 UTC

117's elbow tore open, just as the ground beneath him erupted in clods of ice and dirt. Tracer fire strafed the air as he fell flat on the snow. He fired ahead blindly with his submachine gun, hoping to send his assailants scattering. But they were well-trained, and weren't distracted so easily.

Fantomas must have known they were coming. That was the only explanation for why they were discovered so soon. 117 didn't know how. They jumped at such an altitude as to remain undetected. Their ski down the mountainside had equally been quiet and without incident, the four of them barely making a sound as they swept across the snow-covered dunes. All seemed to be going well as they approached the base's rear entrance, until the first shots rang out in the night sky.

The guards at the entrance advanced; 117 could almost feel the heat of their machine guns as they got closer. Their shots were wide, grazing the air around 117 like mad hornets--trapping him against the drift of snow he fell into. Like a pack of wolves, they fanned out, circling their prey and leaving no room for escape. 117 found himself staring into the barrels of four automatic weapons, cornering him from all sides. He imagined bullets tearing into him, perforating every angle of his being...

A stream of gunfire sounded off, but not from the guards. Eva Kant swooped down on her skis, the submachine gun alive and kicking in her hands. The stream dropped two where they stood, causing the other two to scatter. Diabolik sprung behind one, knifing him at the base of his spine before throwing the blade at the other. The last guard dropped, and Diabolik skied over to re-trieve his knife.

Eva Kant bent over 117 to inspect his arm. "Not as bad as it looks," she said. "In one end and out the other. Clean."

"Still hurts like wildfire," 117 said, sitting up with a growl. His arm flared, but he ignored it for the time being. Eva Kant retrieved a roll of gauze and disin-fectant from her satchel. "No time for that," 117 spat through gritted teeth.

"I've become accustomed to treating gunshot wounds in record time. Now hold still..."

"We caused enough of a ruckus to bring the whole house down on us now," Diabolik said, rejoining the party. "So much for the element of surprise."

"It was like they knew we were coming. Like they were—Ah!"

New embers of pain flared up where Eva Kant dabbed the disinfectant on his arm. "Like they were tipped off in advance," she finished for him, starting to wrap the gauze around his arm tightly. "I notice Mr. Logan is currently unac-counted for..."

117 looked about, and saw nothing around them but the dead men, lying in red stains on the snow. Kriminal was nowhere to be seen. "Damn it all. I should have known..." 117 seethed where he lay, so much so that he was surprised the snow beneath him didn't turn to vapor. A siren echoed from within the rear en-trance--the jig was up. An army of goons was likely bearing down on them at that very moment. He felt his plan slip away, as if trying to catch melting snow with his bare hands. All because 117 had made the critical error of leaving Kriminal alone for more than ten minutes. "I knew better than to trust that thug, and still this happens..."

"Time enough for self-flagellation later," Diabolik interrupted. "More guards will be here any minute. We need to be on the move."

Eva Kant took a length of cloth and tied the ends together. She looped it over 117's neck, and placed his arm in the make-shift sling. The pain mercifully abated to a dull throb.

"That'll hold it for now. Can you shoot with your left hand?" she asked.

"Well enough," 117 said, standing with a grunt. He let his anger subside for the moment, turning his attentions back to the task at hand. There were innumerable problems to be dealt with, but 117 didn't allow the weight of them to sink his nerve. He organized their severity in his head, seeing them as a list to be tackled one-by-one.

"We can still turn this to our advantage," he said. "They'll know we're here, but the bulk of the guard will be drawn to this point. If we can somehow sneak by them, it should make traversing the base undetected easier. If only we could find another way in..."

"Three steps ahead of you," Diabolik said. He produced a small map of the facility. "From one of the dead guards. There's an air duct nearby. Slim, but not so much that a body couldn't squeeze through. It looks like our ticket in, but..."

"But what?"

"It's a vertical shaft. We'll have to shimmy our way in," Diabolik said, acting out the motions with his arms on either side, reaching up one after the other. "Meaning you'll need two working arms..."

"So much for that," 117 said, motioning to his arm in the sling.

"We could still make it work," Eva Kant said, taking the map from her lover. "Look here: the shaft goes horizontal at this point, over a hallway leading to this entrance. If Diabolik and I go ahead, we could plant explosive charges on either side, bring the roof crashing down on top of them. That will clear the bulk of them, and Diabolik and I could pick off the stragglers. After that, you'll be able to waltz right in, Hubert."

117 stalled. If the plan were to work, Diabolik and his companion would have to leave *right now*. The window for success was incredibly small, but still 117 hesitated. Could he trust the two of them on their own?

Eva Kant seemed to sense his trepidation. She placed a hand on his shoulder. "We won't leave you hanging, Hubert. I promise."

He sighed. "Sure. Why not see how worse all of this can possibly get?"

"You'll know the signal when you hear it," Diabolik said, with a lift of his eyebrow. He and Eva Kant took off, leaving Hubert standing alone in the snow.

November 7, 1964, 02:50:19 AM CEST +0200 UTC

Kriminal shed the layers of his ski suit, and quickly dressed himself in the yellow and black skeletal jumpsuit that was his trademark, slipping on his skull-faced mask last. He was to present himself before the high priest of their most sacred order of super-crime, and thus wanted to be properly dressed for his rite.

78

Ditching the French fool and the Italian tarts was easy enough. *You should never make the mistake of trusting a Kriminal*, he thought with a chuckle. He expected the absolute worst out of everyone, and they never failed to surprise him with the depths of their naïveté. The world was nothing more than the meat of a rotting oyster, with the pearl at its center available only to those willing to tear their way through to get to it. Infiltrating a secret team of spies and pulling one over on them, in the process humiliating the lawmakers and sterling chiefs of justice of the world? Fantomas would have to admire such cunning and ruthlessness. Perhaps he would even make this skull-faced disciple his new right hand, putting Kriminal in the seat of power. Not to mention the perfect position to turn his knife to Fantomas himself, making Kriminal the new high priest of crime and terror...

But that was a matter for another day. Kriminal traversed the hallways until he came to what appeared to be a luxuriant dining hall. The chandeliers hung nearly twenty-five feet above, electric candles dulled in their arms of polished brass. The massive table and chairs were covered in dust-lined white sheets, with a massive fireplace at the head of the room, long grown cold from disuse.

Kriminal felt a presence behind him, and spun around on the balls of his feet, his hands raised to his skull-masked face in defense. A chilled silhouette stood absolutely still in the corner of the room, black-gloved hands folded over themselves and draped nonchalantly just beneath the navel.

"Did I startle you?" a voice echoed from nowhere in particular, creeping in at the edges of a room like a dagger being slid into soft flesh.

Kriminal shook involuntarily. The temperature of the room seemed to have dropped considerably. "Too many years looking over my shoulder, is all," Kriminal replied, dropping his hands and relaxing his posture.

"I remember those days. Always on the run. Always on the loose, someone or other on my tail. Cops, reporters, rival criminals... when you're at the top of the mountain, there's always someone looking to push you off. But you know how I've survived all these years? How it is I've stayed at the top of the heap?"

"How's that?"

The silhouette stepped forward, revealing its featureless face of pale green. Wearing a black shirt, suit and tie, it had the general shape of a man, but sat uneasily in those definitions, as if the man's body it sat within were nothing more than a vessel for a demon that could tear itself free at any second. A slit opened on the gargoyle face, carving a sinister grin into the visage.

"Fear," Fantomas said, with hints of laughter in his deep, hypnotic voice. "If you can make them fear you, you can make them do anything. Terror and fear are the only currency of any value in this world of ours. The secret oil that keeps the gears beneath everything we know grinding smoothly."

"I got that covered," Kriminal said, pointing to his mask.

Fantomas only smiled in response, before changing the subject. "You led the others into the trap, as previously agreed upon?"

Kriminal nodded. "Like lambs to the slaughter. They didn't know what hit 'em. I was able to sneak away with no problems."

"Good," Fantomas replied.

Kriminal waited for him to continue, but there was no further response. "So, what'll you be needing now? Anything you want, I think my resume speaks for itself..."

"Oh, of that I have no doubt," Fantomas said. "But while I appreciate your help in this little endeavor, I am afraid your services shall be no longer required."

It was everything Kriminal could do to keep from lashing out. He vibrated with anger. "No longer required? Now, listen here, I put my arse on the line for you. It's not easy playing double agent for the other side..."

"Yes, but you see, there is the issue of loyalty. An excellent back-stabber is still, after all, a back-stabber. Normally, I wouldn't worry, as long as I can hold them in place with fear. But you're not a man who scares easily. I don't have any other use for you."

Kriminal tore his mask off, letting Fantomas see the rage boiling underneath. "Maybe it's just as well, then. Maybe I can just save myself the trouble and kill you now, absorb this little empire of yours..."

Fantomas' head tilted to the side. Cold blue eyes burned deep within his sockets. "Really? You think you can take me, now?"

"I'm thinking more and more you're not the real deal, just someone with a lotta fancy tricks banking off a famous name. The real Fantomas would have to be a geriatric by now, anyway." Kriminal reached to the back of his belt, and retrieved his knife. "So, yeah... I'm thinking I could take you."

A long, slender knife appeared in Fantomas' hand in the blink of an eye. He held it up to his face, regarding its keen edge like a former lover. "It's been a long time since I've used one of these." He placed a finger to the knife's tip, tracing the blade down to its hilt. "I can remember every last one, you know. Every kill I ever made with a knife, all the way back to my early days in Whitechapel..."

"Now I know you're full of it. Fantomas didn't become active until the early twentieth century..."

"Fantomas, like evil, is immortal," the gargoyle replied, twirling the knife in his hand. "You can mark my words: there will always be a Fantomas."

"Big talk," Kriminal said, trying to hide the quiver in his voice. He may just be an imposter, a pretender to the throne... but he still had the name. The idea that he truly was Fantomas burrowed itself in the back of his mind and refused to leave. Kriminal held his knife out, and took a hesitant step forward. "Let's see if you can back it up..."

Fantomas' feet shifted on the ground to a wider stance. He raised his free hand for balance, bending the wrist that held the knife upwards before him. The thin slit in his face grew even wider, and his blue eyes glimmered like coals in a dying fire.

"All right, then. Have at it."

November 7, 1964, 03:00:37 AM CEST +0200 UTC

"How many more do we need?"

"Last one," Eva Kant said. She set the primer on the last explosive, and crawled back through the crawlspace, sliding down the vertical portion to meet Diabolik at the ventilation shaft's opening.

"We're set then?" he asked.

"All it takes now is the push of a button." Eva Kant retrieved the detonator from her belt, undoing the clasp at the tip to reveal a shiny, red button beneath. The clap of heavy boots thundered through the floor. Fantomas's guards would be in position within seconds.

She felt Diabolik stirring beside her in the dark of the shaft. "What is it?" she asked.

"I'm afraid I'm going to have to take that detonator from you now, Mademoiselle Kant," a voice that wasn't Diabolik answered from behind. A flash of steel briefly alighted in the darkened shaft. One second, Eva Kant saw Diabolik reaching for his knife; the next, the hilt of another was sticking out of his thigh.

Before she could call out, she felt the cold edge of a blade at her neck. "The detonator, if you please," the voice from the darkness said in her ear, barely above a whisper.

"You want the detonator?" she asked, thumb quivering over the red button. She heard the guards passing through the nearby hallway. A bead of sweat ran down the side of her neck, wetting the knife held against it. "All right, then…"

November 7, 1964, 03:01:00 AM CEST +0200 UTC

The ground shook beneath 117 as a portion of the ceiling collapsed within the base's interior. He wrapped the shoulder-strap of his submachine gun around the elbow of his good arm, and rushed into the open hanger at the rear entrance. A wall of rubble enshrouded over two dozen of Fantomas' guard, with a few stragglers caught just ahead of the blast. 117 picked them off quickly and cleanly. He continued on, his vision blurring from the detritus in the air.

Through the smoke and dust, the familiar form of Eva Kant came stumbling through. She fell to her knees, coughing, covered in soot and dirt and bleeding from a cut on her forehead. 117 bent to help her up, but she pushed him away.

"Still in there," she said, through bouts of coughing. "Needs help… he's still in there…"

117 heard the sounds of a struggle ahead, and slowly made his way through the thick layer of smoke enveloping the hall. Two figures became visible just ahead, shadows locked in combat. Knife-blades glinted through the smoke. A muffled grunt echoed through the wreckage. One of the shadows fell. The other grabbed it by the collar, and dragged it through the rubble. 117 steadied his submachine gun, finger grazing the trigger as the dust and smoke parted...

Limping, Diabolik stepped forward, and dropped the fallen Fantomas at 117's feet.

"Who's the third-rate knockoff now?" he said, sheathing his knife at his belt. Eva Kant pulled herself up from the floor, and ran into his arms. He slumped, bleeding profusely from his thigh. She eased him to the ground, and immediately set about dressing the wound.

"I think that's enough to earn our pardon, don't you?" Diabolik called out to 117.

"Don't go celebrating just yet," 117 replied. "Mission's not over until we see the Minister to safety."

"Oh, come on. I just bested the most notorious criminal of the twentieth century! His goons will be scattered and confused now."

"If it's really him," 117 said, unable to take his eyes from the comatose form of Fantomas. He was severely wounded, but still alive. Inspecting him closer, 117 noticed a seam running down the back of his smooth head.

"If it is the real Fantomas," Eva Kant said, biting one end of a bandage to tear it in half, "then all that signifies is that you've bested a man well into his nineties, darling..."

"Hardy-har," Diabolik threw back, as Eva Kant tied off the bandage on his leg.

117 reached down at the inhuman face and pulled. A soft rubber mask gave way, revealing a familiar, blandly handsome face underneath.

Eva Kant stopped what she was doing, raising her eyebrow. "Mr. Logan?"

117 nodded, looking back and forth between the wounded Kriminal and the rubber mask dangling in his hand. She helped Diabolik to his feet, stabilizing him by throwing his arm over her shoulder.

"Not the genuine article after all, eh?" Diabolik said. "Oh well... At least we know who's better with a knife *now*."

"An outcome we were all dying of anticipation to see," Eva Kant said dryly. Diabolik ignored her.

117 produced a pair of handcuffs and locked Kriminal's wrists behind his back. He opened his canteen, and splashed water over the comatose man's face.

Kriminal sprung to life, his eyes wide upon his pallid face. Trembling, his face twitched as he spoke softly. "Twenty steps back, thirty steps right, turn and again to the left," Kriminal mumbled over and over again, until his words ran into each other and became indecipherable.

"The hell's the matter with him?" Diabolik asked.

117 snapped his fingers in front of Kriminal's face, to no effect. The thug kept on, babbling incoherently and with his wide eyes fixed at some indistinguishable point.

"Don't really care, to be honest," 117 said. "In any event, we're not out of the woods yet. Diabolik, you're wounded, so you stay here with the half-wit. Mademoiselle Kant and I will finish the mission at hand."

"I told you, I don't take orders," Diabolik said. "And you're wounded, too."

"Yours is worse," 117 said. "And it's not an order. Think of it as a… special request."

Diabolik sighed. "Anything happens to her, and…"

"Oh, please. She's already saved both our lives tonight. Now that I've worked with the two of you, it's clear to me who the true brains of your little operation is…"

"A mind every bit as exceptional as the exquisite form that holds it," Eva Kant said with a smirk. Diabolik remained silent. "Let me make sure his bandages are tight enough before we go," she said, going over to inspect Diabolik again. 117 walked ahead, looking for a spot where the rubble of the wrecked ceiling wasn't piled so high.

As he searched, 117 felt a distinct change in the room's temperature. Everything seemed to grow… colder. The hairs on his arms raised, and 117 felt it behind him. Before he could turn, the point of a knife pressed itself against the base of his spine.

"You know who this is, don't you?" said a voice as smooth as silk.

117 remained absolutely still. "Unless you've managed to hypnotize another into pretending to be you…"

The voice chuckled. "Quite clever. Just like using my own bastard children against me. But also quite desperate. Foolish, really. You think men like us are so easily swayed into your confidence? That weak-minded fool would sell out his own mother, if it meant a small fortune."

"Then you both have something in common."

"*Heh.* That's more true than you know. But I'll tell you something else. You, and the governments of the world you represent… you're all the same. All you had to do was pay a small offering to get back your precious little official, and what do you do instead? Send little monsters of your own to steal him back in the quiet of the night."

"You left us no choice…"

"Ah, that's it, isn't it? The old 'desperate times call for desperate measures' ideal. But the truth is that you always have a choice; you just never fail to make the ones I want you to. Civilization has grown so complicated, and yet pushing it in the direction I wish remains as easy as it has ever been. All one has to do is insert the knife in the exact place, and twist it just so. Then the victim does whatever you wish."

"Is this all a game to you?" 117 asked. "You have half of Europe in a stir…"

"Yes, and you see how easy it was to do. But I think I'll let you have this round. The seed of fear has already been planted. I think I'll sit back and see how it grows. I'll be back in time. I always come back."

A small laughter slipped through the cracks of the silence around them, and the knife vanished from 117's back. He turned, gun at the ready, but saw nothing behind him.

November 7, 1964, 06:35:09 AM CEST +0200 UTC

"All things considered, Hubert, I'm amazed you actually pulled it off…"

"Glad to know you always believed in me, chief."

117 slumped in his seat, saw the French Alps become nothing more than lumps of sugar dotting the ground in the distance behind them. The Garde des Sceaux had finally calmed enough to fall into a gentle snore, although he warned everyone involved that there would be hell to pay as soon as they found themselves back in the capitol. Countless departmental oversights had been the cause of his exhausting (and quite embarrassing) abduction, and he would see to it personally that they all would be going through "rigorous restructuring of agencies and their processes." Translation: heads will roll like they hadn't since the time of Robespierre. As long as it would allow 117 to sleep for a week, he didn't care.

"We'll be shipping the Englishman back to his own country. He's their problem now. And I've already put a warrant out for the Italians, through Interpol and everyone else who would care to know."

I like you, Hubert, Diabolik had said, right as Eva Kant turned her gun on 117 upon returning with the Minister. *Pray we never meet again.*

And with that, the two of them made off into the night together. There wasn't anything 117 could do, really. The mission was over, and a success, at that. After Lesignac and the exfil team arrived on sight, it was discovered that several dummy accounts set up for SDECE agents abroad had been thoroughly drained of all funds. Oh, well… They did fulfill their promise in safely rescuing the Minister, so there was that. It would be a lie for 117 to say he never wanted to see Eva Kant again, but knowing that such a meeting would invariably involve her black-clad, eye-browed boyfriend, he was all right with the idea that they would never cross paths again.

117 closed his eyes. He tried to sleep, but never quite managed to drift off. It was that last bit, something that stayed with 117 throughout all the years to come. Whenever he couldn't sleep, whenever a job went south or a new threat

came across the wire, the words would find him wherever he was. The words that had seemingly appeared on the wind, belonging to a creature that 117 was not entirely sure could even be described as human:

I'll be back in time. I always come back.

Matthew Dennion revisits John Carpenter's classic 1978 film Halloween *and, in the best* Shadowmen *tradition, comes up with a wholly unanticipated twist. For those who may be unfamiliar with the Black Coats, the name "marchef" is a contraction of "Maréchal-des-logis-chef" (literally "marshal-of-lodgings"), a sub-officer rank used by some units of the French Army and roughly the equivalent of sergeant...*

Matthew Dennion: *A Purpose in Life*

Haddonfield, Illinois, 1963

The wind kicked up and blew several fallen leaves into Michael's mask as he walked down the street in his clown costume with his pillowcase in hand. The pillowcase carried far less candy than he was hoping for, but it was still early on Halloween night. In fact, the sun was just beginning to set, which was Michael's cue to start heading home.

Michael's night had to be short. Despite the fact the he was only six years old, he was out Trick-or-Treating by himself. His family did not have time for him tonight, just as they did not have time for him on any other night. His parents were at a party, and his sister was making herself up for her boyfriend, who would come over when she was supposed to be babysitting him. Another young boy might have gone out Trick-or-Treating with a friend and his parents, but Michael did not have any friends. He mainly kept to himself at school in a self-imposed friendlessness. It was not the other students who made Michael uncomfortable, it was Michael that made Michael feel uncomfortable. He simply felt out of place in his own skin. It was only on this night that he felt anything at all. When he put his mask on, he was no longer the empty shell that was Michael. With his mask on, he was something else, and that made him feel slightly more whole.

Michael had almost made it back home when the porch light on the house across the street suddenly turned on. He knew this to be the universal sign of a neighbor indicating to children that his house was now open for candy seekers. Michael began walking up the steps to the porch. The man in the house was new in town. He had only moved in a month ago. Michael heard his father talking to the man, who had introduced himself using a military title: General, Sergeant, Colonel... Michael couldn't remember for sure.

In Michael's mind, the strange thing was that he remembered the old man at all. Most people Michael met were like shadows that only existed in his consciousness while he was looking at them. As soon he turned his gaze from them, they no longer existed in his mind, but the old man was different. He stood out

86

to the boy. When Michael first saw him, he felt a surge of admiration and respect. It was the first time in his life that he had felt the desire to interact with another human.

When he came to the door, he knocked quietly.

The old man opened the door and Michael whispered:

"Trick-or-Treat."

A smile spread across the old man's face.

"Why, Michael! Happy Halloween! Come in, my boy, please come in! I have a very special treat for you on this night."

The old man turned and walked into his house as Michael silently followed him without a second thought. The Old Man sat down in a chair and motioned the boy to take the seat across from him.

The Old Man interlaced his fingers, and leaned forward.

"Michael, do you remember my name?"

Michael simply shook his head in response.

The old man laughed. "That's alright. You will know it well enough in time. I am Colonel Bozzo-Corona."

Michael simply stared at the Colonel, unable to take his eyes away from the charismatic figure.

The Colonel stared into Michael's soulless eyes.

"Michael, you came to my door seeking candy, but I can offer you much more than sweets. I know you, Michael. I know how unbearable life is for you. There is nothing in your existence that offers you a purpose. You have no friends, a family that is indifferent, and, more than that, you feel out of place in society. You know that you are not like all the other children. You may think of yourself as an outcast, but in fact, you feel disconnected because you are unique! You and I are special amongst the gathered throngs that people this planet."

The Colonel stood up and continued to address the boy.

"You can feel that what I am saying is true. You mind works differently than those of the other children; you perceive the world in ways that they do not. Even physically, you are starting to realize that you are different from the others. You are physically stronger than your classmates. Your reflexes are faster. Michael, would you like to know why you posses these abilities?"

The boy nodded affirmatively.

The Colonel smiled. "To understand what you are, you must first understand who I am. I am the leader of the Black Coats, the most powerful criminal organization in the world. For centuries, I have ruled them and used that power to control the criminal underworld. A man in a position such as mine must have ways to enforce his decisions. Allow me to introduce you to the man who enforces my will."

The Colonel snapped his figures and, from the dark room behind him, a hooded giant stepped into the living room. He was covered in muscles and carried a massive scimitar. Michael stared into the giant's eyes and immediately recognized the same soulless eyes that he himself possessed. He said nothing. He simply stared at the giant as if he was looking in a mirror for the first time.

The Colonel walked to Michael and placed his hand on the boy's shoulder.

"Michael, this is the Marchef. He is my enforcer and my high executioner. He is the instrument of my will personified. The Marchef will spend his life in glorious service to me. The rewards for his service are numerous. He is gifted with immense strength, stamina, and durability. No normal human can match his physical abilities. His greatest gift, however, is a purpose in life. It is his role to destroy those who would oppose me. You can sense it, can't you Michael? The connection you have to this man. The two of you are one and the same..."

Michael held his gaze on the Marchef while the Colonel continued his revelation:

"One day, the Marchef will no longer be able to carry out his duties. He will either die, or grow too old to carry out my wishes. This has occurred numerous times during my reign. When one Marchef is relieved of his duties, there is always another prepared to replace him. The dark forces of the universe determine who is destined to be the next Marchef. We have studied the signs, Michael, and there is no mistake: you have been chosen to be him. You will replace this man just as he replaced his predecessor. The physical attributes that he possesses will be bestowed upon you. You will be able to overpower any adversary, and wounds which would be mortal to most humans will be a mere annoyance to you. These gifts will all be yours, but the greatest gift, the gift of a purpose in life, cannot simply be bestowed—it must be accepted! You must choose to become the Marchef; you must choose to become a member of the Black Coats, and my most trusted follower."

The Colonel leaned closer to Michael and whispered in his ear:

"This choice is not made by simply agreeing to it. There is a price to be paid, through an act on your part. It is a simple exchange: in order to join the Black Coats, in effect, to become part of my family, you must first sacrifice the family of your birth." The Colonel continued with calculating precision. "A simple task for you, Michael. I have watched the interaction between you and your family. They tolerate you at best, and ignore you most of the time, whereas you are apathetic towards them. Go, my boy. Go and leave Michael Myers behind... Go and take the first step towards becoming the Marchef!"

Michael stood up and walked out the front door.

Night had fallen as he walked across the street to his house with a blank look on his face but his mind opened to a new direction in life.

Smith's Groves Hospital, 1978

The guard led Michael through the hallway to the visitor pavilion. It was a first for Michael. The only visitor he had ever had was his psychiatrist, and he'd stopped showing up years ago.

The guard led him to a thick plastic window and told him to sit down.

When Michael looked up he saw the face of the Colonel looking back at him, holding a phone connected to the wall in his hand.

He motioned for Michael to pick up the phone next to him.

Michael picked up the phone, but did not say a word; he simply waited for the Colonel to speak first.

The Colonel smiled.

"It's almost time for you to take your place at my side as the Marchef. The Black Coats have eliminated your parents. There is only one thing that stands in the way of you fulfilling your destiny. You have another sister; she is called Laurie Strode and still lives in Haddonfield. Prove yourself worthy to be the Marchef, escape this hospital, and slay your sister. Let nothing stand in your way! Do you understand your mission?"

Michael nodded affirmatively and hung up the phone.

Brian Gallagher has used Marie Nizet's Captain Liatoukine—from her ground-breaking 1879 novel Captain Vampire, *available from Black Coat Press, ISBN 978-1-934543-01-6)—to introduce us to the complex and murky world of vampire politics, moving progressively forward in time. While each story can be read independently from the others, the sequence is most impressive, starting with "City of the Nosferatu (Volume 10), "The Trial of Van Helsing" (Volume 11), and "The Stake and the Sickle" (Volume 12). Here is his latest installment...*

Brian Gallagher: *The Berlin Vampire*

Berlin, Soviet Sector, 16 June 1953

He had been killing Germans soldiers the last time he was here, thought Boris Liatoukine. Now he was back in Berlin—the Eastern part—where he expected to kill more Germans. Previously this had to do with the struggle against Hitler—and, of course, taking control of a chunk of Germany.

At the moment, the Germans seemed to be less than grateful for their induction into the glorious workers' paradise enjoyed by the people of the Soviet Union and elsewhere. The workers were striking—they seemed displeased with the rule of the local communists, the *Sozialistische Einheitspartei Deutschlands* (SED), and thus must be taught the error of their thinking. With the assistance of Russian tanks, of course—the power of which the locals would be aware.

Not that the Russian KGB vampire Boris Liatoukine entirely blamed them. Communist rule was, indeed, rather dull. All very ordinary and low grade—how he longed for the imperial courts of old, the genial atmosphere and the privileges of his then-high rank. Still, the Germans should know their place.

He looked at his newspaper—from the decadent West Berlin he enjoyed visiting.

It appeared that there had been some murders. Three people had been found largely drained of their blood. The "Berlin Vampire," they called the perpetrator.

What the newspaper did not report—because it had been kept secret by the SED—was that a number of such murders had also happened in the East. Liatoukine had no doubt that this was the work of a vampire, the primary reason he and his superior, Von Bork, were in Berlin.

A knock on the door distracted him.

"Come in," said Liatoukine.

A burly guard shoved in a handcuffed prisoner and sat him in front of the KGB officer and then left. The man in front of him, had been arrested a few days ago. He was a trade unionist who had demanded better living conditions.

He had few family, just a wife. This was why he had been brought to him. Liatoukine was not interested in this man's case. He simply looked at him.

The unfortunate trade unionist looked back at him. Why the silence, he thought. Why is he staring at me? He looked at this man—clearly a Russian. He had a pale face and black beard, but the eyes—they were like a cat's.

He could not take his eyes off him. He felt himself start shaking. His vision started to blur—his head seemed to move down, giving some sight of his hands—which were flaking away? He saw his hands as bones, and then saw no more.

There was no more to him but ash.

Liatoukine looked down at his handiwork. Liatoukine was a vampire—but living energy was what he took, not blood. He had feasted well. Not for nothing was he called "Captain Vampire" by some—despite now having the rank of Major.

He rang the buzzer. The guard came back in and was unsurprised by what he saw. Liatoukine said to him, "I have executed this man. As you can see, I have also cremated him—thus saving his widow some expense. Let it not be said the proletariat are not cared for!"

They both laughed.

Later that day, Liatoukine called on his superior, Von Bork. Their specialty was supernatural matters—dealing with any threats of that nature, but also using dark powers in the furtherance of Soviet aims, both at home and abroad.

He entered the spymaster's office, which, of course, was rather larger than his own. They were in an old German military building, taken over for Soviet purposes. It still bore the marks of war damage, despite some rebuilding to make it habitable.

Von Bork beckoned him to be seated. A man advancing in years, he had operated a spy ring in Britain for Imperial Germany just prior to the of outbreak of the first world war. He had been undone by the detective Sherlock Holmes and returned to Germany in disgrace. The communists there found use for his skills. He never looked back, and was now senior in the KGB. He had accumulated a number of supernatural operatives, Liatoukine included.

Liatoukine did wonder how, despite his advanced years, Von Bork managed to seem so fit and energetic. The German gestured to Liatoukine to sit down, which he did.

"Major Liatoukine, you have eaten, I understand?" he said.

"Yes, Berlin cuisine was better than I expected," the Russian vampire replied.

Von Bork smiled. "Good," he replied. "Moscow now wants us to assist more with the anti-state activities of local subversives. Still, we must not lose sight of this 'Berlin Vampire.' We have had information that these killings are directed by the West—the British MI6. The aim is to further destabilize the situation here. So far, they have failed. However, we must still capture the perpetrator."

Liatoukine considered this for a moment. This was not MI6's style, to use a vampire in such a manner. It was known that their equivalents there considered them too unreliable for such work. However, he was aware that the KGB had excellent sources from within the British security agency, and this was not likely to be bad information, unless Von Bork was not being entirely truthful. Liatoukine stroked his beard and said: "From newspaper reports in Berlin, the vampire has struck at least three times in allied sectors. That is less than the seven times we know of here, but why would they have their own vampire commit murders in the Western sectors?"

Von Bork seemed to have been ready for this question, and responded: "We think it is possible her bloodlust has taken over. "

"*Her?*" asked the Russian vampire.

Von Bork smiled. "The vampire is Countess Marcian Gregoryi."

Gregoryi! Liatoukine's mind raced. She was an old foe of Liatoukine's, once participating in a plan to eliminate his influence in the Sepulchre, the vampire city known as Selene to the humans. She had fled when that plan had failed. That was in 1913. He had not encountered her since. This was not unusual. The two world wars, whilst providing much death, also wiped out many vampires and, indeed, many humans who had opposed them. There were far fewer vampires and other supernatural beings now than there were in 1913. Where had she been all these years? There had been reports, sightings from his own sources and those of the KGB unit he worked for, but nothing confirmed.

"Has there been any information from the Sepulchre?" Liatoukine asked.

"Nothing. However, as she is working for MI6, she may well be avoiding the Sepulchre."

Liatoukine bristled. It was not for humans to refer to the city as such; he could not care less if they called it Selene or whatever. It was an affront, but it was a way for Von Bork to exercise his power over him. Liatoukine had tried to fight these communists and failed; they later found him and made him work for them. Liatoukine was playing a long game, waiting for circumstances to change.

"We have not heard from the city for a while," he said.

The German spymaster ignored the comment. "Find Gregoryi. Our superiors have much to question her about."

Back in his own office, Liatoukine pondered the situation. Did he detect a reluctance to discuss the Sepulchre? And why did their superiors want to talk to the Countess? They usually left such matters to them. He would have to question her first.

However, how would he capture her? She seemed to be moving between Eastern and Western sectors. He had issued a description of the Countess to checkpoints. This was hardly infallible; she may have made some cosmetic changes, and he certainly didn't what clothes she was wearing. He simply hoped that the guards would pay more attention to a beautiful woman crossing the checkpoints. However, she may not be moving around in a conventional manner. A vampire with her powers could cross borders without being detected.

Liatoukine considered the problem further. As a vampire, she could well be disguised as a human; as far as he could recall, she was one of those—like himself—who could, to a greater or lesser degree, operate in the sunlight. Then again, she could simply be holed up in various places. With her powers, it would be much easier to hide in various places—there were enough ruined buildings in both parts of Berlin left over since the war for her to hide in.

Liatoukine had looked at the police reports of the vampire murders. All most informative, and yet there were no reports of anything unusual, bar the killings themselves. There was always the possibility that there were details not included in the reports—matters so odd that the policemen writing them up would not wish to mention them in case it might cast doubt on their own competence. It would do no harm to go out on the ground and speak to the police directly. However, he knew he had to move fast. The political situation was decaying rapidly. He knew very well that Soviet tanks were to deployed to crush this German uprising—and that he himself may have to assist, regardless of the high priority of the current mission. The Countess would no doubt exploit the chaotic situation. As perhaps he could.

The Russian vampire made his way to the scene of the latest killing, not too far from the Brandenburg Gate. Naturally, some of the locals knew what had happened, but not the whole of the city, due to the information blackout—some word was spreading through subversive lines, but generally the public in East Berlin was unaware. The killings in West Berlin were more publicized due to the free press there. The RIAS—Radio in the American Sector—had not broadcast anything about the killings in what they called the Soviet Zone of Occupation.

Liatoukine went to see the policeman supervising the investigation locally. A Sergeant Schmidt. He was not in overall charge, but was the man who knew the area. Liatoukine met with him, not in an office, but in a local bar. This had not gone down well with East German higher ups, but they kept their objections to themselves. Now was not the time to stand in the way of the KGB.

"My dear Sergeant," Liatoukine began, having bought the policeman some schnapps, "I have read your notes on this murder. They are most efficiently presented."

Schultz nodded his head in a way that denoted his thanks for the compliment—although this was not the first time he had been commended on his efficiency by a Russian. Was it a genuine compliment or some sly remark on his being a German, he wondered.

Liatoukine gave nothing away on this. "The victim was a young woman, an Andrea Gruber, aged 20. You believe that she knew her attacker, perhaps?"

"Yes," Schultz replied. "Despite her throat being ripped out, there seemed to be no other resistance. She was unharmed in any other way. Her body was discovered in the morning. No one heard anything during the night either."

"You have spoken to her friends?"

"Friends, acquaintances, her comrades at work, they all seem to have alibis of one kind of the other, and we can't seem to find a motive. However, we are probing deeper. Naturally, we are seeing if any of them had any links with the other victims." He then added hurriedly "Of course, we are simply trying to eliminate all possibilities—we are aware of the view that the criminal is an agent of the imperialist West."

Liatoukine could see that this policeman thought little of the Western agent theory. He wondered how much coordination had gone into this investigation, given the secrecy involved. It was perfectly likely that only he and a few others had had full access to all the police reports. The Countess, of course, had mesmeric powers of seduction. Her victims would naturally put up little resistance. Male or female. He continued his questioning:

"Sergeant, aside from this murder, has there been any other strange occurrences? Matters that appear a little odd? We live in unsettled times—oddities may be a clue to subversive activities."

So that was it, thought Schultz—this was political. Like a number of regular police, his sympathies lay with the workers, and not with the SED and their quota mentality. Nevertheless, political or not, murders were being committed, and it would certainly not do to hold back.

The Sergeant looked at the Russian vampire. "There were..." he paused, his face clearly displaying some concern as to what he should say next.

Liatoukine made a gesture with his hand—suggestive of asking the Sergeant to continue. Which he did.

"...This may seem foolish, but some of the locals reported a green tint on their windows for the previous couple of nights—they could not detect the source. This came to us from the housing officials. But we could see no connection with the murder."

But Liatoukine did! Although he did not display any emotion, his mind was racing again. Some vampire's presence could be detected by strange green lights in the vicinity. They were often those who had strong connections with the Sepulchre—and Gregoryi certainly had that in the past. He himself had managed to master this embarrassing problem of late, but clearly the Countess had not. He now had a way of anticipating her next move.

Whatever the reason for her killing frenzy, she was still familiarizing herself with the local area before striking—still operating with some degree of caution.

Liatoukine moved fast. He sent a message to all police stations and through various channels asking for reports of such green lights. The request made vague mentions of them coming from Western spies using special cameras. It was nonsense, but no one queried it. Liatoukine wondered if those hunting the Countess in the Western sectors where using the same method. There could be no way of knowing where she would strike next—it could well be in the West.

He received a few reports; the witnessing of the lights coincided with the killings in the East, except for one, the previous night, 15 June. That could mean that, tonight, on 16 June, she might strike. He had to be ready. However, today was not the best day to lay a trap for a vampire...

Liatoukine was summoned to his superior's office.

"Have you not seen this?"

Von Bork waved a newspaper at his subordinate. He had. It was a copy of the day's *Die Tribune*. An article about compulsory work quotas had caused protests from construction workers building the Stalin-Allee boulevard. RIAS broadcasts were not helping either.

Von Bork was clearly feeling a little harassed. "It is likely we may have to intervene on some level. I cannot give you the men you require to trap Gregoryi. I have been explicitly told that the hunt for her now takes second place to the current political situation. Those SED fools seem to have been taken by surprise and have little idea what to do. All our personnel, including our more specialized ones, are to be put on stand-by to deal with matters as they arise."

Liatoukine knew that "specialized" was a euphemism by those higher up the chain of command for operatives such as himself—used to maintain secrecy, and as a form of mental denial of the reality of the supernatural.

Liatoukine leant forward across his superior's desk. "The Countess can cause further trouble by more killings—creating lack of confidence in the authorities here. She is a priority on that level."

"Quite so, my dear Major. That is why I can spare you six operatives. Not what you want, but all that can be spared. If any questions arise, then of course we are hunting for a western agent provocateur. See to it that no such questions arise if you do not capture her tonight."

With that, the Russian vampire took his leave. He found it quite interesting that Von Bork was keen enough to give him six people at this time of crisis. It could be his natural desire to capture the Countess as part of his duties, but Liatoukine sensed it could be something more. Perhaps Von Bork would also like to talk to her before handing her over to their superiors?

Liatoukine took his specialists to the streets around Bernauer Strasse. It was here that green tints had been reported on people's windows. There was a problem in that the area was next to the French sector. The Russian had already made up his mind that, if necessary, they would cross into it. They already had, whilst scouting the area earlier. It occurred to Liatoukine that, perhaps, the Countess had more recently targeted the Soviet sector due to secrecy; the killings in the Western sector had created some media interest—and thus pressure to find the culprit. Here, in the Soviet sector, there was a press blackout and people would not be so on guard.

It was now shortly past midnight. Liatoukine's operatives were well versed in secreting themselves in such urban areas. The day had proved eventful, politically. Whilst looking out for any signs of Gregoryi, he and his team had observed various workers protesting against the government. The Russian vampire was well aware that many of the factories had been dismantled and parts taken back to the Soviet Union. Liatoukine was no real communist, but he did approve of looting. However, he did wonder if things had gone too far. After all, if the Germans were allowed to create a bit more wealth, there would be more for Russia to take.

Liatoukine doubted that the Countess would make any kind of move during the day, with so many people milling about due to the political situation. The protests against the regime appeared to have petered out late in the evening. Liatoukine did not believe that would be the end of it—he was certainly aware that his Soviet comrades had moved tanks and men to areas of strategic value in the whole of East Germany.

In the last couple of hours, things had been quiet. His team had kept an eye on the few people who walked past. Such people were suspicious and should be questioned as to why they were about at this hour—but he did not want to scare away the Countess. Further, they served as useful, albeit unwitting, bait. However, the specialists were taking it in turns to venture out—observed by at least one other colleague. They were all in radio contact.

Liatoukine himself was atop a building, from where he could see more. A crackle on the radio and one of the specialists voices—a man called Ageykin—came over, "One of the street lights near the church is glowing green," he said.

This must be it! And yet, so close to the church? This was the neo-gothic Church of Reconciliation on the strasse. Vampires had difficulties with consecrated ground. Perhaps she was thinking of escaping to the French sector, reasoning that any pursuer would not follow her there? An error if so.

He ordered Ageykin to go onto the street and walk towards the street lamp but not beyond the church—and told everyone else to converge swiftly and as covertly as possible to him. His specialist would be used as bait—a duty the man understood and was well armed for.

Liatoukine had expected to get to the scene in but a couple of minutes—but then heard the radio again:

"Contact! Contact!" the specialist was screaming.

The Countess must have struck the moment the man broke cover. He scaled down the building he was on and ran to the scene. He was there a minute later.

In that minute, much appeared to have happened. With his enhanced abilities, he took in what had happened. Ageykin's weapon had been discarded but he could see no empty shells. One part of Liatoukine's mind considered this—the enemy had been able to deal with the specialist before he could use his weapon. However, his mind was mostly focused on what was happening on the steps of the Church. The specialist had been making his way up them, fleeing what was behind him.

And what was behind him was not the beautiful form of the Countess Gregoryi. No—this was some decaying creature in barely human form. The head was little more than a blackened skull with eyes, with putrid fluids dripping from the eye sockets. It seemed to be clad in some kind of military fatigues.

Steam was coming off the creature—as if it were burning? Perhaps due to proximity to the church? The specialist had not been able to deal with it and had run towards the church—a good strategy, but not enough. The creature was upon him. It had fangs and bit deep into Ageykin's throat.

Liatoukine bounded up to them and grabbed the thing. It dropped the unfortunate specialist and smashed its fist in the Liatoukine's face. The Russian dropped onto the ground, but picked himself back up quickly. As he did so, he saw the creature change. The blackened skull with fangs regenerated, white flesh appearing, and growing and long healthy hair flowing. It was the face of the Countess Gregoryi!

As her flesh grew back, she hissed in pain—the church was clearly causing her much pain. Before the Russian vampire had gathered his wits, she ran past him, kicking him savagely in the head and knocking him firmly back down. By this point, another specialist was present, with the others converging. The one in front brought out a crucifix rather than fire his weapon—mindful of the original instruction to capture if possible.

The Countess simply broke his arm, but clearly winced in pain at the cross, which fell to the ground. She grabbed the man, flew upwards and swiftly disappeared.

Liatoukine did not have that power. The Countess had eluded him. The specialist she took would soon be dead. However, Ageykin was still alive. He may be able to shed some light in the matter. His team gathered the wounded up and disappeared. It had not been a good night.

Liatoukine and his men had returned to their base. Von Bork was less than pleased with the night's events. In his office, he asked Liatoukine to give him the full details.

"Major Liatoukine, are you finally getting old? You and six top specialists were unable to deal with a single vampire?"

The Russian defended himself:

"The circumstances were not quite so simple. As I have already related, Countess Gregoryi has appeared to have changed into something else—or appears to be cursed. It gave her some new-found strength."

Liatoukine knew that this was not quite true. Her strength and powers were much the same as previously. She had always been formidable, but he had underestimated her—his pride coming before his strategic intelligence. And he had indeed been taken by surprise by her horrific new form. What lay behind that, he didn't yet know, but guessed that it was important.

The phone rang. Von Bork took the call and relayed to Liatoukine what he was told:

"The body of the specialist has been found. His remains were thrown into the Graf Spree. He appears to have been drained of blood, of course. He is in our sick bay. Perhaps this is an opportune time to look on Ageykin?"

Like most members of Von Bork's organization, Ageykin was Russian—very few human members were not, unless they had some extra skill. Von Bork considered non-Russians untrustworthy, and was especially careful about his supernatural workers, who had usually been forcibly recruited. However, it was inadvisable for any underling to point out Von Bork's German origins.

They found the Doctor just outside the sick bay. Liatoukine recognized him—Sitnikov. In his 40s, he was experienced as a combat medic having fought during the Great Patriotic War. He was also used to handling sensitive matters. He could keep his mouth shut, which is why Von Bork had recruited him. Still, Liatoukine was surprised to see him here. Was he not stationed elsewhere?

"Comrade Doctor, how is Ageykin? " asked Von Bork.

"Dead," Sitnikov replied.

Liatoukine was surprised to hear this.

"The man's wound's were severe, but I did not expect him to die so soon; he should have survived."

"Yes, he may have pulled through, but there appeared to be complications. He seemed to be suffering from some curious after-effects, causing some blistering on his face. It appeared that the Countess infected him with something. I have some more tests to run; come back in an hour or so. I should have some more answers then."

Von Bork nodded. "Very well. In the meantime, current events must be attended to."

He strode off back to his office, no doubt preparing to set some of his forces against the local German protestors—early indications had suggested that the previous day's unrest would continue. The Soviet army may be busy today. The Russian vampire had noted that Von Bork seemed strangely lacking in questions. The doctor closed the door of sick bay behind in a manner suggesting he did not want Liatoukine to see what was in there just yet. Swiftly, the Russian put a hand on the door before it closed, pushing it open a little to ensure the Doctor's head popped around to see what was happening.

"Doctor Sitnikov, I am surprised to see you here," said the vampire. "I thought you were stationed in our outpost in Kazakhstan?"

"I was. Comrade Von Bork summoned me here to help in the event of any political problems that may arise here, in addition to this business with your 'Berlin Vampire.'"

Liatoukine let the door go. "Thank you, comrade, I was simply curious."

And he was now even more curious. He would spend the next hour looking at Doctor Sitnikov's file—to which, of course, he had access.

The file did not yield much: honorable war service, and then some work with their department, treating those wounded by the supernatural, and researching the biology of such creatures. He had spent some time recently in Kurchatov in Kazakhstan, attached to the military there, whilst also being a liaison officer for their unit in the region. There was nothing obvious as to why Von Bork would have summoned the man. Liatoukine closed the file and got up to head to the sick bay. The hour was already up.

The Russian vampire was not surprised to see Von Bork already there—no doubt, already briefed. The German stood near to the door, almost blocking Liatoukine's way as he entered.

The room was small, but not so much that Von Bork would have had to stand back so far from the beds. Liatoukine understood the reason why in a split second. On two of the beds were the corpses of the specialists. In front of both beds was the doctor, clearly wearing a protective suit of some kind, complete with mask. He held some form of instrument in one hand and, with the other, he was motioning Liatoukine back. He took off his mask and spoke:

"Ah, Major, there you are. Let me show you what I have just demonstrated to Comrade Von Bork." He put the mask back on and waved the instrument at the first corpse—Ageykin. There was a ticking sound. He then moved over to the other one. The noise became louder. He turned back to the KGB men, taking off his mask again. "That was radiation. These men have been in contact with something radioactive. Do not be alarmed—there is not enough here to damage any of us provided we are careful. Indeed, Ageykin may have survived the dose had it not been for his other injuries. As to what this radioactive source is, I can only speculate that it was something on Gregoryi's person—or herself."

"This radiation may have caused Gregoryi's change in form," speculated Von Bork. "Perhaps a process akin to what we know as a mutation? She may have been subject to radioactive experiments by the West. We must find her and get the truth from her."

Liatoukine nodded his agreement. "The problem remains as to how to locate her," he said.

"That should be less of a problem now," the doctor said. "You have been tracking your target with sightings of reflection on window. Now you can track her with radiation detectors."

"Excellent," said Von Bork. "Major, you will be in charge of this operation. Send our men around the city—have them dressed as civilians. Their cover to the German authorities will be that of spying on the counter-revolutionaries. Indeed, they may as well file reports on such activity as well. Kill or capture the

Countess, Liatoukine, but try not to get too close to her."

Von Bork strode off, leaving any double meaning to his last phrase in the air. The Russian vampire swiftly realized why the doctor was there; his file said he had previously been stationed in Kurchatov, the base for the Soviet atom bomb testing site of Semipalatinsk. He had been involved in studying the medical effects of radiation. It was also convenient that a number of radiation detectors were so readily available. Von Bork knew more than he had been telling...

Liatoukine planned swiftly. As they were to provide intelligence on the subversive events of the day, as well as hunt for the Countess, he could use more specialists, and could even bring in some regular Soviet Army on the pretext of finding 'Western saboteurs.' Red Army tanks were already starting to move on the streets—Moscow had no confidence in the SED and its police to deal with the political situation. They believed the German authorities had no firm grasp on the matter.

Liatoukine could only concur. A procession of workers was already heading out to confront SED party leaders. News of the uprising had spread throughout East Germany; people were coming out on the streets in Bitterfeld, Halle Leipzig, and elsewhere. A radio car had even been taken over with comments such as "Goatee's got to go"—a reference to the SED leader Walter Ulbrecht's beard. Liatoukine cared nothing for the German leadership. He was annoyed, however, by disobedience of subject peoples to Russia, no matter what their grievance. Such people should be firmly dealt with—and the Red Army was going to do it. They had crushed Germans before, after all.

His priority now, however, was to find the Countess. He would help repress the Germans later. A number of supernatural operatives could not be used due to their inability to work in the daytime. Even his own powers were reduced.

As the day wore on, unrest continued. Liatoukine observed with pleasure Soviet tanks move against protesting crowds, breaking them up.

Strong traces of radiation had been found in the area around the Church of Reconciliation—it was important to find similar traces. The matter was compounded by the fact that, the previous night, the Countess had flown away. Liatoukine's main concern was, what if she had gone back to the West? If this had happened, his resources would be limited; he could hardly lead Soviet tanks in there—no matter as much as he wished to do so.

But never became necessary. There had been major clashes with protestors at Unter der Linden and in Potsdamer Platz. Now, his operatives detected some radiation at Potsdamer Platz. These had been larger readings. Presumably, the Countess was hiding amongst the protestors—perhaps in plain sight, Was it a deliberate ploy? Liatoukine doubted that she was aware of their new tracking methods, but would she stay in the area after the disturbances had been dealt with?

Suddenly, his phone rang. Von Bork wanted to see him immediately.

"Major Liatoukine, there have been new developments," Von Bork said as soon as the Russian vampire entered his office. He was standing and made no intimation that they should sit.

"One of our tank crews sent out to deal with the subversives returned to its barracks. Its crew is dead, except for the driver who had been ordered under hypnosis to return unobtrusively. He is of little use of us; he is not responding to our questions. The inside of the tank is full of radioactive traces. Countess Gregoryi must have somehow gotten inside and took her fill before leaving. We have no witnesses of a woman doing this—but however she did it, the situation has now changed. Our superiors are demanding that she be destroyed. Not only does this represent an attack on the Soviet Union, but, given the current situation, this can only create greater problems."

"Destroyed?" asked Liatoukine. "We still need to find out how she got into the state in which she is. Draining so much blood means that whatever is afflicting her is also draining her own energy at a rapid rate. We need to know how she came into contact with radioactive material."

"Liatoukine, that no longer matters," Von Bork impatiently responded. "Senior command want this problem dealt with right away. They do not care at the moment about the origin of the Countess' present condition. It has been made clear to me that, if we do not deal with it soon, others will be given the task of doing so. I would say that we have about 24 hours—if even that. How do you intend to find her?"

The Russian vampire paused before answering. Did their superiors really not care about how the Countess had suddenly become radioactive? Or Von Bork? This was surely important on so many levels—not least, the effect that radiation was clearly having on a vampire. Their superiors and Von Bork had obviously some idea of what had happened—and now urgently wanted her liquidated rather than have her complicate the situation in Berlin. It was he who had been kept unaware of what had really been going on.

The trouble at Potsdamer Platz had died down by late evening. Soviet tanks had done their work in crushing the protestors. Indeed, the German uprising throughout the country had been largely put down.

Aside from members of the security forces, the only people around were Liatoukine's own specialist staff—dressed in plain clothes.

Had the Countess left the area? This would surely be the logical thing to do, unless she was thinking of hiding somewhere where she thought she they would not look? Did she suspect they could find her via radiation traces? Then again, perhaps her condition caused her to behave erratically?

The Russian looked around the square. Nothing suspicious, his own men taking further radiation readings, a patch of mist, bored Soviet troops, the drab buildings, the—

Mist?

A patch of mist was drifting towards a stationary T-72 tank. Of course! Some vampires had the ability to turn into mist. It was a rare skill. Count Dracula himself had been said to have possessed such awesome power. This was no doubt how the Countess had been able to enter the previous tank. Now she was using the same trick again.

Why was she acting in such a fashion. though? As if she wanted to be caught? She could use this formidable power—albeit one that was said to take up much energy—to enter people's homes. Why tanks?

Liatoukine let the mist enter the tank. Then he rushed to it—clambering on top of it. He swiftly instructed his specialists not to interfere. He wanted to deal with the Countess alone. The tank crew was exiting, already in a panic. He jumped inside, a stake in his hand, confident he could deal with the Countess.

Too confident! He received a bullet between the eyes. His regenerative ability kicked in—but he was confused, his brain functions being impaired. He sensed, but did not fully comprehend, that he was under attack. Then he felt a pair of fangs penetrate deep into his throat.

He heard a scream, and, for a few moments, he felt nothing. It was enough time for his brain to regain some senses. In front of him, he could see the Countess vomiting blood and observe what seemed to be some kind of energy flashing around her face. A dead soldier was slumped at some controls—she had managed to kill him and drink some blood in the time it had taken him to get inside the tank. Her frenzy suddenly calmed. They looked at each other. Her appearance looked young and beautiful—as he remembered her from long in the past—but then he could see some patches of burnt blackness starting to form on her face and neck.

He recognized the energy flashes. They came from his body—he saw them sometimes, when he was injured. Then he understood her behavior. She had lured him into a trap—to get his energy presumably in the hope of curing whatever was ailing her. She confirmed this immediately.

"You were my last hope," she said bitterly.

Liatoukine could feel his head regenerating—she could no doubt see that, providing a contrast to her own lack of healing. She dropped the gun she had used against him. Liatoukine could see she had virtually given up.

"It seems my type of blood is not to your taste," he said, "if indeed you can call the energy that courses through my veins blood. More immediately, you are of course, surrounded. And I suspect your mist trick has already left you weakened—otherwise, you would have already employed it again to make your escape."

She nodded and said, "And so, you intend to destroy me. One day, your masters will come for you, given that humans have destroyed most of our kind."

Something in the Russian Vampire's expression gave away the fact that he may not quite know exactly what she was talking about.

"Oh, Boris, how it is that you have been kept in the dark? Do you not know of *Operation Tropic*?"

He looked at her levelly. "Perhaps you would care to enlighten me?" he said. He was not in the best of moods; not only was he not being fully informed of what was going on, but he had walked into a trap—not dissimilar to the ones set for him in the past.

She smiled—although that must have caused her slight pain, given that her face seemed to be gradually blackening with burns. "I can give you a memory of everything—as we vampires can."

Vampire had certain psychic powers, and could transfer memories to each other. Liatoukine realized that she could leave some matters out. Nevertheless, he would have the knowledge of this '*Operation Tropic*' within a moment, and given that time was not on his side, it seemed to present an excellent solution.

"Very well. Communion!" he said.

"Communion!" she replied.

And, in a moment, he had the memory. The memory was naturally edited, and entirely from her point of view.

London, January 1953 (Six Months Earlier)

The Countess stared across the table at her superior. He was an Englishmen simply called Control. Not his real name, but a code-name. She was a bit fed up with every other spymaster in the British secret services calling themselves "Control," "M," "Hunter" and the likes. Was it some English humor thing?

"This is not a course of action that I find credible," she said.

Control leaned forward to her. "Not at all. It seems to suit everyone, my dear Countess."

His use of her title was not intended to display any respect. Rather, he used it to emphasis her powerlessness. She had worked for the wrong side during the humans' last World War. The British had captured her, and, utilizing certain mystical techniques at their disposal to ensure her loyalty, had more or less recruited her to serve their MI6. This was not to her taste—she had hoped to flee Europe for a while. Still, it was better than working for the Soviets, whom she detested even more than the Western Allies.

"How so?" she asked.

"The atomic bombing of the Vampire City, or The Sepulchre, or Selene, whatever the bloody hell people call it, will remove a terrible threat to all humanity."

The Hungarian vampire rolled her eyes.

Control grinned. "Oh, very well. Stalin tells us that is why he wants to do it. Of course, we know that he thinks the city can't be trusted. He believes it colludes with us now, and probably did so with the Germans during the War."

The Countess groaned inwardly. For all she knew, the allies did deal with the Sepulchre. However, the fascists—and she had worked with them—were largely clueless about such matters, despite having access to territories, people and information involved with the supernatural. They followed their own lunatic mysticism. After the war, the West and the communists had gathered up what remained of Central Europe's supernatural heritage that hadn't been destroyed by two world wars, including her, of course.

Control continued. "We and the Cousins don't want the Soviets having any further access to the Vampire City—we would certainly enjoy the secrets of that place, but that does not seem feasible at the moment. Better it is wiped out rather than possibly offer the Reds anything useful at this time."

The Countess was not going to let this go too easily. "They do have secrets; the Sepulchre could still be useful to us if we could persuade the Russians to stay their hand, and open our own lines to it, perhaps via Tito?"

Tito was the communist dictator of Yugoslavia, on whose territory the Vampire City was situated. He was not on the best of terms with Stalin.

"Countess, this city has provided little of use to the Soviets, bar a few operatives. One of our own citizens in the late 1700s managed to create havoc there. The most recent national security threat from such creatures came in 1893, from Count Dracula, and that was seen off by a group of civilians.

"As for Tito, he is going along with it. He does not want Stalin finding some pretext to roll his tanks into Yugoslavia. What's more, Tito is as much a strongman as Stalin. He wants no opposition of any kind, and he will be happy to see the Vampire City gone. Of course, if they'd done a deal with him, that might be different, but their deal is with Moscow—a rather more powerful political center than Belgrade. One of the reasons this is a joint operation is that it make Tito feel better about it. Another, incidentally, is that Stalin wants to show us that he is capable of using atomic weapons. He will hardly listen to us, even if we were inclined to prevent it. Politics aside, you will be on the mission representing us. Don't even think about arguing. This can't go wrong—and on our side, you are the asset we have who has the most experience with Selene."

This was not something she had wanted to hear. She did not care much for the Sepulchre; their collusion with communists did not sit well with her—being against God was one thing, but taking her rights and properties for their own personal enrichment was another. Nonetheless, she was aware that humanity's wars had smashed the supernatural, especially in Central Europe. Indeed, the humans had seen that part of Europe effectively and simply divided between East and West. Was the end of the Vampire City in her long-term interest? For her, being immortal and dead, the long term was something that she could appreciate. However, there was perhaps a way to turn matters to her advantage...

Yugoslavia, March 1953 (Three Months Earlier)

The Countess found herself in Tito's Yugoslavia. The Sepulchre was in the

Vojvodina area, and sealed off. It was meant to be a military site—but, in reality, it was sealed off to keep people away from the Vampire City. There was plenty of vegetation around it. Keeping the secret thus far, since the emergence of cameras, had been something of feat. Of course, the existence of the City had had been rumored, and indeed a number of perfectly authentic photographs had managed to appear over the years. The Countess had seen them—and also the many other obviously fake pictures with different depictions of the City which the Yugoslav secret service and its Serbian predecessor had given to the gutter press to create confusion and disbelief.

The Countess looked around at her group, all dressed in Soviet military fatigues. Most were Russian, but some were not. She was there for the British—an MI6 officer was also there with her.

She recalled the recent briefing. Supposedly, under the long-standing Soviet-Selene Accord, the Russians were delivering books and documents that had originated from Dracula's castle and the library of the Scholomance—the school of dark arts the Count had attended. Vampires would study them and pass on their insights to Moscow. However, the large sealed casket on the lorry did not carry any such materials. It carried an atomic bomb.

It had to be done by land—dropping it from the air might run afoul of the various defenses the City employed against aircraft. Such defenses may not be of much use, but certainty was required, even if that involved risking people on the ground.

"Apparently, it's God's will that the City appears for but an hour a day. Presumably as warning to us humans. Do you believe that, Countess?" the voice came from her MI6 colleague, breaking her chain of thought. He was called David and was part of the MI6 team that dealt with the supernatural—a department of low importance staffed only by enthusiasts. She knew David had a view on beings like her—and that this act was something he almost certainly had no problems with.

"God is not an area I consider much. Why it materializes for an hour a day is mystery. Some vampires consider it does so to absorb energy from the Earth to power it," she responded.

"We'll certainly be giving it a lot of energy today," he said laughing.

She looked at him. It was a look that had struck terror into many people over the centuries—often the last thing most of them ever saw.

He laughed again. "Don't look at me like that. The actual material that Selene thinks it's getting provided us with the control we have over you—we can make you stake yourself if we want to."

Ah, so that was how they had control over her. Information gleaned from the great Count or his old school. Her will was often her own, but she was unable to flee or to disobey orders. Still, the power MI6 had was not absolute. She could not mesmerize David or look into his mind. However, she could sense things. Yes, he hated her, but deep down he desired her. She was beautiful—she knew this, of course. And he wanted her very badly. Perhaps these mixed feelings were to do with his bloodline? She had heard him been referred to as Harker—a slip by Control, who perhaps thought she was out of his hearing. She had little doubt he was related to the couple who participated in the murder of Dracula. Had the Count not had a certain hold over the woman Mina Harker?

Yes, a tiny weakness for vampires there. She would one day take great pleasure in giving him his desire. She would seduce him, turn him into a vampire and make him serve her forever. If he somehow survived the day that is. Whatever the precise nature of MI6's control over her will, she did not think it would extend into the Sepulchre. She had not been there for decades, but she had been in its vicinity in the course of her duties, and she had felt the spies hold lessen. What would happen if she entered it? MI6 kept her well away from entering the City, or indeed any centers of supernatural activity. They believed she would fail as an infiltrator. Her talents were sparingly used against human enemies of England, and the occasional mystical nuisance.

The City started to materialize at 11 a.m. as it did every day. The strange, abstract shapes of the Vampire City formed out of thin air.

"We are on," David said.

The carrying of the collection into the City had involved much negotiation. It would not be given over at the gate. It would be transported by the military into the heart of the City, at which point they would be given a receipt for it and leave. The vampires were used to Soviet bureaucracy.

The City fully materialized and its dark, sinister gates opened. The small convoy—a Soviet military car with she and David sitting in the back, an armored personnel carrier carrying the load, and another military car—moved slowly forward. Then the APC came to halt, breaking down. This was planned—after 30 minutes, the convoy would resume. The vampires would see nothing suspicious in this. They also expected that sort of thing from the Soviets.

After the "repairs," the convoy moved forward. It would take about ten minutes to get to the center of the City. The bomb was timed to go off a few seconds after it dematerialized back into whatever dimension it spent most of its time. Control had said the atomic explosion would have no effect on Earth whatsoever. The Countess recalled the void outside the City—there seemed to be nothing there. And vampires who had ventured too far into it had never returned.

The convoy moved into the City. Suddenly, the Countess could feel her freedom return. MI6's mystical hold had no longer any effect here—the real reason they kept her away from the Sepulchre. She instinctively gasped in pleasure. David noticed the change in her and brought up a stake. Should she kill him and warn the City? She leapt out of the car and flew upwards and towards the City center. She looked backwards briefly—the convoy was speeding up.

She flew down into the heart of the Vampire City, to its version of City Hall. A small delegation was there. She recognized the one who was in charge—

Baroness Phryne.

She landed gracefully in front of her—looking odd in her Soviet military fatigues. Phryne recognized her immediately. "Countess! how good to see you after..."

She cut him off. "Baroness, we have little time. The humans are betraying you. They are delivering not a collection of books and documents—but an atomic bomb. All the great powers have agreed to destroy you. You must get it away from the City—it is timed to detonate almost immediately after dematerialization"

"Don't be absurd—we have had an alliance with the Russians for decades now. We have heard, Countess, that you now work for the British? It would be in their interests for to create discord."

There was no time for this, thought Gregoryi. "If I am lying, then there will be no atomic explosion when you get it out of our city, and I will be your prisoner."

The Baroness looked at her warily. The convoy was arriving swiftly, and stopped. David got out of his car.

He went straight up to them. In perfect Russian he said: "This is a British agent—she is here to get you to reject the collection, claiming it's an atom bomb. Their operatives outside the gate are now being arrested."

Baroness Phryne looked at him warily also—although she knew a couple of the officers with him, she did not know this man. One of the officers she recognized waved a radio and said: "It's true—our comrades have had to subdue them."

David said: "We have to get back to help—and your city is leaving in a few minutes." He pointed to the Countess, "Her, we're happy to leave to your justice."

With that, he and the others headed back to their cars and drove off.

There was no time to unravel any of this. Baroness Phryne motioned to her minions to take hold of the Countess. But she smashed them away and lunged for the cab of the lorry. She got in and tried to start the vehicle—but all that happened was a loud bang. The wheels had collapsed. The lorry was immobilized. Phryne's servants grabbed her and pulled her out.

She flung them aside with ease, and said to the Baroness. "Look—they have immobilized their own vehicle! Why would they do this? Why? We must physically move the bomb ourselves."

The Baroness was frozen in indecisiveness. Gregoryi ran to the back of the lorry and leaped in—and was then repelled backwards. On the large casket containing the bomb was a silver cross. A number of them had been strewn around the lorry. Along with garlic and bottles of holy water. Such tools were standard weapons carried by the Soviets in the vehicles they used when entering the Vampire City. They were no doubt hung there the moment she had escaped.

The Countess staggered back in and knocked the cross off the casket, burning her hand. She screamed out in agony.

"Help me, you fools!" she commanded the vampires.

They tried to get in but were repelled. Even Baroness Phryne could not seem to get in.

She realized then there was no hope. They could perhaps move it in time, but they could not face the pain and fear of dealing with the crosses and holy water. The water had even been splashed on the casket. Her will was far stronger—she could, but was unable to move the bomb alone.

Survival was now the objective. She flung herself out of the lorry and flew down the road. She could see the convoy ahead, still not out of the City. They had been slowed by attacking vampires. Someone in Phryne's entourage had presumably taken her seriously and got word out to stop them. Much good that would do. The humans were giving a good account of themselves—with silver bullets and weapons firing stakes. She could see their vehicles smash through the gates and out. She was flying hard and fast to catch up—she would be back under MI6 control and they may very destroy her, but she faced certain death if she stayed.

The Vampire City was already starting to dematerialize! She flew down to the damaged gate which had had been closed, but, due to the damage sustained by the convoy smashing out, was not locked. She wrenched it open with all the strength in her possession.

She later saw an image drawn of what the Soviet troops outside saw at that moment. A black skeletal silhouette of her—unrecognizable—against a blinding white flash. They had to describe it, for their eyesight had been damaged.

The bomb had gone off slightly early. It was not known why. However, the blast took place after most of the City had already dematerialized. It was not widely known if opening the gate would provide entrance and exit for a few seconds more. The flash out of the gateway was momentary—and not even completed. It was enough to leave behind some radiation, but easily covered up.

She had been vaporized, but her dust had been blasted out. After a few days, she somehow reformed. First, she appeared as mist, and then floated away from the area—this ensured she was not noticed by the observation team left to see if the City would return. Her survival had been achieved by sheer force of will; the Countess refused to die. Only when she was safe did she change back to a solid form—a blackened skeletal form. She came across a peasant later and drained him of his blood and reformed back into the beautiful woman she had once been.

However, soon she deteriorated back into a blackened husk, requiring ever more blood to regenerate. She killed her way back to London. Her condition horrified her, but the atomic blast had one positive effect—it had severed the mystical hold MI6 had held over her.

She found David Harker, seduced him, and brought him under her control—but she did not turn him into a vampire. She did not wish to trip any of the supernatural alarms MI6 employed. Those alarms were not much use in any event. MI6 were lax in such matters and she wouldn't have been surprised to learn that the KGB had compromised the entire spy agency.

David revealed much to her. Selene, it seems, had been obliterated. It had not manifested itself in weeks. He also told her of the existence of Von Bork's little KGB operation. A group, it seems, that had played no part in what the British had called *Operation Tropic*. Other Russians had led this attack. Von Bork was believed to have valued the agreement with the Sepulchre too much. David further mentioned the existence of the energy vampire, Boris Liatoukine, who worked for Von Bork.

The Countess knew she was deteriorating; she could not absorb enough blood from her victims to heal completely and defeat the radiation that had damaged her so. Perhaps she could absorb Liatoukine's special energy? Surely that may work. David certainly thought so.

They knew Von Bork had a major outpost in the Berlin sector of the Soviet Occupation Zone, which he and his top people visited regularly. It was a simple matter for David to go to West Berlin on a pretext, providing support for the Countess. She would kill people to draw Liatoukine into a trap. This was supposed to happen only in the Soviet sector, but her needs drove her to kill in West Berlin. David let it be known through various lines that it was the Countess who may be responsible for the killings to further entice Von Bork's group to take an interest—especially Major Boris Liatoukine.

Berlin, 17 June

The KGB vampire was finished with the memories the Countess had imparted to him. He looked at her for a moment, feeling as near to shock over the destruction of the Sepulchre as he would ever get.

"That information is most useful to me. Presumably you think you will get a bit of revenge in some way if I use it?" he said.

She nodded her head. The burns were rapidly taking her over now. "It is over for me, Liatoukine. I do not have the energy now to turn into mist. Whatever is in you has accelerated the process. I only have hours left. Kill me."

Liatoukine considered this. It might be useful to take her in, to see how she died from radiation. Much information could be obtained on radiation's effect on vampire physiognomy. However, did he really want Von Bork to have such knowledge? No. He had no intention of absorbing her energy due to the radiation. Somehow, he still had his stake in his hand. She braced herself, and he smashed the stake into her heart. She held his gaze even whilst turning into radioactive dust. He regretted her passing. She had been a formidable foe.

Soon, he met again with Von Bork. The German was pleased with the turn of events. "The subversives have been crushed and we have eliminated the Countess. Did she tell you about the Sepulchre?"

"Yes," the Major replied. "Why did you not tell me of this *Operation Tropic*?"

"Major Liatoukine, as you know, we are not entirely appreciated by some. I was informed of the plan. Stalin was still alive then and I made no objection, of course, although our superiors knew full well I valued the Accord with the Sepulchre. Stalin apparently believed we had no agreement with the City. 'You cannot have a binding legal agreement with those who are already dead,' he reportedly said. Legally, I suspect that is actually quite true.

"I was strictly informed not to pass on the information about the bombing to my operatives. I certainly did not want to draw any further attention to us—we may have faced another purge."

Liatoukine could hardly disagree—Stalin's era had seen a number of attempts at liquidating them. However, those who had tried to instigate such proceedings were often found dead from "natural causes." Yet, there had been some close calls. They had only pretended to mourn Stalin's death.

"However, our liquidating of this radioactive Countess when others failed will prove our usefulness again," Von Bork continued. "Her escape from the City was not something anyone knew about, and it is good we have cleaned up the mess of others. Incidentally, I am pleased to see that your regenerative powers were able to deal with your exposure to her radiation."

Neither man mentioned anything about informing the Germans of the radioactive traces now around Berlin—such a thought did not even cross their minds. The Russian vampire still had more to say:

"The destruction of Selene was foolish; we could still have learned much. The Accord had been useful over the years."

"Major Liatoukine, if you have some grievance, perhaps you would like to take it up with the leadership in Moscow. You can see how they deal with problems." He pointed at the outside world beyond the window, where the Germans had been crushed by Soviet tanks.

Liatoukine, of course, would not be taking the matter further. Of course, he had long wanted to control the Sepulchre, and, in due course, he had expected to do so. The bombing had taken place on 5 March, the day of Stalin's death - his last gasp an atomic blast. The communists had cheated him. Still, he always knew it was possible the humans would destroy the Vampire City in time, with the help of their superior weapons. It was a setback to his ambitions.

Nonetheless, he had certain knowledge that he had not known previously. He now knew that the MI6 officer David Harker was no doubt still susceptible to vampire influence; perhaps he could be manipulated again one day. He also knew that the British had artifacts taken from Count Dracula and the Scholomance, no doubted looted after the War. It would be useful to eventually get hold of them at some point. As an immortal, he had time.

Like Brian Gallagher, Martin Gately has also assembled a series of tales over several volumes of Tales of the Shadowmen, *but his feature Gaston Leroux's sleuth, Joseph Rouletabille, published however in a diverse chronological order. "Leviathan Creek" (Volume 8) takes place in 1916. "Rouletabille and the New World Order" (Volume 11) takes place ten years later, sandwiched between parts 1 and 2 of "Rouletabille vs. The Cat" (Volume 10). "Rouletabille on Mysterious Island" (Volume 12) takes place a year later, in 1927. With this new installment, we jump back in time to an earlier segment of the young French journalist's life, located just after* The Perfume of the Lady in Black, *when he is summoned to the Tsar's Imperial Court for the adventure known as* Rouletabille chez le Tsar *(aka* Rouletabille in Russia, *or* The Secret of the Night)...

Martin Gately: *Rouletabille Rides the Horror Express*

(Inspired by the script Horror Express
by Arnaud d'Usseau and Julian Zimet)

The following report to the Royal Geological Society by the undersigned, Alexander Saxton, is a true and faithful account of events that befell the Society's expedition in Manchuria. As the leader of the expedition, I must accept responsibility for its ending in disaster. But I will leave to the judgment of the honorable members the decision as to where the blame for the catastrophe lies...

Professor Sir Alexander Saxton, FRS, MCIfA

Prologue - Outer Manchuria, winter 1906

It had been a hard trek across the ice fields, but Saxton's spirits were high. The foothills were now in sight. And somewhere in those hills was the cave that a silk merchant in Peking had described to him nearly five weeks ago. The merchant said that he had sheltered in a cave system during a snow storm and stumbled upon the partially decomposed body of an ancient man-like creature encased in ice. The story had fired Saxton's imagination, and the merchant's obvious sincerity had defused the geologist's natural cynicism. In addition, the man had wanted no payment for the crude map he drew of the cave's location; in turn, the local guides Saxton had procured in the nearby town of Xiang-Jing seemed well aware of the cave and what it contained. Quite why they had not drawn the authority's attention to the ice creature he did not know—at this time.

Nearly two hours later, Saxton and his guides stood at the ragged mouth of the cavern. He removed his thick fur mittens and lit the portable limelight lantern he had brought with him. The searing cone of silver projected by the lantern illuminated the interior almost as brightly as natural daylight; the harsh light glinted prismatically off the millions of tiny ice crystals on the cave's smooth walls.

Saxton allowed one of the guides to ease in front of him, and the man led him unerringly to where the creature lay. The silk merchant had not exaggerated. This was an anthropoid creature from out of the remote past. Saxton marveled at it. While it was not perfectly preserved, the level of protection created by the ice was extraordinary. Decomposition had twisted the waxy flesh of the thing's face into a terrifying sneer. And its eyes were still in place—remarkable! He was unaware of the discovery of any human-like creature with the eyes intact. This find would make his reputation, and the Royal Society of Geologists would surely agree that the diversion away from the study of alluvial deposits, with which he had been tasked, was well worth it. Of course, the matter did not truly fall within the field of geology; more properly, this was paleontology, or some weird offshoot of it. While it was quite obvious that the ice creature was flesh and bone, not stone, he resolved that he would refer to it as a fossil, particularly when speaking to the uninitiated and ignorant. Also, if the Chinese authorities misunderstood the nature of the find, and believed it to be a recently frozen man, he might be caught up in weeks of wrangling. Far better that it be thought of as a fossil by all concerned.

He turned to the guide.

"Fetch the tools from outside. We are going to have to cut it out of the ice and carry it back to the town," said Saxton.

Trans-Siberia Station, Russian Concession, Harbin - three weeks later.

In some ways, Joseph Rouletabille had never felt happier. The appalling affair of the Living Bombs was retreating in his memory; it was months now since he had become entangled with the affairs of General Trebassof. Following that, the French journalist had been a little surprised when a call for his assistance had come from China, though he shouldn't have been since the Russian Concession had both Russian and French language newspapers which dutifully recorded his exploits. Yes, General Wang, whose role was a combination of military governor and minister for trade, had heard of Rouletabille, and required his assistance in finding the hidden den of a group of Dacoits allied to a certain *Devil Doctor.*

Rouletabille had worked more or less undercover with an Irish soldier, Captain Sean O'Hagan, who was serving in the concession's International Regiment. Ultimately, a raid had been organized on the tunnels the Dacoits had constructed beneath freight yards of the Chinese Eastern Railway. During his time in China, Rouletabille had concluded that the foreign concessions within the country were marvelous, cosmopolitan and egalitarian institutions. Perhaps they were even a blueprint for the future organization of society. After all, crime was very low and the corruption of public officials almost unknown, or was he just viewing this particular jointly administered enclave through rose-tinted *pince nez?*

In the office of the Trans-Siberian Rail, the calm was rapidly disappearing from the voice of Professor Sir Alexander Saxton. He pointed speculatively at a filing cabinet with his walking cane, while addressing the station master.

"My name is Alexander Saxton. If you check your records, you will find the telegram I sent you three weeks ago requesting both a single private berth and space within a freight car."

"I'm sorry," replied the official. "There isn't a single seat left."

Saxton's outburst of fury was delayed by the arrival of Dr. James Wells, a fellow academician and acquaintance of Saxton's. The doctor was accompanied by a rather portly and matronly woman of about sixty, who generated the aura of that rare creature: the female scientist. Wells' extraordinarily gaunt face relaxed into a friendly smile

"Professor Saxton, I presume," greeted Wells, in mock imitation of Henry Morton Stanley.

"Dr. Wells," said Saxton, coldly. "What the Devil are you doing in Harbin province?"

"I might ask you the same... Actually, I'm here collecting both zoological specimens and bacterial cultures," said Wells, who then gestured in a chivalrous way in the direction of the lady at his side. "This is my assistant, Miss Jones. She is a superb technician."

"For a woman, he means," said Miss Jones, self-deprecatingly.

Miss Jones extended her hand and Saxton just about managed to shake it politely; inside, he was still seething that he had not been allocated a private berth and space in the freight car.

Miss Jones looked Saxton up and down. Why, he didn't seem English at all; he looked more like a displaced Italian nobleman. He was six feet five inches at least, and his face was adorned with a thick, dark moustache. He was compellingly handsome, and so very obviously as volatile as a volcano.

Suddenly, Wells seemed to have the attention of the station-master.

"I realize that I'm asking the impossible, but I need two private berths on the next train to Moscow and space for three animal crates." As he said this, he passed the man a thick bundle of pale turquoise Chinese banknotes.

"Of course, sir," said the station-master, immediately returning to his desk to write out the travel warrants.

Wells turned back to Saxton.

"In China, it's called 'squeeze,' I believe," said Wells.

"And in Britain, we call it bribery and corruption," condemned Saxton.

Saxton advanced on the little station-master's desk with fury in his eyes, clutching his walking cane as if it were a club. With a single sweeping action, he knocked the typewriter, desk lamp and document basket off the desk and onto the floor with a crash. The official recoiled in fear, anticipating that he was about to take a beating from this madman.

The door into the office opened yet again. This time a platoon of International Regiment Soldiers in their distinctive peacock blue uniforms marched in; leading them was a European officer with a flaming red moustache.

"Captain O'Hagan, sir," said the officer to Saxton. "General Wang asked me to find you and see if I could make myself useful."

Saxton knew the seemingly omniscient General Wang only slightly, and had not thought to rely on him for favors, though he had, as a matter of courtesy, sent him a message describing the importance of the ice creature fossil find. He was extremely pleased that International Regiment troops would be on hand to move the crate and guard it.

Saxton noticed that the station-master was now filling out a reserved ticket travel warrant for him, just as he had for Wells.

"Your ticket, Excellency," said the little man, assuming expediently, although incorrectly, that Saxton had some form of diplomatic status because troops had been deployed to assist him.

Saxton shook Captain O'Hagan's hand warmly.

"You're a sight for sore eyes, Captain. I have an extremely valuable archeological find for transportation aboard the Express. Your men are just what I need."

Rouletabille had not seen O'Hagan, arrive on the station platform because he had been paged loudly to the local telegraph office. The message was from the French Diplomatic Bureau located within the French Concession in Shanghai. The telegram used plain text, but was couched in such a way that it was obvious that he was being asked to undertake a mission which would greatly benefit his government.

He considered it for a moment, then surreptitiously burned the telegram whilst lighting his pipe. Further along the crowded platform, a man caught the journalist's attention. His body language was furtive, and this stood out quite noticeably in the hustle and bustle of ordinary passengers and merchandise sellers. The man now loitered by a large padlocked and chain wrapped crate. Rouletabille could not see his hands, but the movement of his shoulders was highly distinctive. The man was picking the padlock.

Rouletabille continued to move nearer. Then, he became aware that there was another man at his side, keeping pace with him. It was a tall bearded Russian dressed in the distinctive black robes of a *strannik*—a religious wanderer. The holy man had obviously noticed, or sensed, what the brazen thief was now doing, and he, too, was moving in to apprehend him.

Rouletabille and the Russian exchanged a look; seemingly, they were allies on the side of right. But before they could reach the man picking the lock, he suddenly cried out and collapsed face down onto the rough flagstones of the platform.

Rouletabille suspected that the thief was shamming, and felt for his pulse. But the man was dead. The holy man turned over the body. The journalist wondered how he could have been so horribly mistaken. For the man could not have been a thief—he was blind! He had no pupils, no corneas. Both eyeballs were just a mass of white scar tissue, as if his eyes had been seared or cauterized by a red-hot poker.

The holy man began chanting incessantly in Russian, praying for the thief's soul. After a few minutes, the curious crowd parted to allow a policeman to approach the corpse. This was Inspector Pavel Mirov of the Trans-Siberian Express Constabulary Force.

"Why pray for *his* soul, *strannik?*" asked Mirov. "He was just a filthy sneak thief."

"You knew him?" said Rouletabille. "Yet surely, he could not really have been a thief. He was blind."

"He could see well enough when a policeman was after him!" spat Mirov. "It is Grashinski, the failed locksmith. His father was Russian and his mother Chinese."

Mirov moved closer, and was obviously shocked by the dead man's blank white eyes.

"I'll be damned," said Mirov.

"This *is* the work of the Devil," said the holy man.

Simultaneously, Rouletabille and the *strannik* started to pull the chains from the crate in order to get it open and see what was inside it. In his mind, the Frenchman was already forming a hypothesis: it was quite possible that someone was inside the wooden box and had squirted acid through the small rectangular aperture that he had now noticed in the side of the crate, and it had gone into Grashinski's eyes.

Saxton, who had just come out of the office, was appalled to see the two men seeking to open up his precious crate.

"Get away from my property," he bellowed.

Again getting ready to wield his cane as a weapon, he had completely forgotten that O'Hagan and a platoon of armed men were standing ready to back him up.

"Is this yours?" queried the French journalist. He had imagined the crate as belonging to some local crime lord, perhaps smuggling a wanted confederate out of the concession to the comparative safety of Moscow.

"It reeks of evil. Whatever is inside this box is unholy and must be destroyed," said the *strannik*.

"What is in the crate, Excellency?" asked Mirov.

"Merely fossils," said Saxton. And then adding by way of explanation, "Ancient bones that have, over time, become stone by way of a natural process of molecular petrifaction."

Mirov and the holy man both looked unconvinced, but Rouletabille was fascinated.

"What sort of bones? Animal bones?" he inquired, but his question went unanswered.

"It's just a laboratory specimen, of no value to a thief," assured Saxton.

"Everywhere there is a place for God," said the holy man, enigmatically. "Even on this stone floor," and with that, he stooped down, removed a small piece of chalk from his pocket and drew a cross on the flagstones. "But where the Devil is, the cross cannot be marked."

The holy man reached up to the wood of the crate, pressed hard and attempted to draw the cross again. This time, no mark was made at all. Mirov's face registered surprise, but Saxton was merely appalled at this display of charlatanry and superstition.

"A puerile conjuror's trick," said Saxton. "Captain O'Hagan, would you get your men to put the crate onto the train as carefully as humanly possible?"

While the troopers strained with the box, O'Hagan took the opportunity to say a proper farewell to Rouletabille.

"It has certainly been a pleasure working with you, Joseph. I hope you don't mind if I look you up if I'm ever in Paris?"

"My friend, I will show you all of the sights," promised Rouletabille. "A man who has not seen Paris has not lived."

Rouletabille wrestled his wallet out of his pocket to check his travel warrant reservation, and then started to make his way along the express train, looking for his carriage. He glanced back down the platform and saw that Mirov's uniformed men were already carrying away the body of Grashinski the locksmith. It looked as if he would have to place the mystery of the blind thief into the 'unsolved' section of the filing cabinet in his study.

In the freight and baggage car of the Trans-Siberian Express, Dr. Wells was already inspecting the placement and integrity of his animal crates and the smaller cases of culture specimens. Everything seemed to be in order. At that moment, the troopers carried the large crate containing the ice creature up the ramp and into the car under Saxton's watchful eye.

Without warning, a deep roar reverberated through the train car. It came from nowhere and everywhere—permeating every iota of Saxton's being. He looked suspiciously at Wells' small live animal crates. But rats, hares and juvenile deer do not roar. He moved closer to the crate, but the sound had stopped.

Bidding Saxton farewell, O'Hagan led the troopers away, leaving Saxton to his puzzlement. The scientist unlocked and swung open a rectangular door at the top of the crate which revealed the ice creature's head. Wells was at the far end of the freight car, feigning a lack of curiosity. Saxton put his hand to the anthropoid's face. The thing was starting to thaw.

Wells approached as Saxton was re-locking the door in the crate.

"What are you going to astound the scientific world with this time, old boy?"

"You'll read about it in the Academy's annual report. It is a most unique and remarkable fossil," said Saxton.

"You're joking! It's not a fossil! You've got something alive in there. A moment ago, it was growling," said Wells.

"You're badly mistaken," said Saxton, condescendingly.

"Well, if it's a fossil, you won't need to feed it," Wells teased.

"The occupant has not eaten for roughly two million years," said Saxton.

"That's one way to economize on the household food bill, I suppose," grinned Wells.

Wells exited the freight car just as two more people entered and the train started to move. The first was Maletero, the baggage man; the other an unfettered vision of loveliness, the Countess Irina Petrovski, an extraordinarily beautiful noblewoman in her late twenties. In one arm, she clutched a small white poodle, and with her free hand, she gently held a long red velvet bag—the sort in which a lady might place her most treasured valuables.

"You have a safe place for valuables?" she asked the quietly whistling Maletero.

"Yes, Countess, I shall make you out a receipt," said the baggage man, hurrying off towards his corner desk.

The Countess commenced to walk past the ice creature's crate, at which moment her little dog started to whimper horribly.

"Excuse me," she asked Saxton, "something is making Alinka afraid. What do you have in that crate?"

"Nothing that would interest Alinka, Madame," said Saxton.

"Then perhaps it *you...* but normally she likes Englishmen—all we Poles do" smiled the noblewoman rather charmingly. "Oh, yes—England, Queen Victoria, Sherlock Holmes, crumpets…"

"I admire Poland, Ma'am," said Saxon. "I believe that there is a bond between our countries."

"Yet, we Poles also have long memories—my husband the Count often mentions how your King Henry sided with the Lithuanians against King Jagaila of Poland in 1389."

"I hope that you and your husband will accept my profoundest apologies for that betrayal," said Saxton with grandiose sincerity. He had become totally entranced by her beauty.

Rouletabille had paused at the restaurant car only long enough to order soup and a sandwich, and then made his way along to his berth. The *strannik* had also been in the restaurant car ordering food, and the Frenchman was able to learn that his name was Father Pujardov, and, perhaps more surprisingly, that he was a passenger in a private first class coach allocated to Polish nobility.

At the moment Pujardov walked past Rouletabille, the express crossed a set of points at high speed and the holy man momentarily stumbled against him. The journalist could not resist satiating his curiosity regarding Pujardov's trick with the chalk, so he picked the pocket of his robe and relieved him of the item. Pujardov, oblivious, simply apologized and strode off to his coach.

Once he was out of sight, Rouletabille paused and examined the chalk. At first, it seemed perfectly ordinary, but then he saw that one end of the chalk had received a thick hard coat of white enamel paint. Pujardov was perhaps little more than a harmless charlatan. The trick had been a pre-rehearsed one, and the journalist could not help wondering in what other circumstances he had used it, as well as what else was in his repertoire.

Rouletabille slid open the door into his berth and found a blond man in his mid-thirties already settled in at the little table playing chess with himself.

"I hope you don't mind company, my friend," said the man. "This train has been overbooked and the conductor is doubling up everyone in what were supposed to be private berths."

"Not at all," said Rouletabille. "And I see that you play chess. What better way to pass the time as we journey through the Siberian wastes? I am Joseph Rouletabille."

"And I am Oleg Yevtushenko, an engineer," said the blond Russian. "Now will you play red or white?"

Back in the freight car, Wells pressed several turquoise Chinese bank notes into the hand of Maletero, the baggage man.

"If someone were to drill a little hole in this crate in the night and see what was inside, I'd be very grateful," said Wells.

The woman had no ticket and was therefore desperate to avoid the relentless advance of Conductor Konev up the train. She knew that the Express was completely full, but was desperate to find some hiding place. The door to Berth 8 was partially open and there was no luggage at all inside it. That meant the passengers must've missed the train, for everyone was in their respective carriages by now. Possibly if she hid in, or under, one of the bunk beds she would escape Konev's attention?

She stepped swiftly into the berth and shut the door behind her. Should she lock it? No. That would only arouse the conductor's attention. The berth had a small cupboard for luggage; she might be able to squeeze into that. But before she had a chance, the door was opened again. Through the portal stepped a gaunt, kindly faced man with smiling eyes.

"You must help me," she implored.

Wells shot her an admiring glance and did not allow himself to be distracted from storing his suitcase on the rack.

"My dear young lady, what could I possibly do to help you?" he asked.

"You see, I have no ticket," said the woman. And her eyes widened as if to emphasize her extreme helplessness; while as the same time, she arranged herself to show off the nubile form that lay beneath the tight blue silk of her Chinese-style suit. The transaction offered was most apparent: "Cover for me and I'm yours." Wells was instantly aroused at the thought of it. For the price of a sheaf of turquoise notes pressed into Konev's moist palm, he could be spending himself inside her all the way to Moscow.

Tears welled up in the woman's eyes. She was obviously just about to lose control. She pressed herself into his body for comfort.

"There, there…don't cry," said Wells.

The woman's scent was intoxicating. In another few seconds, he would have to start maneuvering her towards the lower bunk. He wondered idly if there was a do not disturb sign for the door.

"I had to get out of Harbin…there is a man there, an evil Chinese Doctor… I barely escaped with my life from his women's quarters," said the woman.

Suddenly, the door opened again and this time Saxton entered and immediately started securing his luggage on the rack.

"Sorry, dear fellow, you're in the wrong pew," said Wells, rather diplomatically. "You see: Berth 8," he continued, showing his ticket.

"I have a ticket for Berth 8 also—for the upper berth," Saxton confirmed, as he ascended into his allocated top bunk, after putting his case and hunting rifle in the luggage rack.

"This young lady is in trouble," explained Wells.

"Well, what would you like me to do about it?" asked Saxton. And then, realizing that it would be ungentlemanly to cast out a damsel in distress, he added, "I am sure we shall get along swimmingly."

He unfolded a French language copy of the *Harbin Times* from under his coat and started reading.

In the comparative warmth of the freight car, the thaw of the Ice Creature's body continued and its brain became more active with each minute passing.

Back on the platform, it had sensed the presence of the locksmith Grashinski and scanned his mind. It might not have bothered to absorb him, except for the ability to open locks, which was one which might prove essential before the night was out.

Experimentally, the Ice Creature moved its right shoulder. With the state of decomposition of the muscle tissue and the degraded nature of the nerves, this movement virtually amounted to an act of telekinesis. The Ice Creature slid its hand out of the small rectangular door in the crate and felt along the chains until it reached the steel bulk of the padlock. It extended the long brown decaying limb as far as it could out of the crate until it lighted on Maletero's work table. The hand, like some great hairless spider, explored the table, selecting and discarding potential tools with which to pick the padlock. The fingers found a steel nail. That might be of use. And then, with strength that Grashinski would never have been able to muster, the nail was bent in the center at a ninety degree angle to make it into a more effective lock-pick. Accessing the whole of Grashinski's experience, the Ice Creature started to work the lock. Almost immediately, the shank clicked open, and the chains fell away.

Maletero rushed from his corner desk towards the crate and looked into the rectangular aperture with alarm registering on his face. The set of fiery red eyes within it transfixed him. His brain seemed to boil, his eyes started to bleed profusely. Then his eyes turned milky white. He was dead. Eerily, the dead lips of the Ice Creature strained into a pucker. And the thing started to perform the tuneless ditty Maletero had been whistling earlier in the evening. Finally, it was free of the crate!

The effort of absorbing a psyche, the effort of killing, had put a considerable strain on its system. What if it were discovered now? What if it were cornered? It might be destroyed by the soldiers or the policemen on this train. It now devoted all of its remaining psionic power to regenerating its bodily functions. It had not waited with insane patience for two million years to have its life snuffed out now. It had to make it to a city. It needed not a train full of people, but millions of humans; only then would it be able to recreate its hive mind and extend its consciousness to the god-like proportions that were required. It flexed both its hands. It was starting to regain proper control of its body. The hominids had progressed well over the last two million years; yet, where might they be now if they'd had the benefit of guidance from the cosmic demiurge soul which dwelt inside the Ice Creature? They might already be traveling amongst the stars...

The Ice Creature placed Maletero's body inside the crate and re-chained it before finally snapping the padlock back in place. This would stall the humans for a while. They would simply waste time looking for the baggage handler. And all the time, the express train was moving relentless across the Siberian tundra, every second bringing Moscow nearer. The Ice Creature created a space at the back of the freight car, hunkered down and hid itself beneath canvas and old blankets and waited to regenerate.

Hours passed, and with its brain thawed and repairing itself, the thing experienced sleep—proper sleep—rather than just the suspension of it consciousness for the first time in epochs. Naturally, it dreamed of its ultimate return to the interstellar depths.

Eventually, the sound of raised voices caused the Ice Creature to awake. Using its telepathic powers, the being scanned the vicinity. The Siberian-Express Policeman, Inspector Mirov, was quizzing the two British passengers—Saxton and Wells—trying to ascertain the whereabouts of Maletero.

Wells admitted bribing Maletero to open the crate. Mirov demanded that the crate be opened, but Saxton impetuously threw the padlock key out of the freight car window, infuriating Mirov, who then placed the scientist under arrest. Then Konev, the conductor, was called upon to smash open the front of the crate with a fire axe.

Within moments, they had discovered Maletero's corpse within the crate. The Ice Creature was impressed with the humans' reasoning. Even though they were facing a being returning to life from suspended animation, something totally outside of their experience, they had drawn the correct inferences and conclusions from the information at hand. These modern-day hominids were promising. It must not underestimate them.

Mirov directed two armed Siberian Express guards to lock up Saxton.

"We'll search this train and find it—and destroy it," he said. "We mustn't alarm the other passengers."

Later the Ice Creature eased itself from its place concealment, stretched its taut limbs, and walked out of the freight car into the train proper. It needed a strong and vital new body to transfer its consciousness into until such time as they reached a teeming metropolis. The ape-man that it currently inhabited had served his purpose. What he needed now was to be able to blend in. He briefly considered transferring its consciousness into a sleeping child, but how much better would it be to become a figure of authority in this new world. Almost without warning, the armed guard was right next to it in the corridor and was already starting to un-shoulder his rifle. The Ice Creature's eyes burned again. The guard fell. Blank eyes staring, and blood flowing from his eyes, nose and mouth.

Yevtushenko and Rouletabille had decamped to the restaurant car, not so much because they were hungry, but because they wanted to drink some champagne. And they were not the only ones. A gaunt-faced Englishman and a Russian beauty in a blue silk suit were also quaffing champagne. Somehow, Yevtushenko and Rouletabille had got onto the subject of religion—something the journalist normally avoided. And he had made the somewhat unsettling discovery that the Russian engineer was an atheist.

"Why so surprised my friend?" asked Yevtushenko. "In another hundred years, religion will be all but dead. Faith will be replaced by science. No proper scientific theory requires the involvement of God. There is no room for God in Newton's work on gravity. Likewise, there is no need to involve God in our thoughts and theories about how life arose on Earth. The answers lie in Darwin's writings, not a Bronze Age book of fables."

"But when you look at the beauty of the world and the goodness that man is capable of, how can you doubt the existence of the Almighty?" asked Rouletabille.

"When I look at the world, I see a desperate and savage battle for survival by all the creatures within it. And when I read the Bible, I see the handiwork of primitive men, the beginnings of a basic moral framework. Why, the Ten Commandments themselves don't forbid the keeping of slaves, or even the act of rape. Moreover, it is a random collection of contradictory writings with no insight into the true nature of the universe. Not one. If it just contained one or two revelatory facts... I don't know... that the sun is really a star, or that the earth rotates around it, then I would be more hesitant perhaps. But as it is, I can see that it is a book of ignorance rather than wisdom," said Yevtushenko.

"The theory of evolution seems to me immoral," observed Rouletabille.

"Yet it is a fact. And there is no morality in a fact," said Yevtushenko.

Somewhat dumbfounded, and with his head slightly aching, Rouletabille glugged the contents of his champagne goblet.

At that moment, Inspector Mirov strode rather anxiously into the restaurant car and went up to the gaunt Englishman. A brief conversation ensued during which Mirov ascertained for certain that the Englishman, whom he called Wells, was a doctor. Dr. Wells was not enthusiastic about leaving his meal of boiled salmon, but ultimately he did so. To Rouletabille, this could mean only one thing, a crime—most likely, a murder—had happened aboard the train. The hairs on the nape of his neck stood on end. While his main interest was always to serve justice, it occurred to him that enormous kudos might be gained from being the first amateur detective to solve a murder on a moving express train before it arrived at its destination.

Wells knocked and then slid open the door to Berth Six.

"Miss Jones, I shall need your assistance with an autopsy," he instructed.

A storage car was partially cleared and the dead baggage man, Maletero, and the dead guard were laid out side by side. Miss Jones held the swinging electric light still while Wells sawed open Maletero's cranium with Mirov looking on. As had happened with Grashinski on the platform, Miss Jones had to be assured that Maletero was not a blind man—the white eyes struck her as possibly some kind of genetic abnormality. Wells levered off the top of the skull and Miss Jones gasped.

"Smooth as a baby's bottom. Not a single brain convolution. He has lissencephaly," said Miss Jones.

"Yet, I saw this man earlier today and his mental functions were perfectly normal," said Wells. "Which is quite impossible if he'd been born with this disease, plus he'd have been unlikely to have lived past the age of two. No, something did this to him—today. And if Saxton's living ape-man fossil is really responsible, then it is capable of attacking people and severely damaging their brains. I'm not sure how. I suppose a virus isn't out of the question, but shouldn't we all have been affected?"

Wells closed his eyes momentarily and visualized the scene in the baggage car.

"After it killed Maletero, it locked him in the crate using the chains and padlock. How would an ape-man know how to do that? And before that, it escaped from the crate. But even Maletero didn't have the key. How did it get out?" asked Wells.

Mirov considered the problem fast and was horrified by his own deduction.

"It had the skills of the first man it killed—Grashinski, the thief—the locksmith!" he whispered.

"My God," began Miss Jones. "It's capable of leeching thoughts and memories from within the human brain—if it gets closer enough."

The Ice Creature clung with all its strength to the roof of the train. The humans had not yet thought to check the outside. Perhaps they were not quite so advanced as it had first thought. But after a couple of hours, the thing regretted its decision to climb out of the train. It was starting to refreeze. Its limbs becoming stiff, it was getting more difficult to think. It had to get back inside. And carefully, very carefully... If it fell into a chasm, or landed in a bank of snow, it might be frozen for millennia again. The thought horrified it. It had to make it to where there were more people. The hive mind must be restored.

With Saxton now arrested and held under guard in a different berth, Wells wasted no time attempting to seduce the ticketless woman who called herself Natasha. A more willing seductee, he could not have wished for. As soon as she saw him move in for the first kiss, her hand went to the belt of her blue silk pants. A moment later, she sloughed them down to her ankles and stepped out of them. Wells tugged open her jacket. She wore nothing beneath it. As they kissed, he rubbed her left nipple hard between thumb and forefinger, erecting it. She broke away from him, turning her back to her eager lover as she braced herself between the side of the bunk and wall against the movement of the train. Her gorgeous smooth behind was being proffered to him. She was ready to be taken.

Afterwards, she dressed swiftly and excused herself to the bathroom along the corridor. She performed her ablutions perfunctorily and then headed for the freight and baggage car. Wasting not a second, she removed from her pocket a notebook and set to work opening Maletero's safe where the valuables were kept. Inside was the small velvet bag the Countess had asked the baggage handler to lock away securely back at Harbin Station. She grabbed it, closed the safe and got ready to leave.

The cold dark hands of the Ice Creature grabbed her arms, restraining her with immense strength. The thing's eyes glowed like cherry-hot metal in a blacksmith's forge as it leaned in to consume her mind. The Ice Creature commenced to drain her memories... first the mundanity of her mission for the *Devil*

Doctor to steal from the safe, then the overwhelming intensity of her orgasm with Wells just minutes ago...

For the first time since its release from the caves, it paused in its desire to attack. It remembered its own last coupling with a female some two million years ago. Mounting the coarse-haired ape woman from behind and thrusting deep into her. Ejaculating explosively, then finding that her vaginal muscles had clamped down and locked them together. They had been cleaved together as one until the sun rose. It would have to tear the human apart to get her off if that happened now.

The Ice Creature pulled open the woman's jacket and took Natasha's left nipple between clawed thumb and finger and rubbed it hard in imitation of the memory it had devoured. Despite terror and partial brain damage, it erected. The Ice Creature was aroused too. It was secretly pleased that its generative organs still functioned. The claws ripped away the silk and then forced her thighs apart. There would be time to filch the rest of her memories after coition. It turned her to face the wall...

"Natasha? Natasha, are you there?" asked Wells as he entered the semi-darkness of the freight car. The horror of what he saw then would stay with him always. The Ice Creature had pinioned the girl to side of the carriage and was violating her in the most appalling way imaginable, grunting repetitively as it did so. She was close to death.

Wells turned to flee, but the ape man took hold of his arm with phenomenal strength, and it felt like it was going to be torn out at the socket. Wells felt the thing's baleful red eyes turn upon him.

Suddenly, a shot rang out. The bullet struck the creature, and it released Wells from its grasp. The Doctor ran out into the corridor, past Inspector Mirov, who stood there, clutching his smoking automatic.

The Ice Creature continued to advance. Mirov fired again, this time aiming for the anthropoid's brain—and hitting one of its eyes.

The thing's mind was thrown into turmoil by this attack. All of the regeneration of the Ice Creature's body was being undone by the impact of the bullets. With a supreme effort, the thing's consciousness started to abandon the body that had served it so well for so long. Scintillas of thought flowed from it and out towards the only available vessel within range: Mirov.

Almost immediately, the consciousness detected the weakness of this body, as compared to that of the ape-man. Huge amounts of genetic material would need to be rewritten to make this form more robust. It started with the arm. The cells divided and divided; a swiftly commenced metamorphosis, and easier that it had expected—the modern hominids and the Ice Creature were, after all, very closely related.

Just seconds after the transference of consciousness had been completed, the skull of the Ice Creature exploded in a welter of blood and whitish matter.

Rouletabille lowered his revolver, and stepped forward to feel for a pulse on the girl's throat. There was nothing.

"Are you all right, my friend?" he asked Mirov.

Mirov simply nodded, and thrust his disproportionately large claw-like hand into his jacket pocket before the Frenchman could see it. The Inspector replaced the automatic in his shoulder holster and then picked up the velvet bag with his human hand. He could feel a heavy rectangle of metal within the bag. This was something important.

"You," he almost growled, unaccustomed as he was to using human vocal cords, "are the French journalist. This... is something important. The dead girl was trying to steal it. Come along, let us take it to Count Petrovski. Help me, I am feeling weak."

Rouletabille assisted the Russian policeman along the train to the luxurious carriage where the Count, Countess, and their personal *strannik*, Pujardov, had their quarters.

Count Petrovski weighed the metal in his hand.

"Steel—harder than diamond. That's why thieves and spies are after it. The French, the Germans, the English—even a Chinese criminal organization. But they are wasting their time. What matters is the formula, and that is up here." He pointed to his temple.

"What happened to the girl—the spy?" asked the Countess.

"The creature... the fossil, or whatever it was, killed her. It was quite horrible," said Rouletabille.

"But there is no more danger. Between us, the young Frenchman and I killed the monster," said Mirov.

"You think evil can be killed with bullets? Satan lives," smiled Pujardov. "The unholy one is still among us."

With the creature dead and the danger over, Saxton was released from custody and co-opted into assisting in an autopsy on the anthropoid.

Saxton jabbed a scalpel into the left orbit of what was left of the creature's skull and popped out the eyeball.

"What are you hoping to find within its eye?" asked Miss Jones.

"Perhaps the means by which it attacked and absorbed memories and abilities as per Mirov's theory," replied Saxton.

"Yes, its eyes were glowing when it attacked Natasha," said Wells.

Saxton swiftly removed part of the aqueous matter from within the eyeball with a syringe, squirted it into the petri dish, and then viewed the result through Wells' miniature brass microscope.

"I recall that a similar experiment was done with the last of Jack the Ripper's victims—to see if the eye had recorded the image of the killer. But it was not successful. Here however... look for yourselves..." said Saxton.

"Good Lord," said Wells. "I can see Mirov and the young Frenchman. But the image is flickering, changing, now great fields of ice… other ape-men and prehistoric creatures—like something out of the Pliocene. Now, some sort of map of the world. No, wait… it's an image of the Earth from space. The whole of the thing's memory is recorded on the fluid in its eye."

"And perhaps not just its memory," broke in Miss Jones. "Perhaps the last surviving vestiges of its consciousness. We must be careful."

"The consciousness within the creature was undoubtedly alien. It obviously journeyed here through the trackless depths of the interstellar void countless millions of years ago," said Saxton.

The door to the carriage slid open and Pujardov entered.

"What are you doing?" he asked.

"You may find this interesting, holy man," said Saxton. "Through the microscope, you can see a view of the Earth from the heavens."

Pujardov looked through the microscope's eyepiece and was amazed.

"Where does this picture come from?"

"From inside the creature's eye," said Saxton, pointing to where the eye lay abandoned on the table.

"It is as in the holy writ. Before the Fall, Lucifer was in Heaven, looking down upon the Earth. It is the Eye of Satan! It must be destroyed!"

And with that, Pujardov grabbed the eye and ran from the carriage, frantically chanting prayers as he went.

"Is he quite mad?" asked Saxton.

"I'll go talk to him," said Miss Jones, "and see if I can get that eye back."

Miss Jones headed for the baggage car, which seemed to her an obvious place for the *strannik* to hide.

Mirov spotted her and was curious as to what she was doing. He followed her into what had once been Maletero's domain.

"What are you looking for, Miss Jones?" asked Mirov.

"Not what—who. Father Pujardov ran off with the anthropoid's remaining eye. He thinks it's the eye of Lucifer or something. There's a thousand rubles in it for you if you help me get it back," said the female scientist.

"A thousand rubles for an eye?" queried Mirov.

"There's something in it... Pictures, images of long ago and of the Earth from space."

"Who else has seen such pictures?" asked Mirov.

"Just Dr. Wells and Professor Saxton," replied Miss Jones.

Mirov pulled down the blind on the baggage car's only window. Even in the semi-darkness, Miss Jones could see that the hand Mirov used was not human.

It was to be the last thing she saw, apart from Mirov's glowing red eyes.

Miss Jones' corpse crumpled to the floor—her eyes boiled white by the process of the removal of her memories and knowledge. Blood flowed freely from every visible orifice. Standing over her, Mirov became aware of someone kneeling next to him in the darkness. It was Pujardov, offering to him the anthropoid's eye on a white handkerchief.

"Have pity... have pity," begged Pujardov. "Are you going to kill me?"

"Fool," condemned Mirov, "there is no knowledge in your head worth having—just paltry fables and parables which impede rational thought. You would be a pollutant in the hive mind."

Mirov took the handkerchief-wrapped eye from Pujardov and threw it into Maletero's stove. He left the holy man kneeling there and went to find Wells and Saxton to tell them of the death of Miss Jones.

Moving through the restaurant car, Mirov found that the passengers were in a panic. There had been too much death on the train, and many were demanding that the train be stopped so they could get off. Notwithstanding that they would freeze to death, or if they survived the cold, be at the mercy of wolves and bandits. They had to reach Moscow. Mirov needed hundreds of thousands of people at least to form the hive mind properly, to create the beacon that would bring his own kind back to collect him. So he did the only thing he could and threatened shoot anyone who spoke of leaving the train.

Rouletabille re-entered his berth.

"What's all the fuss out there?" asked Yevtushenko.

"Passengers wanting to stop the train. There's some talk of another death caused by the Ice Creature. Though I can't see how. I shot it through the head. Anyway, the police inspector seems to have it well in hand," said Rouletabille. "Hmmm. This is mystery that needs solving. I'm going to see if I can find the two Englishmen."

The journalist paused only to light his pipe and then was gone. Yevtushenko went back to playing himself at chess. Red was moving in for the kill on the opposing king.

Rouletabille found Saxton and Wells in a booth at the far end of the restaurant car.

"Gentlemen, *has* there been another death?" asked the Frenchman, sitting down with them

"Yes, my assistant, Miss Jones," replied Wells, ashen-faced.

"Is the creature responsible? Is it alive or dead?" pressed the journalist. "Do you have any idea?"

"I don't," admitted Saxton. "But I've wired ahead for the express to be stopped at the next station."

Suddenly Mirov was looming over them.

"You had no authority to stop the train!" screeched Mirov, almost hysterically. Then he rushed on down the carriage and out of sight.

It occurred to Mirov that he might be able to countermand the instruction for the train to be stopped if he got to the telegraph room quickly enough. As he neared the door, he saw that Pujardov was loitering in front of it, then he started to feel the train decelerate. It was approaching the station. It was all too late. The sudden transference of consciousness into Mirov had been too traumatic. He was still nowhere near ready to create the hive mind, even in an embryonic form. He had now to seem as inconspicuous as possible to those who arrived on the train. If they discovered that he was responsible for the deaths, he would undoubtedly be executed and his consciousness would be snuffed out forever.

"Tell me who you are. Tell me, and I will serve you," pleaded Pujardov

"I am the Devil," said Mirov. "And you are my acolyte. I have come to reclaim this world and enslave everyone on it. They will all become part of me." It was only a partial lie, tailored to the holy man's pre-existing beliefs.

"I knew it. I knew it," said Pujardov to himself.

If the Devil had come to take over the Earth, he would have to ally himself with the Dark One, at least for the time being, simply in order to survive. If it looked as if God was going to win, he would switch sides. Better yet, perhaps he could engineer the redemption of Lucifer. The Devil had been an archangel once, and perhaps he would be again. If he could turn the Devil back to righteousness, his own place at the right hand of God was assured.

Rouletabille, Saxton and Wells continued to ponder how the Ice Creature could have killed Miss Jones after it had been shot through the head.

"The best we can surmise is that, millions of years ago, something, some form of intelligence, came to Earth from another planet, perhaps another galaxy. It entered the body and brain of an Earth creature—the ape-man—in order to survive," explained Saxton.

"And this thing from another world survived in the fossil and came alive again?" asked the Frenchman.

"Exactly," confirmed Wells.

"Then it seems to me that the animal I killed was only the host. The alien intelligence transferred somehow to another host. It's inside someone... somewhere on this train," deduced Rouletabille.

"You're a damned clever detective for a journalist," said Wells. "But the difficult part will be discovering who is now the host."

"That's our next step," said Saxton.

"But what if one of you two is the monster?" asked Rouletabille.

"Monster? We're British, you know," reassured Wells.

Awaiting the arrival of whoever in authority was going the board the now-stationary train, Mirov had taken refuge in Yevtushenko's berth. The engineer had welcomed the visitation, and the two were engaged in a game of chess. To his surprise, Mirov found he was winning.

"You know how to measure Earth's gravity?" asked Mirov, conversationally. "I mean, what I want to know is: can gravity be overcome?"

"If you mean, can man get beyond the gravitational field of the Earth into space—not yet, but one day soon," replied Yevtushenko. "There is a mathematics professor called Tsiolkovsky; he has ideas about rockets, machines that can fly free of Earth's gravity."

"You know him?" asked Mirov, intrigued.

If instead of creating a hive mind beacon, he could build a vehicle, perhaps marshalling hundreds of thousands or even millions of people under his control in the attempt, as well as all the industrial resources of this planet, he could get back to his own kind even sooner.

"Know him? He is like a father to me. But tell me, why is a man such as yourself..." before the engineer could finish, Mirov was reaching to pull the blind on the door into the berth and turn down the lights.

"This is just supposition, but from everything you have told me, the eyes are always the key. The creature's memories were recorded in its eyes... the eyes of the victims go white... just like the ones of the boiled salmon they serve in the restaurant car," said Rouletabille.

"Hmmm. I noticed that too," said Wells. "It's the only thing we have to go on. Let's check the eyes of all of the passengers. I have a magnifying glass somewhere in my case."

Saxton looked out on the snow-covered station platform. There were a handful of Cossack soldiers covering all the doors of the train with their rifles.

"What are they waiting for? We've been here for ages," said Saxton.

"They're probably waiting for the arrival of the local garrison commander. He won't be based here, but some distance away," surmised Rouletabille.

"Let's get on with this quickly. Can you imagine what a Cossack officer is going to make of a quest to find a creature from outer space by looking in people's eyes? He'll think we're all certifiable," said Wells.

Methodically the three of them worked their way through the train with a bogus story of checking for a highly contagious, but easily treatable, eye infection. There was nothing unusual about anyone's eyes. But the journalist was concerned that two people could not be found: Yevtushenko and Mirov.

Then, suddenly, about twenty Cossack soldiers boarded the train. They searched Rouletabille and confiscated his revolver, before forcing people out of their berths and herding them towards the restaurant car, where the immense swaggering figure of a Cossack captain waited in his braided coat, cutlass at his side and a cheroot between his lips.

Count Petrovski and the Countess were also manhandled at gunpoint. The Count presented himself immediately to the Cossack commander.

"I am Count Marion Petrovski, and this is the Countess Irina."

"I am Captain Kazan of the Imperial Siberian Regiment. Please return to your carriage, Excellency. You are, of course, exempt from my investigations. Two of my men will escort you."

As the two Polish nobles left, Mirov was ushered into the restaurant carriage by a soldier.

Two things occurred to Rouletabille: firstly, the Express had moved off and was accelerating powerfully. It seemed to be moving faster than on any previous stretch of the journey. The other thing was that practically everyone on board was now together in the restaurant car. The journalist leaned in close to Saxton to whisper in his ear:

"What if the host's eyes look different in darkness? We are all here, pretty much. I can test the theory instantly. I'm going to back away for the light switch... after that, I'm heading for the engine. Monster or not, my every instinct tells me this train is running out of control."

Saxton merely nodded.

Bizarrely, Captain Kazan seemed to be trying to interrogate the passengers en masse, as if the solution to the mystery might somehow present itself.

"Who are the killers?" began Kazan. "Who are the troublemakers? Who are the foreign influences?"

Mirov relaxed. This fool was not going to be able to expose him. All he had to do was remain quiet. Mirov was perhaps looking too pleased with himself since suddenly he seemed to have the Cossack captain's full attention.

"And who are you? The police inspector?" asked Kazan.

"Yes, Captain. Mirov is my name."

"Mirov, Mirov... A good Russian name. How excellent to have a reliable man at my side."

At that moment, Rouletabille reached the far end of the restaurant car. He placed his hand against all four light switches and flicked them off. The journalist didn't wait to see the result of the experiment. Wells and Saxton would have to be able handle the host. The Express was now going so fast he feared it would derail at any minute. Slipping between two Cossack soldiers in the darkness, he disappeared out into the corridor.

In the restaurant car, Mirov's eyes glowed demonically in the darkness. He was caught. The game was over.

Kazan was aghast. Everyone in the carriage could feel the palpable waves of malevolence emanating from the thing which inhabited Mirov's body. Every human mind present had some semblance of precognition of what the creature wanted to do to the human population—the hive mind, the enslavement, the construction of the vehicle to escape gravity, and more particularly, satiation of the carnal lusts it had developed while in corporeal form. The visions of what the creature had in mind caused a good portion of the women to faint and the men to vomit at the thought of the mass degradation and orgiastic depravity.

From somewhere, Pujardov cried, "Beware the wrath of Satan!"

Shots rang out from rifles and Kazan's automatic pistol. Terror reigned.

With the way to the engine car blocked by Cossack soldiers, Rouletabille opted to climb out of his berth's window and onto the roof of the train. He might've been surprised to learn that this was one of the creature's favorite methods of moving about the Express.

He crawled on his belly along the snow-crusted metal of the carriage top with the train juddering beneath him. Within seconds his fingers were numb. If he survived, he was going to have severe frostbite. After what seemed an age, but could've been no more than four minutes, he reached the end of the carriage. It was the penultimate carriage before the engine car. In less extreme conditions, and had he felt rather more swashbuckling, he might've jumped the gap between the two in heroic fashion. Instead, he descended the steel ladder carefully. Twice the skin of his palms stuck to the frozen metal of the rungs, and he had to wrench his hands off painfully.

Finally, he ascended the ladder of the last carriage, then wormed his way along towards the wood tender. He dropped down as quietly as he could into the heap of split logs. In the engine car, he could see the engine driver and stoker lying dead—their eyes blank and rimed with blood.

Yevtushenko was controlling the train, moving like a man possessed, stoking the fiery boiler and checking the controls. Instantly, he seemed to sense the Frenchman's presence. He turned. And even with the wildfire light of the boiler, Rouletabille could see that the Russian engineer's eyes were glowing like branding irons.

"Rouletabille! There is a brain worth feeding on. Your ability to solve problems... your deductive skills... you will be an essential component of the hive mind. Come and be one with me..." shouted the creature within Yevtushenko.

"I thought you'd be inside Mirov! He was alone with you just before I killed the ape-man."

"I can be in more than one place, human. I can be *two* people. I can be everyone. As you will see, my friend."

Rouletabille jumped down from the tender car and attacked the thing.

Ten minutes ago now, the dying Mirov, shot multiple times by the Cossacks, had crawled away into the baggage car and found himself reunited with Pujardov. Saxton and Wells, crouched by the door, had heard the chilling words from Pujardov:

"Come into me, Satan! Thy will be done on Earth as it is in Hell!"

And then they heard no more.

"Rouletabille, was onto something when he made the link between the creature's eyes and darkness. I think it can only use its power to drain minds in darkness. Every single attack it had made has been in darkened conditions," said Saxton. "I'm going back to the berth to get my limelight and hunting rifle."

Yevtushenko cracked his head hard against the boiler hatch door, knocked off his feet by the journalist's sudden onslaught. Rouletabille recovered the shovel from the deck and smashed the engineer across the face with it. He was fighting for his existence, his very soul, as well as for the souls of every human being on Earth. He tossed the shovel to one side. The creature was stunned, if only momentarily.

An idea formed in the Frenchman's mind. In other circumstances, it would have been horrible, and yet here, he had no choice. Lifting up Yevtushenko with both hands at his collar, he started to shove the engineer's head into the furnace-like interior of the boiler.

The creature began to recover itself. Its eyes tried to glow brighter. Rouletabille could feel the alien being raking the surface of his mind. He could feel his tear ducts starting to hemorrhage...

And then it was over. Yevtushenko's hair caught fire. His eyes were scorched by the flames from the boiler. The burned and blackened eyes sealed the creature's malign consciousness in the dying body. This part of the thing had been defeated.

Captain Kazan addressed Saxton as he returned to the restaurant car with the limelight and his rifle.

"We are just soldiers... How can we be expected to kill the Devil?" asked Kazan.

"It isn't the Devil, just a kind of living contagion. We must stop it from reaching a population center or it will overrun the Earth. Yet, perhaps I can reason with it. It is a rational creature. Give me five minutes then send your men in to rush it," said Saxton.

In the darkness of the baggage car, Pujardov stood stock still, his eyes crimson coals. Saxton swung the funnel-like beam of the limelight onto him, keeping him covered with the rifle in a single-handed grip.

"Who are you?" demanded Saxton.

"In words, it's difficult," said the thing within Pujardov. "I am a form of energy occupying this shell. I came with others like myself. I was left behind. An accident. I survived in protozoans, fish, vertebrates. The history of this planet is part of me. Pull the trigger and you will end it."

"Then what am I to do with you?"

"Let me go. I can teach you how end disease, pain, poverty..."

"I wish I could trust you," said Saxton.

But the creature was already reaching for the limelight, and then smashing it to the floor.

Kazan's strong hands grabbed Saxton and pulled him away from Pujardov and out of the baggage car. Kazan pulled his saber and charged Pujardov, simultaneously discharging his automatic.

"Attack it!" shouted Kazan, and his men unhesitatingly piled in behind him with bayonets fixed to their rifles.

"No, don't confront it in darkness!" begged Saxton.

Rouletabille had discovered that all of the locomotive's controls had been deliberately jammed by Yevtushenko. He could find no way to apply the brakes or slow the train down. The boiler was banked up with fuel, so he decided to uncouple the engine from the rest of the train. The journalist watched from the caboose of the passenger car as the driverless loco shot forward like a rifle bullet. Then he ran to the telegraph room since Russian trains always have a map of the route there. Tapping the Morse key, he requested that the points be changed about two miles ahead. He calculated that the train's momentum would take it at least that far, and it would come to rest in the small rail yard of a salt mine.

Meanwhile, Saxton and Wells were barricading the door of the baggage car while the rest of the passengers milled around in a state of near hysteria. Pujardov was killing the Cossacks. They could hear everything. There were shouted profanities, whispered prayers, and finally Kazan begging for his long-dead mother to rescue him with a quality in his voice that is reserved for the doomed and the damned.

Rouletabille rushed to the assistance of the Englishmen. Past the barricade and through the little window into the baggage car, he could see an army of red eyes. All of the Cossacks were under the creature's control. In a few moments, they would be seeking to break out. There was only one course of action. He partially depressed the baggage car's emergency locking brake. At this speed, the brake shoes would be worn away in a few seconds, but it would slow the car down. Then he disconnected the baggage car from the restaurant car. The car dropped back.

They crossed the points into the salt mine freight yard. Rouletabille leaned out to see if they were about to strike the buffers at the end of the line. What he saw struck him with horror... He had potentially brought them all to their deaths. The train line was heading straight over the edge of a crevasse into a salt pit.

"Everyone! Jump for your lives!" shouted the Frenchman.

By the time it reached the edge of the abyss, the train was going only a little more than a moderate running pace, and all the passengers made it off safely. Pujardov succeeded in smashing through the barricade at almost the exact moment the baggage car sailed into empty space, before impacting on the great blocks of rock salt below.

A little later, Saxton, Wells and Rouletabille stood on the lip of the salt pit.

"There's another one," said Wells.

Saxton shot at the broken bodied Cossack who was crawling through the salt and snow. Even at this distance, they could see his blazing eyes.

Rouletabille put his hand in his jacket pocket. For a moment, he thought he had lost it in the jump from the train, but no, the ingot of super-hard steel was still there. At least, his mission for the French government had been a success.

Most of the passengers were warming themselves by the fires in the miners' quarters, but the Countess Petrovski was wandering around the rail yard.

"Alinka! Alinka!" she called plaintively.

Hiding crouched beneath a salt truck, some distance away, the little dog ignored her mistress. Alinka did not want the Countess to see her eyes.

Micah Harris is no stranger to making good use, in the pages of Tales of the Shadowmen, *of various otherworldly and demonic forces imagined by Arthur Machen, H.P. Lovecraft and William Hope Hodgson. With his latest tale, he delves into the supernatural world created by Raymond De Kremer (1887-1964), better known as Jean Ray, who created both the warlock Cassave and the mysterious religious Order of the Barbusquins for his classic horror novel* Malpertuis *(1943). Ray was already a prolific writer who had authored numerous stories for young readers, as well as comic strips, detective and horror stories, in Flemish-language magazines under the nom-de-plume of John Flanders, when he was asked by a Belgian publisher to take over the adaptations of the popular* Harry Dickson *series (two volumes released by Black Coat Press). His tales of the* fantastique *have become horror classics. They include the novel* La Cité de l'Indicible Peur *(The City of Unspeakable Fear) (1943), and short story collections such as* Les Contes du Whisky *(Whiskey Tales) (1925),* Les Cercles de l'Epouvante *(The Circles of Terror) (1943) and* Les Derniers Contes de Canterbury *(The Last Tales of Canterbury) (1944).*

Micah S. Harris: *The Goat of Saint Elster*

Caerleon, Wales, The 1790s

I. The Return of the Barbusquins

The tavern door thrust inward, interrupting the sawing of cutlery and hoisting of tankards. The monk followed, appearing in the doorway like an apparition.

"The Devil has come down!" he proclaimed. "England will fall to those who yet dance upon the heath! Woe unto the people of this isle!"

Frowns were exchanged around the room, then all turned as a group to glare at the panting monk. One did not speak in public in such an incendiary manner, not in this day and time of revolution across the channel.

Only two men reacted differently to the priest's arrival and announcement. They were strangers to each other, but both recognized something more in the monk's words than the threat of revolt—a clue to that which had brought them to Caerleon, though for far different reasons.

Both rose and made their way toward the monk, followed by suspicious eyes. One of the men appeared a holy man himself, robed with a hood that lay gathered about his shoulders. When raised, the hood would swathe even his chin, so that, at first glance, it would appear the monk was bearded even though he was clean-shaven. A sheathed broadsword hung at his hip. His forehead was high, accented by a receding hairline. He was tall and gaunt with sunken cheeks, but his eyes, when not contemplating trouble, were no strangers to glints of mirth.

The other man was a Falstaff in girth. He wore a heavy beard of brown hair, which, along with that on his head, was touched with silver. Each took an elbow of the distraught monk and eyed the other to take stock of this unexpected ally.

"Here now, good man," the heavy man said. "You are obviously upset, but you can't just burst in shouting doom down upon England, not in this day and age."

"In the monastery in the wood, by what remains of the Roman road," the monk said to the heavy man. "The contagion is yet contained there. There is hope, but we must act with haste!"

"You need to calm yourself," the gaunt monk said. "Come with me to the back, and I will try to help you."

"As will I," the heavy man said, and his and the gaunt monk's eyes met again.

"Who are you, friend?" the gaunt monk asked.

"Quentin Moretus Cassave," the heavy man said.

"My name is Brom Cromwell," the gaunt monk said. "Lately of France."

"Ah! I am come from Belgium. Well met."

They led the distraught man to a table in the back, where the tall monk had been sitting. The man had calmed down now, and the patrons of the tavern saw that the note of panic he had sounded was apparently a false one. They returned to their eating and drinking. Brom Cromwell turned his attention to Cassave.

"I noticed you earlier," he said as the three were seating themselves, and pointed at a tusked boar head mounted on the tavern wall. "You were carefully studying the work of the tanner on that boar's head with the appreciation of a connoisseur."

"Hmmph. The boar was once well esteemed in these parts by the Celts as the form of their god Moccus. I wanted to see that his memory was well-attended."

"And how did you find it?"

"The jowls sag due to inferior stuffing of cloth or sawdust or cotton. The tanner displayed no understanding of the boar's underlying anatomy or the correct application of underwire. Further, his approach to his subject is too cold, too mechanical." Cassave shook his head and winced. "That boar exhibits no personality whatsoever! That fool tanner managed to labor under both the fallacies of atomism and the transubstantiation of matter at the same time. It's as though he's never even read Paul Belon's text from 1555... What?"

The corners of Brom's mouth were turned up, touching his gently rutted cheeks, and the glint of mirth was now in his vivid blue eyes. He pointed the fingers of his folded hands at Cassave:

"You, sir, are one most erudite in the craft of tanning the hog."

"I noticed you earlier as well," Cassave said. He pointed at the rosary with a crucifix that was wrapped around Brom's wrist. "You appeared at your vespers... or perhaps you just kept falling asleep."

"Oh, no, no. I was making a mental picture of the inside of the tavern. Testing my memory."

"And how did you find it?"

Brom tapped his forehead and grinned. "Perfect recall. Mind still like a steel trap." He turned to the young monk. "Now, good fellow," Brom said. "You know who we are, but who are you? What has happened in your monastery?"

"*His* monastery?'" Cassave asked. "I thought you had recognized one of your own order."

"Not mine. I am of the Barbusquin Order of the Cistercians."

Cassave cocked his head. "That Order is a myth."

"So I have heard," Brom said and grinned.

"Next you'll be saying that you have truck with the Eldila."

Brom's grinned again. "Only on occasion," he said.

"The Revolution seems intent on making a myth of your Order—if it wasn't one before."

"The Reign of Terror is determined to wipe out of *all* forms of Christianity—such is the extent of its madness. You know of the atrocities of the Vendée?"

"Certainly—but *madness*?" Cassave said. "The Revolutionaries are men of reason, and it is reason's time! Surely, you must acknowledge that your corrupted Christian faith has failed in achieving the universal goals they promote: *liberté, égalité, fraternité*?"

"*Ou la mort*," Brom said. "That is the last part of their slogan. Do not let the tail fall off. Now, sir," he addressed the distraught monk, "what has happened at your monastery that has sent you fleeing from it?"

"They have joined the dance on the heath," the monk said.

"All these histrionics over your fellow monks taking up a reel?" Cassave asked.

The monk turned and grasped Cassave's forearm. "Understand me: they dance to the piping on the heath."

Both men leaned into the monk. "Whose piping?" Cassave asked. "Could it be Pan's, perhaps?"

At this question, Brom cocked his head, then detached the monk's hand from Cassave, causing the man to turn to face him. "You need to start from the beginning, my friend, and calmly, please, if I am to know how to help you."

Staring into Brom's eyes, the monk began to calm. "Yes," he said. "It's just—what I have seen—I cannot say it, but indirectly."

"So, there is no one actually *dancing on the heath*, then?" Cassave asked, folding his arms and leaning back in his chair. "No Pan pipes? No... Pan?"

"I must speak of these things in a figure, sir," the monk said. "I must—to describe it literally—such words on my lips would be an affront to God!"

"From the beginning then," Brom said.

II. The Curse of Old Lady Netty Gat

"I am called Frater John, and I have lived in the monastery since a lad of twelve, having taken my vows and withdrawn into the community which has been my world now for nearly ten years. My order is that of Saint Elster, one given to prayer and fasting. We farm our land, raise our own livestock, make our own clothing... we are an island of righteousness in the fallen world that surrounds us. But now, the serpent has been loosed and felled our paradise as well..."

"You speak in figures," Cassave said. "Who do you mean by *the serpent*? Pan?"

"We knew him'er as Old Lady Netty Gat."

Cassave frowned. "*Lady Netty Gat*?"

"Old Lady Gat, sir. That be right."

Brom and Cassave looked at each other for a silent moment. Then Brom grinned. "*Gat* is old English for goat—particularly the female goat."

"But you said you knew *him'er* as Old Lady Gat," Cassave said. "What do you mean by *him'er*?"

"Yes. Old Lady Netty Gat be *both*, sir."

"Hermaphrodites are not uncommon among bred goats," Brom said.

"You are one most erudite in the lore of goats, sir," Cassave said.

Brom smiled again and shrugged. "Our order, too, was self-sufficient as that of Elster. We also farmed and raised our own livestock here in England, though my interests lay more in the Cistercian furnaces we were also developing. The industrial revolution would have arrived much sooner than it has, had not Henry taken our monasteries and lands."

"From the tone in your voice, you sound as you were there, sir," Cassave said with a tilt of his head.

Brom Cromwell's blue eyes glinted. "I am older than I look, I will admit."

"No man bred Old Lady Gat," Frater John said. "She roamed freely to and fro since the Earth were young, until Saint Elster pinned her on our grounds, and there she remains..." Here, Frater John stared into space, his face contorting. "...Unto that wretched day."

"You have yet to tell us what exactly has overtaken your monastery," Cassave said. "You spoke of the old Roman road before. Now, I have heard that it led to an ancient temple of Pan in pagan times. Is your monastery built near that site?"

"Our monastery sets upon its foundations, sir," Frater John said.

Cassave slapped both palms down on his heavy thighs and smiled. "Ha! I knew it! Something older than Christ has risen up, and Pan has taken his revenge on Christ's disciples! That is the cause of what distresses you, eh?"

"I have spoken of those things as I only can, sir, in a fig..."

"In a figure, yes, we know," Cassave said, crossing his arms. "Now, this *Netty Gat*—when she is in her male phase—she is spoke of as Pan, yes? "

"Baphomet-Sammael be his'er's proper name, sir..."

Cassave leaned forward. "*Sammael?*"

"Yes, sir."

"And Baphomet is a satyr." He leaned back in his chair and began tugging his lower lip, speaking in a low tone to himself. "Baphomet could have been how the Templars knew Pan in transposition from Greek to Christian mythos, as the creature adapted to survive..." He looked up to see Frater John and Brom staring at him. "Well," he said and focused on Frater John, "get on with your tale, man."

"You see, Netty Gat be kept pinned so that heshee has little room for exercise. Heshee is fed only the poorest of grains, for heshee must be kept in a weakened state in this yet-naughty world. Heshee is our sacred charge since Saint Elster delivered him'er to us.

"But the monk before his'er last keeper—Father Beaumont—who was of advanced age, who had kept vigil three score years, took an apprentice. This young man had attended seminary in Geneva. Young Charles Wiseman we called him—not because *we* thought him wise, but he thought himself so.

"Young Charles held that the fashion among learned men was now that our holy scriptures were but tales and that our faith stood only on much superstition that was best put away. For the coming world was a new place and our faith must change were it to continue on."

"I have found that it is the nature of the gods to dwindle as their worshippers become enlightened and turn away from them," Cassave said.

"So Old Lady Gat's keeper passed away and young Charles took charge," John said. "He had long felt much pity for the goat. You could count its ribs and its hip bones jutted out. Charles wondered that it could still walk, and that heshee yet lived for such longtime of malnourishment at our order's hands. But Netty Gat found a friend in young Charles, who thought also to grant us the boon of enlightenment.

"Then it came to pass that we sat down to feast at Michaelmass. And we were served the fruits of our labor, and though we enjoyed all the food and beverage of our repast, nothing was so savory as the dairy milk. The very richness of cream was in its taste, yet it flowed with the most proper consistency of milk at its most fresh, full savory. And so cool as though it had been chilled in a brook. The brotherhood partook and were well satisfied.

"Yet, from the first taste, unnatural as a fairy broth it seemed to me, with an under taste that was bitter. If only the others had ceased to partake at that

139

moment as did I... Instead, they freely chose to ignore such temperance that would staunch their pleasure. So, they did drink on until well sated.

"Then we heard the tintinnabulation of the bell...

"Mugs were halted when young Charles entered the mead hall, leading on a leash Old Lady Netty Gat, the bell about his'er neck.

"Fleshy heshee was now, and pranced in on that leash with vigor. And from his'er swollen rows of dugs still dripped hot milk, that hissed when it struck the cold stone floor.

"I tell you, that heshee-goat surveyed us with a sullen triumph in its yellow eyes. Young Charles Wiseman was all a-grin. 'My brethren, you have drunk well, I see, of that milk which I substituted for that of our cows. Behold this goat: from this creature whom I have nursed back to health came the milk you have enjoyed. See you not now that this poor thing which you have feared some demon is but a goat as any other? Come, now, and drink more, for her teats perpetually well with this frothy goodness.'

"Then Netty Gat broke loose from his'er lease. And a voice came from the goat, saying:

"*I, Baphomet, have risen again, and you, my warders, shall serve me, some as my new Knights Templar. These shall become undead and have their eyes plucked out, so that they might not find their way from Hell, and my hold on them will be eternal. Now is Saint Elser's order defiled. Now is my revenge complete.*

"Young Charles Wiseman's eyes widened. He stepped back, saying, 'You have all played me a trick, and this goat is trained. One of you can throw his voice! You mean to disabuse me of my reason, but I will not be made mad as the lot of you!'

"Old Lady Netty Gat turned upon young Charles, saying, *Thy usefulness be at an end!* And heshee charged Charles, shoving him against the wall with his'er horns, and pressed him passingly hard so that we heard his bones crack, and blood did gush from divers places until he was dead.

"Then I fled, and no one did follow. I hid in the forest for long time, a full year, praying, fasting and meditating before I came back to the village nearest our monastery. I disguised myself so that my presence might not become known to the monks. But I soon discovered 'twas good I was not known to the villagers.

"I inquired if anyone had seen the monks of Saint Elster of late, and no one would answer. Finally, one villager said, 'I can tell you are not of this province, young sir, for otherwise you would know that the monks of Saint Elster have become debauched. They have forsaken our Lord, and replaced him with their tutelary: Baphomet-Sammael, deceiver, seducer, that crafty one of ancient Edom.'

" 'How do you know this?' I asked.

" 'They have seduced our good girls away from their Christian homes, luring them with dainties, pretty dresses, and introductions to young men who bring them to ruin. Aye, and the monks do also participate in their ruin. The girls return with swelling wombs and no husbands. Their parents will not then own them. Many drown themselves with the child they cannot feed.'

"Thanking the man, I went to see if it be true what they had said. I did not see Old Lady Netty Gat, but I beheld my brethren as they… they…"

"They what?" Cassave said.

"They joined the dance upon the heath, sir."

Cassave gave a heavy sigh. "You must speak of these things in a figure."

"Yes, sir. I must, sir."

"Then we must see for ourselves," Brom said with a smile at Frater John.

Taking a small bag from within his robe, he pinched a couple of coins and dropped them to the table. He then pushed his chair away and rose.

"I will come with you," Cassave said. "My curiosity has been aroused, as you can well understand, Brother Cromwell."

Brom looked sidelong at Cassave. "The encounter that awaits us at the end of this journey is not one for the idly curious. I would, suggest, rather, that you seek out a fancy show, Cassave."

Cassave frowned. "My curiosity is not that of the idle. I am a scientist, sir. The opportunity to place under rational observation something uncanny, a thing otherwise lost in the ancient past is one I can scarcely pass by. Hold at the door, both of you, and let me collect my things, settle up with the barkeep, and we will go see this thing together."

Brom shrugged. "As you will, then. But, have you faith, man?"

The heels of his hands pressing down on the table as he pushed himself up from his chair, Cassave said, "I have reason."

"As do I," Brom said. "But faith in God and His Christ is necessary as well."

Cassave's eyes gleamed with a cold light, and he raised his chin and sniffed. "Tell that to your fellow Christians who are faced with either being driven out of France or executed because of their belief. See how many of those have learned that faith is a thing that one can do without when reason rules."

From the tavern's door, Boor watched Cassave with narrow eyes as the portly man readied himself for the journey. He noted Cassave paused for a last, brief studied glance at the mounted boar's head. Brom closed his eyes, committing this tableau to memory. Seeing Cassave was now heading their way, Brom turned and exited the tavern.

III. Along the Ancient Road

The moon was the curved sliver of a nail paring when Brom, Cassave, and John began their trek along the "road" that was nothing more than a wide, rough dirt path, rutted by the turning of countless wagon wheels, with loose stones underfoot and sparse grass growing in clumps.

The night sky was greedy with its stars; only a few, distant lanterns shown here and there, lit against the infinitely ongoing dark.

"*So shines a good deed in a naughty world*," Brom said.

"And, as with the stars, so shall good deeds and their effect be ultimately snuffed out by the darkness," Cassave said. "No one will even remember, nor care, that they were ever performed. And those who received some temporary succor by another's efforts on their behalf will fall prey eventually to something they cannot escape. What is the point, then? Everything fades and dies. Even, as I said, the gods."

Brom nodded. "Pagan gods, yes. Their point of reference makes it inevitable. But Jesus Christ is *the same yesterday, today, and forever*. Neither you or I will be lost to the progression of ages, as you say, Cassave, *for God is not a God of the dead, but of the living; for all live unto him*."

"Are you so important, then?" Cassave said, his tone sharp. "Do you think yourself—aye, your entire world—the center of the universe? You seem a learned man; has not modern science disabused you of this vain notion?"

"The Aristotelian-Ptolemaic idea is anything but vain. In Aristotle and Prolemy's system, the *center* is understood as *bottom*. Earth's place is far from exalted." He smiled and clasped Cassave's shoulder. "We are a sunk hole for the universe's lower elements, my friend. And, as for man being at the center of all things, it is your French rebels who promote this anthropocentric view, not the clergy. The Revolutionaries' problem is not that the Christian world view has been *man*-centric but *God*-centric."

"Which god is it that you speak of?" Cassave asked, then raised his palm before Brom could speak. "No, it matters not. Every divinity is even less significant than its followers, for, as I said, they fade away when humanity moves forward. It is true of the pagan's gods; why should it not be true of the Palestinian tutelary, Yahweh?"

"Yahweh of the Hebrews was no tutelary, no entity bound to particular place, but one who possessed Heaven as his throne and Earth as his footstool. As it is written, *the God who made the Heavens does not dwell in a temple made by men*. Recall that graven images of Yahweh in earthly form were forbidden by Moses' law. But the pagans either made their gods in their own image, or the images of nature about them. Yes, civilizations fade, and the Earth and Heavens will pass away. Therefore, the pagan gods had a finite reference point. But as for the Christ—*En Arche ein ho Logos*."

"*In the beginning was the Word?* Then the Word also has a finite reference point though it goes back to the very beginning," Cassave said and grinned.

Brom smiled and raised his finger. "Your Greek is rusty, my friend. Another option for an English translation, one arguably more precise, is: *When all things began, the Word already was*."

"Very well. But within their limits, the pagan gods are most resilient. They shall return."

"Without followers? You said their time had passed because no one believes in them any longer."

Cassave smiled. "Oh, they will have new followers. Followers who do not realize they are keeping the old gods alive."

Frater John, who was walking ahead, suddenly realized that he was trudging on alone. He looked back to see Cassave and Brom leaning against what was left of a medieval wall along the road. He stopped and slowly began walking back to his fellow travelers.

"Friends, we must not pause if we wish to have cover of darkness when we reach Saint Elster," Frater John said.

The three men resumed their journey and soon began to notice Roman bricks scattered loosely over the path. Then they reached a spot where the ancient brick road remained intact.

"Ah, we are close, now," Frater John said. "The monastery be less than a mile away." He looked up at the sliver moon, still high in the western sky. "We should still have sufficient darkness to cover us when we arrive. There, you will observe, my friends, those things that the monks dare do only in the night. That which I can only speak of in a figure..."

"Yes. The *dance upon the heath*," Brom said and sighed. "We know."

Soon, they heard a faint, discordant noise, as though the wind blew through massive organ pipes. As they drew closer, the sound became throbbing bourbon notes before resolving into something resembling a Gregorian chant, but one in which the austere, sober quality became threatening, like the humming of a giant hornet.

No wonder, then, that all three came to a stop. Even Cassave, who had been almost giddy at the prospect of meeting something pagan and otherworldly, became hesitant, staring straight ahead, and tugging on his lower lip.

"Let us move on," Brom said. "But stealthily from hereon. Frater John, we should remove ourselves from the road in our approach. Is there a less visible route?"

"Through the woods to our right be a rough path, with little to no clearing. The darkness is deeper under the boughs, the way uneven, which may cause a tumble. No one will be using it at night."

"Then that is the route I say we take. What say you, Cassave?"

"I like not my girth and an uneven trek. Especially through a dark wood. Go that way if you will, but I shall keep to the old Roman road. I do not think anyone will be watching it. Why should they? From what Frater John says, the nearby villagers fear the monks of Elster, so the monks cannot expect a threat from them. The sounds of their occult ceremonies cover any noise I might make, and this night sky grants enough darkness to conceal my approach as well. Will you not reconsider, my friends? By going through the woods in the dark, you also risk taking a fall."

"What say you, Frater John?" Brom asked. "You know best the lay of the land."

"There is still an element of risk of discovery in Cassave's plan. Through the forest, there is none."

"Then I shall take the woodland path," Brom said.

"And I will keep to the road," said Cassave.

"I will guide you, Brother Brom," John said.

"But we should regroup upon arrival. Frater John, where will we come out of the woods?"

"At the rear of the monastery proper, sir, near our cemetery in the woods."

"Cassave, meet us there."

Cassave nodded with a grunt. Brom and John quickly scrambled down the dirt embankment atop which the Roman road was laid. Then they entered the woods and, immediately, it was as though the night had swallowed them.

Cassave looked after them, grunted again, then began to make his way down the road.

Brom and John pushed their way through low-hanging branches and tore free of undergrowth that momentarily snared their feet. Occasionally, briars and brambles seemed to leap out at them, affixing themselves to both flesh and clothing, causing Brom and John to pause and pluck themselves free.

They now pushed through the low hanging vines and tender low branches of the trees and into the monastery's graveyard. The woods had reclaimed the cemetery, grown up so much that it appeared the older graves had been laid down within the forest without disturbing the trees.

Frater John's eyes brimmed as he surveyed the new graves, and his throat was thick when he spoke.

"There are friends here who have passed on since you left?" Brom said, placing his hand on the young monk's shoulder.

John nodded. "I recognize here the names of my brothers—these were all so young. And died within a month of each other soon after my departure. Did a pestilence sweep through the monastery?"

"Your flight may have saved your life," Brom said.

Frater John leaned in closer to one of his friends' headstones. His eyes widened. "No," he said, and quickly began inspecting two others. "Heshee has made good his'er threat!"

"What do you mean?"Brom said.

"Old Lady Netty Gat, sir! Look!" He pointed at a word chiseled into the gravestones he had examined: "*Abraxas*."

"The Knights Templar' occult word of power," Brom said.

"Netty Gat said heshee would raise up her new knights from our order," John said. "Heshee has done it!"

"Easy, man," Brom said. "If they are interred, they are beyond that creature's power now."

"No! Heshee said she'd put out their eyes so they'd never find their way out of Hell!"

"Only God has the power to condemn to Hell, lad. Be at ease."

But though he spoke thus to calm Frater John, his hand was at his sword hilt, for the Templars' word of power on those gravestones troubled him.

"Listen," Brom said and paused. Then: "How long has there been no singing from the monastery?"

"I know not, sir " John said. "I ceased to pay attention as my ear became accustomed to it."

From the direction of the monastery came the piercing crowing of a cock under darkness. Brom drew his broadsword from its sheath. "Something is happening; something unnatural. Stay close to me, John."

A near-distant rumbling was moving closer. Then the ground beneath the men's boots was trembling; full-on tremors followed as thundering from the ground below grew louder, the shaking of the land sending them reeling...

Robed and hooded undead men on horseback erupted from the three recently dug graves, spewing clods of earth skyward that rained down and pelted Brom and John as they dropped back.

The Knights Templar had risen.

IV. The Blind Dead Strike!

The undead Templar Knights rapidly encroached on Brom and Frater John. Their equally undead horses reared, forelegs kicking, one hoof striking Brom's forehead. He stumbled backward, and Frater John, arms raised and waving, thrust himself between Brom and the hooded dead man on horseback. The Templar Knight reared his horse again and pummeled John's chest with its fore hooves. He fell to the ground. The dead man reared the horse once more, this time to come down on John and trample him to death...

Brom Cromwell ran forward, and, with a sweep of his broadsword, sliced off one of the horse's forelegs at the first joint. The horse was dead as its rider, but it still required four legs to stand up. And it could feel pain. With a shriek, it toppled over, sending its rider tumbling over the ground.

Now the two remaining Knights Templar inched forward on horseback toward Brom. He backed away, aware that the Knight Templar he had felled was already rising behind him. The hollow sockets of the still horse-mounted knights tilted down unseeingly at him. Brom grinned.

They put your eyes out, so that you could not find your way out of Hell.
You have to hone in on sound like those blind hopping vampires that plagued the
Shanhai Pass back in 1699—those Jiangshi!

Bending down, he grabbed up a large, hard dirt clod that had been flung out of the grave when the Knights rose. He threw it beyond the cemetery and into the surrounding forest where it beat the undergrowth before coming to a stop.

The blind knights on horseback turned their horses and charged after it. Then as Brom snapped a twig under his boot, and the Templar Knight on foot behind him charged. Brom whirled about, swinging his broadsword and halting his enemy's blade mid-arc. The Templar Knight withdrew his weapon, but before he could attack again, Brom was on top of him. He hacked down hard, unrelenting, again, again, *again*, beating back the dead man whom he allowed no moment to raise and regain mastery of his weapon.

Then he heard behind him the trampling of hooves: the other two knights were returning, honing in on the sound of battle. Seizing an opening, he sliced off his opponent's sword hand. The Templar Knight shrieked and withdrew. Before his enemy's weapon could hit the ground, Brom snatched it out of the air and turned to face the two Knights Templar on horseback just as they reached him.

A sword in each hand, he met both blades as they dropped, immediately halting their descent. But now, he was on the defensive, and his enemies on horseback presented him with less than an even playing field.

Riding abreast, they were driving him back. He could not pause to look back to see where they were herding him. Then a gray hand lashed out from behind, grabbing one of his wrists. The undead Templar Knight he had disarmed had returned for his sword.

Struggling with his assailant, Brom could no longer effectively defend himself against the two on horseback. A slash to his arm from above, and the reflex from pain caused him to loosen his grip on the revenant's sword. The Templar Knight wrested it away.

From its decayed throat something croaked out that the two on horseback recognized as an order. They drew back. Bent, heaving from exertion, Brom faced the undead knight.

"I'm glad you were right-handed," he said beneath his breath.

The Templar Knight raised his sword in his left hand, then twirled it about adroitly before bringing it to a stop pointed straight at Brom.

"Ambidextrius," he sighed. "Even in death. Just lovely. Of all your faculties to have retained..." He sighed and rolled his eyes heavenward. "Why, oh Lord, why?"

Taking a deep breath, Brom raised his broad sword over his shoulder, then drove himself forward.

Swords clashed, slashed, thrust—with no wound dealt on either side. But now Brom was again the one driving back, manipulating the Templar knight to where an old headstone had almost sunken entirely into the earth over the decades, leaving only six inches still above ground.

The revenant's heel hooked on the raised tombstone...

...and toppled backward.

Brom's sword swung out, severing the Templar Knight's head in the second the undead creature hung in the air. The remnant's body folded, and the head struck the ground, rolling until it came to rest against another tombstone.

"Brom! Beware!" Frater John cried out, and, in the next moment, Brom felt the dart stinging his sword arm.

Immediately, he knew the dart's tip had been coated in an apothecary's preparation. His arm quickly numbed and his sword dropped from torpid fingers to the ground.

The two on horseback were now rushing Brom, ignoring John who was on his knees.

Rising, John trained his eyes on the revenants. Brom, seeing the boy apparently planning to tackle the undead from behind, shouted, "Frater John! Run! You can't help me now! Watch and wait for an opportune time!"

John hesitated, then turned and dashed into the forest. Brom could hear him crashing through the woods.

Good. If they pursue him, they'll have to do so on foot and lose the advantages of horseback.

Brom snatched up his sword with his hand which still retained feeling; he was not left-handed, so his swipes were awkward and easily outmaneuvered. The Templars repeatedly beat down on him with the butts of their swords' handles. He felt his own sword tumbling from his failing grip as the blows to the head succeeded in stealing his consciousness.

V. A Prisoner Underground

His eyes opened first on a lit candelabrum of six candles, setting on a crudely hewn wooden table. The candles were the only source of light in the room. Then Cassave's full face with its bearded jowls appeared beside the candelabrum.

"My friend, you are awake at last!" Cassave said. "Tell me: where is Frater John? Have they captured him as well?"

Brom's brow wrinkled and his eyes narrowed. "Where are we?"

"Imprisoned in the monastery cellar, I'm afraid."

"So you have no idea where John is?"

Cassave shrugged. "He may be imprisoned elsewhere. I suppose it makes sense that they would deal with John separately. Perhaps give him an opportunity to rejoin the order. He is one of their own after all." He paused, stared ahead and tugged his lower lip. "Unless..." he turned back to Brom. "...did he escape?"

"Perhaps..." Brom said. "We parted ways, I was beaten unconscious by these undead Templar knights who attacked us, and have no idea of what happened to him next."

He felt his hip, found both his sword and its sheathe gone. He sighed. *No real surprise there.*

"But what is the plan? There is always a plan, isn't there, in these type of situations? With you adventuring types?"

Brom shrugged, rolled the shoulder of his wounded arm, and massaged it with his other hand, finding the numbing was all but gone. "If there is, it is entirely of his invention."

Cassave nodded, licked his lips, and stared ahead into space again. "So he may still be out there, making ready to effect a rescue, armed with nothing but his wits..."

"*Angels and ministers of grace preserve us,*" Brom said as he continued to rub his arm. Then he rose, pleased to find himself steady on his feet.

Cassave burst out into laughter and wagged a forefinger at Brom. "Very good, my friend. If he is our only chance, we are as good as dead, eh?"

Brom smiled without mirth and nodded.

"Or, at least, *you* are."

Brom cocked his head. "What did you say?"

Cassave reached out and patted Brom's shoulder. "I am saying you were right. I should not have taken the Roman road. I was taken before I reached the monastery. My very life was in danger... so, I had to make a deal."

Brom crossed his arms. "Which involved telling these evil monks that I and their former frater were coming via the less traveled route."

"I had no idea they would call up their blind dead to deal with you. They sound like horrible, horrible things."

Brom pointed. "The two who did me in are right behind you in the doorway."

Cassave glanced over his shoulder. "Oh. So they are."

"They're with you, aren't they?"

Cassave tucked his head and grinned, flickering flame gleaming in his eyes. "I've formed a new alliance since you last saw me, yes."

"I thought as much, when you made no remark on my first mention of these undead knights. You don't have Frater John, do you? You were feeling me out for information earlier by playing my fellow captive."

"We shall have him, soon, I think, with or without your aid. As you said, he does not come across as the most competent rescuer. And his face is well known here."

"You should look to yourself, my friend. Why do you ally yourself with beings whose existence is an affront to God?"

"God was always your concern, my friend, not mine."

"Yes, you were always concerned with *gods*—plural."

"Oh, dear Brom, you do not know the half of it."

Arms still crossed, Brom smiled. "Well, you are so enamored of the Enlightenment, why not enlighten me?"

Cassave smiled back. "I believe I shall. You, I think, shall appreciate what I have accomplished. I do not say, though, that you shall like it."

VI. Cassave's Great Experiment

"I am a very old man," Cassave said, then nodded at Brom, "as you insinuate you are as well. And, as you also say, we are both younger than we look. In my time, I have learned much, and ridden the crest of each new wave of knowledge, from medieval alchemy to that mix of magic and science that was the Renaissance, to the rise of the preeminence of reason in the present age. Each yielded its own peculiar aspect needed to resolve the great mystery. Thus I became a thaumaturge, great in power. And my mastering of these disciplines, various and sundry, led to my ability to find and resuscitate the dwindled gods of pagan days.

"I see the doubt in your eyes, but I tell you it is true. Their hour now is, in the enlightened new age that opens before us. And will they find worshippers? I tell you, they shall in the post-Christian age."

Brom's tone was sardonic: "The future you predict sounds more like the *pre*-Christian age."

"The *future*? My friend, it has *already* begun. The Enlightenment is here! I think that is how I was able to find the goddess that I did, found her spread as dew on a green field. She was in a vineyard in Marseille, where the tilling of the soil had uncovered her fallen idol, with its lion's head and woman's body. This is the Phoenician's Tanit-Astarte, their representation of the goddess first known to men as Ishtar. I had to cut the image free from the vines that choked it to the ground. And when I had ripped away the last vine that grasped the idol, I heard a gasp, and seeking out its source, found nearby the essence of the forsaken goddess herself, deflated, and stretched thin along the ground.

"Through my knowledge of alchemical sciences as well as sorcery, I was able to rescue her, collecting what was left of her essence in a stitched-skin of a woman suit. This suit I was able to transport easily, as it folded most flatly..."

Brom Cromwell started. "What?" When he saw that Cassave's expression was unyielding, he grimaced.

Cassave chuckled. "I see the distaste in your expression. But the obtaining of these skins is no different than the efforts of those who obtain corpses to increase our knowledge of the human body. Their work is for the betterment of humanity, and my own shall surpass theirs when I am done. Really, Brother

Brom, it's not as though those whose skins we employed had any further use for them."

"*We?*"

"My kinsman Philarète is my collaborator. He has a gift for tanning and animal preservation. Under his tutorage, I developed my own skills in the craft. The skin he had prepared, I had alchemically treated to receive the essence of the goddess. I held her in that vineyard, newly reborn in my arms, watching her eyes open and blink uncertainly until they focused on me.

"I was a stranger, but all was strange to her, so she welcomed my concern and accepted my aid. It became clear that she had no memory of who she was—*what* she was. Although… there were times I would see her gazing into space with a haughty expression, as though recalling her superior position among humankind, seeing as one the crowds that reached back through the ages, a forest of peoples stretching beyond the horizon, with arms like uplifting boughs holding the bloodied babes, birthed and slain in her honor.

"But when those moments passed, she was again a lost woman. Later, I told her that her name was Etienne de Lys, and she was much relieved when I found distant relatives of hers in France who were eager to take her in. Of course, they were in truth *my* relatives, childless ones, to whom I delivered the divine waif. They were very wealthy, and the form which we had prepared for her was comely, so she soon moved about in the aristocratic circles in Paris.

"I kept up with her progress, waiting for some sign that the goddess had emerged. I found none. Rather, she pursued a most mundane path. She married one Pierre de Saint-Ange, a much older man. By this time, she had become a confidante of the young women with whom she consorted. Thus, I assumed her life was chiefly of talk of clothes, and shoes, and whoever's latest tryst.

"Despite this lack of encouragement, I did take opportunity to personally reacquaint myself with my foundling when business brought me to Paris. Under pretense of wishing to surprise my 'niece,' I happened to come upon her unawares, and purposed to seize the opportunity to take a frank account of her.

"I found the new Madame de Saint-Ange in confidence with a young woman to whom she referred as 'Julianne.' Julianne was on her knees before Etienne, her head nestled in her lap. I watched as Etienne gently hooked Julianne's chin and raised her head to meet her eyes.

" 'Do not over distress yourself, my dear. Stop it! It would only spoil your figure, and its removal is no more than the paring of a nail, or the cutting of your hair. Are you mistress of your head but not your body? The difference is arbitrary. *All* is arbitrary. Do not fear infanticide—it is an imaginary crime, no different than evacuating any other matter from our bodies.'

" 'But my dear Madame de Saint-Ange,' Julianne said, "perhaps I have tarried too long. Perhaps it is already recognizable as a baby.'

"My Etienne shook her head. 'Were your child in your arms, the right to destroy it would be yours. It is a privilege secure in nature. Have you not observed a runt of a litter is denied its mothers' milk that the more robust spawn should survive? How it is most natural that maternal instinct should be suspended when there is need?'

"I saw Julianne's tear-smeared face as she looked my way, staring into space. 'I would rather rescue and nurse the abandoned runt.'

" 'Then do it!' Etienne said, grabbing her young friend's head between her hands, turning her face to her, then releasing Juliette's head with a shove. 'Save the bitch's whelp and bring the pup for my blessing, but never tell me again that you are with child unless it is to seek remedy for this misfortune as you do now! Otherwise, I tell you, Julianne, I will cease to be your friend at the moment you conceive!'

"I would not have thought that the adamantine, fierce rancor I witnessed in Etienne's voice and face were possible in a human being. I was much encouraged.

"I watched as Julianne produced a handkerchief to wipe her face as she nodded. 'Good,' Etienne said, taking a card from her person and passing it to her young friend. 'Show this to the man at the door at the back of the Rue Morgue.'

"Julianne regarded the card. 'What means this triangle with the straight line across the apex and the circle atop the line?' she asked.

" 'The man at the door will know. That is all you need know to gain you entrée into the Tophet. Do not worry, dear. I will join you there. And in a week or so, we shall have a ladies' day at the baths, eh? We will both have applied a fashionable depilatory plaster. Your lover will be much pleased.'

"The Tophet! I heard her say the Tophet! And what she described on the card was the ancient sigil of Tanit—her *own* sign! I was well satisfied without need to approach my former 'ward.' I knew then all that I needed to. I knew triumph! I had seen the goddess returned in this present age, in all her terrible, austere beauty of blood, mystery and glory! And so I have been encouraged to press on to achieve an even greater incarnation!"

Brom frowned. "Before we met in the tavern, you were already seeking this monastery, were you not? You knew it was built where Pan's temple once stood. You hoped to find here a tangible manifestation of Pan himself—or Baphomet-Sammael, as it were. To turn him loose upon the world as you did Tanit-Astarte." He unknitted his brow, smiled, and with his hands behind his back, stepped toward Cassave, leaned in over his shoulder and said in his ear, "You know that is completely unacceptable."

"Do you think so?" Cassave said, and returned the smiled as Brom leaned back.

"Oh, yes. You see, I also was seeking this monastery before we met. I had heard of its resident satyr and came with intent to destroy it. To seek out these pagan things that linger yet and plague Christiandom, *that* is the express mission of a Barbusquin."

"Hmmm," Cassave said, then made an ostentatious survey of their surroundings. "But you'll admit, you are in no position to frustrate my endeavors."

"I am bound," Brom said. "But God is not bound."

"Your Yahweh has no power here! At most, he is a mere, local tutelary of Palestine."

"Did you not hear young John say that the villager to whom he spoke identified Baphomet-Sammael as the tutelary of ancient Edom? So he was. But Edom crumbled into history, and, by your own belief, Baphomet-Sammael crumbled with it. More, this is the isle of Britain, so how does the tutelary of Edom come to have power here?"

"Baphomet-Sammael, that great spirit, came out of the desert to the shores of the Tiber, and thus gave its patronage and power to Rome," Cassave said. "The Greeks recognized him as their Pan, and so he became known as he lived and grew large with Rome's dominion. So Pan came to Britain. So here he has also revived. And now the hour has now come for Pan to walk among men clothed in human flesh!"

Brom cocked his head and regarded Cassave with eyes narrowed. "You are *not* going to provide another pagan creature with human skin," he said.

Cassave smiled. "Correct, Brother Brom: *you* are going to provide another pagan creature with human skin."

VI. A Murderous Monk with Knives

Brom was left alone, locked in the cellar, to contemplate his coming flaying. With effort he turned his thoughts from the horrific fate. Instead, he took stock of his surroundings. The basement room was fairly large, with wine barrels stacked on their sides, half-way to the ceiling along the wall to his left. A lit, bright candelabrum, the only source of light in the room, remained at the center of the long table. There, he supposed, was where he would be stretched out.

Elsewhere, the room was cluttered with cast off furniture and abandoned décor. He found a crucifix, discarded no doubt by one of the reprobate monks of Elster, picked it up and dusted if off.

"Ah, Lord Jesus," he said, looking at his crucified Christ, then draw the cross to his chest. "Help me now. Give me guidance that this evil be not loosed upon the world."

A stuffed boar's head lay on its side on the floor. He petted it: "Didn't I see you at the tavern?"

Brom paused, shut his eyes, remembered and nodded. Opening his eyes, he noticed something on the floor. He picked it up: a small, golden pig, crafted by ancient hands.

"*Moccus*," he said. "Cassave was coming for you here as well. Then before Pan, the Celts worshipped you on this spot." He looked again at the cast aside Boar's head: "You've come down in the world."

Then he narrowed his eyes on the boar's small tusks. He extended his forefinger to one horn, pricked the tip of his finger, then tried the other one and found it similarly sharp. He then grasped one tusk in each fist, and began working them back and forth and around, until the veins on his forearms plumped. The boar's tusks began to loosen in his grip.

After a few more minutes, he broke free first one and then the other, smiled, and put one in a pocket on either side of his robe. He then patted the boar's head again, and began to look about the room.

He took stock of each object, noting its place. He closed his eyes to picture the surroundings, opened and tested his recollection. He repeated this as he laid down on the floor.

And then, the crucifix by his side, an exhausted Brom fell asleep.

He awoke to the sound of footsteps heading his way. Two sets.

He climbed onto the table, moved the candelabrum to the corner of the far end, and obligingly stretched out on his back.

Then the door opened, and an undead Templar knight walked in.

Now a monk entered the room, wheeling in a small table holding the honed flaying knives, someone's brownish blood scabbing them. He locked the door behind him, then put the key in a robe pocket.

The monk was a bald man of pasty complexion and bulging eyes, plump and with a sheen of perspiration that glowed in the candelabrum's light.

"You should know," the monk said, producing an already damp handkerchief and swabbing his moist, pasty face with it, "that I asked for this task. I have much experience in the skinning of game. More than a mere chore to me; it always gave me pleasure, though I never spoke of my private joy. Since I have been released by Baphomet-Sammael—blessed be the name of the great god Pan!—I have indulged openly. On still-living creatures. I have flayed my first human, but one who was dead already.

"You, however, are alive, and shall remain so and awake throughout your ordeal. I tell you this, so that you will know that you are giving me pleasure with your every scream, for every contortion in your face accompanied by your mute, gaping mouth, when your pain has passed beyond the threshold of vocalization. You will beg. Know that will also give me pleasure because you knew the futility of begging before you did so, for you know that I am implacable."

"Yes, that's all well and good, but is that *my* broadsword at that dead Templar's hip?"

Withered lips bared the blind dead man's yellow teeth in a rictus grin.

"That *is* my sword! Look!" Brom, said, pointing at the Templar, and looking back and forth from the blind dead man to the monk. "He's grinning about it!"

The monk cocked his head, and he wondered how Brom could not have understood the threat he represented to his person, why Brom was not begging him, why… he was being ignored. He squinted at the Barbusquin, shook his head, quickly wiped his face again and began once more:

"I asked for this task. It gives me pleasure," he began again. "The skinning of game… No, no, *you* will bring me pleasure. That's it. Not skinning dead game. Skinning you…"

"But skinning dead game *did* give you pleasure. You said so," Brom said. "Earlier."

"With all that begging you are going to do," the monk said, raising his voice, "with your screams, with the yawning mouth beyond the threshold…"

"What are you trying to say, exactly? I mean, that just doesn't make any sense at all."

"You will beg!" the monk shouted. "Know that will also give me pleasure when I know because you knew that I know that you knew… *know* …"

"I'm afraid I can't follow you."

"…You *know*…knew…know that…you knew…"

"…*the futility of begging before you did so, for you know that I am implacable.* Got it!" Brom said, pointing at his head. "Mind like a steel trap. Got it the first time. When I commit something to memory, I never lose it. But, it would seem, you do not share my mnemonic gifts. So, later, when you're the one on this table, and you're wondering, 'How could this have happened? How did I end up here when everything was going so well?'—that's how. That's it. That, right there."

The monk's face was now red, his cheeks puffed, and he shouted to the blind dead man, "Apply the restraints!"

The dead Templar lunged forward. With a swipe of his heel, Brom knocked the candelabrum to the floor, immediately extinguishing the flame and dropping a blanket of darkness over the three of them, as he rolled over the side of the table.

"Fool!" the monk shouted. "He's blind! A dark room makes no difference to him! He'll find you with his preternaturally keen hearing!"

"Not with you yelling in his ear," Brom said, who had moved behind the Templar knight, yanked back the dead man's cowl, and then, pulling the boar tusks from a pocket on either side of his robe, he thrust their pointed ends into the dead man's ears, piercing his ear drums.

Suddenly sensory deprived, the Templar knight staggered back. Brom grabbed with both his hands his sword at the revenant's side. Drawing it free, he then slashed up and out, where he judged from memory the neck would be, and a moment later heard something hit the floor, followed by the sound of a collapsing body.

Then the air whistled with the swift passing of a small blade in an arc before him.

"Oh, I have not forgotten about you," Brom said.

"You will yet feel the bite of my knives!" the monk said.

He swung the knife out again, but now it met the flat of Brom's broadsword, which slapped hard, sending the flaying knife flying from the monk's hand.

Now he swung back and forth at the monk, driving him backward, until the monk found himself pinned in a corner, cringing and shrieking.

Brom grabbed him with one hand by the upper garment and pulled him into his face. "Now, you are going to unlock the door, then step back and hand me the key."

The monk quickly nodded. Brom shoved him forward. With trembling hands, the monk produced the key from a robe pocket, turned it in the lock and began to pull the door back.

"That's enough!" Bram said when it was at the slightest crack. "I don't want to be obvious, you understand. Just to let in enough light. Turn to me, both hands up... that's it. Now, hand me the keys, and I want you to back up to the table. Lie on it! Flat on your back. Good... Now, I believe you mentioned something about restraints?"

VII. The Gadarenes Maneuver

Brom had no sooner shut the door on the dark room that now held the gagged and bound monk than the chanting began. It was the same that they had heard on the old Roman road: a basso note Gregorian style chant, a malicious hum. By the time Brom had discovered a stone stairwell that housed several crude, wooden flights of steps, the sound was rattling the timbers of the monastery. Brom felt he was ascending the inside of a giant's rumbling throat.

As Brom reached the planked landing with the door behind whence the chanting originated, it stopped. Immediately laughter filled its place. Sword at the ready in one hand, Brom cracked the door with the other, peering into the mead hall Frater John had described. His eyes widened and then narrowed, his forehead creasing at what he saw.

The fallen monks of St. Elster were sporting with girls they had brought there to ruin. The girls squealed, many with one or both breasts exposed and their skirts hiked up on their thighs, the monks groping and pinching the women's flesh. Others downed skin flagons of wine, then let drop their deflated flagons to the flagstone floor.

The long tables displayed a glutton's banquet, foodstuffs toppling from their baskets spilling into one another, the table cloth smeared with stains, meats and bits of vegetables strewn over the table's top and gravy dripping down its sides. The monks' robes were also streaked with filth. Uncombed beards had caught and still held crumbs, bits of meat, and were tangled with dried gravy and juices.

Brom looked up. Above this frenzied tableau, mounted on the walls, and ringing the room, were boars' heads in whose glass eyes flickered the flames from the feasting hall's large fireplace.

And presiding over it all was Baphomet-Sammael, the Great God Pan. The goat creature had grown extremely large in size, its length now twelve feet. Rearing back on its high legs, but reclining on a couch, its exposed, gorged belly revealed rows of swollen teats and its spread legs displayed its androgynous genitalia. Its goat head was bowed in sated satisfaction, jaundiced eyes absorbing the depravities of its former jailers.

Cassave was nowhere to be seen.

Frowning and teeth grinding, Brom kicked the door the remainder of the way open. The struck door boomed loud enough amidst the cacophony that those close enough heard it and turned to see Brom's entrance, his sword drawn.

The women screamed, and they and the men with them fled from him. Brom grabbed the table cloth of one of the long banquet tables and pulled it along, upsetting dishes and cups, sending them clattering onto the floor. Heads turned and the monks and their women rose to their feet in his wake, staring after him. But no one moved to stop him; none dared challenge his authority.

Baphomet-Sammael had watched Brom's approach with no remark. Brom brought his sword point down to the floor so that he held it by the pommel, perpendicular to the floor. Then the creature tossed its head at his boldness, and the goat-thing's black upper lip curled.

"You come in the name of the blind god, the idiot god, my misbegotten male offspring! Here! I protect myself from all rebellious masculine energy with the sigil of my name! The sigil of AZ!"

Extending a foreleg, the goat thing sketched in the air with flame two diamond shapes, one on top of the other, and drew a line through the middle. The flaming sigil hung in the air between Brom and Baphomet-Sammael.

Brom nodded. "So you're AZ now... Of a truth, you have had many names," he said, stroking his bearded chin. "Let us see... No. No. Don't help me. Mind like a steel trap... AZ, Baphomet, Sammael. Pan... Oh. I believe 'Old Lady Nettie Gat' was your latest delightful sobriquet? Are you not also Nodens, god of the deep?"

"I am!"

"I have met Buddhists who know you as *Dorje Phagmo*. You are Choronzon, watcher at the abyss. But you were Chozzar first, to the Mesopotamians. Before Pan the Goat, before Moccus the Pig, you were Chozzar the Hog! From beyond the aether, your dwelling place, you came, Ab-human! As you are identified by Saint Sigsand in his book, *Ye Hogge had once a power upon ye earth, so doth he crave sore to come again. But ye Almighty hath upon ye Hogge power, and recall His Christ, for of all signs, the cross alone hath power over ye Hogge and is unto him a horror!*"

Brom dipped his hand into his robe, withdrawing the crucifix he had found in the cellar, and threw it at the flaming sigil hanging in the air. The crucifix struck the sigil, and, with a hiss, the fire was extinguished and Baphomet-Sammael robbed of its shield. The crucifix clanged to the floor and the visage of Christ shone in the goat thing's face. It bleated and dropped to all fours, charging at Brom with lowered horns.

Brom let the rosary he kept wrapped on his arm drop from beneath his robe's sleeve where he had concealed it until now. He grasped the rosary's crucifix along with the handle of the broad sword. As he drew his sword back over his shoulder, he felt an intense vibrating in the palm that gripped the crucifix, as though he grasped a hornet buzzing angrily, crazed to be free and sting. Brom somehow knew not to open his fist but clinch his sword handle tighter. When it came, the sting shot like hot, purifying venom from his hand through his arm, sending the sword sweeping forward, and, as though the blade were red hot, seared off the charging goat's horns as he dodged aside. The horns clattered to the floor.

A gasp rose from the monks who watched, and shame seemed to descend upon them, prickling first their scalps and then their ears and cheeks.

Baphomet-Sammael tossed its head. The stumps of its horns were smoking from their searing. Further, the goat no longer seemed quite as large as it had been before.

Facing the goat, Brom again held his broadsword out, upside down and before him, this time with the rosary and the crucifix dangling over the hilt onto the blade. "In the name of God and His Christ!" Brom shouted. "You are called into account! Come before me, goat!"

Baphomet-Sammael lowered its head, yellow eyes hooded. Obedient, but conscious and resentful of divine coercion, it began to slink toward him. A low, extended bleat issued from between parted black lips, like a dog's threatening low growl. Still, it came closer, now completely returned to its proper size.

Wary of the rosary crucifix, it stopped a few feet away, continuing its threatening bleat. It tossed its head, but with its stumps for horns, only succeeded in an impotent gesture of defiance.

"The monks of Elster have failed in their sacred charge, and are found unworthy." Brom indicated the men around him with a toss of his head.

"We acknowledge our sin," one of the monks cried out. There were multiple words of assent from around the hall. "Lord Jesu, have mercy on our souls!"

"He will!" Brom shouted. "You have confessed and asked for his forgiveness—now only believe! Then make what restitution you can to the families of those women you have ruined; acknowledge and take responsibility should any of your seed come to fruition! Jesu also stands ready to forgive you young women; his compassion on this earth for those fallen of your sex is written in the scripture; his contempt for those who scorn you recorded that the same Word.

Return them yourselves, men of Elster, to the homes from which you seduced them!"

Now he turned his full attention back on the goat. "Your hold here is lost!"

The goat began to moan, tossing its head side to side, the voice of a distressed old woman dragging from its throat: "*Wolde ye swynke me thilke wys?*"

"Do not seek pity from me! You will find none."

The goat shrieked and fell on its back, writhing. It gnashed its teeth and spat its curses up at Brom: "*Agus bas dunach ort! Dhonas's dholas ort, agus leat-sa!*"

"Be gone to your own place!"

Now, the goat leapt back up, froth dripping from its lips, rose on its hind legs, and began to stretch and contort. The head and hind legs remained those of a goat, but the torso and arms were becoming less hairy, more man like. It pawed the floor with one hoof, and tossed its head back and forth.

"It is Satan himself!" a monk cried out and the others wailed in concert.

"Our repentance came too late!" shouted another. "The Devil has come to deliver us into eternal torment by his own hand!"

Brom did not move from before the satyr but steadfastly held his rosary draped sword handle up, the crucifix exposed. "Silence, you fools! Do not allow your fear the mastery over you! You are in the Chapel Perilous—stand your ground!"

Brom advanced with his sword still held handle up, shoving the crucifix at the satyr. Its head recoiled to the side. Then it began a slow chortling, and quickly turned back to look Brom in the eye.

"You show me none but Atys of old!" The satyr hurled the name at him as its goat head nodded at the crucified Christ, one side of its upper lip curling. "Your new God is but a mask for the old!"

"Do you say so? Atys is not crucified, liar. But if you believe it to be so, why do you not look at the crucifix and call him by his true name?"

Brom extended the crucifix further, but the satyr would not look on it. Instead, it threw its goat head backward, opened its mouth wide, and from deep inside issued the chortling of a herd of swine, a churning cacophony of snorts and grunts.

"Chozar of the Mesopotamians? A pallid porcine mask! Ab-human, I adjure you in the name of Jesu, whether demon or creature of deep time it matters not: yield and reveal your true self!"

The satyr let out a barnyard cacophony of goats bleating and pigs snorting, its throat swelling. Then it fell on its face before the crucifix, flopped over and writhed, shouting out:

"I am the Ubbo-Sathla, mistress of form, and from me all forms proceed! I am the primordial genetrix!"

"Demiurge!" Brom retorted. "Little, blind fool god."

"I am I!" the contorting satyr said. "I was at the beginning!"

Brom laughed. "Is that *all*, goat? I say to you, *En Arche ein ho Logos*!" Brom shouted, unwrapping the rosary from his sword. "When all things began, *the Word already* was!" and he cast down the crucifix onto the satyr's chest.

The creature screamed, and where the crucifix struck, its body began to split apart. Divided, it liquidated, spreading over the mead hall floor. The monks and women drew back for fear this ooze might touch and absorb them.

But before it reached their feet, it began to flow back together before Brom. Sizzling, it churned and bubbled, then gelled, becoming an indistinct writhing fleshy mass of bristling fur, scales, talons and rustling pinions. Fins that became wings rose up out of this wad of fish and fowl, reptile and mammal, and beat at the air as though seeking to take flight. Then from this roiling aggregation emerged brutish, sub-human faces whose eyes seemed to light for a moment with consciousness just as they melted back into the agitated, primordial glob.

I am I! I am the Ubbo-Sathla, the goat's disembodied voice carried through the hall. *I am that utter abyss of all being!* The monks chilled at the voice, and they drew closer to each other and placed the women in the middle of them.

"Behold, my friends," Brom said, gesturing at the squirming mass, "the cornfield adder. This thing is no more than an impotent snake I have encountered in the former colonies of America. When encountered, it rears and sways, mocking the action of the cobra. If you do not retreat, it will fall to the ground, bare its fangs, and hiss. Its final gesture is to play dead. *This* Ab-human is afraid and blusters to conceal it, for it knows where the power of Christ will send it!"

"No!"

All in the hall turned in the direction of the voice to see Cassave entering with something like a heavy garment draped over his arms.

"Even Jesus had mercy and did not return those spirits to the abyss when they begged," Cassave said. "He gave them respite in swine of the Gadarenes! Brom Cromwell, I have prepared for this one a body! Follow, now, the example of your master!"

"*Prepared*? You have *stolen*! Who...?" Brom's eyes narrowed.

Grinning, Cassave held out the suit of skin. Hanging over his arms, upside down, the deflated face retained the expression of fear it had held at death, when its possessor knew it was inescapable, and his last sight in this world would be that of his killer. It was the face of Frater John.

Brom's eyes narrowed as he slowly cocked his head then slowly shook it from side to side. "The monk you sent to flay me said he had already performed one skinning. On a dead man!"

"Exactly! Frater John no longer has any use for his skin. Do not interfere with me, Brom Cromwell, I warn you!

Brom's hand tightened on his sword's handle as he regarded Cassave with wild eyes, his face crimson. Then he closed his eyes, took a deep breath, and relaxed his hand on his sword.

The wrath of men does not work the righteousness of God.

"Come Nodens, come Chozzar, come Baphomet, come great Pan! A body I have prepared thee!" Cassave was chanting and the light in the room was dimming as a chill wind began to blow through the mead hall, causing the fireplace flames to ripple and beat the air. A thick, grey fog rolled in, ankle high.

Sword point on the floor, one hand over the other on the handle, Brom bowed his head and began to pray.

Immediately, the darkness in the hall faded to twilight, and the wind stilled to a breeze.

Cassave continued to chant, but looked toward Brom and frowned.

Now the mist seemed to be sinking into the floor, and the turbulent flames in the fireplace were calming.

"What are you doing, Brom?" Cassave broke his chant and demanded:

Brom murmured out of the corner of his mouth, "I'm praying."

"Stop your damn interference! Stop it, or I will strike you down at your childish vespers!"

Cassave took a step toward Brom who made no move to defend himself. He did not even open his eyes. Instead, a smile crossed his lips as they continued to move in silent prayer, and a gust of wind thrust open the shutters of one large window above their heads.

Then descended a tall cone of blue spiraling light, striped with green luminous bands that also turned at their own speed. All who looked upon it felt the earth slip for a moment under their feet. With a vertiginous rush, all sense of size and proportion fled, for the geometry of angels had seized them in the presence of the light. The cone of light flowed into Brom's sword and set it aflame with azure and emerald hues. He withdrew both hands from it at once. For a moment, it stood erect, perfectly balanced on its point, then it turned itself upward, rising in the air, sweeping back and forth before Brom.

Cassave, eyes wide, stumbled back. "An Eldil! The Protective Force—that is ancient enemy of the Ab-human! The chariots and horsemen of Israel of old!"

The presence was wielding the unmooring of his senses as with all the others. He fell to his knees... One hand fell flat against the floor and kept him from a complete collapse. As the still blowing wind whipped his hair about him, he shouted:

"Brom! Do not propel it into the utter abyss! Will you be less merciful than Christ?" Cassave shouted.

Cromwell shook his head, still bowed, his eyes still closed. "No," he said. "I will be no less merciful than my Christ."

There was another gust of wind, this one foul with the scent of a barnyard, and the squeals and snorts of a seething unclean horde of swine, a rapid stamping of many cloven hooves upon the mead hall floor. The monks and their women stepped high, as though expecting to feel the thrust of a herd of swine shoving against their shins.

Then there was silence in the hall. Its occupants looked at each other and at their feet, still expecting to find swine among them. Then someone shouted, "Look!" and pointed up.

The mounted heads of the feral swine were twisting about on their mounts, tossing their tusks at the air, animated by the entity whose name of late was Old Lady Netty Gat. They shook powerfully, so that some of their bead eyes fell from the sockets and tap-tap-tapped over the floor. The boars' maws tore loose their lips' stiches, spilling sawdust, and from around the mead hall their voices united in one squeal, cringe-inducing to hear, like fingertips scratched over slate.

"Damn you, Brom!" Cassave shouted as he rose.

Now the remaining darkness in the mead hall faded, and the light returned to complete brightness. The flaming sword extinguished. Brom reached out and grabbed the sword's handle while it still levitated in the air, then returned it to his side.

"You have to admit," Brom said, sheathed his sword, then grinned at Cassave. "He was becoming a bit of a bore."

He walked over to Cassave. "Give me Frater John's remains. I will not have you desecrating his body."

Cassave gnawed his lower lip.

"Cassave?"

He thrust the folded skin into Brom's arms. "Take it!" he said. "But I *will* win, Brom! You and your ilk are out of step with the advance of history. The old gods *will* return. And I shall usher in an age unknown until now, by breeding gods with humans. Not by the foolish couplings of myth but through the wisdom of man's science!"

"Cassave," Brom said. "This Christian Abby is built where a temple to Pan once stood. The Romans brought him with them. And in the cellar I saw a golden pig image that reveal it as a hallow place of the Celtic Moccus. And for a moment it *was* Moccus' place and Pan's again. Whatever pantheon you introduce will be incorporated into the cycle, and will also have its day then crumble.

"The nature of this present world has always been that of mutability. Never was it intended to last, including whatever man introduces into the cosmic scheme. I wait for a stone not cut with human hands to enter from without and shatter the cycle forever, for a city whose builder and maker is God!"

Epilogue: As It is Written...

Cassave was imprisoned in the basement to be kept as the charge of the monks.

"And do try to do a better job keeping up with this corpulent fellow than you did with Chozar, lord of the abyss," Brom admonished them.

"We shall," said one of the Elster monks.

Brom sighed. "Well, I have this comfort at least: he cannot run very fast."

The monk who had flayed Frater John, whom the monks had found still bound to the table where Brom had left him, was also jailed in the basement. The monks of Elster expressed hopes of turning them both to God, but Brom cautioned them to beware of Cassave's subtlety.

The grave of the remaining Templar revenant was salted by prayer and thus sanitized, severing the revenant's hold on the earth. Frater John's remains, however, were respectfully interred in the monastery's graveyard. He was honored as a hero of faith and a martyr who had brought about the redemption of the abbey of Saint Elster.

While the chapel and monk's cells were ceremoniously cleansed and re-dedicated to God, the mead hall proved beyond redemption. Not that God's power was lessened, of course, but because the monks could never be at ease at its table with the enemy who had authored their degradation watching them through multiple eyes—even if they were only beads.

So, the monks knocked it down into rubble, burying the possessed swine's heads, and within them the goat of Saint Elster, now securely entombed. There to be held, as it is written of Chozar in the Sigsand manuscript:

Until the Outer Monstrosities held between earth and ye moon—the Dark Archon's domain, ye outer atmosphere, that abyss that is the abode of demons, identified by the apostle as 'the Kingdom of the Air'—will have the barrier that now restrains them removed.

Then Chozar, that vile hogg of old, that ancient goat, will rise up in its flesh. For he will also be loosed at the end of all things to walk ye earth with his brethren Outer Ones. For with them, in ye earlier life upon the world over the world did ye Hogge have power and shall again in ye end. In that day when our blessed Lord Jesu does return to trample all his enemies under his feet.

Amen—so shall it be!

I, Sigsand, attest what I have written here by my own hand.

We of the Barbusquin Order affirm what he has written is true.

I, Natvilcius aver that I have from the original autographs, translated it in-to Latin by my own hand.

Travis Hiltz continues to mine some remarkable works of French proto-SF for his inspiration, in this case, Albert Robida's futuristic fantasy Chalet in the Sky *(1925; Black Coat Press, ISBN 978-1-935558-87-3), Charles Derennes' proto-Lost World novel* The People of the Pole *(1907; Black Coat Press, ISBN 978-1-934543-39-9) and, finally, Paul Féval's* The Wandering Jew's Daughter *(1863; Black Coat press, ISBN 978-1-932983-30-2). The resulting, story is one that parallels one of the exploits of a famous time-traveler from a BBC series, proving that there's truly nothing new under the fictional skies...*

Travis Hiltz: *The Island of Exodus*

The 22nd century

The chalet was homey, picturesque—and floating five hundred yards above the ocean. It wobbled slightly, rising further, struggling to get out of the path of the massive, approaching storm. Like some huge, grey leviathan, the storm crept unrelentingly closer.

The aerochalet was a wonder of technology, combining the joys of travel with all the comforts of home. Despite this, it looked tiny and fragile in the face of the ever-growing storm.

The wind picked up, tugging at roof shingles and scattering patio furniture. A side door opened and two teenage boys emerged. The taller of the two, quickly moved to gather up the toppled chairs. The other, shorter and of a more athletic build, moved to the railing, ignoring the efforts of his brother, to instead stare intently at the dense, looming clouds.

"Andoche!" the taller boy shouted, struggling with the chairs, as well as to be heard over the wind. "We can sightsee after we've gotten the patio cleaned up. We still haven't found where the cat wandered off to!"

"Moderan," his brother said, as if he hadn't even heard the other boy speak and not looking away from the threatening sky. "Do those clouds look... um... I don't know, strange, to you...?"

Wrestling three patio chairs at once, young Moderan stacked them by the door, knowing he'd end up doing all the work if he didn't reply to his brother.

"It's going to be a fierce storm," he said, joining his darker-haired brother at the railing. "Uncle said so and Barlotin has voiced some concerns about it interfering with the instruments."

The fact that the aerochalet's stoic pilot had spoken up at all was enough to snap Andoche's attention away from the clouds and back to his brother. Moderan paused and peered at the pursuing storm, running a hand through his sandy-blonde hair.

163

"There's something odd about that lightning…?" he muttered.

"That's what I thought," his brother retorted. "And it's moving very fast… like the ocean, there's a constant sort of… rolling, I guess you might say."

"Very odd," Moderan repeated, thoughtfully.

He was the more studious of the two brothers and had spent time with their scientist uncle, studying this vast empty stretch of ocean and its weather patterns. For this time of year, this storm was a complete deviation.

So intently were they watching the flashes of lightning occurring within the depths of the massive storm front, that neither noticed Babylas, the aerochalet's corpulent white house cat, strolling along the patio until she began brushing up against the boys legs.

Andoche reached down and absently scratched the cat's fluffy head.

"Wind's picking up," he said.

"Wind currents shouldn't be pushing the clouds along like that," his brother noted. "It should be moving more south east and not that fast… that fast…?"

There was a moment of silence and then both boys were snapped out of their contemplation by their sudden realization that they were standing outside, exposed in the path of the oncoming storm.

"Oh dear!" Moderan breathed, grabbing his brother's arm and dragging him away from the railing.

Andoche scooped up the cat and staggered along after his brother.

The two patio tables were bolted to the deck, so Moderan paused only to grab the couple remaining chairs, leaving the potted plants and empty drinks cart to fend for themselves.

With the cat tucked under his arm like an indignant football, Andoche bolted for the side door.

Feeling the rain hitting the backs of their shirts, the brothers tossed furniture and pet inside the aerochalet, and then paused taking a last second inventory of what remained on the patio: what was salvageable and what they might be looking at for the last time.

"Uncle will be pretty peeved if he loses that berry bush!" Moderan said ruefully.

"He'll be even more peeved if he has to explain to mum and father that you got blown overboard!" his brother shouted, struggling to be heard over the wind.

He grabbed his brother's shirt and pulled him inside.

They put their shoulders against the door to shove it closed and then sunk to the floor. They sat, hair wind-mussed, clothing damp, their backs resting against the door as they listened to the storm raging outside.

Several feet away, Babylas sat on a throw rug, looking at the boys with jaded disapproval. Once it had made its feelings known, the cat resumed grooming its fur.

The center of the aerochalet was made up of a wide corridor with doors on both walls. One door, on the left, was flung open and an eccentric figure leaned out.

The boys' uncle, the noted researcher Professor Cabrol, was a thin, older man. He sported a long black mustache to compensate for the desolation upon the top of his head, on which there was only a single, stubborn tuft of black hair.

Over his tunic and trousers, he wore a long dark green garment, a robe with a hood, made from a lightweight material.

He peered over the tops of his glasses, every bit as disapprovingly as the cat had.

"Really, boys!" he grumbled. "See that the chalet is secure and then do your rough housing. Patio cleared?"

The two boys glanced at the door behind them, hearing faint crashes as the wind had its way with the remaining furnishings.

"More or less," Andoche admitted, uneasily.

"Good, good," their Uncle said, nodding to himself. "Barlotin says we are in for a rough night. Double check all the windows if you please. I still need to see to my books and samples. Dinner will be catch as you can, since Melanie refuses to come out from under her bed till the weather has cleared… Phanor is with her, so no need to worry about him."

Having reassured them as to the whereabouts of the aerochalet's housekeeper and dog, Professor Cabrol gave a final nod and retreated back into his study.

The boys looked at each other and then slumped against the door.

"Pets secure and… well, most of the patio furniture accounted for," Moderan muttered. "Most likely, we won't be able to make our nightly call to Mum and Dad, so I guess it's an early dinner and then a quiet night of hoping we don't crash into the ocean…"

"Ever the optimist," his brother chided him.

Just then, the aerochalet shook and tilted, sending the two boys sliding into the wall. The storm washed over the small flying house like a wave. Every door and window rattled and threatened to burst.

They were able to locate the rest of the household by their outbursts. Melanie, the housekeeper, shrieked that they were all going to be drowned.

Professor Cabrol shouted, as he had been unfortunate enough to discover that not all of his books had been secured tightly enough.

Phanor barked to let the rest of them know he had moved from under Melanie's bed and was now stationed under the stairs—if he was needed.

Andoche and Moderan struggled to untangle themselves and got to their feet just as the aerochalet rocked violently back and forth. They staggered around, ending up back on the hall floor. Andoche, being the more athletic of the two, made several more unsuccessful attempts to get up, before giving up and holding onto the floor for dear life, along with his brother.

The storm raged around them, tossing the aerochalet like a tiny ship on the ocean. The boys slid about the floor, crawling at a turtle pace for the relative shelter of their bedroom.

Dinner was forgotten, as every occupant of the aerochalet huddled down to ride out the storm: Melanie under her bed, Professor Cabrol in his favorite chair, wedged into the corner of his study, and Barlotin the pilot with his ever-present pipe, stationed at the controls working diligently to keep them airborne and safe.

The boys climbed into their beds, made several attempts at conversation, but quickly gave up because of the cacophony of the raging maelstrom outside, as well as the rattling of unsecured furniture inside.

Hours passed; the housekeeper eventually grew hoarse from announcing their imminent demise and fell asleep. Phanor and Babylas, their natural, mutual animosity forgotten in this matter of self-preservation, eventually joined her.

The aerochalet shuddered and bobbed, struggling to keep to a course heading for the fringe of the storm.

Barlotin huddled down in the control room, clamped his teeth tightly down upon his pipe, keeping his hands free to tend to the controls, constantly adjusting dials and levers, while keeping at least one eye on the barometer and a half dozen other gauges and instruments, that monitored the systems keeping the aerochalet aloft and functioning.

While the flying house tossed and tumbled, the white-bearded veteran aeronaut kept his feet on the deck and never showed the slightest sign of losing his balance, or even allowing his face to crease with worry.

In fact, his expression never seemed to rise above "mildly perturbed" by events.

Andoche tied the corners of his blankets to the bedposts and, crawling into this makeshift cocoon, was soon rocked to sleep by the storm.

His more thoughtful brother found that, despite his body's weariness, his brain would not let him sleep, and he spent several hours trying to calculate how far and in which direction the aerochalet was being blown off course.

Moderan pondered braving the journey from his bed to the control room to consult with their pilot, but settled for mental calculations and an eventual, fitful sleep…

Which meant that no one in the aerochalet was able to observe that the lightning was not shooting downwards from the clouds, but rather its long jagged ribbons of a vivid purple seemed instead to be traveling up from the ocean below and striking the center of the raging maelstrom.

Hours passed and the storm eventually raged itself out. Streamers of sunlight poked through thinning clouds. The ocean grew calmer.

The aerochalet ceased to rock and sway, which was, surprisingly enough, what woke Professor Cabrol up. He blinked groggily and ran a dry tongue over his false teeth, looking around his den. His attempts to secure his personal library had not been met with complete success, and the floor of his study was strewn with a multitude of volumes and papers.

Getting to his feet, the thin savant tiptoed his way through the field of books and down the main corridor. He stepped out onto the patio, squinting in the morning sun.

Spotting the drinks cart wedged up on the roof, Cabrol frowned in disapproval, before glancing around, making a mental list of needed repairs.

Andoche joined him several minutes later. He looked slightly guilty over he and his brother's incomplete efforts to clear the patio, and went back to his previous post at the railing.

By the door was a speaking tube on a hook. Professor Cabrol pushed the button for the pilot's room and spoke into it for several minutes. He then joined his nephew.

"Barlotin is a bit concerned," he said. "I fear not all our repair work will be of a housekeeping nature."

"Rousing Melanie will be a task," his nephew replied, absently, his attention drawn to the remaining scatterings of cloud and the ocean below.

He then reached over and tugged at his uncle's sleeve.

"Look!" he announced, pointing downwards.

In the middle of the beautiful desolation of the ocean was a single speck of land.

Both men peered intently at the tiny island. The professor stroked his mustache in thought.

"Curious," he muttered, patting his robe pockets until he found his glasses. "I will consult the charts, but we weren't supposed to reach land until tomorrow... We were blown off course... Perhaps underwater tremors pushed that island to the surface...?"

"Well, there's only one way to find out," Andoche suggested, enthusiastically.

His uncle looked skeptical.

"We have an anchorage, so Barlotin can do any repairs and you wouldn't just be sitting around, waiting. Moderan and I could help..."

"Ah! Now we have it!" his uncle chuckled. "You see an excuse to hike and climb and get away from the sedate life of the studious savant."

His nephew shrugged, smiling sheepishly.

Cabrol patted his shoulder.

"See what you can do to clean up out here, while I'll go and have a word with Barlotin. I may question your motives, but your idea is not without merit."

He strolled away to consult with the aerochalet's pilot, leaving his nephew to rouse the rest of the household.

With the help of their faithful dog, they soon had Melanie up and working on breakfast. Andoche then got his brother to help him with not just the post-storm clean up, but with his efforts to convince their uncle that they had to explore this intriguing new little landmass.

While Moderan did not share his brother's enthusiasm for physical recreation, the tiny island did grab his scientific curiosity, so he was easy to convince.

Slowly the aerochalet drifted downwards, circling the island. Its surface was rocky, foliage being sparse and sickly. It sported a stubby central peak, and, on the far side, were a scattering of smaller "islets" separated from the main landmass by a dozen feet of ocean.

Barlotin steered them to a ragged-edged, natural harbor and, when they were several yards above the rocky shore, released the anchor.

Once securely moored, they lowered the stairs and the two young explorers soon stood upon the barren shore.

Their uncle had, reluctantly, chosen to stay and help Barlotin with whatever repairs or adjustments might be needed; Melanie claimed she had too much cleaning to do to go tramping around.

The brothers packed up some food pills, Moderan's notebook, compass and camera, set up Phanor on the patio with some food and water, and headed out to explore.

Andoche tended to hurry, moving quickly from place to place, while his brother went at a slower, more methodical pace.

The ground was rocky and uneven, with no clear paths, so Andoche tended to stumble along his way, while Moderan lagged behind, studying the landscape and pausing to examine the occasional stone or scrap of plant life.

After the second or third time, Moderan had lost sight of his brother, only to locate him when Andoche would exclaim in pain or exasperation; the studious blond boy sighed, put away his notebook, and set a path to reunite with his brother.

He found Andoche sitting on a stone, tending to a tear in his pant leg.

"If you would slow down…" Moderan chided.

"Just because I'm not entranced by every pebble and weed," Andoche grumbled, not looking up from his torn pant leg and bruised knee.

"This island looks to be mostly volcanic rock, which is very porous, and tends to harden into shale-like rock," Moderan explained, absently. "So, it's going to be somewhat brittle and sharp. It's going to get worse on the far side where it's steeper."

"All right," his brother said, standing up and shifting from frowning at his pant leg to frowning at his brother. "Mother will be pleased to hear you are keeping an eye on me and attempting to further my education."

"Fine, keep stomping around," Moderan muttered. "I've always wished to be only child."

The brothers glared at each other for a few moments, before Andoche smirked and made a "after you" gesture. Responding with a mock bow,

Moderan retrieved his compass and started up a narrow channel through the jagged rocks.

They trudged uphill for nearly an hour before reaching a smooth shelf on the island's central peak that gave them a decent view of their surroundings.

Moderan shrugged off his knapsack and took out his notebook. His brother took out a handful of food pills, sorting out the vegetable ones and keeping the meat and sweets ones. He perched on the least dangerous looking piece of rock and snacked while his brother made calculations and scribbled some notes.

"What have you discovered, Magellan?" he asked, after a couple minutes.

"I think this island was pushed up to the surface by some undersea earthquake," Moderan replied, not looking up from his notebook. "Pretty recently, as it is not on any of our charts, and we don't seem to have been blow wildly off course."

"Is that why the ground feels so strange?" Andoche asked.

"Well, this is not common rock," Moderan replied. "And it does seem to be seismically unstable. I've been noting slight tremors since we arrived…"

"I thought something was… off with my balance," his brother mused. "Is the island going to sink again?"

"Maybe… but probably not" Moderan shrugged. "They're just aftershocks, as it settles."

"You sure it was pushed up out of the ocean during the storm?" Andoche asked.

"Looks like it. Why?"

"So there should be no one else on the island?"

"What are you talking about?" Moderan asked, looking over at his brother.

"I thought I heard something," Andoche said, glancing over his shoulder. "Like someone, or something, following us…"

"Doubtful," Moderan said, closing his notebook and helping himself to one of his brother's food pills. "It's probably just tremors or waves pushing stone and gravel around."

"You sure?" his brother asked, doubtfully.

"It's a big lump of rock," Moderan replied, waving a hand at their surroundings. "We have more vegetation on the patio, and there's almost no shelter from the wind and sea. There's no one here but us."

Just as he finished speaking, there was the sound of something moving further up the peak.

Both boys quickly peered uphill. Then Andoche glanced at his brother.

"Was that an earthquake or a wave?" he asked sarcastically.

"That's… but… come on…!" Moderan sputtered, sprinting and stumbling up the rocky hill, towards the mysterious sounds.

Andoche, being the more athletic of the two, easily caught up to his brother.

Further up the peak, the rock was ridged with narrow paths, like gouges in the rock.

The two edged along as quickly as they could.

It opened up to a wider ledge. Dirt and stone trickled down, like a gravelly waterfall, indicating where their mysterious quarry had gone.

"This doesn't make sense!" Andoche protested.

"Uncle finished the repairs and came looking for us?" Moderan suggested, unconvincingly.

"And he got ahead of us?" Andoche asked. "And isn't bothering to call to us? Something is going on here."

Andoche gestured for his brother to be quiet and both young explorers listened intently for several moments. He then pointed, directing Moderan to move in one direction, while he moved in another, in hopes of catching their mysterious quarry between them.

Andoche crept along, making use of the few bits of cover. More sounds of movement came from behind a trio of rough stalagmites.

He bolted from his cover, coming around the rocks in time to catch a glimpse of movement downhill from him. Andoche skidded and stumbled down the rocky slope, exchanging stealth for speed. He stubbed his toes and cracked his shins as he hurried after the other figure, picking up hints and details as he went. It was another man, and he appeared to be bald and wearing some kind of leather garment.

Andoche leapt over some rocks, slid down a stretch of the peak, coming to a halt by striking his shoulder against a boulder. He lunged forward to grab at the other man and a large, green-black tail slapped his hand away. The stranger spun around and Andoche found himself face to face with a lizard-like creature that stood on two legs and had an odd, plastic gun pointed at him.

Moderan crept along cautiously. He was torn between curiosity about whoever was making the noise and anxiety over what would happen when he caught up with him.

Every step seemed blaringly loud. Any time he nudged a pebble, Moderan would freeze, convinced it would alert whoever or whatever he was pursuing and it would pounce on him. After several minutes, the noise faded away. He was sure he could feel a presence just over the next ridge.

He spotted a narrow gully of stone, that ran lower down the peak, and the young student was sure he could crawl along it and be able to approach his quarry.

Moderan got down and crawled, biting his lip every time a sharp piece of rock pressed against his body. He wiggled through a narrow bend, only to have the brittle rock crack and crumble, and he found himself tumbling off the narrow ledge.

As he felt his body leaving the ledge, a hand clamped onto his arm and hauled him back to safety. With impressive strength, the hand pulled him up and gently placed him upon a smooth bench of stone, allowing him to get a look at his rescuer.

He was a man, almost impossibly tall and old. His hands were gnarled and callused. His face was so craggy that he reminded the young explorer more of an ancient tree than a man.

His clothes were at least a century out of fashion and so coated with the dust and dirt of the road that Moderan couldn't even hazard a guess as to what color his suit had originally been.

The tall stranger leaned casually upon an oaken staff as tall and weathered as he was and peered at the boy with thoughtful bemusement. With one hand, he thoughtfully stroked a beard, white as snow, that hung down past his belt. A small smile fought its way out through the expanse of facial hair.

"Well met, young man," he finally said, his voice mild with a slight creakiness that seemed to come from lack of use. "What brings you out to this desolate oasis?"

There was no hint of menace in the question, rather a feeling as if, despite this odd meeting at this far-flung location, the bearded man could only manage a mild curiosity.

"The storm brought us here," Moderan replied. "The island is not on our maps...."

"I should think not," the tall man chuckled. "Your maps would have to be quite recent editions. You say us... how many are there in your flying machine?"

"Who are you?" Moderan asked, bewildered. He scrambled to his feet. Though the bearded man still towered over him. "How are you here?"

"Isaac is my name," he said. "I'm a wanderer and was sheltering from the storm..."

"How?" Moderan asked, suspiciously. "There's no sign of any of vessels or man-made structures..."

"Man-made...?" Isaac chuckled glancing around at their rocky surroundings. "No, I own nothing but the clothes on my back and only have my feet to get me where I need to be."

"That... doesn't make any sense!" Moderan protested. "That answers nothing... you walked to this island? That's... just... impossible...!"

"I've been told that," the bearded man nodded, absently, while making no further effort to explain himself.

"Why were you following us?" The young student asked, switching his questions in the hope of getting at least one answer that made sense.

"I wasn't," Isaac replied. "I was strolling about, looking for a place to sit and rest my feet when you came tumbling along... *Us*...? Are there others wandering around the island?"

"Just my brother. He went... over there as we tried to catch you..."

"That wasn't me," Isaac said, straightening up. "Come along, we need to find your brother before he gets himself in trouble."

He hooked his arm through Moderan's and, without seeming to exert himself, carried the young explorer along. They made their way around the peak of the island. Moderan felt like his feet weren't actually touching the stony ground for most of the way.

Isaac's long legs took them to the other side of the peak within minutes and he was soon skidding to a halt.

Moderan bumped against the mysterious wanderer's shoulder and then peered past him. Strange as his meeting with the bearded man had been, it seemed Andoche's was even stranger.

His brother stood, his back pressed up against the rocky wall, as a man-sized lizard in a brown tunic, was pointing a gun at him.

Both boys were left a bit speechless, by their own situation, as well as discovering their brother had stumbled into one equally strange.

"Hold, my friend!" Isaac intoned, his voice stern.

The lizard creature looked at the bearded man, then his gaze took in the second boy. Beside a frown, Moderan could not read the creature's expression, but it lowered its gun hand, not holstering his unusual weapon, but no longer directly threatening them with it.

Looking directly at Isaac, the creature hissed and growled.

"None of that," Isaac chided the lizard. "These youths are not your enemy. Speak."

The creature glowered at the tall man before speaking, unsure if it was due to anger or merely that it had to pause and mentally figure out how to make the muscles of its inhuman face adapt to speaking English.

"Intruders, this close to departure," the lizard growled. "Is suspicious."

"Is coincidence," Isaac reassured. "A storm like that, any vessel that came within miles of us was going to get rattled around like dice in a cup. Besides, hardly a threatening looking duo, are they?"

The lizard man took in the two bedraggled boys with their dirty hands and torn clothing and even his alien features made it obvious he was unimpressed.

"What of others? They are only ones piloting vessel?"

"No," Moderan said, in a shaky voice. "The crew is just my uncle... a scientist and... um... two that help run the chalet..."

"And our dog," Andoche added.

"Well, there's your invading army," Isaac said, gently. "Best start barricading the windows and doors now."

The lizard man frowned at the tall wanderer, glanced again accusingly at the two boys, then nodded to itself and walked to the edge of the cliff. It adjusted controls upon its stubby gun and then pointing it down peak from the group appeared to fire off a half dozen shots. There was no recoil or evidence of any kind of projectile, just a series of high pitched whines, like are sometimes made by power lines in hot weather.

Minutes later, there was a reply, or perhaps a delayed echo, but either way the reptile seemed satisfied. It holstered its weapon and made itself comfortable on a lump of volcanic stone.

"We wait," it declared with authority. "The mammal young will stay until departure."

Isaac frowned slightly but then nodded.

"Fair enough."

He gestured for the boys to have a seat, across the clearing. He leaned his staff against the stone peak and began to rummage through his coat pockets. He came out with a small crumpled paper bag. He offered it to the brothers. It contained an odd assortment of candies and food pills. Most of them were slightly dusty and mixed in with them were a few buttons, some coins, lint and even a bullet.

Moderan declined with a shake of his head, while his brother shrugged and helped himself.

"You'll have to forgive my friend," Isaac said, while he picked through the candies. Discovering what he thought was a jellybean was actually a pebble, he flicked it away. "His people and yours have a tumultuous history."

The brothers exchanged a look at the tall man's use of "yours," but were still reeling from their encounter with the lizard man to give it more thought.

"But, what are…they?" Moderan said in a hush, leaning in. "Aliens?"

"Oh, no," Isaac chuckled, sitting back. "In fact, the People have more of a claim to this world than humanity. They were walking this world back when dinosaurs roamed."

"Intelligent beings that evolved from… reptiles… iguanodons, I would guess." Moderan muttered, curiosity beginning to overtake his fear. "Lizard people that existed back in the… um… Silurian era…"

"Don't use that word," Isaac frowned. "They don't take well to being referred to that way."

"Where have they been then?" Andoche asked, waving off his brother. " If this… other civilization has been around before the dawn of mankind…?"

"They have kept hidden, fearing what should happen if they were to attempt to share, or perhaps even reclaim, the Earth," Isaac said. "Some colonies hibernated, sleeping away the centuries…"

"Why wake up now?" Moderan asked. "Why come here, to this island?"

"They haven't come here," Isaac replied. "They've been here the entire time. This world has grown old and there have been many changes. Centuries ago, this island was a mountain encased in ice and snow. The planet shifted and their city was then beneath the ocean."

"The island did rise up out of the ocean!" Moderan breathed, happy that his theory had been correct, as well as discovering the answer was even more fantastic then he'd imagined.

"Was it the storm that brought it up?" Andoche asked.

"Rather the other way around," Isaac said. "The People have decided this world has grown too old, its crust mined and excavated till it is thin and flimsy and they have decided to leave it to mankind. They hope, instead, to find their destiny amongst the stars."

"How do you know all this?" Andoche asked, helping himself to the crumpled bag of candy. "How did you get here?"

"Yes, why are we suspicious invaders and you are just strolling around the island?" Moderan added.

"The People and I have crossed paths several times," the bearded man shrugged. "I have earned a slight measure of trust. I, too, have seen this world grow old and fragile, and have offered my assistance to the People's efforts in exchange for passage."

Both boys looked at the tall wanderer wide-eyed.

"You are...?" Andoche muttered, looking from the lizard man to the raggedy wanderer with his wooden staff and dingy bag of candy.

"Traveling in space with an army of lizards?" Moderan said, shaking his head, unsure if he was impressed or flabbergasted. "How... where is their spaceship? This island is a barren rock?"

"This island is the spaceship," Isaac explained, smiling as he savored the boys' reactions. "I am not a man of science myself, but their plan involves using... sonic energy and, I believe, force fields... there are many equations, and I tend to just nod. I have walked every inch of this tired sphere and if the Good Lord will allow it, I hope to stride across the stars..."

He looked up into the sky with a wistful smile on his face.

"They aren't taking us with them, are they?" Moderan asked, anxiously.

"What..? Oh no!" Isaac chuckled. "They just do not trust humans, but are only keeping you here until it's time to leave."

An hour passed, the boys peppered Isaac with questions about the island, the lizard men and the old man himself.

He was vague in all responses, claiming modesty and not having much knowledge of the science involved. He dropped hints of the various previous times he had encountered the lizard men, but Moderan was skeptical, as the math would have meant that the bearded wanderer was hundreds of years old.

The boys were startled by the return of their iguanodon chaperone, now joined by two other of its kind. One clad in a kilt and vest of a shiny leather-like material. The other in a plain tunic who seemed more concerned with studying his wide wristband and the odd, watch-like device attached to it. It hissed to itself thoughtfully. The lead lizard nodded, then growled and hissed at Isaac.

The old man nodded, and ran a gnarled hand through his enormous beard in thought.

"What's going on?" Moderan asked, nervously.

"Time we were all off," Isaac said, getting to his feet. "Apparently, they got a bit distracted by the preparations and had forgotten about you. We are to board, as the launch is imminent."

"What about us?" Andoche asked, leaping to his feet.

The lizard men all started and reached for their side arms.

"Nothing to fret about," Isaac said, making calming gestures to all around him, before turning back to face the boys. "But I wouldn't dawdle, if I were you. Put some distance between yourselves and the island."

"Um…Thank you, I think…?" Moderan said. "Good luck!"

"Come on!" his brother exclaimed, grabbing his arm and hauling him away.

The two ran down the uneven, rocky peak, keeping each other from falling, as the tremors beneath their feet grew stronger. They stumbled along, putting in a burst of speed as the anchored aerochalet came in view, finally racing up the gangplank and leaning against the patio rail for support as they struggled to catch their breath.

"There you are," their uncle said, looking up from his book. "Melanie was convinced you'd fallen into the sea or some such… Had a good explore?"

"Uncle," Andoche wheezed. "We need… to… hnnn… to… to launch… island… lizards… huh-huh…!"

"The island's not stable," Moderan interrupted, realizing the truth would take too long and leave them vulnerable to whatever was about to occur. "Strong… increase in tremors… might be… eruption… we… need to go!"

"All right, all right," Professor Cabrol said, getting to his feet. "Sit, sit, I'll let Barlotin know."

He went to the speaking tube and, after giving the pilot instructions, saw to drawing in the mooring anchor. Grasping the line, he felt it vibrating like a violin string and realized his nephews were not engaging in adolescent hyperbole.

The aerochalet rose once more into the air, as the shaking of the strange little island reached a fever pitch and storm clouds began to reform. The sea around it was soon churned into boiling foam.

The Professor took the boys by the arms and steered them inside, casting anxious, if curious, glances over his shoulder.

"Quite curious," he muttered, sealing the door behind them, and unhooking the interior speaking tube. "Um… best speed Barlotin"

The tempest was not as fierce as the previous night, but no less unusual and disconcerting for the aerochalet's occupants. They retreated to the Professor's den and, each taking a chair, held tight, as the flying house rocked and soared.

After several minutes, things seemed to have calmed down, and the trio moved to the window.

"Well, you were quite right, my boy," Professor Cabrol said, patting Moderan's shoulder absently. "Even with the tremors, I never would have anticipated such a fierce eruption. Hard to say with certainty, so much smoke and ash, but it was apparently forceful enough to have sent a rather large piece of the island skywards. Going to be quite a splash when that comes back down. I'd best go find where Melanie is hiding and then consult the instruments..."

The brothers merely nodded in reply, their gazes locked on events outside the window.

Hours later, the aerochalet was many miles away and floating gently above a tranquil stretch of ocean. Order had been restored, dinner served, and the Professor and Moderan were standing at the rail, contemplating the water and the approaching dusk.

"Quite an eventful twenty-four hours," the older man mused, removing his glasses and polishing them with the edge of his robe. "Not quite what I had planned for this leg of the journey. Might not want to share too many details with your parents... They'd just worry, needlessly..."

The blond student could only nod in agreement.

"It's funny," the Professor mused. "I had planned this little excursion, because that stretch of ocean where we found the island was the site of the Earth's original North Pole."

"Yes, I... uh... believe I'd heard that... somewhere," Moderan muttered.

"You wouldn't know it now, but the pole has been a source of a great deal of not just history, but stories and legends," his uncle continued. "All sorts of tales of lost cities, exotic civilizations, strange artifacts, and even a rather quaint one about an immortal fellow with a big, white beard, who looked after children... fanciful stuff really... makes one wonder where such notions came from."

"I don't know where they came from, Uncle," Moderan said, looking dreamily upwards at the first emerging stars of the night. "I'm more interested about where they are going..."

176

Paul Hugli happily blends real-life historical events with fiction in a vignette tale that spans two worlds...

Paul Hugli: *As Easy as 1, 2, 3...*

Barsoom, 1899 CE (by Earth reckoning)

In the Palace of Helium, the Princess of Mars, Dejah Thoris, stood sky-clad, like the Ancient Egyptians of the Amarna Period over 3000 years before. Similarly to those Earthlings, she only wore a loose garment about the loins and a sparkling of jewelry. It was all she could do not to lift her arms, so aching was her desire for her husband who lay so far away on the sparkling jewel hanging in the Martian firmament that was Jasoom, or, as he said in the strange barbaric tongue he called English, Earth.

The Princess of Mars turned her back to the vast Barsoomian sky and the hurtling moons that sped across the Martian night. Her concerns this night were greater than her burning desire for her husband, or even the safety of her two hatchlings—Carthoris and Tara—who who were out on their own adventures, unaware of the immediate danger which faced Helium, if not, in fact all of Barsoom.

The sun-worshipping Tardids were rallying up for yet another attack on Helium from their bases on the moon of Thuria. These white-skinned, blue-haired demons had the ability to render themselves invisible by sheer mental powers, and who knows what other diabolical scheme they had up their collective sleeves.

She knew of only one man who could stop this invasion, but he was on Earth, distant Jasoom. Barsoom needed their Champion of Justice... Their Prince... Their Warlord, the Jeddack Dojar Sojat... And they needed him now!

Dejah placed her crimson hand on the Gridley Wave Generator. How many times had she done this in the hope her lost hero would respond? How many hopeless times had she sent the beam across the aether in hopes of awakening her sleeping prince? The green-skinned Thark Tars Tarkas had urged her often enough with his wise but savage council, but now...

Now, her strong but trembling fingers activated the wave generator. May the gods of Barsoom speed it across the vast depths of space to awaken the savior of Helium before it was too late.

"My darling," Dejah Thoris, whispered, almost in prayer, "Barsoom needs you... Helium needs you... your children need you... *I* need you... You must hear my call!"

But the only answer was the low hum of the Gridley wave across the silent

Barsoomian night.

John Carter's Tomb – An undisclosed location in the United Sates

In his tomb, sealed from the inside, laying in-state, was the ex-Civil War rebel and prospector, adventurer, and seemingly immortal figure, known to the Tharks as Dotar Sojat, his gray eyes still.

John Carter, who, as far as anyone could remember, had always been thirty years-old, lay in silence, in stasis, neither alive nor dead. The man who had fought for princess and kings, republics and lost causes, the master swordsman of two worlds, the adventurer across time and space, lay, oblivious to the plea his wife had sent across time and space to awaken him.

Unknown to either Dejah Thoris or the sleeping John Carter, an electro-magnetic anomaly was interfering with the transmission of the emergency signal from the Gridley wave. No signal reached across the aether to awaken him.

John Carter still slept.

Colorado Springs, Colorado

On East Pike's Peak Avenue, near Knob Hill, in the dark of night, stood a 4200 square-foot wooden building. Surrounding it was a tall fence with a warning that read: "*Abandon all hope, Ye who enter here.*" Inside the building was a Magnifying Transmitter: a 75-foot diameter coil of tightly wound, hundreds of turns of fine wire. Within this primary coil was a secondary coil of ten-foot diameter. Erupting from the center of the coils, and through the roof, jutted a 142-foot mast, supported by a 25-foot wooden derrick. Atop the mast was a three-foot diameter copper ball.

Before the gigantic coil stood a 6-foot tall gaunt man of 142 pounds, dressed in a great black frock coat, with ebony hair parted down the middle and a thick, well-trimmed mustache. His body was without any jewelry and his white-gloved hands were clasped behind his back. This was Nikola Tesla and this coil was a gigantic version of what was commonly known as a "Tesla Coil."

The great inventor—or "discoverer" as he referred to himself—stood with a second man as he studied a bank of gauges, then stepped back eighteen steps, then to the right six step, then forward three steps. This was typical behavior for the eccentric scientist, who had an obsessive compulsion for the number three and its multiples, such as using six napkins to wipe his dinnerware or employing a three-foot diameter copper ball atop the mast. The man beside him noted his peculiar manner, but said nothing.

"I'm glad you could be here, Monsieur Saint-Clair," Tesla told the French engineer as he studied the gauges. "I know something of your work and I have read your papers on the properties of light. I welcome your observations tonight."

The Serbian scientist's accent was heavy, and, dressed as he was in this fantastic setting, high in the American Rockies, the French engineer could only picture the great inventor as some mythical Prometheus.

"It is my honor I assure you," Saint-Clair said, noting that Tesla, despite his words, behaved as if he were alone.

Satisfied that all was in order, the Serbian nodded at his white-lab coated assistant, Kolman Czito. Glancing down first to make sure he was wearing rubber-soled shoes, he said:

"We're ready!"

Czito closed the circuit mounted to the wall amongst a bank of capacitors. At first, there was nothing; then, came a crackling amongst the coils, an eerie blue glow, and the pungent smell of ozone.

Tesla hurried to the door, looked up and saw bolts of lightning lashing from the copper ball high above on the mast, first at ten feet, then twenty, then on up to 135-foot streaks of an electromagnetic, ion-charged electrical storm. It was magnificent. But, after only a few seconds, he motioned for Czito to open the circuit, and then the electrical fireworks died away, with only a crackling sound and the smell of ozone remaining.

The Great Inventor was pondering his next move when the machine's *cherer*, a glass tube filled with iron-filling, attached to a telephonic receiver, began to sound: *beep... beep-beep... beep-beep-bee*p. It repeated itself, again and again, the same *One-Two-Three*. Then, it suddenly stopped.

The implications for the beeps were astonishing: could this be code signals from Outer Space? If so, who were they and what was their message?

The French engineer had also grasped the momentous event. "Monsieur Tesla," he began. "This cannot be...?"

Tesla's mind worked rapidly. He had read of a young American named Jason Gridley experimenting with radio waves across great distances, but dismissed the claims as mere scientific romance. Could this be the so called Gridley wave, and if so, for whom was it meant?

"Sir," Czito said breathlessly, "there's going to be a power surge if we don't..."

Sensing the moment, Saint-Clair leaped forward and opened the default switch.

Tesla and Czito re-readied the equipment seizing the opportunity that the Frenchman had given them. Then, the Serbian gave the nod and his assistant once again closed the circuit. The giant coil began to crackle, sparks flying as brilliant arcs of electric current danced harmlessly throughout the room, standing hair on end on the three scientists' heads and casting strange otherworldly shadows about the room.

Suddenly, all went dark, leaving only the smell of ozone in the air. Tesla rushed to the great door and peeked out.

Everything was pitch black, even the streetlights in the far city.

He had blacked out Colorado and Manitou Springs entirely.

"We have provided you with quite a show tonight," he told Saint-Clair, "and it might have been worse if not for your quick action. Still, I suspect tonight has seen the last of my welcome locally. Menlo Park may tolerate its wizard, but after tonight, I doubt that Colorado Springs will feel the same."

Tesla would ponder the meaning of these signals for years to come, speculating that they might have originated from Outer Space as the young American Gridley would have it. Still more important for him, it reinforced his obsessive compulsion for the number threes and multiples thereof. The next morning, a reporter would write that Tesla believed the signals were from Mars.

But Mars by then was beyond either the power of Tesla or the Gridley Wave...

Afterword

Dejah Thoris once more held her lover in her arms and felt the reassurance of his strong body as she became lost in his gray eyes. His astral body had hurtled across space, beckoned by the Gridley Wave after all, despite the anomaly that had delayed his awakening.

Man of action that he was, John Carter dismissed the mystery. There were the Tartids to deal with, and adventures to be had, intrigue, cloak and dagger, beautiful dusky red Martian maids to be saved and lusty Tharks to accompany him on his adventures. Science was a pale Earth-bound mistress when compared to the tapestry of Barsoomian romance.

"All that matters is that I am here, and again in your arms," he told his princess of Helium, her breast heaving against his bare chest. "We'll let Jason Gridley worry about the way I came here, and any problems along the way."

"Yes, my prince—for now."

Dejah Thoris was a scientist as well as the hereditary ruler of Helium, and while John Carter was her hero and lover, as well as soul mate, he was better suited to wielding swords than Nth rays, and she, for one, would not rest until she knew what earthly power had disturbed the Gridley Wave signal.

Alas, we know the cause, though neither Dejah nor Tesla would ever know of the other.

In 1919, five years after the death of his writing partner Pierre Souvestre, Marcel Allain wrote The Yellow Document, *which was subtitled by its publisher* The Fantômas of Berlin *to capitalize on the success of their notorious creation. The only problem was that the novel took place in the 1890s before Fantômas had made his first appearance on the criminal stage. In his story "Long live Fantômas" (published in our Volume 3), Alfredo Castelli postulated that Krampf, the so-called "Fantômas of Berlin," was none other than Lord Beltham, himself a murderous sociopath, who in turn made Gurn, his manservant, the next Fantômas, before being killed by him over Lady Beltham. (This was also the plot line reused in our recent Harry Dickson adaptation,* The Man in Grey.*) Rick Lai paints here a very different picture by inserting the "Fantômas of Berlin" in his unfolding saga of the Black Coats...*

Rick Lai: *Eve of Perfection, Eve of Destruction*

The Lofoten Islands and London, 1898

"Fantômas," whispered Paula Hest in horror as she glimpsed her relentless pursuer through the binoculars. There was no mistaking the square head with its massive beard. The man arriving at the Norwegian inn was clearly Dr. Wolfgang Krampft of the German Secret Service. His complete disdain for human life had earned him the nickname of "the Fantômas of Berlin."

Ever since Paula's theft of the Kaiser's love letters in Berlin, Krampft had pursued her. Boarding a ship in Danzig, she had crossed the Baltic into the United Kingdoms of Sweden and Norway. There, Paula had traveled northward to Moskenesøya, one of the populated Lofoten Islands. She had found lodging at the Valkyrie, a local inn. After receiving a telegram from her, Paula's superior wired back from London that he would be arriving at Moskenesøya soon. During her stay at the inn, Paula was in the habit of taking long hikes in the afternoon. While returning from such an excursion, she had spied the recently arrived Krampft.

"Fantômas?" interrupted a feminine voice. "Who exactly is Fantômas?"

The words were spoken by a muscular girl of eighteen. A red bandanna was tied around her flaxen hair. Slightly over six feet, the young blonde towered over the red-haired Paula.

"Eva! Where did you come from?"

"Please don't be angry, Paula. I've been secretly following you."

"Why would you do that?"

"I'm reading the cases of Sherlock Holmes. He could follow criminals without being spotted. I was pretending you were Irene Adler." Eva nervously bit her lip. "Who is Fantômas?"

"How could you have heard that name? My words were barely audible."

"Uncle Hugo had me trained as a lip reader. Who is Fantômas?"

"Promise to keep all this secret from your uncle."

"I promise."

Concluding that her continued survival depended on an innkeeper's niece with romantic notions of international crime, Eva decided to unleash a barrage of half-truths.

"Have you heard of the Pallid Mask?"

"The most dangerous criminal in Europe. The newspapers dub him the Genius of Crime."

"Fantômas is but another name for the Pallid Mask." Paula handled her binoculars to Eva. "Look at the entrance to the inn."

"A new guest has just arrived by coach. My uncle is carrying his luggage into the inn."

"That man is Fantômas."

"You're joking!"

"I'm deadly serious. I'm not a Swiss schoolteacher on vacation. I'm an operative of the Chupin Detective Agency."

"Irina Putine's employer! She's my idol!"

"For the last three months, I infiltrated the Fantômas gang. In my knapsack is evidence that will send all its members to the guillotine. Fantômas has followed me here. I can only defeat him with your help."

"What do you want me to do?"

"Eva, you must pack enough provisions to last a week. Bring them to your sailboat. You're going to take me to a place that Fantômas will never think of going. Vömma."

"You can't go there! The Deathless One will kill you."

"Stop being superstitious. The Demon of the Maelstrom is a mere legend."

"I will take you there on one condition." Eva rubbed a five-cornered stone star hanging from a chain around her neck. A single eye was carved into the center of the stone. "You must wear one of my Stars of Odin."

Inside the Valkyrie, the proprietor was explaining the rules of his establishment to the new guest.

"In this room is the inn's only bathtub, Dr. Krampft. All guests take turns using it. We do not allow luggage brought into this room."

"Why would anyone want to do that?"

"Our other guest has a compulsive fear of being robbed. She wanted to keep her knapsack here during her bath. I convinced her to leave it in my niece's care."

From reading the register, Krampft knew that Paula was the other lodger. The Kaiser's letters must be inside her knapsack.

Situated south of Moskenesøya, the island of Vömma was close to the whirlpool immortalized in Poe's *The Descent into the Maelström*. Due to its sinister reputation, the small island supported no human inhabitants.

"Fantômas will search fruitlessly for me in Moskenesøya until he's convinced that I fled to the mainland," explained Paula. "Another operative of the Chupin Detective Agency will be soon registering at the Valkyrie. His name is Dr. Mabuse. Bring him here. Until his arrival, avoid Vömma at all costs."

"Even if Fantômas leaves before Mabuse comes?" questioned Eva.

"Yes. If Fantômas suspects you of hiding me, he'll fake his departure to trick you into exposing my location. Now you must return to the inn."

"And you must not fall victim to the Deathless One! Promise me not to remove the Star of Odin."

"I promise." Paula touched the necklace she now wore. It was a duplicate of Eva's.

"Farewell, my brave friend. I will return soon."

As Eva's boat faded into the horizon, Paula congratulated herself on easily manipulating the teenager. She then searched for a spot to make her camp. To her surprise, she found a hut constructed on the island. It was at least a century old.

During the night, Paula awoke. Someone—or *something*—was stirring outside her tent.

She reached for her knapsack. Wilhelm II's love letters were still inside. Taking her gun, she went outside. Her eyes scanned the darkness for signs of life.

Suddenly, two hands clutched her throat from behind. The sound of Paula's neck being broken reverberated through the night.

An hour later, the sole living inhabitant of Vömma stood over the lifeless body of Paula Hest. He spoke to the dead woman as if she was still alive.

"Stupid woman! You sealed your fate the moment your feet touched my domain. Eons ago, the Slumbering Kraken fashioned my soul in his dreams. Odin and the other Elder Gods imprisoned me in the remote depths of the Green Abyss. The walls of my prison were not impenetrable. I created gateways between the Green Abyss and the whirlpools of this planet. Emerging from a whirlpool of an inland sea, I consumed three souls. The appearance of the third victim became my own. He was a massive fisherman. His shape served me well until an encounter with an enchanted knife. My physical form was utterly destroyed by the blade, but my soul was hurled back into the Green Abyss. I created a gateway which spat me out though the Maelström onto this accursed isle. The worshippers of Odin shunned my new abode. Nevertheless, two inquisitive mortals violated this restriction. Their souls became my nourishment. I could have swallowed your soul, but the consequence would have been the assumption of your puny form. Therefore, I have allowed your spirit to be fed to the Cyclops of Pain. Your body shall serve as bait to lure a more desirable physique here. Scanning the dead thoughts lingering in your brain, I see a master of subterfuge who is the perfect candidate."

Many notorious criminals had swelled the ranks of the Black Coats, but few were as formidable as the two men dining together in Campden Mansions, Notting Hill.

"This house was originally the property of Louis La Rothière, a freelance trafficker in international secrets," noted the Pallid Mask. "I'm surprised that he sold it to you."

"He didn't," replied Malbodius. "La Rothière currently resides in a trunk buried beneath the wine cellar."

"By staying in London, you woefully neglect your duties as the Satrap of Paris."

"My wife can more than adequately perform them in my absence. My continued presence in Paris became too risky after my poisoning of Rosita Bianchini. I shall gravely miss my false identity of Carl Friedrichs."

"I assume your murder of La Rothière is a prelude to impersonating him."

"Such an endeavor would be foolhardy. His illegal activities are well known to the authorities. My removal of La Rothière stems from two reasons. First, as you may recall, from my cancelled Espionage Hotel project, my ambition to establish a lucrative spy ring as a subsidiary of the Black Coats. I eliminated La Rothière in order to purloin his confidential files. They list several contacts in the espionage branches of foreign governments."

"And the second reason?"

"La Rothière has an excellent wine cellar ready to be plundered. Since there is too much booty for one man, I have invited you to share it with me."

"My dear Malbodius, how unexpectedly generous of you. You must be seeking a favor in return."

"I seek information about Wolfgang Krampft, the so-called 'Fantômas of Berlin.' Allegedly his nickname was derived from a notorious Parisian criminal. There is no 'Fantômas of Paris,' but *the modus operandi* attributed to this mythical Parisian is identical to yours. Explain this anomaly."

"'In 1892, I was posing in Germany as Juan North, Archduke of Hesse-Weimar. My ultimate goal was to become the secret power behind the German throne. I hoped to persuade Wilhelm II to make me the head of the German Secret Service. A competing candidate for that position was Dr. Krampft. The Kaiser secretly has a formidable mistress. She proved instrumental in undermining Krampft's candidacy."

"The ravishing Countess Hermine! I never imagined her playing a role in this unique drama."

"Hermine, a competent spy in her own right, had a fanatical hatred for France. She regularly read French newspapers to fully understand her enemy. Another of her eccentricities was an insistence on speaking French to her lover, the Kaiser. I secretly seduced her in order to subtly undermine Krampft. As the Archduke, I asked Hermine if she had ever heard of the Pallid Mask. To my delight, she had regularly followed my alter ego's exploits in the French press. Hermine even knew that my *nom de guerre* was derived from the disguise worn by the Phantom of Truth in *The King in Yellow*. I joked that Krampft was so ruthless that he could be dubbed 'The Pallid Mask of Berlin.' My intent being to saddle Krampft with a nickname that would make him an object of derision.

"Hermine repeated my joke to the Kaiser. Since her lover had no familiarity with my criminal alias, she cited its association with the Phantom of Truth. The Kaiser was drunk at the time and misheard parts of her conversation. At some point, Hermine used the phrase '*Le Fantôme masqué*' ('the masked Phantom'). The Kaiser thought that she was saying the name Fantômas. Thus, Krampft became known as the 'Fantômas of Berlin.' The ridicule caused by that nickname ruined his chances of leading the German Secret Service."

"Your rivalry with him did not end well," stated Malbodius.

"Krampft uncovered Hermine's infidelity, resulting in a big scandal that was quickly hushed up. As the Archduke, I was arrested under the German equivalent of a *lettre de cachet*. I found myself in prison with a ball and chain around my leg. Of course, I eventually escaped."

"Like you, Hermine was arrested. A medical examination revealed that she was pregnant. Hermine gave birth to a boy."

"I wonder if the child is mine."

"He's not your son. The boy has a withered arm like the Kaiser. The birth of his offspring put Wilhelm II in a merciful mood. He pardoned Hermine, but forced her to surrender the love letters written by him. Krampft burnt them in the Kaiser's presence."

"I don't believe that for a second. Krampft is a master of legerdemain. He would have swapped the genuine letters with a pile of blank sheets prior to the incineration. He would want the letters as leverage in case the Kaiser later turned on him."

"Correct! Like his royal patron, Krampft is susceptible to feminine wiles. One of my agents, Paula Hest, romanced him. After he revealed his possession of the letters, she stole them. Once the Black Coats have the letters, the High Council will be able to bend the Kaiser to its will!"

"Don't underestimate Krampft! He will try to regain the letters."

"That's why you're here. Tell me every fact that you know about this 'Fantômas of Berlin.' Your knowledge will enable me to anticipate his stratagems."

The Pallid Mask briefed Malbodius on the German spymaster for two hours.

"Thank you, my friend," said Malbodius. "I have a parting word of advice. The name 'Fantômas' is a more evocative alias than the 'Pallid Mask.' Since the name was inspired by your exploits, claim it as your own."

"I have already considered such a course of actions. The High Council has dispatched me to South Africa in anticipation of the inevitable conflict between the British and the Boers. When I return to Europe, I shall fully assume the mantle of Fantômas. I also have a suggestion for you. Where do you intend to locate your spy ring?"

"In London. It's the obvious choice."

"You have failed to realize the significance of the current war between the United States and Spain. America's inevitable victory will transform that country into a world power with the potential to surpass every European nation militarily. I recently concluded the Rambert affair in New York, the financial center of the country. You should center your band of secret raiders there."

"You make a compelling argument, my friend."

"Let me deliver a word of caution as well. Rumors of your marital indiscretions are circulating. If you continue this brazen behavior, Sabine will discover the truth."

"My wife's passionate devotion always blinds her to my faults."

"Sabine is the least of your worries. Have you forgotten that she is a member of the Balsamo family? Your sister-in-law has the capacity to be the most vindictive woman on Earth, and your wife's aunt is a member of the High Council."

After his guest had left, the physician known as Malbodius contemplated his destiny. He had been born Erich Heinz Maubeuge in Switzerland. In 1891, he and his nephew Jacques were recruited into the Black Coats by Professor James Moriarty. Following Moriarty's death, his younger brother, Noel, had become the corrupt doctor's patron. Under the alias of Malbodius, Maubeuge had amassed great power, but a major goal eluded him. He had yet to achieve a seat on the High Council. A recent communication indicated that this long coveted prize was finally within his reach.

Dear Erich,

By the time you read this, I will have resigned my seat on the High Council in order to seek my destiny in the monastery of the Rachë-Churân. There are two candidates to replace me, you and the Pallid Mask. The Council will keep the rank and file ignorant of my absence until they have agreed on a successor. I have recommended you as my replacement.

As a token of my esteem, my notebook detailing my experiments in telepathic hypnotism is enclosed. With the exception of the All-Father, you are the only member of the Black Coats capable of fathoming its contents.

Antonio Nikola

Malbodius had an ulterior motive for inviting the Pallid Mask to dinner. The present resident of La Rothière's house wanted to gauge if his guest was aware of their competition for the High Council seat. Clearly, the so-called Genius of Crime was ignorant concerning Nikola's resignation. More importantly, the future Fantômas had inadvertently disclosed a plausible strategy that could torpedo his rival's candidacy. If Malbodius' adultery became known to Madame Sara, she would avenge her niece's honor by engineering the elevation of the Pallid Mask to the High Council.

Accompanying the letter had been a notebook with a yellow cover. It documented Nikola's gradual mastery of the ability to mesmerize others solely through eye contact. This skill was predicated on first establishing a telepathic link with a kindred mind. Nikola had achieved this linkage with his sister. Malbodius attempted to achieve the same result with his nephew, but all their attempts had failed miserably. He searched futilely in Nikola's notations for some explanation for these continued setbacks.

The Valkyrie derived its name from Norse mythology. The inn's sign depicted a blonde woman in silver armor and a winged helmet. She was the warrior entrusted by Odin to select who would die in battle. Standing behind the front desk was the inn's owner, a man of approximately the same height and build as Malbodius. Whereas Malbodius was a clean-shaven man with black hair, the innkeeper was a heavily bearded man with grey hair.

Picking up a pen to sign the register, Malbodius noticed columns for arrival and departure dates for each guest. While his face displayed no emotion, he was shocked to see the name of Wolfgang Krampft. The fact that Krampft had checked out a day after his arrival was troubling. Had the so-called "Fantômas of Berlin" regained the Kaiser's letters? Malbodius had also spied Paula Hest's entry on the register. The lack of a departure date indicated either her continued presence, or her death at Krampft's hands. With a bold flourish, Malbodius wrote a favorite alias, "Dr. Eric Mabuse, London," and the current date.

"I see that you are a doctor from England," said the innkeeper in flawless English. What is your specialty?"

"Neuropathology."

"I am a doctor as well. My name is Hugo Howey. Although I've been managing this inn for the last two decades, I have a medical degree from the University of Stockholm. I studied Swedish Gymnastics as pioneered by the great Per Henrik Ling. Are you familiar with his work?"

"Ling's concepts are starting to gain acceptance under the title of Physical Therapy. Your accent sounds American."

"I was born in Brooklyn. When I was thirteen years-old, Congress passed the 1863 military draft. My father was drafted to fight the Confederates. Being a committed pacifist, he opted to flee the country with his family. Since his mother was Norwegian, he settled in Oslo."

"Your father seems to have been a wealthy man. Couldn't he have taken advantage of the loophole in the draft law allowing the hiring of a substitute?

"My father thought it immoral to enlist another man to die in his place."

"How did a physical therapist become an innkeeper in the Lofoten Islands?"

"It was due to my niece. My older sister married Lars Bjelke, an archeologist from Iceland."

"I read his book, *The Cult of the All-Father*. His cousin was the guide for the controversial Lindenbrock Expedition of 1863. In 1881, Lars led another expedition to verify Lindenbrock's findings. Tragically, your brother perished when his rope broke during the ascent of the Snafell Crater."

"My athletic sister always accompanied her husband on his expeditions. She died in the same accident. Eva, their daughter, was then only a year old. I became her guardian. My theories on physical therapy had gone beyond the treatment of injuries. My focus shifted towards the molding of a child into the perfect physical specimen. Eva became my test subject. The Lofoten Islands with their rugged terrain were the perfect Eden in which to raise this new Eve."

"But you are denying her a proper education."

"I have schooled her in the major academic subjects. Her knowledge of history, geography and mathematics is profound. She is fluent in seven languages: Eva can even read lips."

"And her social skills? Her ability to interact with other people. Isn't she in danger of becoming a shy introvert?"

"I avoided that danger by becoming an innkeeper. Tourists from all over Europe come to the Lofoten Islands to see the famous whirlpool featured in the works of Poe and Aronnax. This inn permits Eva's interaction with people from all walks of life. In fact, my niece will soon be conversing with a London neuropathologist."

This comment was the opening that Malbodius had been waiting for. He now could broach the subject of Paula Hest without raising Howey's suspicions.

"When I signed your register, I noticed that a German woman is lodging here. Is her profession as intriguing as mine?"

"You must mean Paula Hest. She claimed to be a school teacher, but her actions were little better than a confidence trickster. Paula left the inn without paying her bill. Her sudden flight caused another guest, a German doctor, to panic and cut his stay short. The doctor became fearful that Paula had been murdered by the Deathless One."

"Is this creature some sort of local bogeyman?"

"There's a legend that Odin, the ruler of the Norse Gods, banished a race of aquatic demons, the Children of the Kraken, to an underwater chasm. One of these creatures escaped this prison by traveling through the Maelström. The whirlpool deposited him on the small island of Vömma. Because of this myth, the natives of the Lofoten Islands avoid Vömma. There are two documented instances of this taboo being violated by local fishermen. The first case happened near the start of this century. The second transpired last year. Both times, the boats of the fishermen were found floating aimlessly near the island. Inside each vessel was its owner's corpse. The bodies were cold and rigid as if all life had been sucked out of them."

"Do you believe in this monster?"

"He's just a myth! Those two men probably lost control of their boats and succumbed to frostbite. I deal in hard facts, Dr. Mabuse, as will be demonstrated when my book about Eva's training is eventually published. Its title is *Eve of Perfection*. I plan to visit London soon in order to find a publisher."

"I may be able to help you there if you let me read the manuscript."

"I will. Feel free to make any suggestions."

"When can I meet Eva?"

"Did someone mention my name?" asked the innkeeper's niece entering through the front door.

Turning around to view the newcomer, Malbodius was stunned by the beauty of the statuesque teenager.

"We have a new guest," declared Howey. "Please show Dr. Mabuse to his room."

"Mabuse..." muttered Eva.

"Are you familiar with my name?" asked the master criminal.

"There was a Renaissance painter named Jan Gosart of Maubeuge. He was also known as Jan Mabuse."

Grabbing the new guest's suitcase, Eva led him up a stairwell. Once they were inside the supposed tourist's room, the Herculean damsel closed the door in order for them to speak privately.

"Paula told me everything! The Chupin Detective Agency! The Fantômas gang! Everything!"

"Calm down!" cautioned Malbodius. "Tell me slowly and calmly everything Paula told you."

When Eva had finished her recital, Malbodius had words of praise.

"You did very well. If you were 21, I would recommend that the Chupin Detective Agency hire you."

"Thank you, Doctor. I've been an admirer of the Agency since Irina Putine solved the Bluebeard III murders two year ago."

Malbodius smiled cryptically. Under his real name of Maubeuge, he had been publicly implicated in those killings.

"Perhaps one day, I shall have the pleasure of introducing you to Mademoiselle Putine. My concern is that Krampft not only left early, but also mentioned Vömma."

189

"Uncle Hugo drove him to the docks. Krampft definitely boarded a ship destined for Hamburg. Scrupulously following Paula's instructions, I avoided all contact with Vömma in anticipation of your arrival."

"After dusk, you must take me in your boat to Vömma."

Eva touched the five-cornered star dangling on her neck. "Only if you promise to wear a Star of Odin."

"Agreed. Your talisman is more properly called the Elder Sign of Omidom."

"Omidom? You must have read my father's book."

"Since you are familiar with the exploits of the Chupin Detective Agency, you must be aware of our continued conflicts with the criminal organization called the Black Coats. Their supreme leader calls himself the All-Father. I've often wondered if that title was derived from Odin, the All-Father in Norse mythology. I read your father's book in the hope of unearthing some connection between the two All-Fathers. Although I didn't find any evidence of a link, I was fascinated by your father's theory that Odin evolved from Omidom, a deity referenced in the controversial *Deminderon Scrolls*. Did your father find these Elder Signs during one of his archeological excavations?"

"After *The Cult of the All-Father* was published, my father began to gather material for a sequel. Several historical records contained assertions that Odin would take human form to fight alongside his Viking followers in major battles. An eleventh century manuscript written by Cumal O'Brien, an Irish soldier, made the startling assertion that Odin was slain in human form during the battle of Clontarf. O'Brien even described the burial of Odin's body under a cairn. Locating this burial mound in Ireland, my father removed a stone that had been shaken loose from the cairn over the centuries. When a fisherman was found dead near Vömma last year, I broke the burial stone into three pieces and created a Star of Omidom from each. According to the *Deminderon Scrolls,* the Stars of Omidom can be used to repel sea monsters. Let me get your Star."

Eva briefly left. Upon her return, she handed the amulet to Malbodius whose right hand gripped it by the chain. "I'll see you at nightfall."

Left alone in his room, Malbodius grabbed the stone with his left hand in order to bring it closer to his eyes. A slight electrical jolt flowed through his body. His eyes flickered as a series of visions flashed through his brain.

A huge anthropomorphic being with vulture-like wings flew among the stars. His head resembled a starfish with a single gray eye. Its tentacle-like arms had talons attached to their wrists.

On a world of three suns stood a gigantic statue of the one-eyed creature. Prostrating themselves before the idol were several winged beings whose star-shaped heads housed five eyes.

A brutal battle was fought between two armies under a single sun. One army consists of the five-eyed denizens from the planet with the three suns. The opposing force was composed of winged combatants with octopus-shaped heads. The fighting stopped when a huge shadow passed over the armies. It was cast by two giant flying monsters wrestling in the sky. One of the fighters was the one-eyed titan. The face of its opponent sprouted tentacles.

The winged entity with only one eye shrank in order to take on the semblance of a man with grey skin. The left eye socket of the grey man was empty while the right contained a large ashen eye.

Dressed in armor, the grey man rested motionless on the ground. A group of bearded warriors piled stones over his body.

The images suddenly ceased. Malbodius realized that he had experienced his first true telepathic moment. Perhaps the Star of Odin was the key to unlocking the secrets of Nikola's notebook.

Malbodius then considered the proper course of action to take regarding Eva Bjelke. Regardless of what he found on Vömma, he would have to kill her. He couldn't run the risk of her telling others about the connection between him and Paula. Malbodius deeply regretted this decision. His regret stemmed from his desire to seduce her. It would take time to persuade such a naïve girl to share his bed, and time was a luxury denied him.

Leaving the boat, Eva and Malbodius walked cautiously on the rugged surface of Vömma. The doctor was armed with a gun

"There's a hut over there," said Malbodius. "If this island has no human inhabitants, who could have built it?"

"The Deathless One!" answered Eva. "He must use it as a lure for his prey!"

Reaching the hut, the duo found Paula's corpse outside. Her knapsack was lying near her body. Bending down, Malbodius examined the body. Her neck's broken. She wasn't wearing the Star of Odin."

"The Fantômas papers were in her knapsack," responded Eva. "Are they still there?"

Malbodius rummaged through the knapsack: "The papers are gone. It wasn't The Deathless One. It was Krampft."

Eva shook her head.

"No, I killed her!" she said.

Delivering a devastating leg kick, she knocked the gun out of her companion's hand. Her right hand smashed into the doctor's stomach causing him to drop to his knees. Eva shoved Malbodius backwards. Lying on his back, Malbodius felt Eva's right boot pressing on his neck.

"Paula always carried her knapsack with her except when she bathed," explained Eva. "Her suspicious attachment to the knapsack aroused my curiosity. Searching it during her bath, I found the Kaiser's letters. Paula never realized that I knew her secret, not even when I compared her to Irene Adler, a woman who possessed a different monarch's romantic correspondence. Paula's falsehoods about the Chupin Detective Agency and the Fantômas gang were very amusing. It wasn't difficult to deduce her true allegiance. When she mentioned your surname, I thought of Jan Mabuse, the pseudonym of a painter from Maubeuge. I also remembered reading of a Dr. Maubeuge, who played a major role in the Bluebeard III crimes solved by the Chupin Detective Agency. You must be that notorious agent of the Black Coats.

"When I fashioned the Stars of Odin a year ago, I had a strange reaction when my fingers touched the completed carvings. My mind was flooded momentarily with images of a Cyclopean being with a star-shaped head and a man with grey skin. The same figures haunted my dreams in the subsequent months. Gradually I realized that the history of Odin was being shown me. A monstrous being from beyond the stars, Odin took on the form of the Grey Man to walk among the Vikings. This avatar of Odin was imprisoned in a burial mound during the eleventh century."The Grey Man began to converse with me in dreams. He recruited me as his high priestess. In order to break out of the confines of his cairn, Odin needs to replenish his strength by feasting on souls. I would provide those souls by sacrificing victims wearing the star-shaped symbol of my god. During these ritual murders, the slayer must also wear an Elder Sign. Paula was my first sacrifice. I lied about having made three Stars of Odin. I only constructed two. You are wearing the Elder Sign that I removed from Paula's broken neck. I could have taken Paula's life when I brought her here during the day. However, Odin demands that his sacrifices happen only at night. A second trip to Vömma was required to eliminate Paula.

"I removed the Kaiser's letters from the backpack, and brought them back to the inn. I sold the documents to Krampft for a modest price. Wanting to leave the inn quickly, he asked me to suggest a suitable pretext. It amused me to advise Krampft to cite the Deathless One legend. It was very easy to manipulate you into coming here. You shall be my second victim."

"Harlot of Odin!" interrupted the naked figure standing in the doorway. "I decide who lives or dies here!"

The intruder had the body of a man with dark blue skin. Except for two eyes and a rudimentary mouth, its face was lacking in features.

"The Deathless One!" shouted Eva lifting her foot from the doctor's throat. "Be gone, Demon of Cthulhu, or be annihilated by the power of the Elder Sign!"

The monster from the Green Abyss laughed. "Star-stones are only effective when they are fully infused with the power of an Elder God. Eons ago, Odin had such power. Eight centuries of incarceration have caused his strength to wane. Your recently created Elder Sign is merely a communicator to an impotent deity!"

Malbodius remained immobile on the ground. He could barely move due to his physical battering at the hands of Eva. All Malbodius could do was watch the confrontation between the murderess and the ancient predator.

The Deathless One underwent a metamorphosis. Its azure skin lightened in tone, and its body ceased to be masculine. The Deathless One was now a woman with a face like Eva's."

"When you first came here, I assumed you were a puny woman. I didn't realize the truth until scavenging through your victim's fading memories. Your muscular flesh fulfills my needs. Being a female is a new experience for me."

"Experience my fist!" yelled Eva as she delivered a devastating uppercut to her doppelganger's jaw. The Deathless One was knocked off its feet. Grabbing her opponent's throat with both hands, Eva smiled. "Let's see if your neck muscles are as strong as mine."

Before Eva could act, beams of lights shot forth from the macabre twin's eyes into her own. Eva's muscles stiffened as her eyes flickered wildly. Her hands released her hold on her adversary.

"I shall consume your will, your memories, and finally your soul!" predicted the Deathless One. "I shall walk among mankind as you! I shall devour the souls of other mortals beginning with that wretch on the ground! I am your Lord and Master! Acknowledge my supremacy! Say my true name!"

"My Lord and Master is..." mumbled Eva. "My Lord and Master is Khosatral—No! My Lord and Master is... Mabuse!"

Malbodius had successfully used the Stars of Odin as a conduit to link his mind with Eva's. A giant concrete wall was projected inside Eva's brain to act as a barrier against her replica's mental attacks.

"Strike, Eva! Strike!" screamed Malbodius.

Eva's hands clutched the Deathless One's throat once more. Without hesitation, the innkeeper's niece snapped her enemy's neck. The Deathless One collapsed. Its body underwent a metamorphosis. No longer resembling Eva, the creature reverted to its earlier masculine form.

"Eva," commanded Malbodius, "Lift me up and take me to the boat. We must leave this island."

"Yes, my liege."

Eva complied with the doctor's command. As the boat sailed away from the island, Eva heard a voice whispering inside her brain.

"You are my high priestess! You swore to sacrifice Mabuse to me. Fulfill your oath. Kill him."

"You impotent Cyclops!" screeched Eva. "You failed me when I needed you most! You are no longer my god! Mabuse is my god!"

Removing the necklace bearing the Elder Sign, Eva cast it into the sea. Malbodius did the same with his own Elder Sign

On Vömma, the Deathless One stood up. He had successfully repaired the injuries to his neck. The mortals had absconded, but this was only a temporary setback. Someone else would inevitably visit his island, and the passage of time was meaningless to an immortal predator.

As Dr. Mabuse, Malbodius remained in the Lofoten Islands for three weeks. He and Howey became great friends. With the innkeeper's permission, Malbodius mailed *Eve of Perfection* to a London publisher. A telegram arrived announcing the acceptance of the manuscript. In order to sign the contract, Malbodius booked passage to London for Howey, Eva and himself aboard the *Macedonia*, a steamship with a predominately Danish crew. Malbodius justified his selection of the vessel on the grounds that his nephew was a member of the crew.

While the *Macedonia* was crossing the North Sea, Eva Bjelke and Hugo Howey looked up at the stars.

"Uncle, what will happen to me when your book is published?"

"You will become an instant celebrity. I am already drawing up plans for you to accompany me on book tours."

"You wish to treat me like some sort of freak!"

"Eva!"

"Don't you realize that this is the first time in my life that I've been outside the Lofoten Islands! I want to see the world! I dream of searching for gold in the Yukon, diving for pearls in the South Seas, and climbing mountains in Tibet."

"If that is what you want, I won't stand in your way. I'll relinquish my control over your inheritance from your parents. You're free to travel wherever you want."

Eva's eyes filled with tears. She kissed her uncle on the cheek just before she broke his neck.

The crew of the *Macedonia*, actually a gang of professional smugglers, attached weights to the corpse and threw it overboard. While her uncle was being given an unceremonious funeral, Eva went to her cabin. Malbodius was waiting inside. "It is done, darling," she said.

A version of the final meeting between Dr. Howey and Eva was added as a concluding chapter to *Eve of Perfection* as it was being prepared for publication. It altered the facts by having Howey survive the encounter. The man known as Dr. Mabuse was totally absent from the narrative.

A photograph of Hugo Howey had been mailed with the initial draft of *Eve of Perfection* to Bridewall Press. When the editors of the publishing firm met their new author, they did not recognize him. Dr. Howey apparently had shaved off his beard.

Malbodius personally delivered a report of his recent activities to a meeting of the High Council in London.

"Krampft's murder of Paula Hest regretfully deprived us of the Kaiser's letters, but my time in the Lofoten Islands was well spent. Subject to your approval, I have laid the foundations for a major spy ring, the Secret Raiders, inside the United States. *Eve of Perfection* has the potential to be an extremely popular book on both sides of the Atlantic. As Hugo Howey, I shall be welcome in the homes of the most prominent people in America."

"I agree with your assessment, my boy," said an old man with parchment-like skin. "I perused the excerpt you submitted. It reads like a novel by Balzac rather than a scientific treatise. Arrange for a French translation as soon as possible. We may want to re-locate your Howey persona to France sometime in the future."

"I shall do so, All-Father."

"I wish to discuss this Bjelke woman," interjected Madame Sara, a blonde woman who looked much younger than her actual years. "How did you recruit her?"

"My nephew Jacques seduced her aboard the Macedonia. She had the potential to be an assassin whose fighting skills will surpass even the Pallid Mask's."

"Where is Bjelke now?" asked Sara.

"She and Jacques are being transported by the *Macedonia* to Canada. In accordance with the conclusion of *Eve of Perfection*, they will travel to Dawson City in order for Eva to create the impression that she is participating in the Yukon Gold Rush. A massive fire in Dawson City will break out shortly after their arrival. With my nephew's assistance, Eva will create the illusion that she died heroically saving lives during the blaze. News reports of her apparent martyrdom will provide publicity for *Eve of Perfection*. In the wake of her apparent demise, Eva will adopt the alias of Ragna Rokstrom."

"A play on Ragnarok, the twilight of the Norse Gods," declared the All-Father. "Your proposal also has you posing as a one-eyed man to your subordinates in order to restrict knowledge of your Howey identity to a few lieutenants. Is this Cyclopean incarnation a reference to Odin, the All-Father? Do you seek to usurp my title?"

"No disrespect is intended, All-Father. Eye-patches have long been a method of disguise."

"Of course, my lad. I was merely teasing you."

"If there are no further questions for Dr. Malbodius," said Noel Moriarty, "I suggest that we debate this proposal in his absence."

Moriarty's colleagues concurred. Malbodius waited outside the Council's meeting room for a half hour before being summoned back.

"Congratulations, my boy," announced the All-Father. "Not only is your proposal accepted, but you have been elected to the High Council."

Malbodius had played his cards well. He had successfully deceived the High Council to secure his promotion. His seat was only the first step in a scheme to become the dominant power in the Black Coats. When that day came, he wondered what his name would be. Malbodius, Mabuse, or something else?

In "The Adventure of the Orcival Rain," published in our Volume 12, Nigel Malcolm introduced us to the team-up of an aging Monsieur Lecoq and a lonely Doctor Watson, missing his famous partner after his disappearance over the Reichenbach Falls. Nigel returns to this winning combination with yet one more investigation by this dynamic duo, this time taking place in London and involving that most modern of contraptions: the automobile...

Nigel Malcolm: *Maximum Speed*

London, 1893.

Many long term readers of my adventures, as well as general readers of the newspapers, will be aware of my esteemed friend, Mr. Sherlock Holmes' three-year absence from Baker Street after he disappeared at the Reichenbach Falls, presumed dead, and before he reappeared in my surgery, before my very eyes, to finally destroy the remainder of Professor Moriarty's criminal network.

Many readers have speculated upon what Holmes did during this hiatus. Some of these outlandish speculations contain a grain of truth, whilst others could not be further from the facts. Even I, the great man's Boswell, know not everything. At that time, I, like the rest of the public, thought him to be dead.

It is generally assumed that life for me, during this period, was uneventful. However, this is also untrue.

It was the late summer of 1893—a rather bleak time for me, as my beloved wife Mary had passed away only a few months before. Life was joyless and miserable.

Work is the antidote to sorrow, so I soldiered on, building up my medical practice and, occasionally, acting as a police surgeon. It was in such a capacity that I was called to a police morgue one afternoon to perform an autopsy upon a large and wealthy man.

Inspector Lestrade was not there when I first arrived, but Constable Japp informed me that the victim was a Mr. Bartholomew Daniels of the Marple-Daniels company.

As I was concluding my work, I heard the Inspector and another man approach.

"I am just finishing, gentlemen," I said, before turning round to see not just Lestrade, but also Monsieur Lecoq.

"Doctor Watson, this is Monsieur Paul, a former Commissioner from the Sûreté. This is a matter for the French police apparently," said Lestrade, with some irritation.

I was amazed to see this figure from my past. He noticed my surprise.

"Good afternoon, Doctor Watson," he said.

"Oh yes," I replied, recovering, "Good afternoon, Monsieur…?"

"Paul," prompted Lecoq.

"Ah, yes. Well, gentlemen, Mr. Daniels died from inhalation of a gas un-known—at least to me. I would like to bring in and consult some colleagues of mine from St. Bart's."

Lecoq walked up to the corpse and smelt the man's face.

"The gas you speak of is the fumes of burnt gasoline."

"Gasoline?" I echoed, astounded.

"Yes," he replied, drawing himself up to his full height and becoming al-most theatrical. "Mr. Daniels was asphyxiated by gasoline fumes from a motor engine!"

"So he came into contact with one of these new-fangled automobiles. That puts him in a very select group," said Lestrade.

"I would have expected death to come more from being trampled under-wheel rather than inhaling its fumes," I remarked.

Lecoq clearly had a different opinion on these contraptions.

"Ah, Doctor, you have a most negative opinion of progress," he said. "The automobile is an incredible invention that should revolutionize the very way we travel."

"I am not against progress; I just fail to see how these things are as safe or reliable as a good old horse and cart."

"Do you have any leads, Monsieur Paul?" interjected Lestrade, drawing us back to the situation at hand.

"Well, seeing as this is Mr. Daniels of Marple-Daniels, I propose we go and interview Mr, Marple."

"I'll leave you to it, since it's your case; I have to go to court in an hour."

"Oh? What have you done?" asked Lecoq, possibly joking.

"I haven't done anything. I'm scheduled to give a statement," replied Lestrade, irritated.

He walked away. Lecoq moved closer to me so we could talk confidential-ly.

"How did you recognize me?" he asked.

"Because we met not four years ago, and I have an excellent memory."

"But I am wearing a different disguise," he said, before becoming less cer-tain. "Am I not?"

"I think you were wearing that same wig when we met in Orcival."

"And I thought it one of my best wigs! I'll have to get some new disguises. Anyway, what else did your post-mortem reveal?"

I turned back to the cadaver.

"This unfortunate fellow preferred a pinch of snuff to smoking, of which he abstains. He writes his own correspondence and is a keen gardener…"

"Yes, yes, but anything unusual? Bruising for example?"

"Yes, there are bruises on his wrists and upper torso consistent with the victim being tied to a chair or some such—by at least two assailants."

Lecoq looked at the body thoughtfully for a moment. Then he looked at me.

"Doctor Watson, would you like to come with me to the Marple-Daniels offices? It's time to question Mr. Marple."

"Well I... I have no other pressing engagement," I stammered, surprised to be given this invitation by the great French detective. Unsure whether I should step back into this world, but equally excited, and also wanting to avoid going back to my now soulless marital home, I agreed.

"Yes, yes... I would be delighted."

Lecoq chuckled.

"You British people are always so vague and uncertain. Come along, Doctor."

In the time it took for me to remove my apron and don my jacket and bowler, Lecoq had left the building and managed to hail a hansom cab.

As it rattled through the streets, I turned to the French detective and asked him about his involvement in this case.

"Why are you interested in this murder?"

"The Patent Office in London, and its French equivalent in Paris, were broken into within a few days of each other, nearly two weeks ago. Intelligence from the criminal underworld connected this with the Black Coats. At that stage, I was asked to look into the matter. However, my investigations revealed that their High Council have little knowledge of this matter, and no part in the theft.

"Then I read in the newspapers that the patent for the motor engine had been sold to the Marple-Daniels company. Bartholomew Daniels gave an interview in which he boldly announced that he wanted to use it to develop the automobile invention further. I have to tell you, Doctor Watson, that the patent already belongs to a Mr. Rudolph Diesel, and so this is fraud. So I came over here to investigate. When I arrived, I heard about Daniels' death earlier this morning. It would be astonishing if the two events were not connected. Do you know much about the Marple-Daniels company, Doctor?"

"Very little, I'm afraid. I have had no cause to become interested in their business before now."

"It was set up about four years ago. It specializes in building, developing and promoting new inventions and technologies. Part of their business includes purchasing, or seeking exclusive rights to, patents. Bartholomew Daniels was quite ruthless and predatory, while his partner, Albert Marple, is more cautious—it could be why Daniels went into business with him. Marple seems to prefer spending as little time in London as possible, given that his wife and three daughters live away from London, and he joins them during the weekends and school holidays."

"I believe it is the school holidays now, so presumably Marple is away from London."

"No. He is here, in the city. And no doubt, this murder inquiry will keep him here."

Our cab drew up to a building. Marple-Daniels occupied the second floor. We were let inside and found an office in disarray. It transpired that the usual secretary had been taken ill earlier that day and been sent home. Her replacement had arrived not long before us. Yet, this new secretary—a Miss Loveday Brooke—managed to remain composed and calm amidst the chaos. Still young, she showed a plain maturity. She appeared as sober as her Quaker-like dress sense.

Miss Brooke eventually showed us in to see Albert Marple, a middle-aged man with sad eyes—sad from the earlier news, no doubt. With him was his daughter of three and ten, clearly out of school because of the holidays."

"Miss Brooke, would you be so kind as to take young Jane here to the Savoy for tea? Never mind the office, I will look after things here."

Miss Brooke hesitated for a moment, but then complied.

"Certainly, Mr. Marple."

Marple waited until the woman and the girl had left the room and shut the door. Then he ushered us to sit down and the brave face he had put on in front of his daughter and staff disappeared.

"How did he die?" he asked, bewildered and jittery.

Lecoq told him. He also told Marple that the patent was forged, and that Bartholomew Daniels had been murdered. Marple almost convulsed with the shock. He just stammered that he couldn't believe it, repeatedly. We tried to question him further, but he did not have any more information, other than the patent was sold to him by Lord and Lady Bristol, who had had dealings with Daniels rather than him.

I do not normally recount my adventures out of the order in which they occur, but just this once, I will switch to the account of Loveday Brooke, who told me later on what was happening just outside the door of the office while we were interviewing Marple. For she and Jane Marple stood right by that door, listening intently to our conversation.

When she told me about this later I was appalled both by the eavesdropping, but also by Miss Brooke's decision to let the thirteen year-old be exposed to such things. Although she insisted that Jane was made of much sterner stuff, and coped with the situation well, I am still unsure, because, as Loveday described the situation, Jane gasped as she heard us discuss Daniels' murder.

Miss Brooke silenced her with a finger to the mouth, and, eventually, after they'd heard enough of the conversation, she led her away by the arm.

"Do not worry, Jane. I am absolutely certain that your father did not murder his business partner," she said, seeing the confused look in Jane's eyes. "We should go into the file room."

They left the room and walked down a short corridor to a room full of filing cabinets.

"Papa is not a murderer. It's simply not in his nature," said Jane.

"It is only right and proper that his own daughter should think so," replied Loveday, kindly.

"But even if I weren't one of his daughters, I can see—anyone can see—that he is not capable of something as cruel as murder. It is rather like Abe Saunders at Sunday School. The teachers were so convinced that he stole that apple, but it was only later they discovered he couldn't have done it. And he had such a gentle nature. Besides, Papa would be too obvious a suspect. He wouldn't be able to disguise his involvement. He is too obvious, don't you see?"

Miss Brooke listened to this rambling monologue with increased astonishment. This bird-like young girl showed brilliant powers of observation and deduction—although of a very different sort to the less intuitive, more coldly scientific, sort displayed by Sherlock Holmes.

"That is very impressive reasoning. I, too, believe your father to be innocent. Perhaps you can help me search through these files for hard evidence."

So, taking care to not make too much noise, they searched through the various filing cabinets.

Meanwhile, Lecoq and I left for the evening. It was now beginning to get dark, so we decided to postpone the rest of our inquiry. Instead, I suggested that we dine at Simpson's in Piccadilly.

We chatted very cheerfully about Lecoq's illustrious career, and he demonstrated that he had read many of my accounts of Sherlock Holmes' work. It seemed as if the intervening four years since we had met, Lecoq's opinion of Holmes had become kinder. He had, for the most part, got over Holmes' embarrassing *miserable bungler* comment, acknowledging that he himself had once displayed the arrogance of youth.

Eventually we parted company for the night, but not before Lecoq said to me:

"Meet me tomorrow at Manuel's café on the corner of White Horse Street, near Green Park, at nine o'clock."

It was enough to make me feel good about returning home, where I went to bed happy, and rose from my slumbers the following morning with energy.

I stepped into the café at the agreed time and spotted Lecoq just as the smell of fresh coffee met my nose. Loveday Brooke and Jane Marple were both with him, sitting around a table for four. Lecoq beckoned me over and I took that fourth seat, while Miss Brooke very kindly poured me a cup of coffee from a pot on the table.

"You have met Miss Brooke already, Doctor Watson."

"Of course! Thank you, ma'am," I said to the lady, as I accepted the cup.

"Miss Brooke is my spy inside Marple-Daniels," Lecoq continued, before adding irritably, "and despite the fact that she was supposed to be taking Miss Marple to Hyde Park this morning, they both have joined us."

"Do not be so begrudging of Jane's presence, Monsieur. She has proved to be most helpful," said Miss Brooke.

"You have wasted no time at all, Miss Brooke. You have converted even this child to your cause," I said, with perhaps a trace of disapproval in my voice.

"Jane was a willing convert, Doctor Watson," she replied.

"I became friends with Ebenezer Dyer during one of my previous visits to London," said Lecoq. "He has since left the police and now he runs a private detective agency. Since I cannot disguise myself as a young woman—not any more, anyway—I needed someone to infiltrate Marple-Daniels for me. Mr. Dyer selected Miss Brooke. He also had a word with the usual secretary and persuaded her to take a few days off, so he could switch her with Miss Brooke. The poor woman didn't need much persuading. Have you made much progress, Miss Brooke?"

"Yes, I have," she replied, reaching into her bag and pulling out a piece of paper. "With Jane's help, I have looked through all the correspondence and documentation sent to and from the company. It is all quite straightforward and innocent—by business standards, anyway. All, except this letter originally sent to Messrs. Marple and Daniels by Lord Bristol, claiming that he owns the patent for the motor engine, which he was willing to sell for what he calls a 'reasonable price.. It is signed by him, but the main body of the text, the handwriting, is clearly that of a woman's."

Brooke showed us the letter. The three of us examined it.

"How on Earth can you tell that?" I asked, astounded.

"Oh, surely, Doctor Watson, you can see the difference between a man's handwriting and that of a woman! This handwriting is more fluent and elaborate than the spidery scrawl of a man. And the signature denotes that the pen was being used by someone who holds it differently than the author of the rest of this letter."

"You make it all seem so obvious," I exclaimed. "How could I not have seen it?"

Loveday Brooke looked at me with an amused look in her eyes.

"Perhaps you see, Doctor Watson, but you do not observe."

I chuckled.

"Yes, I used to be told that rather a lot," I said.

"Let me have a look at that," said Lecoq impatiently, snatching the letter and examining it closely. "I have studied the science of graphology—the study of handwriting."

Then Jane broke her silence, having sat there, almost unresponsive in that particular way the teenaged have, seemingly in a world of her own.

"The handwriting is similar to that of my school friend, Christine. She is so confident and self-possessed. Arrogant, even. She once smuggled cigarettes into the dormitory, you know, and yet brazenly denied they were hers, even when she was caught out."

"Well, we're not after a schoolgirl who is smuggling cigarettes here," muttered Lecoq, before being struck by an idea. "Of course! Arrogant... brazen... *Mais oui, bien sûr!*"

We all looked at him expectantly.

"It's Josephine Balsamo! But why would she want to perform a confidence trick?"

"Maybe she needs to raise money quickly?" I suggested, being slightly familiar with the activities of several villainesses who have called themselves Countess Cagliostro.

"Possibly. I'll have to check if the supposed 'Lord and Lady Bristol' are still staying at the Dorchester," said Lecoq, looking at the address on the letter paper.

"Monsieur, I took the liberty of making discreet inquiries at the Dorchester yesterday evening," said Miss Brooke. "I discovered that they will be staying there until the end of the week."

"Excellent! Then your work for me is done, and done admirably! I will commend you highly to Mr. Dyer, Miss Brooke. You no longer need to remain at Marple-Daniels."

Jane looked at Loveday disappointedly. She had clearly formed a strong attachment to her over this short time, as young people often tend to do.

"Come, Doctor Watson, we have work to do," Lecoq added, before finishing his coffee swiftly and picking up his hat and cane.

I struggled to gulp down my scalding coffee—the French detective must have had a mouth made of leather. Making my excuses to the two ladies, I hurried after Lecoq.

We visited Lestrade's office at Scotland Yard, before making our way to the Dorchester. Outside, we saw, certainly for the first time in my life, an automobile. I was not overly impressed by the sight. It looked to me like a bulky carriage that was missing a horse. However, Lecoq seemed to be quite enchanted by it.

"Ah! Such an amazing technological achievement. Karl Benz is a genius!" he said, admiring the outer structure of the thing, before peering in to the front where there were levers instead of reins. "Maybe there will come a time when I can finally have a go in one of these things."

"Shall we go inside?" I suggested, slightly worried that he was about to climb inside the vehicle and ride it around.

I managed to usher him into the hotel foyer, where we agreed to wait for our prey. As we did so, we were joined by Lestrade and three plain clothes policemen. I had my back to the entrance, but Lecoq had a clear view of who came in.

Eventually, I heard an alien, croaky sound from outside the hotel.

"You hear that, gentlemen? That is the sound of an automobile—the sound of progress!" said Lecoq.

"Don't tell me there are now two of those infernal things outside," I said, before seeing Lecoq sit up.

I looked over at the entrance and saw a couple walk in and approach the reception desk. They seemed relaxed. The man was bearded and rather anonymous-looking, but the beard may have been false. His wife was enchantingly beautiful and supremely self-possessed.

Lecoq sprung to his feet and strode over to the couple. I, too, stood up, ready for action.

"Lord and Lady Bristol?"

They looked round at him.

"...Or should I say that I do not know who you really are, Monsieur, but you, Madame, are Josephine Balsamo, the so-called Countess Cagliostro! I arrest you both for the murder of Bartholomew Daniels and fraudulently selling a false patent."

"How dare you accost us like this!" thundered the man, clearly British.

"I don't know what you mean," said the woman.

"Let's go over to the corner of the room," ordered Lecoq.

"No! Tell us here and now of what exactly you are accusing us!" thundered the man, before looking around frantically as I, Lestrade, and his men slowly approached.

"Very well," replied Lecoq. "The two of you—and maybe some other accomplices—went on a burgling spree, breaking into houses in search of patents. You burgled the Patent Office in France and in Britain. This was with the aim of selling forged patents to unsuspecting entrepreneurs. But one such person, Bartholomew Daniels, found out what you were doing, and so you killed him. The murder weapon you used involved a car and some kind of hose pipe. I arrest you both for burglary, forgery, fraud, and murder!"

The couple could see us closing in on them. The woman suddenly pushed Lecoq violently away, and they both ran out of the hotel before anyone else had the chance to react.

The three policemen, Lecoq and I ran after them. Outside, we saw a second automobile, which was obviously theirs. They climbed expertly inside, started the engine, and rode away.

The three policemen looked dumbfounded. Lecoq was the first to react. He ran over to the first automobile and climbed into it.

"Quick, Doctor Watson!"

Instinctively, and without a moment's hesitation, I climbed in beside him. By now, Lecoq had started the engine and, within moments, we started moving.

In the near-distance, the other car chugged down Park Lane. We drove after them in pursuit. They disappeared around Hyde Park Corner.

"Hold on, Doctor!" shouted Lecoq. "I shall accelerate to 12 miles-per-hour—the maximum speed this beast can go!"

The phrase *maximum speed* chilled me. I hung on for fear of being thrown off as we swung round a corner, narrowly missing a hansom. Horses had an instinct for safety. Trains ran on rails. However, the automobile seemed to have nothing to restrain it. The thing was highly dangerous.

"You mad fool!" I shouted, "No one can survive going at this speed!"

Lecoq seemed to ignore me as he swung the handle that steered the car and hurtled around Duke of Wellington's Place.

It was a logical assumption that our prey had turned left into Grosvenor Place. I held on tight as we swung round. The wheels slipped on horse manure.

We roared down the street, passing angry horsemen and their startled steeds, as well frightened pedestrians. Lecoq overtook an omnibus and, further down the road, we could see the Countess and her accomplice driving their automobile just as recklessly as we were diving ours.

"Where must they be heading, Doctor Watson?" asked Lecoq. "You must know this confusing city better than I. Why couldn't you British have a more geometrically planned city, like Paris?"

"Slow down, for Heaven's sake!" was all I could reply. Then we saw ahead of us, the other car heave leftwards. "They must be heading for Victoria Station," I said.

We rode on, eventually coming to the railway station, where indeed the other car had been abandoned.

Lecoq stopped our car in front of the station's entrance. I jumped down and felt an almost irresistible urge to get down on my hands and knees to kiss the ground. However, Lecoq broke into my thoughts:

"We must split up. You take the platforms on that side of the station while I take the ones on the other! Hurry!"

So we ran off in opposite directions and dashed up and down the platforms.

Eventually I saw one train pull out of platform three, and I ran over to it, knowing that I would be too late to catch it. I arrived at the platform in time to see the train disappear into the distance, and, at the far end of the platform, Monsieur Lecoq, throwing his wig onto the ground and stamping on it in sheer rage.

For a moment, I feared that such a fit of excitement and physical exertion might be dangerous for a man of his advanced years. However, he soon seemed fine. In fact, he seemed to have the fitness and constitution that would make a man half his age envious. Perhaps he was sustained by the thrill of the chase. Or, what Holmes would have called *the Great Game*.

Inspector Lestrade and the police, having procured a four-wheeler, soon caught up with us on the station concourse. I explained to Lestrade and his colleagues what had happened, occasionally interrupted by angry oaths from the French detective.

"They'll probably try to head for the coast eventually. I'll inform the authorities at Dover. Oh, and Calais, too."

We all made to leave the station.

"I'd better return to Paris. That may be where they're headed," said a calmer Lecoq, seemingly unaware of having annoyed Lestrade by implying the Inspector wouldn't catch the fugitives. "It appears that our adventure together has come to an end, Doctor Watson." He proffered his hand and I shook it. "I will write to you to let you know how the investigation ends," he said, rather optimistically, as it would transpire.

There were no more burglaries or murders related to the patents, so in that sense at least, the affair was concluded. However, Monsieur Lecoq never caught Josephine Balsamo. Later, I found out that her gentleman accomplice was Simon Carne, the famous *Prince of Swindlers*, as he would later come to be known.

However, as I returned home from Victoria Station on that day in 1893, I found myself reflecting upon the remarkable Monsieur Lecoq. A man who was still active in his sixties and who had still plenty to offer the world. I also reflected upon Miss Loveday Brooke, a woman who had only recently embarked upon what was quite clearly her calling. Even young Jane Marple had a gift for crime detection, if she ever chose to pursue it.

Life carried on, and I felt as though I was living again.

Mary Shelley's ground-breaking classic Frankenstein *(1818) was adapted into a stage play in 1826 by Henry M. Milner under the title,* The Man and The Monster; or The Fate of Frankenstein *(which opened on 3 July at the Royal Coburg Theatre in London), which in turn was re-adapted as a French play by master fantasist Charles Nodier (with Antoine Béraud and Jean Toussaint Merle), who recast the legendary scientist as a sorcerer, and his Monster as a mute killer created via alchemy with the help of a Genie. (Available from Black Coat Press in* Frankenstein & The Hunchback of Notre-Dame, *ISBN 978-1-932983-38-8.) Then, in 1910, came the 16-minute Edison Studios' short film, written and directed by J. Searle Dawley with Augustus Phillips as Dr. Frankenstein, Charles Ogle as the Monster, and Mary Fuller as the doctor's fiancée. Christofer Nigro decided to revisit these two early versions of History's most famous monster in the story that follows...*

Christofer Nigro: *Bad Alchemy*

Castle Frankenstein, Darmstadt, Germany, 1898

Ludwig von Frankenstein sat quietly in the darkened chamber of his study, penning his latest journal entry under the illumination of a single kerosene lamp. His scheming mind pondered numerous thoughts and theories that would have been considered profane by most individuals other than himself. The sheer enthusiasm he displayed for copiously committing his obscene thoughts to paper bordered on the obsessive.

After all these years of intensive study and no small expenditure of my inheritance, I believe I have succeeded in gathering all that I need to repeat the alchemical experiment used by both my esteemed father, Charles Victor von Frankenstein, as well as our ancestor from the Italian branch of our noble lineage, Zametti Pretorius, to create artificial human life.

Since the 16th century, several men in my family have been bequeathed with both the superlative intellect and inner drive to create the next step in human evolution, something Darwin himself could not have conceived in all his limited writings. Examples of my genealogy who have followed in the illustrious footsteps of the master alchemist Paracelsus have included Count Johann Ferdinand von Kufstein, Johann Conrad Dippel, and Septimus Pretorius. Each succeeded in creating living miniature humans called homunculi.

My great uncle Victor Frankenstein, of the Swiss branch of our lineage, utilized a combination of advanced surgical techniques, galvanic forces, and arcane chemical concoctions to stitch together and bring to life a powerful being of great size, perhaps never realizing the alchemical nature of some of the materials which enabled him to accomplish that miracle. My great-great-great uncle Zametti, however, used entirely alchemical and hermetic methods to create not a miniature version of a human, but a giant entity my father referred to as a magnumculus. *My father, likewise, created such a being.*

I, too, have inherited both the intelligence and the unbridled will to engage in such forbidden science. I plan to utilize the methods of my ancestor Zametti and my father Charles Victor von Frankenstein, but not to create a magnumculus *of my own. Rather, I am going to actually* recreate *the two* magnumculi *originally formulated by my ancestor and my father...*

Ludwig's writing was interrupted by the creak of his study door opening. His young wife Julianne stepped into the room carrying a tray with a glass of wine and a repast.

"I thought you may want something to eat, my dear," the attractive auburn-haired young woman said. "You have been locked up in here since yesterday afternoon, so I took it upon myself..."

"You took it upon yourself to disturb my work, is what you did!" Ludwig screeched. "What did I tell you before, you thoughtless little wench? When I am sequestered in my study or the laboratory, I am not to be disturbed! Must I make the extra household expenditure of securing a lock for these doors?"

The young woman's lovely countenance frowned. "I am sorry, my dear, I was just concerned for you. You've hardly eaten over the past few days..."

"That is because I have been busy. Now do not bother me again, or next time, I will throw you through that door!"

Julianne's supple lips began to tremor as she struggled to hold back tears. "Very well, and I apologize again. I'll be... in the front room working on a new shawl if you do happen to need me."

"I won't! Now begone!"

Ludwig made it clear he meant business by throwing a glass flask at his bride. She dropped the plate to cover her eyes while the brittle container hit the wall and smashed to pieces just an inch away from her face. She was very thankful that the flask was empty and not filled with some type of corrosive fluid. The alchemist returned to his writing without saying another word after he heard his wife shut the door behind her.

Soon, all of Ludwig von Frankenstein's hard work, and even harder monetary expenditures, were coming to fruition as he stood before a huge metal crucible. It was there that he intended to recreate the two alchemical monstrosities that had previously known unnatural life three centuries apart from each other.

Unlike his ancestor, Zametti, and his father, Charles, he would not reject the respective creatures; he would embrace them for what they were and give them a purpose for existence, even if that sole purpose was to see to his personal advancement. He would feed them, provide them a place to live, and be akin to a father to them.

What more could any intelligent being brought into this world want? Other than a reason to exist, that is, and I shall provide that for them. They will owe me everything in return.

Since Ludwig rarely entertained any company socially, he fell into the habit of speaking to himself during important lab work. He learned that this practice helped him focus his thoughts by providing a private theater for his ego.

"Everything is now prepared. All who practice alchemy or any of the hermetic arts must understand the importance of the element of focused thought on the planned result; how the human mind uses symbolism to create a final product that mirrors his intentions. This factor is every bit as important as the physical ingredients one will use in the process."

The alchemist had the specially designed six-foot-tall, five-foot-wide cast iron crucible carefully heated until the pure mineral water within it roughly approximated the temperature of a horse's womb. He displayed a proud smile as he approached the large vessel with a sealed cucurbit in each hand.

"I now add the following ingredients: human semen that has been allowed to putrefy in a tightly sealed container for a period of 40 days, and a distillation of human and animal blood. These are essential for the spontaneous generation of life, for these two fluids, above all others, are infused with the life-force that respectively seeds and animates all living things. This is why succubi and vampires, respectively, seek them for sustenance."

He poured both substances into the crucible's bubbling mixture. The alchemist then retrieved an airtight canister which he opened to produce a stored mandrake root.

"Though Paracelsus himself discredited the notion of animal life springing forth as a result of preformationism, the notion was only untrue in a purely literal sense. In order for a being in a human shape to arise, something representing said shape needs to be used to create a sympathetic template, and nothing serves that purpose better than the mandrake."

The botanical specimen was dropped into the boiling crucible. The loud bubbling sound was now producing a visible brown froth. Next, he produced a vial containing a thick, black, noxious-scented substance that was known as Dippel's Oil.

"Ah, my somewhat distant relative Conrad Dippel, how thankful your successors are that you invented this substance. Of course, this particular distillation of bones additionally contains the herbal supplements of a truly exotic subspecies of the *gingko biloba* plant, known to be the oldest botanic species that still survives on this planet."

The froth in the brew bubbled up even further, almost resembling a small pit of lava as the obsidian-colored liquid was poured into it.

"Normally, this broth would take forty weeks with a continued daily infusing of these substances to spawn life. However, I shall add one very important step to speed the development and 'birthing' manifestation of each creature to less than a half hour of time."

The scientist opened a small box and produced two more professionally carved waxen figurines, these being representations of two very specific individuals: the two *magnumculi* created by Zametti Pretorius and Charles Victor von Frankenstein, respectively. The details for sculpting were acquired from the written reports of several eyewitnesses, the first one including Zametti's close friend, a gypsy leader named Janskin and the former's betrothed, Cecilia, both of whom survived an encounter with that monster; the second had Charles Victor von Frankenstein and his wife as among the few eyewitnesses.

"I spent a fortnight under the full moon of each evening with these two figures sitting on the rocks surrounding Castle Frankenstein. All these stones have unique magnetic properties and all lay upon a mystically charged dragon's trail, as such a creature was said to inhabit this area in the 11th century before being slain by the knight Lord George. There I used a variety of ancient rituals to collect the discorporated essence of these creatures which were still floating about the planetary ether. Due to the nature of the creatures' creation, my parents were able to focus the power of thought to discorporate him. How ironic that I shall be using this same method to *recorporealize* him."

It was then that Ludwig prepared for that risk-fraught final step. To that end, he looked towards an object set on a nearby table which resembled an obsidian-colored rock.

"I will have what is owed me by virtue of my father's legacy, and I will put to good use that which his pedestrian will could not handle. My good sire, you could have had the mightiest servant imaginable, but you recoiled in horror rather than nurturing the beast. Our long departed Zametti and Victor Frankenstein, as well as others in our lineage, showed a similar weakness of will. I, however, shall prove worthy of the legend carved by the Franks."

With this decided, Ludwig von Frankenstein gathered his courage and approached the shard of the Black Stone. He put his hand on it to prove he feared going to no lengths to acquire what he believed the universe owed him. The energies he felt surging through his arm as he did so was comparable to electricity.

"This rock was taken from nothing less than the actual Black Sarcophagus. Right from the secluded woods in Venice where Zametti Pretorius found it. Within it is the essence of one of the *djinn*, those otherworldly beings who can grant virtually any type of arcane secret to those who know how to trap them. The Genie of the Black Rock gave a small sample of a certain elixir that is the final necessary ingredient to Zametti, and a bit more covertly, to my father. It is time for me to create the Triangle of Solomon."

The alchemist then began using chalk to draw the three-sided geometric figure in a special area of the laboratory floor. Within it was drawn the three sacred names of God: Tetragrammaton, Primeumatron, and Anaphaxeton. Three sections of letters that combined to spell out the name of the warrior/protector archangel Michael were drawn near the Seal of Solomon symbol in the center. It was there he placed the rock.

"King Solomon was given the means to control the *djinn*, and now that method has been passed on to others. With sufficient effort I should be able to extract the essence of the Genie through that shard and materialize him in the middle of the triangle. There, in theory, he should be trapped and forced to obey me before being allowed to return to his own realm. It is time to start the summoning."

Ludwig von Frankenstein took a very deep breath and began the task at hand.

The alchemist spoke a series of commands and biddings in Arabic, Syrian, and Sanskrit, along with intensive channeling of the energies with which the local area was infused. These were all done in conjunction with powerful visualization and focus of intent on his part. He stood within a protective circle surrounded by four lit candles, each representing one of the four directions and four of the five elements of antiquity to guard and balance the forces he called upon.

After several minutes, a strange stillness and quiet came over the laboratory, followed by thunder and lightning directly outside the castle. A cloud of dark smoke began billowing forth from the shard, where it gradually condensed into the ebony-attired form of the Black Genie of the Rock. The inside of the triangle was filled with flame as the *djinn* took corporeal form within the geometric construct.

Ludwig forced himself to remain calm. "Welcome to my plane of reality, friend," he said to his otherworldly guest.

The Genie looked him over, as if noticing something familiar. "You share the blood of... *them*," he said with overt contempt. "Moreover, you share their ambitions. Which would indicate you are *no one's* friend."

Ludwig giggled. "You mention ambition as if it is inherently bad."

"You misunderstood my words. Ambition is not intrinsically immoral, but can be judged by which purpose it is focused upon. And yours, like those of your two relations before you, are not focused towards a purpose that could fit any definition of altruism."

"You object to the creation of life?"

"I object to your reason for creating it in such a fashion. My only satisfaction in being forced to aid you in this endeavor is the certainty that it will lead to your ruin."

"My father, who had also utilized your services, lived 'happily ever after' with my mother, I should say."

"Only because he rejected the evil he wrought, as he truly felt love for the caring mate he had in his life. You, it must be said, are incapable of such feelings, and you will not allow your own caring mate to provide you this opportunity for salvation."

"Ha! As if my fortune in any way depends upon that woman!"

"You scoff her value at your peril. And, alas, her own. I shall take a measure of joy in watching your undoing from my side of the veil."

"Enough of this! Hand me the vial. Then you may be free to return from whence you came."

The Genie reached into a pocket hidden in his obsidian cloak and produced a jar filled with a light green liquid. He placed it securely on the floor just within the perimeter of the triangle's bottom horizontal line.

"You may now depart, entity of the otherworld," the scientist demanded with focused conviction.

"I gladly depart to leave you to the fate you have writ for yourself," the Genie said as he began discorporating back into a dark smoke-like substance and appeared to be quickly sucked back into the substance of the rock. More thunder and lightning accompanied his departure from the material plane, and the flames within the triangle briefly increased their intensity before snuffing out entirely.

When Ludwig was certain no trace of the sinister *djinn* remained on the material plane, he summarily dismissed the elementals guarding the quarters of the circle and ended the ritual entirely. After it was completely safe to breach the circle, he grasped the jar and its precious contents in his hand. He could scarcely believe what he now held in his possession.

Ludwig wasted no time in walking over to the large crucible and poured the contents of the jar within the frothing concoction. The substance mixed with what had already been deposited in the brew, and the lathering effect further intensified. He then walked through the open metal doors of the chamber, which he had placed the giant cauldron, and yanked them shut. He was confident the iron chamber would prove secure, as it was constructed by his father when the latter had conducted his own experiment in spontaneous generation.

Ludwig then peered through a small portal located in front of the chamber to watch as the amazing process was completed.

As a short span of time passed, a set of skeletal arms rose from the broth, to be quickly followed by a second pair. Two full skeletons, covered by what appeared to be red strands of gristle, stood up painfully, revealing mutual heights exceeding seven feet. Muscle began rapidly covering the bones of both beings until they were entirely sheathed in flesh. Layers of epidermis quickly covered the exposed ligaments, though such skin seemed a deathly white rather than the healthy pink of normal human coloring.

Each being shook their enormous heads to mitigate the strange sensation of eyes forming within previously empty sockets. It was by now clear both entities were of the male gender. This unnatural genesis concluded with strands of hair emerging from pores atop their skulls like grass sprouting from dirt in an accelerated motion. The creature on the right had hair taking a long and lustrous form, draping over his upper back like a cloak; the creature on the left, however, spawned a shock of a sandier color that wasn't long in back, but rather spiraled out the top of his head in an unruly mess.

The two man-monsters howled in joint euphoria as their essences were pulled from the ether and fully restored to a strange form of corporeal existence. They both moved their gnarled fingers in front of their grotesque visages repeatedly, as if seeking to confirm the authenticity of the sensations they were once more experiencing.

Once each had made this confirmation to their satisfaction, they finally took notice of their mutual presence. The two creatures then sloshed through the bubbling stew to attack each other. Both exhibited immense strength of roughly equal proportion as their mammoth hands locked onto the face and throat of the other, thus resulting in a stalemate.

Their attempt to rip each other to pieces was interrupted by the clanging sound of the chamber's steel doors being pulled open. Ludwig rushed in and shouted them to attention.

"Cease your violent actions immediately, both of you! You are family, and I am your father! I restored the miracle of life to both of you! I am your reason for being, and you owe me absolute loyalty and obedience!"

The two creatures stopped struggling against each other and moved to study the man before them. The memories of their previous existences were now rapidly returning in full clarity, and they remembered brief lives consisting of pain and rejection. This time, however, they were apparently offered acceptance from the one who restored them to the world of material existence. As far as they knew, such a harsh tone was natural from one who cared for another. It didn't make them feel good, but it did make them feel *accepted*. If acquiescence to the will of another was what was required to receive this, then they would simply have to follow that person's demands. At least for now.

Ludwig reached over and handed the giants a pair of large but simple garments of strongly hewn cotton, specially tailored to individuals of great size.

"Both of you, get out of that cauldron and get dressed. It is time to introduce you to my wife, and to the castle in which you will be living."

Julianne von Frankenstein was quick to heed her husband's calls to the door of his laboratory. She rarely received much attention from him outside the kitchen and bedroom, and she was excited at the prospect of his sharing with her the product of the long labors of work that demanded most of his time. She arrived to find him standing by the open door.

"Julianne, our home has two new residents," Ludwig announced. "They were previously created, respectively, by my great-great-great uncle Zametti and my father. I have reconstituted them to full physical form from particles of cells floating in the ether."

Before Julianne could in any way assess the veracity of her husband's words, two giant figures emerged from the door. Both had to bend to get through the opening, and she had never before seen any men as large as these two. Nor did they resemble any person she had previously laid eyes upon in a general sense. Each had ghastly pale skin, yellow-colored eyes, and faces of grotesque appearance.

The pair of creatures looked upon the young woman before them and were instantly struck by her beauty. They smiled and walked over to her, each one trying to bump the other aside to reach her first.

Though Julianne was terrified, she had read the legends of such beings connected to the schemes of her husband's relatives. She suspected he had been working on something of this nature, and her love for him forced her to be prepared. If accepting these beings were what was required to be viewed as supporting his life's work, then, by the grace of God, she would do so.

Despite shaking intensely as the monster with the head of scraggly hear moved his huge finger over her face to gently twist it around one of her auburn locks, she compelled herself to smile.

"It is... my pleasure to meet you, and you are welcome here. But you must both be given names. You can take our last name, of course, but you will need your own forenames." She looked at the giant before her. "Since you were created by my father-in-law, I shall call you... Charles."

Her voice obviously had a soothing effect upon the newly christened creature. He smiled in response, exposing an unsightly set of crooked yellow teeth, but still Julianne maintained her composure, and never visibly winced.

The second creature, this one with more a skeleton-like face and the thicker flowing hair shoved the first monster aside to have his turn at admiring Julianne. He reached out to her with his own pasty white hand. Julianne took it in her own and gave it a tender squeeze.

"And you, my big friend... since you were created by Great-Great-Great-Uncle Zametti, we shall call you... Zam."

The first monster, Charles, then moved forward and shoved Zam back. The second monster angrily responded in kind, sending his "cousin" up against the wall. Snarling in anger, Charles clasped his enormous fists together and prepared to rush his equally monstrous kin.

"Now, now, boys, that will be quite enough," Julianne said, moving between the two. "You must get along, for I am here to care for you both. Is this understood?"

The two ceased their hostile movements towards each other as soon as the beautiful Julianne bade them. She touched each of their barrel chests and pushed them in opposite directions. They slowly backed away from each other and gently wrapped their fingers around her far smaller and softer digitals.

Ludwig then stepped in and pushed Julianne away from them. "You do not command these creatures; I do! Mind your place in this house, woman!"

The young wife gasped in surprise as she was shoved. "I am sorry, my dear. I did not mean to infringe on your..."

"Well, you did! Remember what I said about minding your place!"

Julianne simply looked at the floor and sobbed, "I am so sorry. It won't happen again."

The monsters each held an expression which suggested they were even more taken aback by their "Father" Ludwig's vehement actions than his wife. Why would a man treat such a beautiful and kind soul in such a way? It was a question that would bear greater significance as time passed.

Over the next few months, both Zam and Charles von Frankenstein proved quite intelligent and able to absorb knowledge quickly. With Julianne's attentive lessons, the two had swiftly learned to read and articulate themselves verbally, showing a particular propensity for poetry. Though they enjoyed learning, that activity paled before their delight of simply being in the company of Julianne. Both creatures remembered, from their past lives, beautiful women who had been repulsed by them, and this young woman's kind ministrations were both refreshing and invigorating. For her part, she found their company to be a recompense for the time Ludwig refused her any attention.

Julianne thus came to resent how her husband used Zam and Charles to perform all the necessary labor around the manse. This included retrieving wood from the nearby woods and cutting it for the stove, moving heavy lab equipment, and being used as security against the intrusions of wild animals and human trespassers. The efficient and brutal manner with which these two tore everything from roaming wolves to armed trespassers to shreds with ease horrified the young woman.

However, commanding these beings to do such things seemed to fill her husband with a chilling power trip. She had seen a gentle side to the monsters, and it was this side of them she wished to nurture forth. Alas, her husband wouldn't have it, and she realized it was only a matter of time before he sent the two *magnumculi* on errands of brutality against those who had merely insulted him. And there were too many of those to count, both in the halls of academia and the social circles he only occasionally cared to frequent.

All of this would come to a tragic culmination, which began one afternoon during a chess game between the two monsters. It all started when Charles angrily threw a pawn at his cousin during a game.

"You cheat!" the creature shouted.

"I did not!" Zam retorted. "You are just angry that Julianne gives me better lessons! That is why I win!"

"Julianne does not fancy you better! Because you are the ugly one!"

"Do you truly believe *you're* some vision of beauty, cousin?"

Charles growled in anger and pushed Zam. The second creature pushed him back, sending him crashing into an expensive end table, which served to shatter all of its glass knickknacks and porcelain statuettes onto the floor. Julianne, who was preparing meals in the kitchen, ran into the front room.

"Boys, what is the meaning of this?" she shouted.

"Zam said you love him best and that is why you teach him to play chess better!" Charles grumbled.

"Charles said I'm ugly and you love him best because of that!" Zam hollered.

"You boys need to stop with this!" Julianne insisted. "I love you both equally. You are both my family!"

It was then that Ludwig bounded into the room, as he was disturbed from his study by the commotion.

"What is this ruckus?" he asked. "Dear Jesus, what have you two fools done to the knickknacks? They cost a fortune! And you shattered them because of your constant fussing over which of you my wife favors!"

"We are sorry, Father," Zam said. "We do not mean to bicker; it is just that..."

"I shall tell you what it 'just is,' monster!" was the alchemist's irate response. "Both of you vie for that woman's attention, when in reality neither she, nor any woman, would have an ounce of love for either of you! She only pities you two for your grotesque appearances and clumsy nature! She uses you both to practice the teaching skills she regrets never being able to put to use! She only tends to you to ingratiate herself to me!"

Both Zam and Charles looked down, feeling as if their synthetic hearts were being torn from their bulky chests. This was far from the first time their tendency to cause such accidents had enraged their "father," and his pejorative tirades were becoming too much to bear. They were each secretly beginning to wonder if tolerating such behavior in exchange for the approval of another was truly worth it.

Julianne became incensed at her husband's cruel words, having been subjected to them often enough herself. She reluctantly decided to speak up.

"Ludwig, please refrain from saying such things," she pleaded. "I certainly do love both of the boys."

"You dare contradict me in front of them?" Ludwig was so livid that he struck Julianne across the face. She fell against a small table, the impact of which knocked an expensive Indian vase to the floor. "Damn it, you would have to fall against that table and break yet another expensive belonging of mine!" He then kicked the young woman in her right shin, causing her to scream in pain.

Charles and Zam both stood with their fists clenched, which indicated they were filled with building anger.

"Stop that!" Zam demanded.

Ludwig scowled at the far taller entity. "What did you say? Did you dare give me an order?"

"You hurt those who love you!" Charles added. "You do nothing to earn our respect and loyalty!"

"Earn?" Ludwig said. "I do not have to earn anything from you! I brought you two into this world, you owe me everything! As does this woman! I have given her a home, and all she needs to live on!"

Zam snarled. "Giving us food and clothing may satisfy our stomach and skin, but love and respect are needed to nourish the heart. You... starve us in a most crucial manner!"

"Ha!" Ludwig scoffed. "My wife has been reading you too much of that insipid poetry! Your leisure time is now over, and you will be punished for sassing me. Both of you out into the forest, and do not return until you bring me no less than two thousand kilograms of wood each. Let us see if even the pair of you can have your muscles torn from overwork!"

Julianne wiped the blood trickling from her split lip as she returned to her feet.

"Ludwig, please do not do this," she implored. "I will accept a punishment in their place. This was my fault, not theirs."

"Oh, you shall receive a punishment, all right," the scientist said. "But *with* the two of them, not in their place! The whole useless lot of you are at fault here!" He then shoved her against the wall again.

"That is enough!" Zam decreed as he grasped Ludwig's wrist in a devastating grip.

It was now the scientist's turn to shout in pain as he felt his carpal bones being crushed. "What are you doing, you fool? Release me at once!"

"No!" Charles bellowed. "Do not release him, cousin! He has gone too far! Let me have part of him too!"

Juliane leapt to her feet in horror. "No, boys, please! Your father does not mean to be that way; he just overworks and it makes him irritable! Please!"

However, the moment she ran up to Zam and put her hand on his towering shoulder, Julianne saw that her husband's arm was no longer attached to his body; a bone jutted from the torn flesh of the stump as it dripped blood on a nearby table. She then looked to see her husband writhing on the floor in indescribable agony as Charles crushed the alchemist's chest with his enormous boot while he ripped off the man's left leg along with a portion of his groin. A spectacular spurt of blood accompanied this action, and the costly Venetian rug was spattered with a wide crimson stain.

Ludwig's final scream reverberated through every corner of the large manse. Julianne stood in shock, yet she swore she could hear distant cold laughter emanating from... somewhere.

"Fitting," she heard the Genie of the Rock say from beyond the veil.

Then all went silent as she fainted.

After she awakened, Julianne discovered to her continued horror that the act of dismembering their ersatz father's body had changed the boys' behavior for the worst. Though they both continued to love her dearly for her kindness, that feeling now took on a new form. They refused to allow her to leave the house unattended for any reason, not even to secure water from the well outside or to ride the horse.

"We shall do all that is required to maintain this castle," Zam told her. "You need do nothing save for continuing to teach us words and read us poetry."

"And the cooking!" Charles reminded her. "We so love the meals you create on that stove. My cousin and I shall provide all the wood you ever need for that. We will also see that the garden continues to yield produce and that the horse is fed."

Julianne didn't want to provoke them into anything more stern than this, such as confining her to her room. She loved these two as if they were her children, or at least two errant younger siblings. However, the rejection they both endured in their past lives, and the cruelty enacted against them by her husband in this one, had twisted them. Despite their positive responses to her love and care, her husband's behavior had torn open the emotional scars they had incurred in the past.

Now they were extremely fearful Julianne would leave them, especially after the terror they knew she felt upon seeing them slaughter her husband. They realized that, despite any love she may still have for them, it was now punctuated by fear, since she saw what they were capable of if provoked.

For her part, Julianne didn't want to risk antagonizing them any further by protesting her situation. Instead, she pretended to be accepting of it until she finally formulated an escape plan.

As much as it pains me to even consider doing this, I cannot leave myself at their mercy any longer. I so loathe to manipulate their insecurities and rivalry with each other for my attentions, but they leave me no other choice. Dear Lord, please forgive me for what I must do.

Early the next afternoon Julianne asked Charles to play a game of chess with her, while Zam was asked to go into the forest to fetch wood for dinner. She took one of the monster's pawns with a rook as she began setting her scheme in motion.

"Charles, I am quite concerned for you because of your cousin," she said.

"How so?" the giant replied.

"Well, I think he has come to realize how I love you much more than I do him. His ugliness, both in appearance and behavior, has caused me to favor you. I know it was he who goaded you into killing your father in the first place. So I worry for both you and myself."

Charles grumbled loudly as he dropped a pawn from his massive white fingers. "I always knew you preferred me! I assure you, fine Julianne, that he poses no threat to either of us. I shall see to it!"

"Thank you so much, my wonderful big man," she said, moving her hand gently over his own. "I was certain I could count on you."

Soon after Zam returned, Julianne approached him as Charles was placing the wood into the stove.

"Zam, I am so concerned for you," she said through quiet sobs.

"What is the matter, dear Julianne?" the monstrosity queried.

"It is your cousin. I fear he has come to suspect how I love you more than him. His curt behavior towards you, his inferior mannerisms, and yes, that hideously untidy excuse for hair on his head; well, I just cannot love him as I love you. I so worry he will... make some type of move against us both should the truth be confirmed to him."

Zam crushed a porcelain coffee mug in his hand as if it were hollow cardboard. "Trust me, dear woman, I assure you that will not come to pass! I always knew you loved me best! I shan't allow that fool to render what we share asunder."

She forced tears to pour from her eyes. "Oh, thank you so much, my brave fellow. I knew I was safe with you at my side."

Julianne realized that all she needed to do after that was to quietly sit back on the imported Hitchcock chair in the living room to await what she knew was all but inevitable. She would have to time things just right once the fracas started.

After Charles finished his task at the stove, he walked out of the kitchen to see Zam standing before him with folded arms. He instantly took this as an attempt by his cousin to stand between him and Julianne, unable to accept whom she loved best.

"Step aside, Zam," he demanded. "I do not want you so close to Julianne."

"Oh really, cousin?" Zam replied defiantly. "Is that, perhaps, because you would seek to do her harm for what she and I have together, but which you and her do not?"

"You deluded monstrosity!" Charles exclaimed. "Your ugliness of face and spirit has reviled her enough! Now allow me to go to her side!"

"No!" Zam hissed. "It is you who are deluded! You shall not offend her any longer with your unruly head of hair and vile disposition!"

Charles responded to that with a strong bash to the side of Zam's jaw. The creature flew into a nearby dining table, smashing it to pieces. However, unlike anyone else ever hit by Charles, Zam stood up again with nothing worse to show for it than blackish blood streaming out the side of his mouth. With a scream of rage, Zam charged his cousin, slamming into him with the force of a charging bull. That blow sent Charles crashing through the thick oaken doors leading into the kitchen as if they were composed of paper.

Julianne stood up and prepared to take leave until Charles was suddenly hurled out of the kitchen and onto the coffee table a few inches from her feet, reducing it to splinters. The huge monster turned to the woman as streams of black ichor poured out of his shattered nose.

"Fear not, Julianne, for I will not allow my cousin's rage to carry over to you!" he said.

"It is *you* who threaten Julianne, vile brute!" Zam rejoined as he ran out of the kitchen. "Step away from her now!"

"You were the one who threw me next to her, you feeble-minded bastard!" Charles shrieked in reply as he leapt back to his feet and attacked his cousin anew.

The two monsters began pummeling each other furiously with each blow strong enough to crush an ox. The interior of the living room was soon spattered with their foul-smelling onyx-colored blood. Finally, as the two continued their efforts to tear each other to pieces, they both went smashing through a wall leading directly into the library, effectively placing them out of Julianne's presence.

Seeing her chance, the young woman quickly stood up and ran from the house, heading directly for the enclosure where the horse was kept. She quickly untethered the stallion and jumped on its back, prompting the strong animal to begin running down a path she knew would lead through the woods and into Darmstadt.

Julianne's eyes were flowing with tears as she pushed the horse onwards, for she couldn't help but be filled with regret for leaving behind the two pathetic creatures bent on each other's destruction over the kind of love for her which her late husband never had felt.

Who better than John Peel, one of Doctor Who's best authors, to craft both a locked room mystery and a time travel conundrum? For the uninitiated, Bob Morane is a long-standing French adventure series created by Henri Vernes in 1953. Bob has had several time travel adventures, starting in 1957, when he met the Time Patrol from the future, and later pitting him against the diabolical Monsieur Ming, a.k.a. The Yellow Shadow, whom we met earlier in Matthew Baugh's story.

John Peel: *Time to Kill*

Paris, 1960

"I have a dead body on my hands that I can't explain."

Bob Morane looked at his bank manager, André Durand-Mareuil, and merely raised an eyebrow.

His friend Bill Ballantine, on the other hand, whistled loudly. "Crikey! That must be a bit hard to explain to the police," he commented.

"Quiet, Bill," Bob admonished the burly, red-headed Scotsman. "I have a feeling Monsieur Durand-Mareuil is going to fill us in." They were in Bob's apartment on the Quai Voltaire in Paris, and his landlady had served tea just before announcing the banker. Bob offered the banker a cup of tea, but Durand-Mareuil shook his head.

"There really isn't that much to... ah... fill in," he said, sadly. "And Mr. Ballantine is quite right—it is difficult to explain to the police, and to my bank's Board of Governors. They're not at all happy about the matter, I'm afraid."

Bob rather liked Durand-Mareuil—he'd always been very helpful in the past when he had faced urgent needs to raise funds to gallivant all over the world in some of his more extreme cases, and he felt sorry for the man, who clearly hadn't managed to get much sleep.

"Well, why don't you tell us what you can?" he asked.

"You may already have heard some of this," Durand-Mareuil replied slowly. "The victim was Albert Carrigan."

The name was indeed familiar. "The millionaire?"

Bill sat bolt-upright in his chair. "I read something about that in the papers yesterday! He was shot to death in a bank..." He realized what he was saying. "Oh—*your* bank..."

Durand-Mareuil nodded sadly. "My bank. More specifically, inside my security vault."

"I can't see the problem, then," Bill said. "Whoever did it must have been seen by dozens of people."

"Nobody saw him. Nobody *could* have seen him."

Bob had been in plenty of interesting moments during his time in the Military, and even more in his days since, as a kind of freelance adventurer. He could always tell when something interesting was on the cards, and his intuition was signaling strongly now.

"Perhaps you'd care to explain that rather cryptic comment?"

Durand-Mareuil frowned slightly. "I don't think you've ever been in the bank's security vault, have you?"

Bill laughed. "We've never had the kind of money to need to."

"Quite. Well, it's where all of the safety deposit boxes are kept. Many people store jewelry, stocks and bonds, that sort of thing in our boxes. Mr. Carrigan has—*had*—several with us. He would come into the bank once a week, on Wednesday afternoons at two o'clock precisely."

"He'd been in that habit for some time?" Bob asked.

"Oh, indeed—since before my time, in fact, so over five years."

Bill chewed his lip. "Always dangerous to get into predictable habits."

"Quite so," the banker agreed. "Last Wednesday, Mr. Carrigan came into the bank as usual, and, as always, I accompanied him into the vault, along with one of my security guards. Mr. Carrigan and I opened the door to the box he wished to use. The guard and I then left the room, and the guard closed and locked the door."

"Forgive me a moment," Bob said, "but allow me to ask an obvious, if foolish question: there isn't any other way into the vault, I take it?"

Durand-Mareuil shook his head. "Just the one door, which the guard locked. He remained outside the door for thirty minutes. Mr. Carrigan always stayed for precisely that length of time. I returned when the time had elapsed, and we opened the door together. And inside, we discovered the body of Mr. Carrigan. He had been shot once, through the heart, and was quite dead."

"Crikey!" Bill muttered. "That must have been unsettling. Did he shoot himself, then?"

"He couldn't have done, because there was no gun in the room."

Bob hesitated before asking the obvious question. "I don't like to cast doubt on anyone, but how trustworthy is that guard?"

Durand-Mareuil smiled bleakly. "Yes, the police wondered about that, too, obviously. Their initial theory was that my man had opened the vault door, shot Carrigan, and then closed the door again."

"That *is* the logical conclusion," Bob agreed. "But I take it that was also impossible?"

"I'm afraid it was. You see, the security vault is adjacent to the cash vault. Our chief cashier is locked within that vault while the bank was open—there is a barred door, and his desk is immediately behind it. If any money enters or exits the vault, he and the guard have to open that door together. So while he waited for Mr. Carrigan to finish, the guard was seated just outside this door and in the

221

full view of my chief cashier the entire time. Both men insist that the security vault door was not opened again until I returned."

"They could be in cahoots," Bill suggested.

The banker shrugged. "But to what end?" he asked. "The two men do not socialize; they do not even know where the other lives. Both have worked for the bank for more than a decade, and have always been steady, reliable men, otherwise they would not have been in the positions of trust they occupy. Neither of them have any reason to kill Mr. Carrigan."

"Couldn't they have stolen something from the strong box?" Bill asked. "Some fabulous jewel, or something?" He sounded quite excited.

Durand-Mareuil shrugged again. "It is always possible," he agreed. "The bank has no record of what was kept in the box, of course. But as soon as we discovered the body, I telephoned the police. I remained with the guard until they arrived. Before either the guard or the chief cashier were allowed to leave the bank at the end of the day, they were both thoroughly searched." He coughed, embarrassed. "As was I myself, and quite rightly so. The security vault was checked, and the cash vault. Nothing out of place was discovered anywhere. As far as they were able to ascertain, the motive for the murder was not robbery."

Bob smiled widely. "Monsieur Durand-Mareuil, you couldn't keep us out of this now if you tried." He grinned at Bill. "A classic, eh? A locked room mystery. No way for a murder to have been committed, no possible killer."

"And no clues, either, it sounds like." Despite his pessimistic comment, Bill's grin was just as wide as Bob's. "Sounds right up our street."

The banker's relief was evident. He pumped Bob's hand enthusiastically. "Thank you, thank you. Are you able to accompany me right now? The sooner this mystery can be cleared up, the happier my Board of Directors will be."

"I can't guarantee I can solve it," Bob said, "but I think Bill and I can spare some time, eh?"

Bill nodded. "I'll say." He rubbed his large hands together. "I can't wait to take a peek at the scene of the crime." He looked anxiously at Durand-Mareuil. "We *can* see it, can't we?"

"I've already spoken to the police. They have it sealed off for the time being, running fingerprint tests and such like, but they have agreed to allow you access as representatives of the bank. You will, of course, be recompensed for your time."

Bob smiled. "I think this mystery in itself is going to be payment enough," he said.

"But we accept your generous offer," Bill added, hastily. "Er—it *will* be generous, won't it?"

"Quite so."

"Jolly good."

The bank was just around the corner, so it didn't take them long to walk there. The main floor was conducting business as usual, though there were a couple of policemen watching over things. The handful of customers in the bank were trying not to be caught staring at the officers. The policemen nodded politely to the manager as he led Bob and Bill toward the stairs that led down toward the basement vaults.

As he did so, Bob had a curious sensation that he was being watched. He'd learned never to ignore his instincts, so he glanced around. One of the customers as the central table, standing with a deposit slip in his hand, was looking directly at him. He was an elderly man, with long, white hair (and an errant curl giving him a slightly wild look), carrying a gnarled walking stick under one arm. Bob had never seen him before. He frowned. The man didn't seem to be bothered to be caught staring, and inclined his head slightly in acknowledgment before bending to fill out the form.

Odd. But probably not relevant to their case.

The bank was one of those grand old buildings, filled with artistic flourishes. There were chandeliers on the main floor, and pedestals with fresh flowers. The stairs leading down were wide and marble-covered. There was a bank guard stationed at the head of the stairs, clearly to ensure nobody without official cause got to descend, but he knew Durand-Mareuil, naturally, and stood politely aside for them.

Bob looked carefully around as they walked down. At the foot of the stairs, there was a small area illuminated by another ornate chandelier. Directly in front of them was the cash vault. The barred door was of steel, some six feet tall and about eight across. It looked quite impressive. Behind it, he could see the chief cashier's desk—an ornate wooden affair, with ball and claw legs. The man himself was seated at it now; he was a fiftyish, greying man with the look of a goblin. He was clearly trying to get his work done and ignore two more policemen stationed in the hall.

Outside that door was a small desk and a chair. The bank's security guard was seated there, trying to look uninvolved, though he was clearly uncomfortable. Bob could see that Durand-Mareuil's comments had been entirely accurate: the two men would have been in full view of one another the entire time Carrigan had been in the vault. Unless they were working together, then it was impossible for either they or any other person to have entered the vault to kill the millionaire.

Bob finally turned his attention to the security vault itself. At the moment, the vault door was wide open, but it was a standard door, some six inch thick metal. Nobody could have shot Carrigan through the door, and nobody could possibly have opened it without being seen. All that was left was to enter the vault and look around to see if they could find anything that the police might have missed.

"Who is the officer in charge of this case?" Bob asked.

"Need you ask?" came a familiar voice from inside the room. "A case that is inexplicable and potentially career-damaging if I fail to solve it? Who else would they give it to?"

Bob's face broke into a broad grin as he walked into the vault and shook his old friend by the hand. "Commissaire Maigret!" he said, delightedly. "I don't know why they bothered to consult with me. I'm sure you must have the case completely solved by now!"

Maigret grunted. He had his pipe firmly clenched between his teeth though it wasn't lit. "Oh, I have it all solved, my friend," he agreed. "Except for who did it, and how."

Bob knew Maigret's methods of old. "Don't tell me that you don't have a suspect already."

Maigret shrugged. "Indeed I do—the dead man's nephew, Donald Carrigan. He's absolutely the perfect suspect: he likes the high life, he gambles on cards that he plays very badly, and is in a large amount of debt. He stands to inherit millions from his uncle's death."

"And yet?" Bob prompted.

"And yet, he has an unshakable alibi," Maigret said sadly. "At the precise time of the murder, he was losing money at baccarat in the casino at Royale-les-Eaux. There were dozens of witnesses to this fact. He was quite certainly not in Paris at the time of the killing, and, in fact, will not arrive back here until later today—accompanied by Janvier."

"I see your problem," Bob murmured.

"And I am afraid I see yours." Maigret waved his hand about the room. "Feel free to search for clues. If you uncover any, I would be most grateful, because my men and I have found nothing of significance."

"What about the bullet?" Bob asked. "Did you recover that?"

"Yes," the Commissioner said. He took his pipe out of his mouth, looked at it, saw that it was empty, and then replaced it. "Like everything else in this case, it is a puzzle. It is of no known manufacture, and has a rather unique set of patterning on it. It was fired by no gun either I, or anyone in my department, can identify." He shrugged. "As if there were not enough problems with this case."

Bob glanced about the room. It was about twenty feet by sixteen, and the ceiling was about ten feet high. There was a table and single chair, closer to the left-hand wall than the right, but no other furniture. The room was illuminated by another of those omnipresent chandeliers—rather brightly, in fact. Three of the walls were lined, floor to ceiling, with small doors that each had two key holes, and behind which the owners' safety deposit boxes resided. The fourth wall contained only the large security door. The walls either side of it were bare.

"Let's eliminate the absurd first," Bob suggested. He tapped the bare wall. "I take it that there's no possibility of a hidden panel behind this?"

Maigret looked over at Durand-Mareuil, who shook his head. "The walls consist only of two inches of covering over four inch steel."

"I really didn't imagine that there were secret passages, but it's as well to be certain." Bob shook his head. "There doesn't seem to be any other way into this room."

"What about the ventilation system?" Bill asked, cheerily. "In the movies, people are always crawling about them."

Maigret smiled dourly and pointed with the stem of his pipe at a rather small grille set in the ceiling about six inches in from the wall. "It's six inches across. Feel free to try and fit inside it." He eyed the burly Scot with a faint smile.

"OK—not that way, then." Bill thought for a moment. "But what about the gun? *That* would be less than six inches long. If the killer had somehow rigged a gun with a remote-control device so he could place it in the vent and then fire it…" He looked rather pleased with this suggestion.

"Well," Maigret admitted, "that's certainly an idea that had never occurred to the police." He didn't look impressed, however. "The problem with that idea, my friend, is that the vent is *behind* the table where Mr. Carrigan sat, and he was shot from the front. Horizontally, not vertically. The gun must have been placed about…" He walked to the right hand end of the room and stood in one corner. "Roughly here." He used the stem of his pipe to demonstrate. "Just at the level of a man standing here, holding a gun."

Bob scowled. "I've run into some pretty rum things in my time," he said slowly. "And I can think of only one solution that *might* answer all of the problems." He gave a slight laugh. "The only trouble is that it's even more absurd than the crime—at least on first glance."

"And what is that?" Maigret raised an eyebrow.

"That there really was a man standing there with a gun—but nobody could see him."

"An invisible man, you mean?"

Bob shrugged. "I know it sounds impossible, but, well, Bill and I have witnessed any number of things I'd have thought were impossible. Technology seems to be advancing so swiftly these days…"

"I agree, it sounds foolish, but let us consider it," Maigret said. "Let us postulate the existence of an invisible man…"

"With an invisible gun," Bill said, helpfully.

"As you say, with an invisible gun. He walks through the bank unseen and down into the vault area. When Monsieur Durand-Mareuil here opens the door, he somehow manages to slip inside and waits in the corner. When he is alone with Carrigan, he shoots the victim and then waits for the vault door to be opened and slips out again. Unseen the entire time."

The bank manager shook his head. "Even granting such a silly idea," he glanced apologetically at Bob "we would have *felt* someone brush past us, for the door is not large, and was closed behind us when we entered. I had to open it again when I left, and closed it immediately behind me."

Bob sighed. "Well, it was just a thought." He shrugged. "In that case, I'll admit that I'm completely baffled for the moment." He saw Durand-Mareuil's face fall. "Cheer up, sir! I'm only baffled for the moment. Ideas often come to me later. If you're quite done here, Bill, what say we go back home and think for a while? It's about lunch time, as my stomach is reminding me."

Bill, never averse to the idea of food, nodded his agreement, and they said their goodbyes. As they trudged up the stairs to the bank lobby, Bill turned to Bob. "So, what do you make of this?" he asked.

"Nothing, as yet," Bob admitted. "It seems to have no possible solution. But since we know that Carrigan *was* murdered, then obviously there must be an explanation of some sort. We simply haven't seen it yet."

They emerged onto the main floor of the bank. As they headed toward the exit, a figure moved to intercept them. Bob glanced at him, and realized it was the elderly gentleman who had been looking at him earlier. He held up his stick to block Bob's path.

"Please excuse my imposing myself upon you, Commandant Morane," the man said, politely. "If you would be so kind, I would appreciate the opportunity to speak with you."

Bob shrugged. The man seemed harmless enough, but he clearly had something on his mind. "By all means," he agreed.

"It's about the case that you're on," the stranger said.

And now Bob had him pegged: a retired gentleman with too much time on his hands who read the papers and fancied himself an armchair detective. "I think you'd better leave that to the professionals," he suggested, as kindly as he could—and, he had to admit, a trifle hypocritically, since he himself was hardly a professional.

"Advice you'd do well to take yourself," the man replied, testily. "Believe me, Commandant, this is outside the normal order of things."

"Look," Bob said, in a gentle manner, "I'm sure that you're very good at solving locked room mysteries in detective stories..."

"Your *locked room* isn't locked," the stranger snapped. "You've just come from there yourself."

"It's not locked *now*," Bob agreed, "but it was locked two days ago."

"A room is only ever locked in three dimensions," the man stated. "There are more—you live in four."

Bob smiled. "Don't you?"

"I dislike being confined." The old man reached into his pocket and pulled out a business card which he handed across.

Bob glanced at it. It bore only two words: *DOCTOR OMEGA*. "No phone number?"

"I am not reachable by phone. I... travel extensively." The old man touched the card. "If you need to contact me, tap the card against any piece of metal—the message will reach me wherever I am."

"Are you an inventor… Doctor Omega?"

"I am much more than that, young man." The old man straightened himself to his full height. "Now, if you wish to solve this case, all you need do is to meet me in the vault next Wednesday, shortly before two p.m."

"And then you'll explain everything?" Bob said, smiling.

"I shall do much better than that," Doctor Omega retorted. "You shall witness the murder taking place." His eyes twinkled as he added: "I suggest you bring a camcorder to record it for evidence."

"A what?" Bill asked.

Doctor Omega considered. "Oh dear—what's the day again?"

"Friday," Bill replied.

"No, no—I meant the *year*."

Bill laughed. "You don't know? It's 1960."

"Ah, quite so, quite so." He tapped Bill's chest with his walking stick. "Then I suggest you bring one of those Super-8 film devices." He inclined his head. "Good day, gentlemen."

"You're not going to tell us your theory?" Bill asked him.

"Theory? I have no *theory*, Commandant—just the truth. And there would be no point in my attempting to explain *that* until you have seen what will happen on Wednesday next. Until then." He spun about and marched from the bank.

"Well," Bill said, laughing, "I don't know how you do it, Bob, but you do manage to attract the weird ones."

"I'm not so sure he's crazy, Bill," Bob said slowly. "One thing he said makes a strange kind of sense."

"Well, you're ahead of me, then," Bill confessed. "I thought he was just rambling—a senile old man. Means well, but…" He tapped his temple. "Not all there."

Bob sympathized with his friend's view, but shook his head. "It's that business about us living in four dimensions, and the door being locked only in three…"

"So?"

"Don't tell me you've forgotten about our little adventure with Professor Hunter's time machine!"

Bill shuddered. "How could I ever forget that? Being chased by dinosaurs…" His eyes widened. "You mean he's suggesting that somebody used a time machine to go back and kill Carrigan?"

"Something like that, I imagine. Though there isn't enough room inside that vault for one of Hunter's machines to fit. And I can't imagine anyone simply sitting still when a time machine appeared and a man climbed out—and Carrigan was killed sitting at that table…" Bob shook his head. "And there's something else…"

"What?"

227

"Doctor Omega, as he calls himself, knew my name and my rank. We haven't mentioned the latter to anyone. And he obviously knew we've had experience with time travel. How could he possibly have known all that?" He couldn't make sense of it himself—yet. "I have a strong feeling that we're going to run into the good Doctor again—probably on Wednesday…"

Over the next several days, Bob and Bill had plenty to occupy their time. Bob tried to puzzle through the facts of the case, but got nowhere. More than once, he'd picked up the business card Doctor Omega had given him and then, sighing, put it down again. On the Monday morning, he'd called in at the prefecture de police to see Maigret and ask about the case.

The Commissioner shook his head. "I'm afraid we know no more than we did on Friday. I did meet with the nephew…" He lit his pipe and took a few puffs. "Every instinct I have tells me that he is the guilty man, and yet he has thirty-seven witnesses who saw him at the moment of the killing and who can testify to that in court."

"Could he have hired an assassin to shoot his uncle?" Bill suggested.

"Of course—anyone might have. But we still have that same problem—how did anyone kill Mr. Carrigan in a locked room?" He gave Bob a weary smile. "I am almost ready to believe in your invisible man, my friend."

Bob gave a short laugh. "And I am about ready to believe in something even more fantastic," he admitted. He told the detective about his meeting with Doctor Omega, which made Maigret sit up.

"That would explain this, then," he said.

Reaching into the basket of papers on his desk, he extracted an envelope. From it he took another of Omega's business cards, and a brief note, which he handed across to Bob. It read:

Please be so kind as to meet me in the bank security deposit vault shortly before two p.m. on Wednesday. Commandant Morane and Mr. Ballantine will be present.

"Sure of himself, isn't he?" Bill remarked.

Bob smiled. "I think he's relying on our curiosity, Bill. But he's right—I wouldn't miss this for the world."

Bill scowled. "Do you really think he can deliver what he promised?"

"We'll know in two days," Bob answered.

On the Wednesday, Bob and Bill arrived at the bank at one thirty. Durand-Mareuil was in the lobby, pacing nervously, when they arrived and hurried to meet them.

"Monsieur Morane! Thank goodness you are here! Such goings-on in a respectable bank!"

"Steady on," Bob said. "What do you mean?"

"The police are here again, and have asked me to keep the general public out of the vault for the next hour or so. And there's a strange old man prowling about—he's one of our customers, to be sure, but he's behaving very oddly. And he seems to want to give orders, too."

So, Doctor Omega was here! Bob clapped the bank manager on the shoulder. "Whatever the Doctor told you, I suggest you do. Bill and I are going down to the vault now also, so we'll keep an eye on everything."

Durand-Mareuil looked like he was going to erupt again, so Bob added: "And, relax. With a little luck, we'll have unmasked the killer within the hour, and everything will be able to return to normal. Come on, Bill."

And he hurried down the stairs before the nervous man could protest again.

He could see why Durand-Mareuil was so nervous—there were about a dozen uniformed gendarmes in the basement. Several of them were carrying chairs into the security vault. The others allowed Bob and Bill to pass after checking their credentials.

Inside the vault they found Maigret directing the traffic, with Doctor Omega standing in the background.

"What's going on?" Bob asked.

"Your friend here," Maigret said, pointing at the Doctor with his pipe stem, "says we have to simply observe. In that event, I aim to be comfortable and not simply stand about waiting." Once the four chairs he had required were in place, he waved off the gendarmes. "You two stay here," he directed. "The rest of you, upstairs, and give us some room."

When the room was clearer, he flopped into one of the chairs. "That's better." He glanced up at Doctor Omega. "Now, are you going to explain any of this?"

The old man shook his head. "Not quite yet, my good man—I fear that you would not believe my tale. Once you have seen what is to happen—what *has* happened—ah, *then* I promise to explain everything."

"Now, just a minute," Bill began to protest, but Bob held his arm.

"Let him have his minute, Bill. If he can explain this mystery, I think he's deserved it."

Doctor Omega beamed. "Thank you, my young friend. Now, did you bring your movie camera?"

Bill unslung the bag he was carrying over one shoulder. "It's right here, Doc."

"Good, good. Now, if you set it up here and aim it in this direction..." Then he glared. "And don't call me *Doc*." He indicated a place behind the chair set at the table. He watched as Bill took out a folding tripod and extended it to take the cine camera. "Right! How much film is in there?"

"About twenty minutes."

"Then do not start recording until our killer approaches the table," the Doctor instructed. "Until then, we shall simply wait."

"I'm glad I thought of the chairs," Maigret muttered. He nodded to the one beside him, and Bob sat down also. Bill joined them once he'd finished setting up his camera. Maigret gestured to the fourth chair. "And you, Doctor?"

"Not for me, no. I shall sit here." He settled himself in the chair at the table. "Where our unfortunate victim sat exactly one week ago."

"That's a bit morbid," Bill muttered.

"Now," Doctor Omega said, firmly, "whatever happens, I wish to assure you that I am perfectly safe. Do not interfere with what you are about to witness, any of you. This must play through precisely as it happens."

Bob felt his excitement rising. He had no idea what was to happen—though the Doctor clearly did—but he sensed that it was the final event in a chain forged a while back. It was for moments like this that he lived for—the excitement, the uncertainty, the mystery...

They didn't have long to wait. At five minutes past the hour, there was a noise in the outer hall, and then a man stepped into the vault. He stopped dead as he saw everyone present. Maigret gave a smile. "Donald Carrigan," he said, softly. Bob raised an eyebrow—the prime, impossible suspect.

"What is this?" Carrigan asked the vault guard, who had accompanied him. "I must be alone in here." He held up the small case he was clutching. "That is my right! Clear these men out of here!"

Doctor Omega turned to regard him. There was a faint smile on his lips. "I am sorry, Mr. Carrigan. If you are uncomfortable with an audience, perhaps you would care to come back later?"

"Yes. No. Yes." Carrigan the younger stood stock-still. He was starting to sweat. "Get out, all of you! I must be alone!"

"Mr. Ballantine," Doctor Omega called, and gestured at the camera. Bill hopped up and started it going.

Maigret stood slowly up. "I am Commissaire Maigret," he said. "I am afraid you cannot order me to go anywhere." He sat firmly down again. "I stay."

Bob grinned. "I've nothing better to do this afternoon."

Carrigan was sweating profusely now, and clutching his case tightly. "No," he moaned. "No—I *must* be alone."

"That is not going to happen," Doctor Omega stated. He glanced at his watch. "You have only three more minutes—you had better get busy..."

The young man was moving in a very jerky fashion, like some reluctant puppet being drawn by unyielding strings. He walked, shaking to the other side of the table, where he placed the case with trembling hands. He was sweating a stream now, and his eyes were wild and terrified. It took him three attempts to open the clasp on the case, and his hands trembled as he drew out an odd-looking gun. The part he clasped looked like a normal pistol, but attached to the barrel was a bulky tube-like structure that looked like an over-fed silencer. There were pulsing lights on it, tinier than any Bob had ever seen before.

Carrigan raised the pistol and pointed it directly at Omega's heart.

Bob gave a cry and jumped to his feet, but the old man's hand slashed out. "Stay!" he commanded. "Remember what I told you! I assure you, I am in no danger."

Shaking horribly now, Carrigan was forced to use his other hand to steady his grip on the pistol. Then, with a wild cry of terror, he fired.

Bob was terrified for a second, expecting to see Doctor Omega to collapse, dead. Instead, absolutely nothing happened. There was no sign of a bullet, and the old man was obviously totally unharmed. It made absolutely no sense.

With another cry, Carrigan dropped the strange pistol to the floor. "You fiend!" he hissed. His hand, no longer shaking, thrust into the case, and he pulled out a second pistol, this one a normal-looking Luger. He raised it and pointed it at Doctor Omega. "I don't know how you did that..." he began.

Bob saw the look of fear on the Doctor's face and realized that this was obviously not part of the old man's plan. He sprang forward and delivered a forceful blow to Carrigan's stomach. The man gasped, and folded as Bob wrenched the gun from his hand.

"Thank you, my friend," the Doctor said, wiping his brow with a handkerchief. "I must confess, I did not think he would have a second gun."

"Just glad to help," Bob said.

Maigret motioned to his two gendarmes, one of whom grabbed hold of Carrigan, who was still whooping for air. "It's nice to see that my instincts were not wrong," he said. He glanced at Omega. "I have a strong suspicion that I really do not want too clear an explanation for what I have just witnessed."

The Doctor smiled. "Probably not." He indicated the movie camera. "You have film of Mr. Carrigan there firing the gun. It has his fingerprints on it, and your ballistics department will be able to match the bullet to that gun—which has only the one bullet missing, the one that killed his uncle a week ago. I believe he will confess his guilt rather than go to trial, so that should prevent any necessity for a clearer explanation of what happened here." The second gendarme had carefully picked up the gun. Omega pulled on a pair of white calfskin gloves. "Ah—if I might?"

The policeman looked at Maigret, who nodded. Omega took the pistol and unsnapped the odd device on the end of the barrel, and then handed the pistol back to the officer.

"It's probably better that this not be left here," he said, gently.

Maigret nodded. "I have my killer," he said. "I have my evidence. I will sleep better without an explanation." He picked up Bill's camera. "I'll return this to you later," he promised. He nodded, and the gendarmes preceded him, dragging the shaking Carrigan.

Bill turned to Doctor Omega. "Well, may *he* doesn't want an explanation, but I do! What just happened here? And why on Earth did Carrigan fire that gonzo gun with so many witnesses present?"

"The inexorable force of Temporal Destiny," Doctor Omega replied solemnly. Seeing Bill's blank expression, he chuckled. "Invite me home for tea, and I shall explain everything," he promised.

A short while later, the three of them were seated comfortably in the apartment on the Quai Voltaire with a fresh pot of tea and some small cakes, courtesy of the landlady. Bill couldn't keep his calm any longer.

"All right!" he exclaimed. "We have tea! We have cakes! Now may we have an explanation?"

Bob couldn't help laughing at his friend's vexation. "Well, the first thing is that our friend here is obviously a time traveler."

Doctor Omega smiled. "I knew you would deduce that, my boy. Capital! Yes, I am indeed a wanderer through the dimensions."

"A time traveler?" Bill said, looking surprised. "How do you know?"

"From what he said. Don't you remember? He said that *we* travel in four dimensions—not himself. And the fourth dimension is time. And he didn't know the year, or what recording capabilities we had."

"I thought he was just cra..." Bill caught himself in time and shut up.

"Yes, well," the Doctor said, shifting uncomfortably in his chair. "Anyway, onto the explanation I promised you. As a wanderer through the dimensions, I have the capability of detecting other time travelers. My ship arrived here just over a week ago, and my instruments detected a waning temporal field, so I investigated. It was not far from Royale-les-Eaux, and I found a dying man." The old man frowned. "He was a member of a rather... ah... unpleasant organization. There was—or, from your point of view—will be... It's very difficult discussing temporal matters—languages these days aren't formulated to speak of things that haven't yet happened for you, but are in the far past for someone from the distant future... Oh well, in about three hundred years, there will arise a dictator who will make Hitler and Stalin look like amateurs." He paused. "You *do* know about Hitler and Stalin, right?"

"Yes," Bob said, grinning.

"Oh, good. As I say, I sometimes lose track... Well, this dictator-to-be was killed under mysterious circumstances, so this... temporal group decided to send a man to assassinate him. But they did so rather cleverly. The dictator was—as all such men are—paranoid, and was surrounded by bodyguards constantly. The group realized, though, that *after* his death there wouldn't be a guard. So they built a weapon..."

"That gun!" Bill exclaimed.

"Precisely, young man—that gun. It was programmed to shoot a single bullet exactly one week into the past. The idea was that the assassin would arrive one week after the dictator's death and fire the gun, thus killing the man one week earlier."

"But something went wrong, I take it?" Bob interjected.

"Indeed. When the would-be killer arrived, he was set upon by a group of soldiers who stumbled upon him accidentally. The man was shot and mortally wounded before he could perform his task. He did, however, manage to trigger his return device. But that, too, had been damaged by firing, and it malfunctioned, dropping him onto the road near Royale-les-Eaux some ten days ago.

"He was found by Donald Carrigan, who was driving to the casino. Carrigan found the man delirious, and heard this fantastic story about being a time traveler and owning a gun that could fire exactly one week into the past. Now, Mr. Carrigan is an amoral and lazy young man, with no love for anyone but himself. He left the dying man, but took his weapon. Obviously, he then hit upon the plan to murder his uncle.

"He would create a perfect alibi for himself for the time of his uncle's murder. He knew of his uncle's habit of visiting the bank vault every Wednesday at exactly the same time, so there was his chance! All he would have to do was to go to the bank one week after his uncle's murder and fire the gun..."

"And the bullet from it would travel a week back in time and kill his uncle!" Bill said, excitedly.

"Correct." Doctor Omega steepled his fingers and stared over them at his friends. "Unfortunately for him, though, I, too, discovered the time traveler before he died, and also heard his rambling tale. Naturally, I did not know the name of the man who took the gun—merely that someone had, with the intention of using it. Then, I read a few days later of the most mysterious death of Mr. Carrigan and understood immediately. I presented myself at the bank, and the rest you know."

"Except for the most important bit!" Bill exclaimed. "I get that Carrigan the younger came to the bank with the intention of shooting the gun that killed his uncle—but, when he saw us, why didn't he leave? Why did he stay and reveal his own guilt?"

"Because he was an amateur messing about with time!" Doctor Omega explained. "Such matters should be left strictly to the professionals. You see, my boy, time is unforgiving. Albert Carrigan was murdered last Wednesday shortly after two o'clock. The gun that did it *had* to be fired, then, today at precisely the same moment. It was the only thing that could happen. And though young Carrigan struggled mightily against it, the force of temporal destiny drove him to commit the crime—even with all of us present as witnesses. The crime *had* been committed—therefore it *had* to be committed."

"I think you've strained my brain," Bill complained.

Bob smiled. "It is a bit hard to grasp," he agreed. "And it's lucky Carrigan didn't work out how to change the settings on the gun—that would have messed everything up, wouldn't it?"

Doctor Omega chuckled. "It might have," he agreed. "But, as I said, he's a very lazy young man who would much rather steal and kill than work. I knew he wouldn't take the time to attempt to understand the weapon he had."

233

"Still, it took some nerve to sit in front of that gun while he fired it," Bob commented.

The old man chuckled. "I have faith in the workings of time, my boy. Now, if I might trouble you for another of those excellent little cakes...?"

Frank Schildiner has taken on the mantle of Jean-Claude Carrière, penning the adventures of Gouroull, Carrière's version of Mary Shelley's classic monster, in The Quest of Frankenstein, *published earlier this year by Black Coat press (ISBN978-1-61227-429-4), and in next year's* The Triumph of Frankenstein. *Here is an incident featuring Gouroull that didn't make it into the books...*

Frank Schildiner: *The Taking of Frankenstein*

Late 1935

Humans were odd little creatures. Gouroull found them endlessly bizarre, despite his much extended existence. They fooled themselves into believing almost anything, even that they were capable of stealth.

The human version of furtiveness was a mummer's dance, slow attempts to move in silence that sounded like elephants attempting to tip-toe. They followed this with low, soft breathing that every animal and insect could hear for miles, and the result was ludicrous at best. Their scents alone would mark them for any creature with a properly working nose.

Take the group of humans shadowing Gouroull these last few days. Their behavior was ridiculous as they followed him through the Texas scrubs. Did they believe that, by hiding in the small trees and under bushes, he would be fooled? Did they not realize the stench of the spices they used in their half-rotted meats could be smelled for miles? Apparently not, since they still pursued him and performed complex hand gestures to replace speech.

In this situation, there were two directions Gouroull could take, physically and metaphysically. A box canyon was ahead, a perfect location for an ambush on their part. He would be at a disadvantage, but Frankenstein's most lethal creation was unafraid. Physically, he could turn west and take a different, more rugged path.

But in making this choice, he would also be determining how he would approach the humans circling about him like a pack of flies over a corpse. If he chose the rugged approach, he would kill all these men and proceed on his way. If Gouroull walked into the box canyon, another choice might be made.

In the end, Frankenstein's monster chose the canyon. He had an interest in what would occur next. It was apparent to him that the humans operated under a severe misapprehension. These men, when viewing Gouroull, focused on his inhumanity. Taller than any human, with chalky gray skin, black lips and terrible yellow eyes, Victor Frankenstein's creation was not a man. But they appeared to believe he was naught but a shambling corpse, a barely functional brute. They were very wrong, and would learn as much in a short time.

Therefore Gouroull was unsurprised when a heavy cargo net dropped over his head. He made a brief show of grunting and struggling feebly, watching as these black-clad men wrapped the net tighter about his body. The leader barked orders in a tongue Gouroull didn't understand, and then stepped forward. He held a bamboo pipe in hand and blew a fine powder in the face of Frankenstein's monster. Gouroull watched the man for a moment, and then closed his eyes, his body falling limp.

It was three days later when the team of dacoits returned to the hidden temple of their master. Their assignment—to track and capture the creature known as Gouroull—had been far simpler than they had imagined. Tales of the terrible depredations of this monster were legendary around the world. To find he was nothing more than an oversized brute was slightly disappointing, but they did not complain. They merely bowed to their master and backed out of his laboratory.

Their master smiled as he sat on his wooden throne, staring down at the fallen Gouroull. His assistant, a short pug faced man with a white streak down the center of his head, stood the side. His face seemed to twitch slightly before he spoke, an odd mannerism that didn't appear conscious.

"What are you planning on doing with it? It's just a corpse." The man's voice was low and strong, the voice of one who possessed little fear of his fellow human being.

The one on the throne was an altogether more unique figure. Taller than his counterpart, he possessed a high bulging forehead and eyes filled with a strange mix of intellect and cruelty. Dressed in a long yellow robe, he behaved as if he was the undisputed leader. There was a suspicious, crazed quality to him. He subtly twitched and his eyes scanned all about the room, all the while attempting to behave as if he was a king or an emperor. This gave him an air of paranoid megalomania, made him look capable of terrible acts if his will was denied.

"Just a corpse? You look ,but you do not see, my dear Xavier. This corpse, as you call it, is so much more. You see a dead body, but the great Wu Fang, Master of the Sacred Order of the Golden Dragon and the Chang Li, sees so much more. This detritus is the product of the genius of a man whose intellect almost reached my exalted levels. His name was Victor Frankenstein and this being is his creation. Some of my countrymen have met this monster. The reports of its power and lethal qualities intrigued me."

The man who called himself Wu Fang spoke in a purring tone. There was malice in his every word, the purr of a cat as it toys with its prey.

"Never heard of him. What are your plans?" Xavier asked, stepping closer to the net-enshrouded Gouroull.

"Wu Fang will dissect this deceased beast. Then the secrets of reanimation will be made clear. And then I shall build an army of such monsters. Wu Fang's first act will be to destroy the enemies that have plagued our plans. The first to die will be Val Kildare. That Federal fool shall die in agony. Then Michael Traile, who disrupted our agent's plans. He, too, shall be torn limb from limb. Then this decadent country shall fall when an army of the undead brings a reign of terror to every city!"

Wu Fang raised his hands and began to cackle, his madness unchecked.

That was all Gouroull wished to hear. The sleeping powder of the dacoits was merely an amusing, wasteful attack. Victor Frankenstein's creation didn't breathe. Such potions were utterly useless. But Gouroull wished to know who was pursuing him—and why. Now that he knew, he would end this forever.

Opening his vast maw, his razor sharp teeth clamped down on the net. The heavy fibers ripped like tissue paper. Reaching out with his massive hands, he shredded the remainder of the net. Rearing up, Gouroull reached out and snapped Xavier's neck in a simple twisting motion. The odd-looking scientist had a confused look on his face as he died, and was tossed aside by Frankenstein's monster.

Wu Fang backed up, his eyes wide open. He scrambled about for a weapon, grabbing a small scalpel. He held the tiny blade in front of him, his hands shaking as the massive figure advanced towards him. Gouroull's alien yellow eyes locked in on Wu Fang's, causing the crime leader to shudder involuntarily. The inhuman menace which lay in those amber orbs filled him with terror. He opened his mouth to scream for his loyal followers.

Which was when Gouroull pounced. Before a sound emerged from Wu Fang's lips, a huge hand covered his mouth and lifted him off the ground. Gouroull grinned, his teeth glinting in the light. He then slowly moved closer, bringing Wu Fang up with almost gentle hands. His movements were nearly affectionate—until his fangs clamped down on the villain's carotid artery. Gouroull ripped the gang leader's throat out and dropped him to the ground. Wu Fang tried to gasp, but died unable to utter a sound.

Gouroull walked out of the laboratory, following the scent of the dacoits. Tearing them to bits would finalize this chapter. Then, he would return to his original plans. There was much for him to do...

The story so far: An unlikely but stalwart crew of heroes, Chandu the Mystic, F. X. Gordon a.k.a. El Borak, and Hareton Ironcastle, has been brought together by Sâr Dubnotal to thwart Count Dracula's mad scheme to locate the fabled City of Z buried deep in the Amazon jungle and use a pre-cataclysmic machine to summon the Powers of the Outer Dark and destroy the world as we know it. The Vampire Lord has succeeded in bending the Great Psychagogue to his will by turning his medium, Annunciata, into a vampire; but the three adventurers are hot in pursuit. Now, read on....

Sam Shook: *Bringer of the Outer Dark*
The Eldritch Stones - 2

The Amazon Rainforest, 1929

Hell. That was the only word Ironcastle could use to describe that green inferno in which he and his compatriots marched.

Abandon all hope, ye who enter here, he mused to himself.

Things had been smooth at first for them; along with a company of brave Brazilians, Hareton Ironcastle, Francis Xavier Gordon, and Frank Chandler had found the rainforest to be mere child's play compared to the dangers they had faced in adventures past. It was no Gondokoro or Yolgan, that much was certain. Amongst the tangled vines and trees, so tall they blocked the very sun, Ironcastle felt right at home. For Gordon, this wasn't his usual haunt, but with a rifle in his hands and his scimitar and a six-gun by his side, he felt as though he could take on anything. Chandler was thrilled by the experience as well. At first, they thought the task would be daunting, but soon they discovered there was an odd beauty to the roaring, great Amazon River, and its curious wildlife. Squirrels, capybaras, coati, and even monkeys would peek around trees curiously to witness the explorers.

At first, the insects and occasional jaguar were the only things that presented danger. The men who accompanied them were able to either convince the various tribes they came across to let them through, or they would give the tribal leaders tribute in exchange for safe passage. Ironcastle found Fawcett's advice here to be useful. People are far less likely to kill you if you don't look like you're going to kill them.

Gordon was especially impressed with Pedro, an older fellow who would later shoot himself to free his mind from the terrors he witnessed in the deeper forest. Before then, though, Pedro had used his guile and silver tongue to get them out of a sticky situation with a few chieftains. It reminded Gordon of his past exploits when, with charm and diplomacy alone, he could get the aid of all sorts of people in the East.

As for Ironcastle, he didn't blame the tribes for their wariness; numerous "civilized" men had done horrendous things to their people. Furthermore, they had been terrorized by the "Pale Man," or as we call him, Dracula, whom he and his companions were desperately hunting. Overall, though, the small band of travelers believed that they were prepared for any threat that came their way.

But that was two weeks ago.

When they reached the deeper parts of the forest, when the dead began to stalk them from the dark places, and madness was all around, the three explorers soon found themselves to be quite alone. One by one, their company had fallen. Gabriel had his blood drained by an errant vampire. Poor Leonardo, the last one to stay with them, had run screaming into the night when insanity finally had taken hold of him. Gordon had called the deserters "cowards," but Ironcastle harbored no ill will towards them. Truth be told, if the situation were not so dire, this would be the last place he would want to be.

Again, he thought it was nothing like Gondokoro, but that is because Gondokoro was nowhere near as terrible as this place. The deeper forest was alive—and it was evil. The vines grew in tentacular shapes, and would try to grab the adventurers. The spells of ancient Muvian sorcerers still infected the soil and the plant life. The kapok trees grew tall, but something was ineffably wrong about them. Gordon would grip his rifle tighter as he passed one. Chandler looked uneasy around the trees, and Ironcastle found that, whenever he looked at them, there was a certain anthropomorphic quality about them. He could almost swear it looked as if they were contorted into a picture of unspeakable suffering.

Stones were marked with maddening symbols, and the outposts of the Mi-Go were scattered and overgrown throughout. Birds and other wildlife seemed to avoid this place. Not even the mosquitoes, which had harassed them in the early parts of their expedition, were bothering them now. There was nothing but the wind between the trees, only rarely broken by an intermittent comment by one of the men.

They were almost out of supplies, but they pressed onward. Sâr Dubnotal guided them with messages to Chandler, and the three men were determined to reach him and stop his captor.

"So," Chandler said, picking up his pace to be even with Ironcastle, "Dubnotal has informed me that we're catching up."

"That's good news," Ironcastle replied.

"Unfortunately," continued Chandler, "it's because Dracula and his 'children' took a day to feed on a village out this way. As far as the Sâr knows, there were no survivors."

Ironcastle sighed. This creature was the vilest of things he had encountered. He looked again at the Staff of Solomon. Soon, they would drive it into that monster, and perhaps rid the world of his dark influence.

From what he could tell, the sun was setting; they'd need to make camp soon, for though no wild beasts stalked them, there were worse things that could come out of the gloom. As he pondered these thoughts, he also wondered how the Sâr fared…

Sâr Dubnotal walked side by side with Count Dracula, his old nemesis. After his manic episode in the automobile, the vampire had returned to the demeanor that Dubnotal was used to: quiet, cunning, and calculating. He was looking healthy, more so than when the Sâr had first seen him. That was also the reason, the Sâr figured, why he hadn't changed his appearance when they had encountered one another, back in Rio. While working with El Borak, feeding off of blood would have been an impossible task, being in the desert and such. Since gorging on those poor villagers, though, that had changed. He could alter his appearance at will.

As he looked behind him, the Sâr could see Annunciata closely following the Count, like a loyal pet. He hated himself for letting that happen to his medium. She was like a daughter to him, and he had failed her. Above all else, he loathed that thrice-damned villain, Dracula. Dubnotal had faced the Count's fiendish children many times in the past. He had seen the numerous lives ruined by his dark influence. Yet, they had only met face to face a couple of times prior. Those times, however, are stories for another day.

One of the vampires in Dracula's command came up to him, and the two began to confer. Dubnotal took this opportunity to try to speak with Annunciata.

"Annunciata," he said.

She didn't even acknowledge him.

"Annunciata," he repeated.

This time, she looked at him, but still didn't reply. Unfortunately, any conversation they might have was interrupted by Dracula.

"Tell me, *El Tebib*, how is your arm?"

It hurt like the devil, but Dubnotal kept a stern façade, and said, "About as one would expect after one's radius has been fractured."

"Not well, then, I take it?"

The Sâr refused to dignify that question with an answer.

"Just be grateful I didn't remove your arm entirely."

Something was slightly peculiar about Dracula. It wasn't like him to work so overtly. He would brag of being of the Székely people, talking about their "heroic blood," and so on. Perhaps he was acting on his boast? The Great Psychagogue doubted that, though; he could see through the Count's cordial mask and amicable conversation.

"Tell me, my old enemy," he asked, "what brings the greatest of vampires out from skulking in the shadows like a coward and into this part of the world?"

Dracula shot him a look of utter rage, and then calmed himself.

"My friend," he replied, "I've little idea what you mean."

"There's no point in hiding the truth from me, Count. You're not the sort who actively seeks out such risky voyages. You are the devil in the details, and work from the darkness. I know you well enough to know there's more to this than you are letting on. You say my many victories have made my senses dull. I think your many defeats have made you desperate. So tell me, what drove you so far from your home to take up this errand?"

Dracula's face was like a statue. Despite the vampire's cool manner, the Sâr saw something that looked like dread behind his eyes.

"You know the sort of places where one find the knowledge imparted by the stones, *El Tebib*. After all, you are the Great Psychagogue... It could not have been but one moment that they spoke to me, but their starry wisdom still burns in my mind..."

Dracula was many things: immortal, warrior, nosferatu, and necromancer, but even one such as him was not immune to the eldritch forces from beyond.

"So that's it then. You had commune with the Great Old Ones."

With a toothy smile, Dracula replied, "They do have an effect on you, don't they? To sate your curiosity, the ulterior motive you seek in me is compulsion. True, I may wish to activate this machine, so I may be always at the height of my power, but once this task is fulfilled, the compulsion the Old Ones gave to me will be gone. I know not how, but I know it will."

Dealing with Dracula was already a dangerous enough proposition, but dealing with a half-mad Dracula could only be worse, the Sâr thought. Suddenly, he heard a droning buzz behind them. Normally, hearing some animal life in this God-forsaken place would have been welcome, but he recognized this as the same sound he'd heard in front of the Copacabana Palace Hotel.

"Mi-Go!"

Dracula and his servants turned and, from behind them, appeared seven of the Fungi from Yuggoth. With his good hand, the Sâr began to make a mystic sign, but, as he looked about him, he saw that neither the Count nor his minions looked alarmed.

"Fight, you fools! They are upon us!"

Dracula merely laughed. "Oh, *El Tebib*, they have been following us since yesterday. You said it yourself: once Gordon and I got our hands on the black stone, they would continue to chase us. I struck them down, and now they live again and are mine to command."

Looking at them a bit longer, Dubnotal saw that the Mi-Go had been somehow mutated. It seemed that their bodies did not react well to the Count's dark kiss.

"Go," Dracula said to them.

The monsters droned out something in reply, and shambled off. Dubnotal feared the worst.

In the camp, the three men were huddled in a raggedy tent. The weather had turned sour. Though rain was not uncommon here, this storm came completely out of nowhere. Fog, too, had rolled in, and they could barely see from beyond the edges of their camp. Chandler was again speaking to the Sâr, sharing esoteric advice that neither Ironcastle nor Gordon fully understood. Nonetheless, this was the only thing that gave them any semblance of hope in this foreboding time. When everything else closed in around them, they could always at least count on the Great Psychagogue.

"I am reaching out to the mind of Sâr Dubnotal," Chandler said, gazing into his crystal ball as he always did whenever he had contacted *El Tebib*. "Sâr, can you hear me?"

A moment later, Chandler heard a voice in his head: *I can.*

Chandler breathed a sigh of relief. Every time he tried to contact Dubnotal, there was always that fear in the back of his mind that there would be no response, that the Count would have... He pushed the thought from his mind. There was no need to worry as long as the Sâr was alive.

I apologize, Chandu, I cannot give you any words of hope. I can give you a warning. Not but a moment ago, Dracula has set his servant...

The Psychagogue's voice suddenly stopped. Chandler's heart sank. He feared the worst.

"Sâr Dubnotal? Sâr?... Sâr?"

I... something... interferes... how?...

Then an unfamiliar voice assaulted Chandler's mind. It was ancient and its wretched laugh chilled him to the bone.

Hello, Chandu. We have met, but I fear we haven't been formally introduced.

"No," mumbled Chandler, eyes wide, "it can't be!"

My name is Count Dracula.

"How...?"

I have lived long, Chandu, and I know many things. I know sorcery and forbidden knowledge. I have fought in wars long before you were even an idea. I have made pacts with the Devil that would be beyond your understanding. Do you think that mere thought transmission would be difficult for me? Young fool! I could hear everything that you and El Tebib *said to one another.*

"What... Why haven't you stopped us? Why risk us catching you?"

Because if El Tebib *knew from the beginning that it was hopeless, I'm sure he would be willing to give up his life to prevent me from finding the machine. Make him think there is hope that you will catch me, make him think I am not clever enough to figure out his game and...*

"And he becomes more compliant. You should not have given away your plan so easily."

I would not have told you if there was any way for you to stop me. We are on the doorstep of the City of Z, and I have a gift for the three of you. Can you hear the droning? Your death is nigh. Farewell, Chandu, I suspect we shall not speak again.

Ironcastle and Gordon looked puzzlingly at Chandler. He sat with a forlorn look on his face. Normally, he of all people was best at keeping his sanity, especially after communicating with Sâr Dubnotal.

"Everything's alright?" Gordon questioned.

Suddenly, the all too familiar buzzing rang out through the trees. They could hear it even through the deluge and the thunder.

Ironcastle leapt to his feet and grabbed his elephant gun.

"We have company," he shouted.

The horrid beasts descended upon the camp in a fury. They tore through the adventurers' shelter, smashing a kerosene lamp which they had used to light the area, burning the tent. Fortunately, the men were already out of there and fighting.

But something was wrong.

Ironcastle had shot a Mi-Go with both barrels. Gordon had put a bullet each in the heads of six others, and unloaded six rounds into one's torso. Yet, none of the creatures fell. They kept fighting despite their grievous injuries. Ironcastle pulled out his own revolver and fired at them; Gordon blasted them point blank with his Lee-Enfield, but these failed too. Then, Ironcastle drew his hunting knife and began viciously stabbing the Mi-Go, but they were like a wild boar that refused to die. Chandler crushed one's neck with his boot. Even still, the creatures would not fall.

Ironcastle was getting desperate. He embedded his knife into one of the creature's skulls, and went for the last weapon he had available: the Staff of Solomon. The moment he hoisted it, the Mi-Go recoiled in fear. Now, he saw what had happened. These monsters had been turned by Dracula. He struck one with the Staff. The eyes of the carved cat-head burned with emerald fire, and the Mi-Go was instantly reduced to ash. Gordon ceased his relentless bludgeoning with the butt of his rifle. He had never seen a weapon of such power before.

"You waited until now to use that?" he complained.

Ironcastle flashed a grim smile before driving the staff through another Mi-Go. Soon, the night was filled with the shrieks of the eldritch beasts.

After their encounter with the Mi-Go, the three adventurers had not gotten a wink of sleep. The storm had still not let up. They supposed it wasn't much different from the night before, or the one before that... It was the Great War all over again. They were completely exhausted, but knew they would carry on.

It was while they were packing up their undamaged supplies that Gordon asked Chandler, "Tell me, what did the Sâr say to you last night? You looked like you'd seen Hades."

The mystic didn't want to kill any courage they had left, but he knew he owed them the truth. "Gentlemen, I'm afraid I can't mince words. This has all been a trap. We were drawn into this place in order to bait the Sâr into complying with Dracula's scheme."

Chandler could practically see the life fade from his compatriot's eyes. "As if that weren't bad enough, he has always been able to overhear my conversations with Dubnotal, and can get inside my head to drive out our friend's mental voice. We have no more guide and our foe is about to reach the City of Z. We were doomed from the start."

Upon hearing this, Ironcastle removed his slouch hat, ran his hands across his scalp, and rubbed his eyes. For a while, the three men stood in silence, before Ironcastle eventually said, "So, there is no hope for us?"

It was unusual for any of these men to admit to the grim reality of the situation. How many times in their lives had they survived by the skin of their teeth? How many times had they looked death square in the eye and said "Not today"? How many times had they been saved by one thing or another at the last minute? And now, it looked as if their luck had finally run out. This time, there was no way out. Ironcastle thought about their state of affairs. Without Sâr Dubnotal to guide them, they had no chance of finding the mystical city, and they didn't have enough supplies to turn back and get help. They weren't even sure they had enough to keep moving forward! Dracula had won. They were too late. They weren't in the habit of giving up, but did they even stand a chance?

Gordon looked at his scimitar. He mused on how he always thought he'd die to a Jezail bullet, or an Englishman's revolver. Had he come so far, only to perish such a long way away from both Texas and the Arabian Peninsula?

Chandler thought about his sister, his brother-in-law, his nieces and nephews, and Nadji. He thought of her most of all. She would wait, growing old as she hoped, praying for his return, even when she knew it would be impossible.

Ironcastle thought back to his time in Gondokoro when Muriel had rescued all of them; had she not been there, they would have been goners. He wished she was here now. He could see her in a black veil, along with Sidney and Philippe dressed in their best, as the members of the Gun Club all had a drink in his honor. Tears would stream down his daughter's face. He couldn't bear the thought of it! He hoisted up the remains of their supplies, and began to march through the mud.

"Our Father in Heaven, Thou art my rock and my fortress; therefore for Thy name's sake lead me, and guide me." He began to pray, quoting the Book of Psalms. He trudged, step by step, though fatigue made him want to quit, he forced himself to go on.

"Pull me out of the net that they have laid privily for me…" ten feet, twenty feet, forty, sixty. Step by step, he continued in the initial direction they were heading towards. It was no guarantee, but he wasn't going to give up. He would not die here. He would not!

Soon, Gordon and Chandler followed him.

For nearly half an hour, he continued like this. Marching and praying. At last, weary, starving, and bereft of hope, Ironcastle stumbled and fell backwards into the mire. He whispered out over and over again, "For Thou art my strength… for Thou art my strength… for Thou art my strength… don't… let it… end… here…"

Several miles away, Dracula looked at the great golden walls of the City of Z, marked with arcane glyphs. Even in ruin, it was still beyond belief. At last, all of his planning, all of his research, all of his patience, had paid off.

"*El Tebib*," he said, "you have proved invaluable to this expedition. Now there's but one more duty for you to perform. Find us the machine hidden amongst these ruins."

One of Dracula's minions shoved the Sâr forward. The Great Psychagogue would try to stall for as much time as he could, though he didn't have much hope left. He feared that he might have to pull out his trump card… but if he did, then the world would regret it.

When Ironcastle woke up, he was somewhere warm and dry. He could hear that it was still raining outside. To his left, Chandler lay unconscious, and to his right, Gordon was talking with a woman he didn't recognize. She was about a little taller than him, dark-skinned, and wore a white tunic with a gold belt. Around her neck was a stone amulet with an eldritch symbol carved into it. He thought they were talking, but when his vision cleared, he could see that they were gesticulating and drawing symbols on the ground. He supposed that each was trying to overcome the language barrier.

Gordon was a patient man, but he was getting tired of this elaborate game of charades. He could keep at it all day, but it seemed they could find no common ground, even with the symbols. After a few more minutes, a man wearing a jaguar pelt around his waist walked in, carrying a wooden bowl. He took a sip himself, then gave it to the woman, and then handed it to Gordon to drink. Thirsty, the explorer obliged. As he did so, he heard the man and woman arguing in their native tongue. Then, quite suddenly, after finishing the sweet tasting liquid, he heard the woman say:

"I mean, do you have any idea if the elixir will work, Aeon?"

Gordon coughed, choking on the fluid. *Did she just speak English? Fatigue must be getting to me.*

"Of course it will! Have I ever been wrong before?"

Gordon could not believe it. Only a moment ago, they spoke a language that sounded like some form of Spanish crossed with Egyptian, and now, as sure as there was ground beneath him, they were speaking English.

"I'll test it," the one apparently called Aeon said. "I'll start with simple words; I'm not sure how intelligent this interloper is." Aeon got very close to Gordon's face and began to say very slowly: "Do... You... Hear... What... I... Am... Saying?"

"How did you start speaking English?"

"Ah, wonderful, we can understand each other! I knew the elixir worked."

"Yes, Aeon, you've done very well for yourself," the woman said, before mumbling under her breath, "for once."

"Now," Aeon continued, "did you drink all of it, or did you save any for your brothers?"

"They aren't my brothers, but yes, I saved some."

"Fantastic."

Ironcastle lay very confused. It was as if he was hearing only half a conversation. Actually, that seemed to be exactly the case. Somehow, Gordon was able to understand them, and they, him. Gordon walked over, and gave the bowl to Ironcastle to drink. His throat was exceptionally dry; he practically wrenched the bowl from Gordon's hands and took a large swig. When he heard Aeon start speaking English, he was mildly surprised. But he had seen stranger things before this day.

Sâr Dubnotal had done all that he could to stall Dracula, but eventually, after looking at every ruined building, and every remnant, a few of them twice, he had no other option left than going to that one, single door. It was so simple, so unsuspecting... It looked little more than a hatch to a cellar, but there it was, the treasure room.

They dusted it off, and saw a gold lock covered in runes. In it were three indentions. Upon closer examination, they saw how each of the indention had different carvings inside, each corresponding to a different stone. Dracula beckoned one of his minions over, who brought his leather case in which he held the eldritch stones. It was the same leather case in which Dracula, disguised as Professor Webb, had promised to take the stones to be photographed. One by one, Dracula set each orb into place, first the golden orb of Mu, then the black stone of Yuggoth, and finally the ruby of Opar.

The door opened.

In a last desperate attempt, the Sâr reached out to Annunciata:

Annunciata, if you are there, somewhere, I beseech you! Help me end this. I don't think Ironcastle and his company will be here in time.

This time, something seemed to resonate within the medium, as her face suddenly took the look of one who has long forgotten something, but knows it's important. Yet, she couldn't remember.

The time had come. The Sâr had to use the one thing he wished he didn't have to. It would be the cruelest act of his life, but he had no other option. As they descended into that vile darkness, he saw in the dim lights of the eternally burning torches, made of the luminescent rocks of Yuggoth, the gears and mechanisms of that abominable monolith. The object of their search stood before them.

Dracula breathed in the musty air. He closed his eyes, and simply drank in the moment. His long awaited triumph was here! All it would take would be a simple pull of a lever, carved into the likeness (if such a thing exists) of Yig. That was when Dubnotal said something the Count had not expected:

"Voivode Vlad Țepeș, Son of the Dragon, Lord of Vampires, you will not activate this machine. If you so much as touch that lever, you leave me with no choice but to use one of my greatest incantations. I will utter the Deplorable Word, and I will destroy you, and this accursed place!"

For a few seconds, Dracula looked legitimately shocked, but then began to laugh. "No, you will not. If you did that, good doctor, you would bring this entire continent down with us. I do not think you can bring yourself to do it."

Dubnotal kept his icy gaze upon the Count, "Try me."

After Chandler had woken up and taken the draught, the adventurers had become acquainted with their rescuers. After Ironcastle had collapsed, Gordon and Chandler had attempted to carry him. They had spotted a nearby hut, hoping that it was either empty, or home to someone who would help them. It was then that Chandler had attempted to contact the Sâr once again, only for Dracula to do something to his mind, and put him to sleep.

Gordon, mustering all of his strength, had hoisted one man on each shoulder and carried them the rest of the way. That is when he had met the ones they now knew as Aeon and Haz'El. They were cousins, and the only two survivors of the village that Dracula had attacked. Even more surprising, when Ironcastle had asked what the name of their tribe was, for the sake of his journal, they told him that they didn't consider themselves of a particular tribe, but that they were survivors from Mu. They could trace their lineage back to the priest of Shub-Niggurath named T'yog, and, more recently, to some of the sorcerers of the City of Z, whose talent, it seemed, they shared. With this knowledge in mind, the adventurers inquired about the machine, and repeated the story that the Sâr had told them. Once they had finished, Haz'El shook her head.

"While mostly true, I fear this magician-friend of yours has one detail incorrect."

"What do you mean?" Ironcastle asked.

Haz'El continued gravely, "The machine does not make the night unending. It tears a hole in the sky, and brings the Outer Dark, and, with it, the end of all things."

None had anything to say at this point. As if things weren't bad enough. Ironcastle asked her to elaborate.

"The Muvian priests who lived in the golden city believed that history moved around and around like a wheel," she said, illustrating her point by drawing a circle in the dirt. "They believed that when this world would end, a new one would be brought forth from its ashes. When we die, it allows life to continue, like rain watering corn. The sea-raiders marched on us with such a fury; it looked like all hope was lost. The priests decided that it would be better to end this world's cycle, and hope that the next one would be a better one."

"An overreaction, if you ask me," Aeon mumbled.

Haz'El chuckled, before returning to her grave tone. "The ones from Yuggoth and the worshipers of the Yellow King helped create that device to awaken the Dark Outer Gods who would end the world that we know. If the Pale Man activates the machine, then..."

Haz'El shuddered. Aeon finished her thought, "Everything will die. We will look at the sky, and see only those from the spaces beyond: Azathoth, Yog-Sothoth, The Lord of Spiders, The Crawling Chaos, the serpent god Set... We'd pray to Shub-Niggurath for a quick and merciful death. Your magician-friend said the machine was used for two weeks and it destroyed the golden city? No. It was on only for a matter of minutes."

Haz'El finished for her cousin, "You see now the danger at hand. We must stop the Pale Man, at any cost."

"Are you mad?" Aeon asked. "Do you think we have any chance in the slightest against him?"

"What would you have us do, Aeon? Barricade ourselves in our little shack, waiting for the end to come?"

"Well... no, but what can we do?"

"Kill the Pale Man, get revenge for our village, or die trying."

"But how?" asked Aeon. "You saw what he could do, cousin. What hope have we to slay this demon who walks as a man?"

"This," Gordon said, taking from their supplies the Staff of Solomon.

Haz'El and Aeon's eyes widened.

"Atlantean!" Haz'El said.

Gordon nodded, and then said, "I've seen what this weapon can do and I don't think that even the mighty Count Dracula can stand against it."

"That changes everything," Aeon said, with greater vigor. He leapt to his feet, along with Haz'El, and said, "We will show you the way. I know we know not one another very well, but for now, you are our brothers."

With that, the adventurers grabbed their weapons. It was five against the most dangerous of all vampires, and his undead servants. Ironcastle picked up the staff; Gordon smiled grimly. He didn't like their odds, but it was going to be a hell of a fight nonetheless.

Sâr Dubnotal and Dracula stood facing one another, like gunslingers, waiting for the toll of high noon, though, outside, a moonless night had fallen. The Great Psychagogue had said each syllable of the Deplorable Word, save for the last. Dracula stared, fierce and wolf-like, as if waiting for his enemy to make his move. The look he gave Dubnotal practically screamed, *Do it! You have come this far. I defy you to finish that word. Go on. Make South America a modern Atlantis. Finish it!*

Dubnotal looked around. There were no signs of hope. Just as he was about to form that last syllable, two of Dracula's undead minions ran into the room.

"Master! It's... It's..."

"Speak up. What is it?" Dracula commanded, visibly annoyed.

"The guard you left at the entrance; he just walked in to the antechamber... and he... and he..."

"He did what?"

"He went insane; he started killing the others. Then there was some native who ran in and smashed a clay pot, and then the room filled with miasma that killed the rest. I was the only survivor!"

The other minions looked around at one another, then to Dracula, who, in turn, looked at Dubnotal. The Sâr, however, looked as confused as the Count.

Suddenly, six gunshots rang out, and six vampires grabbed at their legs, and fell to the ground. Five people walked into the room: the three adventurers Dracula recognized, and a man and woman whom he didn't know.

Gordon stood there with the barrel of his iron still smoking. The Count shot a deathly glare at them. They shouldn't have been able to make it. There was no way... he noted, however, that the people who accompanied Ironcastle, El Borak, and Chandu were dressed like those from the village. He didn't know how they survived, but he knew that it was a mistake he must correct.

He signaled his minions to charge. As the score whose legs had not been shot attacked, Dracula went over to the machine, and pulled the lever, then snapped it in two so that no one could disable the contraption.

The gears started to whir and dead furnaces lighted themselves anew. Aeon took out the second clay pot, filled with an elixir made with silver shavings, and hurled it at the charging vampires. Almost all of them succumbed immediately to the concoction. Two or three escaped, but they soon met their end by being crippled with lead, then impaled with the Staff of Solomon.

"Dracula!" shouted Ironcastle over the sounds of the ancient monolith, "What have you done? If the machine's allowed to run, then everything dies. There will be no world for you to rule; only a shell left behind by the Outer Gods!"

Dracula scoffed, "Do you take me for a fool, Hareton? Your lies will not work on me."

"You are the fool!" Haz'El cried. "Bringer of the Outer Dark, end this, now!"

"Never! Now, bow before your new god and despair!"

"Go," said Gordon, "help the Sâr turn off this contraption. We'll take care of Dracula." He quickly reloaded his six gun and holstered it. He slung the rifle off his shoulder.

"Let's finish this," Ironcastle said, drawing his revolver. The Staff of Solomon burned with eldritch fire in his other hand.

Chandler stared with grim determination. He thought of Nadji, and it filled him with courage. "Your time has come, Dracula!"

Suddenly, the Count vanished into the shadows. There was a noise from behind them, and there he was! He struck at Gordon, who blocked him with his rifle, but the force of Dracula's blow shattered the wooden frame and bent the barrel. Ironcastle swung at him with the Staff of Solomon, but, with inhuman speed, Dracula twirled out of the way, and leapt onto the wall, hanging on the side like a hellish reptile. Chandler fired his gun at him, but the Count again vanished.

He appeared on the opposite wall, where he tore one of the Yuggoth torches from its sconce, and hurled it at Ironcastle. Gordon shot it out of the air. Dracula believed that, were he stabbed or beheaded by Gordon's scimitar, he *might* die—it wouldn't be the first time cold iron had killed him—but he knew that if he was so much as touched by King Solomon's staff, he would *certainly* die. As such, he wanted to end the fight quickly, but these vermin refused to fall.

Over by the lever mechanism, Dubnotal conferred with the two Muvians psychically. He may not be able to understand their spoken language, but the mind communicated with ideas, not words. Fortunately, being somewhat skilled magicians themselves, they could understand him. Dubnotal questioned if they had any rituals that could stop this. Haz'El reached into her bag and withdrew several parchments. She and Aeon poured over them, until their faces lit up. They had discovered something useful, something which could create a small but powerful earthquake to collapse the building—the same sort of ritual used to protect temples from intruders. If they did that, the machine would be destroyed, and it could never plague humanity again.

Suddenly, they heard Dracula shriek "My children! Kill *El Tebib*!"

The six who had been shot, but whose legs had now healed, started to run towards the Sâr, Haz'El and Aeon, who were doing their best to deactivate the machine.

The three adventurers rushed to aid their friend, but Dracula charged them. He clawed at Chandler, who barely managed to avoid being eviscerated. The Vampire Lord backhanded him, and sent him flying into the wall. Gordon slashed at the Count with his scimitar, but the Vampire dexterously avoided the crescent blade. The adventurer swung at him with all the mastery which only years of swordsmanship could confer, but every time, Dracula managed to avoid his attacks. This, however, enabled Chandler to shoot the Count in the shoulder, and Ironcastle to finally stab him with the Staff.

Dracula let out an inhuman noise, before instantly turning into mist, allowing Ironcastle's attack to pass harmlessly through him; he floated away and vanished.

Meanwhile, Dubnotal had formed a mystic sign to protect his two new friends. Unfortunately, it was no use; the vampires were too fast. They grabbed his broken arm, and he briefly lost his concentration. They mobbed him, Aeon, and Haz'El, and began to scratch and bite at their flesh. The undead cackled in delight.

But for Annunciata, something felt wrong. She hadn't participated in this fight, as if she just couldn't bring herself to harm Dubnotal. Something, a small sliver of conscience in the back of her mind, prevented her.

"Annunciata!" cried the Sâr, "if you are still in there, somewhere, I beg you, please help!"

As this transpired, Dracula rematerialized, now as a large, black dog. He tackled Ironcastle, knocking his revolver from his hand, and clamped down on his shoulder. Gordon lunged at the beast with his sword and pierced the dog's side. It yelped, and Ironcastle kicked it off and picked up the Staff again. Gordon helped Ironcastle up, and Dracula shifted back into his "human" form. As the Vampire leapt to his feet, Gordon hauled leather and put a round between the Count's eyes. The bullet passed through him harmlessly; not even El Borak's exceptional speed could help him here. He looked over to the six vampires who tormented the Sâr and his companions.

Dubnotal was being savaged by the vampires, and again he cried "Annunciata!"

Memories came pouring back into her head, and a tear rolled down her cheek. Just as Dubnotal, Aeon, and Haz'El were about to give in and die, he heard a voice say "Doctor..." He made eye contact with his medium. Another tear rolled down her cheek, and she let out a scream, and charged into the fray. Over from across the way, they heard a cry of agony.

Chandler had fallen to his knees: Dracula had broken his thigh bone. The adventurers stood back to back, as the Count practically danced around them, striking at them, as they attempted to strike back. Gordon would swing his scimitar; if it didn't pass through him as he went into his mist form, Dracula would avoid it easily. Hareton would try to stab at him with the Staff, and Chandler would throw a punch, but none ever hit their mark. They were cut, bruised, bleeding, and simply losing their spirit. Now, more than ever, it was important they destroy the monolith, and, with Annunciata helping slay the attacking vampires, it could at last be done.

Dracula understood what was happening and decided that this distraction had gone on long enough. Gordon and Hareton were too wounded to keep fighting, and had collapsed. He leapt over to where the four occultists worked their magic, grabbing Gordon's ruined rifle along the way. As he left the three men, however, he failed to notice Ironcastle dragging himself over to Chandler and whispering something to him.

Dracula first brought his weapon down upon Aeon, smashing his ribcage, and then, as his cousin ran to his aid, the Vampire Lord hoisted her up in the air. He sampled her blood, before hurling her back to the ground, kicking her in the face. The Count next brought the club down on Annunciata's head. She lived, but would be out cold for a while.

And then there was only one: Sâr Dubnotal gave him a defiant glare. In return, Dracula made a red-lipped, toothy smile, his eyes full of malice.

"Lambs to the slaughter!" he bellowed, "You think you know my wrath, *El Tebib*? Ha! You know nothing, but I will show you!"

Just as he was raising the twisted club of wood and metal to deliver a killing blow to the Great Psychagogue, he heard the voice of Chandu call:

"Dracula! Face me!"

Dracula looked over his shoulder. He would not have his moment ruined; so he picked up the broken lever, and threw it like a javelin to pin the magician to the wall. The projectile whizzed by, barely missing, but Chandu continued to speak, fingers to his temple, looking the Count directly in his burning eyes.

"Dracula, your will is no longer your own."

The Count felt a strange feeling in his head.

The fool dares to control my mind? he thought.

Dracula's eyes burned even brighter, as he said:

"No, Chandu, I fear that *your* will is no longer your own." Then a truly wicked idea came to him. "You will shoot the Psychagogue. Take out your gun," Dracula commanded, "and kill him."

Chandler didn't want to, but he couldn't control himself. Dracula's psychic abilities were beyond any he had ever faced. Slowly, he drew his revolver and aimed it.

"Do it!" said Dracula.

Suddenly, he heard something next to him, but he was too late. An incredible pain shot through his stomach. He looked down to see that Hareton Ironcastle had lugged himself over, Staff of Solomon in hand, and driven the weapon into the Vampire Lord's abdomen. The eyes of the carved cat blazed as Dracula was consumed by flame and crumbled to ash. He shrieked and wailed as he was reduced to nothingness.

Ironcastle looked over to Chandler, who had now dropped his gun and was breathing heavily.

"Honestly," Ironcastle said, "I'm just as surprised as you that he fell for it, old bean."

Time, unfortunately, was still of the essence. Sâr Dubnotal worked furiously at adding the finishing touches to the ritual, until, finally, he felt the ground beneath him begin to shake.

"Quickly," he said, "we must leave!"

Ironcastle supported Chandler on his shoulder, while Gordon helped Aeon and Haz'El, and Dubnotal aided Annunciata. The great stone cogs began to fall around them, shattering in thunderous crashes as they hit the floor. They hastened through the antechamber and the hall, until they reached the stairs.

They emerged from the hatch just as the roof began to fall. As they stood in the wreckage of the ancient golden city, for the first time in weeks, they could stop for a breath, and feel a sense of relief.

Epilogue: The Gun Club, A year later

Hareton Ironcastle sat comfortably in his high backed leather chair by the fireplace. The pure snow of a new year fell and settled gently on the roof. He expected Muriel and Philippe soon, but first, he had to finish his correspondence to Sâr Dubnotal.

In the letter he had received from the good doctor, he was told how, though it had been a lengthy process, but thanks to some help from Professor Van Helsing, the Great Psychagogue had managed to undo the dark magic of Dracula. Annunciata, though shaken, should be fine. Aeon and Haz'El had started a new life with a friendly tribe. Gordon had returned to the East and continued his life of adventure. Chandler had gone back to Egypt to be with Princess Nadji—a warm thought which made Ironcastle smile.

As for the eldritch stones, they posed no more threat. With the machine destroyed, they were nothing more than harmless, but pretty trinkets. Dubnotal had taken the black stone of Yuggoth to study it further. He had sent the gold Muvian orb to the Smithsonian Institute as proof of the ancient continent. As for the Opar ruby, well, Ironcastle looked at a lovely wrapped parcel on the coffee table. He picked up his pen and added to his letter, "I do believe that Muriel and Philippe will love their Christmas present."

Bob Morane (whom we met earlier in John Peel's tale) returns in this vignette from Michel Stéphan, based on a urban legend that one hears in Los Angeles...

Michel Stéphan: *One Summer Night at Holy Cross*

Los Angeles, 1956

In general, Robert Morane knew that he could rely on the steadiness of his nerves. This was not vanity on his part; it was simply that he made it a point of honor to remain in control of himself in any situation. He was still young, and yet had lived more fully than most ordinary persons did in their entire lifetime. He knew that, despite the coolness that had hitherto seldom failed him, there were pitfalls that he should avoid, should he wish to remain the master in any kind of situations.

This was the summer when Robert Morane reached a milestone in his life and took a step too far, gaining a spiritual growth which, frankly, he felt he could have lived without.

It had all started a few days earlier when his friend detective Harry Callahan had earned a promotion that would see him leave Los Angeles to take up a new posting in San Francisco. Since good things often go together, Callahan was also about to marry, which he hoped would allow him to "find a balance in his life," as he'd put it to Bob.

Bob had met Harry through their common friend, Bill Ballantine, after returning from the so-called "Hell Valley" a few years prior. Since Bob happened to be in Southern California, not quite as a tourist, Harry had happily invited him to the going-away party that his soon to be ex-colleagues of the LAPD had thrown for him.

At the beginning, Bob had felt at ease. Harry was a man on whom one could count, of the same caliber as Bill. He had not regretted having accepted the invitation.

But then, there was the alcohol and the other cops... He had nothing against the LAPD, whose courage was legendary and who did remarkable work. But there were maybe a hundred people in a room that became increasingly cramped and uncomfortable. However, as time passed, the men gradually left, often soaked in whiskey. Before leaving, everyone vigorously shook hands with Harry and congratulated him on his impending marriage and his well-deserved promotion.

The hour was late and only a dozen officers remained. All had been drinking heavily. That's when Bob realized and regretted that he had not seen the hours go by and left earlier, maybe not drunk as many toasts. He had been drinking too much and was angry, at feeling himself vulnerable.

Of course, both he and Callahan knew how to handle their liquor. There was no question of staggering about or spilling anything. But, suddenly, under the effects of alcohol, the conversation took a strange turn. The Frenchman never found out whether he had been the victim of a manipulation, a hazing, or a frightful reality that he would have been unable to accept, even if he'd been a lot drunker.

One of the officers spoke to Harry Callahan:

"It's nice to have a Frenchman around, Callahan. I think the French are almost as ballsy as we Americans."

Harry stared at the bottom of his glass. Then his eyes went up quickly to stare at his colleague's face, but, visibly uncomfortable, he did not utter a word.

"Did you explain to your French buddy, Callahan, how we measure courage at the LAPD?"

Harry coughed. All the officers in the room remained impassive, aware that an incident was about to occur. Harry put his glass down and grabbed the wrist of the other cop. His face had hardened dramatically and he replied in an icy-cold voice:

"Don't go there, Fred. That's just between us cops. My friend's got nothing to do with it, and doesn't need that kind of crap. He served in the RAF during the big one. That's enough for me."

"Take it easy," replied Fred, shaking himself free of Harry's grip. "I just wanted to know if the French are as brave as the LAPD."

Bob, watching the scene, was stunned by the underlying violence that was suddenly implied in the tone and the words of the two men. Something unhealthy now hung in the air, and the room seemed to have become too small and suffocating.

As he opened his mouth, Bob realized that, if he had not been drunk, if his mind had been clear, he would never have become involved in the conversation. He would never have asked for more details.

Fred walked slowly towards the Frenchman. His colleagues, pressed around him, created a sort of honor guard. He appeared to move in slow motion. There was total silence in the room.

"Don't, you bastard," Harry swore. "He doesn't need to know."

But Fred continued to advance without saying a word and planted himself right in front of Bob.

He began to whisper:

"Your friend thinks that you don't need to know..."

Bob heard Harry's voice, but it now seemed to come from very far away.

"Myself, I think you're just as good as any of us here, even though we're all experienced police officers. I think you've got guts and are ready to take the test..."

Bob knew that the whiskey he'd drunk had fogged his brain and might be his downfall. He swore he would never touch a drop of alcohol again; would never again be dragged into the kind of party that might turn out to be a trap. If he had had all his lucidity, he'd have refused, of course. But on this day, August 17, 1956, h wasn't in full possession of all his faculties.

"What is this test you keep talking about?" he asked in the same low tone that the cop had used.

"Stop it!" Harry shouted.

"Hey! You're no longer part of the LAPD, pal," Fred shouted back, provoking the approval of three other policemen. "You're now Badge 2211 in the SFPD. You can't do anything here anymore."

"I could smash your face, asshole!"

"Why? Your chum here seems willing enough to take the test. I don't see what's wrong. We all took it!"

Fred nodded to Bob to sit.

"There's no risk of physical injury. All that's happening is just in your head. It only takes courage, the kind that shows how far your mind is able to function properly before sinking into madness..."

When Bob did not answer, he continued:

"I'll tell you everything. At the LAPD, we have a test. Everyone here has taken it and passed..."

"Apart from those who ended up in an asylum," said a voice.

"Yeah, that's right... Apart from those who ended up in an asylum. Do you want me to tell you what that test is all about? Do you want to take a chance to prove your courage?"

Bob barely had time to nod before the other continued:

"A long time, ago, something happened in America... A lot of crazy shit has happened in our country, but this was mostly kept under wraps. In fact, some still believe that it was nothing but is a bunch of baloney, but they're the type who don't ask too many questions... Well, here we go: there was this egghead; his name was Herbert West, and they said he could raise the dead. He'd discovered a serum that he injected into the bodies of the dearly departed, and wham! them corpses came back to life ready to party like a bunch of drunk Irishmen!"

Bob looked over Fred's shoulder at Harry, but his friend seemed to have gone.

"Well, of course, the guy, if he ever existed, is himself dead by now. But we, at the LAPD, found some of his serum, and used it to test our new recruits, to see how far they'd go when confronted by the ultimate terror..."

Bob now believed that this was all part of some strange hazing ritual. He understood the enormity of the thing and, despite his somewhat confused state, did not believe that Fred was telling the truth; so he decided to go along with the macabre joke,

"We've got a place for the test, the west wing of the Holy Cross Cemetery in Culver City," continued Fred. "We have a set of keys. More specifically, Room C of the morgue, where they keep the bodies waiting to be buried. The candidate for the test only has to spend one night in there, with a syringe and a Colt. The syringe contains Dr. West's precious serum, and the Colt only one bullet. The rookie chooses a body from the recently deceased and injects the serum under its skin. The corpse then comes back to life and always starts whooping around the room like a bronco at a rodeo. Then the rookie must fire his only bullet through its brain to stop it and return it to eternal sleep. If he misses his target, he better get out quickly, but none of our guys has ever missed."

"You mean they all passed?"

"I mean they all managed to fire that bullet through the skull of the corpse, but it's true that some fell apart after that."

Twenty-four hours later, the effects of the alcohol having long since dissipated, Bob Morane had the feeling of having lived through a bad dream.

He stood in front of the entrance to the West Wing of the Holy Cross Cemetery in Culver City, with the impression of being a student waiting in front of the principal's office.

The old man who opened the door had obviously been informed of his coming and showed no surprise. This had to be a commonplace event. The cops had their entries even into cemeteries.

"Hello," said Bob. "I have my Colt and the syringe."

"Down the hall to the left. Wipe your feet on entering and try not to damage the walls."

Bob never went back on his word, even if it'd been given under the influence of alcohol. But now that that he was in place, it all seemed like a practical joke.

The cops, the caretaker, even Harry Callahan, were probably lying in wait to see the reactions of the Frenchman in such a grotesque and ridiculous situation.

This is why Bob had lied: he was willing to put himself through this ridiculous test, but would not carry a weapon. Harry had insisted that he take his Smith & Wesson, but Bob had refused categorically:

"Last night, I wasn't in my normal state. I had too much to drink and I agreed to this stupid prank, so I'll go to the cemetery, plant my syringe in a stiff, but I'm leaving right away, without firing a single shot!"

Bob was still angry at having agreed to take the test, but he had only himself to blame.

The caretaker made a sign for him to hurry, adding that he would lock up the place in just under an hour, and Bob would have to "take care of it" before then.

Bob opened the door leading to the Morgue. When it closed behind him, he found himself in a narrow corridor bathed in a wan light that seemed to struggle hopelessly against the darkness. He felt as if he had entered, not a contemporary building, but the hall of an ancient pyramid.

The corridor began an endless descent.

Bob had spent most of the day outside. In this month of August, the sun was shining over Los Angeles. Yet now, he found himself deep in the shadows, in a very special structure.

This was probably part of the test. How far could they go? Bob was absolutely convinced that it was all a vast practical joke, as his fingers clenched the small leather case containing Dr. West's syringe.

Finally he reached Door C. It also amazing: such a long corridor leading to a single door. Bob decided to stop asking questions and entered. The sooner things were finished, the sooner he would be done with this joke.

The door opened without a squeak. The room could have passed for an ordinary office, if not for the size of the drawers on the wall. Each of them contained a fresh corpse, as in any respectable morgue. The air smelled of the characteristic antiseptic odor. There was no mistake; he was in the mortuary of Holy Cross.

Not without some effort, he opened several of the drawers. He had to choose a corpse and prove to these morons that he was up to their challenge.

It was when he opened the fourth compartment that he understood. The cops had everything planned. He found the joke even more lamentable.

Bob sat on a chair, and pulled the syringe from its case. It was in this body that he would inject the serum, because, obviously, it was the one they had chosen for him. What a bunch of idiots!

Before him lay the body of an old man, his features drawn, livid. Someone had dressed him up in a disguise that Bob recognized—the medallion, the cape... the body had been dressed to look like Count Dracula!

It was pathetic!

He would have to inject the serum in that emaciated body.

As a test, it was utterly grotesque and ridiculous.

In order not to prolong the suspense, Bob grabbed the syringe and stuck the needle in the dead man's neck. The yellow liquid quickly spread into the necrotic flesh.

The operation took only a few seconds during which Bob chose not to look.

After his task was accomplished, Bob didn't even bother to close the drawer; he walked briskly toward the exit.

Just as he was closing the door behind him, however, taken by a sudden impulse, he turned around and looked at the body of the dead man.

If there is one chance in a million that this corpse come back to life, he thought, *I don't want to miss it.*

He returned to sit at the back of the room.

Minutes passed. No sounds disturbed the stillness of the morgue.

They must have planned everything, Bob thought. *Yet I haven't seen any-one else since I've been here. They should be watching my reactions, hoping that I panic and run away. They might be waiting behind the door. I'm stupid to have accepted their challenge. Those idiots have disguised the remains of an old man, dressed him up in the costume of Count Dracula! I have never seen a joke in such a bad taste... At least, Harry had no part in it!*

Five minutes passed. Then ten. Then a quarter of an hour. The appointed time had apparently passed and no undead had come forward. Dracula had not left his coffin.

Almost disappointed, Bob resolved to go.

It was in the corridor that the first thing happened. Bob experienced the feeling of not being alone. This presentment quickly gave way to certainty: a presence was there, with him. He began to be on the alert. He made a connection with the body he had left in his drawer, but there was no corpse shambling after him...

Yet, he distinctly heard a few furtive noises, some slight friction seemingly coming from nowhere. Something was moving, perhaps above him, but the darkness that reigned in the corridor didn't allow him to see it.

Bob stopped several times on his way to listen. Each time, it seemed like the *thing* mimicked his movements, making sure not to be spotted.

The final steps it took him to reach the exit seemed to take an eternity.

The caretaker was no longer on duty at the entrance. To Bob's astonish-ment, night was falling. How long had he been down there? Where were the cops? Where were Harry and Fred? The Frenchman lengthened his stride.

Luckily, the glass door leading outside was not locked. A split second lat-er, Bob found himself in the open air outside, much to his relief.

He barely saw a dark shadow taking advantage of the opened door to fly away and disappear into the night.

It is reported that, as the last visitor who had come to pay his respects to the remains of Bela Lugosi was heading for the exit, a surprising event hap-pened in the endless corridor of the funeral home. A gigantic black bat, flying silently, followed him and, when he opened the glass door leading outside, with a few flaps of its lathery wings, the animal escaped into the sky from which the sun had just disappeared.

Jean Boullet.

Bela Lugosi in *Bizarre Magazine* #24-25, Paris, J.J. Pauvert, 1962.

Translation by J.-M. & Randy Lofficier

A new Tales of the Shadowmen *would not be complete without a story featuring that wonderful rogue, Arsène Lupin, and we can always count on David Vineyard to provide one. The following tale takes place rather late in Lupin's career and manages to cast a new light on a classic horror film...*

David L. Vineyard: *The Moon of the White Wolf*

England, 1934

Author's Note: Some elements of this story were changed, characters added, names changed, and incidents rewritten for the classic film version of this story. I have retained some of the original names and the location from that film, though they are not accurate, but changed for legal and privacy issues, in order to protect living descendants of the families involved, but rest assured the following account taken from local records, memoirs, and extensive interviews is the real story. The true story.

> *"Even a man who is pure in heart,*
> *And says his prayers by night*
> *May become a Wolf when the Wolfbane blooms*
> *And the autumn Moon is bright"*
> Curt Siodmak

The throaty roar of the roadster's exhaust filled the still afternoon like an impending storm approaching. Dr. John Silence, alienist, standing in the garden by the little priest and the Spaniard, spoke above the roar.

"That will be Captain Drummond, I'll wager. I hear Colonel Nielson of Scotland Yard sent him down to poke around this queer business. I suspect he'll find no more clarity than we have, though."

The little priest was bent over a small bushm examining a beetle crawling on a leaf, and did not seem to hear what Silence had just said, but beside him, the tall, slender Spaniard looked up.

"You fear he will get no farther than you and the good father have, doctor?" he asked.

Don Luis Perenna was the very portrait of a Spanish nobleman, sword lean and quick of movement. Silence would not have been surprised to discover that the stick he carried contained a length of slender Wilkinson steel beneath the silver wolfshead that topped it.

The little priest stood up and looked around blinking.

"I wouldn't say that our own investigations have been pointless; only that those things we have learned suggest unlikely conclusions."

Silence smiled grimly. "Well, I admit I'm done for. I've seen and heard some queer stories in my time, but this one..."

"Ah," Don Luis said, "our host, Sir John, has heard the good Captain's trumpet call."

Sir John Talbot was a distinguished silver-haired man short of stature but wide-shouldered and deep-chested. He walked with a slight limp, assisted by a walking stick with a silver wolfshead, similar to the one held by Don Luis.

Drummond arrived in the drive with a slight cloud of dust that was soon cleared by the damp morning air. Bounding from the roadster, he was revealed to be a large, hardy man with a pleasantly ugly countenance beneath the soft brim of his felt hat. Beneath his Burbury, his broad shoulders were evident.

"Sir John," he said offering his hand. "Hugh Drummond, I think you were expecting me. At least, I hope so. I'd hate to make that drive again, deuced long drive, been up half the night. Took the wrong turn out of Lanwiyy—sorry, these Welsh names are a bit much for my poor noggin'. It's a wonder I didn't end up in the Irish Sea," he hardly paused, "Colonel Nielson extends his compliments, and his apologies for not being able to send someone more suitable, but I've poked around in the odd bit of the mysterious with some luck, and when the Colonel asked if I could come down... Well, I'm not one to miss out on queer goings on in the woods—any woods."

The young man smiled and his ugly face was transformed.

Silence, Don Luis, and the little priest had walked up behind Sir John.

"Captain Drummond," the nobleman said, "these are my other guests: Dr. John Silence, the noted alienist and occultist; Don Luis Perenna, a man of no small reputation; and this is our religious advisor in this case, Father Brown."

Drummond shook hands with all three, pumping the little priest's arm. "Sky pilot for this affair, hey, Padre? Might be needed at that." He turned to Sir John. "And your son, Lawrence, ain't it? Is he still recovering from the incident?"

"Slowly, but currently he is taking a little walk with Miss Conliffe. He should be back shortly. Meanwhile, may I offer you a brandy?"

"Offer away! I'd slay a Welsh dragon for a flagon of beer though. Thirsty work drivin' this monster."

Sir John smiled a bit narrowly. He was a quiet and reserved man, genteel in the true sense of the word, and seemed taken aback by the boisterous Drummond.

"I think a beer may be arranged."

Sir John led Drummond toward the manor as Silence and the other three hung back.

"So that's the famous ' Bulldog' Drummond?" said the alienist. "One wouldn't say much for his higher functions at this point, but I know Nielson, and he's no fool."

"Not all books have accurate covers," Don Luis said. "Eh, Father?"

The little priest blinked innocuously.

Once they were all gathered by the great fireplace with drinks, Sir John excused himself, leaving the four men alone. It was clear he was giving them time to openly discuss the recent incidents that had led them to this place.

"You chaps fill me in, won't you," Drummond said. "The story I got from Nielson don't make much sense. Gypsies, wolf men, curses—all over my poor noggin'. How about you, doctor? Does this babble have a grain in it, or is it all, as the Yanks say, a bunch of malarkey?" Drummond tapped a cigarette out of his case and lit it with a match from the fireplace before descending into an overstuffed chair with his drink.

Silence delicately sniffed his bubble glass. It was a rather good brandy.

"Frankly, Drummond, I can't say at this point. The facts are clear enough, but..."

"I ain't got a thing agin' startin' with the bare facts," Drummond said dropping his g's consciously.

Silence leaned back in his chair extending his long legs. With his dark hair and sharp pointed beard, he looked faintly Luciferian. Don Luis stood by a window, casually looking out while sipping his brandy. Father Brown, with his little glass of sherry, was looking over some volumes from Sir John's extensive library. It would seem as if the alienist had been elected as storyteller.

"A bit more than five weeks ago," he began, "Sir John's second son, Lawrence, arrived from the States where he'd been attending university, following the death of his brother. No, no, we've looked into that—tragic, but nothing to do with this business. In any case, there was some estrangement that father and son both wanted to put an end to, and it seemed as if they had succeeded. Lawrence even put a new telescope in Sir John's observatory. He has quite a delicate hand for a big man. Any strain that may have been there seemed to have faded. Of course, I have this all second hand from Sir John, Larry, Lawrence, from the servants and some of the family friends.

"There's been an encampment of gypsies nearby. Sir John always lets them use his property when they come, not unusual as you likely know in the country. This lot isn't the usual bunch that comes yearly, but they seemed harmless enough. Young Lawrence wanted to visit the gypsy camp and went with a local girl, Jenny Williams. It was a clear moonlit night and, save for a bit of ground fog, the two should have had an enjoyable evening, but Maleva, the fortune teller—she runs the place pretty clearly—spun a story about seeing a pentagram on young Talbot's palm—the sign that is supposed to appear before an attack by a lycanthrope, a werewolf if you will, and the young man does seem to be highly suggestible. A latent neurosis, my colleagues would probably say.

"On their way home, Talbot said he began to feel they weren't alone, and for once, his anxiety proved well founded. Maleva's son, Bela, had followed the couple and attacked them. There was a colossal struggle. The gypsy was a big man by all accounts and Talbot, while young, is quite powerful himself. Anyway, Talbot fought him off and killed him, but was wounded himself in the struggle."

"Seems straight forward enough," Drummond said. "So what am I missin'?"

"The Devil, Captain Drummond," the little priest said softly while perusing a volume taken down from Sir John's shelves, "is in the details, is it not, Dr. Silence?"

Silence sighed. "In this case, almost literally. Talbot was rather badly injured and quite out of his head for some time. Dr. Lloyd did his best, but the mind doesn't always follow a clear straight path. It was he who called me in as Sir John called in the good Father. Don Luis was already in the area, and when Sir John learned of his interest in the Romany, he invited him to join us. Young Talbot has developed a kind of *idée fixe*, as it were. He's convinced the gypsy Bela was in the form of a wolf when he attacked him, and the Williams girl—I should point out that Dr. Lloyd and the local constable, Colonel Montford, both assured me that the body they found was that of Bela, the gypsy, and while his clothes were torn and he was half-naked, there was no sign of any wolf.

"But young Talbot claimed he saw a wolf, and because he was bitten, and because of what the old soothsayer told him, and because he had borrowed his father's silver headed cane, which is what he used to killed that gypsy, he's convinced that, when the moon is full, he'll turn into a wolf himself."

Drummond shook his head. "I can see the poor devil's problem, but won't he realize it's all nonsense when the moon is next full and he doesn't become a wolf?"

"It isn't quite that simple, is it?" Don Luis said, joining them. "I'm afraid the logic we would apply to the situation may elude young Talbot. Incidentally, I think I spied him and Miss Conliffe returning along the lane. It would be awkward if he were to find us discussing his fate so bluntly. We have some time, but we should get to the point."

"The corridors of the mind aren't always direct, Captain," Silence said. "Talbot has become fixated on this, with the soothsayer Maleva feeding his delusion with her talk of pentagrams, curses, and wolfsbane in bloom. Talbot believes he will turn into a wolf when the moon is full, and he may well become quite agitated. There have even been cases of physical changes, think of the notorious Doctor Jekyll—all natural and quite easy to explain, but no help for that poor damned soul..."

"Not damned," the little priest corrected. "Not yet." His voice was suddenly firm and surprisingly powerful.

Drummond shook his head. "Even a man who is pure..." he quoted the old doggerel softly, then suddenly returned to being his bluff self. "Well, it's quite a pickle, but I don't see what I can do other than stand by Sir John in lieu of Colonel Nielson..."

"Actually," Don Luis said, "your presence may be more fortuitous than you suspect, Captain. For one thing, the local constabulary are busy with a spree of local crime, and may not be able to spare a man to help watch over the lad, and for another, you seem to me the ideal candidate to accompany us this evening in our visit to the gypsy camp to visit the witch, Maleva. Getting in will be no trick..."

"Getting out, on the other hand," Silence said, "will be another thing. The police have insisted the gypsiess remain in their encampment while the inquest and investigation continue, but they're becoming restless being confined and with so many *gagin* about."

"Gay..." Drummond began.

"*Gagin*, Captain," Don Luis said. "Outsiders. Those not of the Romany blood. They've been persecuted across all of Europe, and they have little trust of authority or strangers. Our little visit to Maleva could turn difficult." The faint smile at the corner of his lips seemed to indicate he wouldn't mind if things turned difficult indeed.

Drummond rubbed his hands together. "That sounds a bit more like me. A few cracked heads might well clear this bloody fog away and even put poor Talbot straight. You joining us, Padre?"

The priest blinked. "No, no, I hope your investigation bears fruit, but I am more needed here. I've already visited our Romany brethren to perform my duties; they are of the faith, you know. I had a long and informative conversation with Maleva. But my work tonight is here. This night, above all others, spiritual guidance may prove as important as any physical or intellectual effort we can muster."

Drummond looked puzzled.

"Tonight, Captain Drummond," the meek little priest said with no hint of drama, "tonight is the first full moon since poor Talbot was bitten. Tonight the wolfsbane blooms."

The gypsy camp proved as hostile as Don Luis had predicted. The sullen eyed inhabitants were both wary and angry at the intrusion. Drummond had a little experience with gypsies as a country gentleman, but it usually added up to nothing more than petty thievery, a few confidence games, and, once in a while, a local boy getting too friendly with a gypsy girl. In most cases, the Romany folk welcomed locals visiting their encampment, putting on a sort of county fair atmosphere, palm-reading, selling cheap silk scarves, and lifting a few purses.

Not so with this lot. Drummond could feel the resentment, and several men and women either spit contemptuously as the *gagin* passed, or made gestures that Don Luis had whispered to him were meant to ward off the evil eye. Drummond, who enjoyed a brawl more than most, had no desire for a knife in his gizzard, and more than once, let his hand slide along the pocket of his jacket where his little Bulldog revolver rested. The truth was, he half-wished he had packed the big Webley instead. The tension in the encampment was palpable.

Don Luis seemed unconcerned though. He was a cool character. Drummond had sidelined John Silence while they were still at Sir John's to learn more about the Spaniard, and had been told the fellow had been something in the French Foreign Legion and was involved in some business with the King of Morocco. Watching him now, Drummond didn't doubt it. The fellow was whipcord lean and taut as a bowstring.

Maleva's tent stood beside her wagon at the center of the camp, a large and fairly imposing structure. She was, Don Luis, assured him, a queen among her folk, and not merely an old crone with a bag of witchery and tricks. Near her tent, several large and menacing gypsy men stood guard, sullenly watching, the threat under their heavy dark brows evident. One of them kept them waiting for a few anxious moments outside as the other gypsies gathered around. Then, they were finally ushered inside the close candle-lit quarters, redolent with the scent of exotic powders, cheap perfumes, incense, humid vapors, and an unhealthy hint of something far more potent.

No wonder young Talbot had believed the old crone's witchy predictions. Drummond himself felt the hairs along the back of his neck rise. He had little use for this sort of business.

The old woman sat in the shadows, largely hidden behind a large crystal ball covered by a blood-red silk cloth, embroidered with the symbols of the Zodiac. Other than a beaky nose and thin lips, and the occasional flash of black eyes under the silk scarf that covered her head, little of her features could be discerned. Her hands, despite long cracked nails, were lean and almost masculine, without spots or other signs of age.

"Welcome," she said in a cracked high pitched voice. "Welcome to our little camp, gentlemen."

"A strange sort of welcome," Don Luis said. "I have known the Romany folk for many years across all of Europe and the Middle East, and never have I felt threatened before. You are a queer addition to your tribe, Madame."

Drummond expected her to bristle. The Spaniard's tone was deliberately challenging, but instead she waved a hand in dismissal.

"My son Bela was well loved," she said. "His death has disturbed my people, upset them. You claim to know them, Don Luis. If so, you know they are like children, easily swayed by emotions and passion. They seek justice for my Bela, and they fear—they fear the wolf."

"What wolf?" Silence asked. "There has been no wolf. A few frightened villagers who heard things in the night; the unfortunate incident with your son and young Talbot..."

"Poor Bela. He carried the curse, you know. Many years now. Most full moons, we were able to chain him, drug him, protect him from himself, but this time... I bear no ill will toward the young man who killed him, mind you. He was an animal, a beast in that form and not himself..." She paused to cross herself. "And now tonight... You wonder why my people are hostile and frightened when your police will not let us leave, and we know what is coming. The moon will be full tonight, as you well know..."

"And what *is* coming?" Silence asked.

"It is the night of the wolf," Maleva said. "The wolfsbane blooms. Someone bears the mark of the pentagram. I only pray it is none of you."

Drummond found himself fighting the urge to look at the palm of his hand. Damn nonsense, but in this atmosphere and the old witch doing her spiel... Little wonder young Talbot had fallen for it.

"I've got cure enough for any wolf right here," Drummond said, patting the revolver in his pocket.

"Ordinary bullets will do no good against one of the werefolk. Only silver can stop them. Do you have silver bullets in your gun, sir?" She cackled softly and Drummond felt his spine shiver.

"I do have silver," Don Luis said sharply, slightly raising the wolfshead walking stick. "And I fear no wolf, nor any gypsy magic. I had hoped to speak some sense to you, Maleva, to give you one last chance to see light and end this. But I see that is pointless now. Your little game has gone on long enough, and tonight, it ends. Tell your people it is over. Tonight, the White Wolf will have his say—at long last."

The old woman almost recoiled at his last words.

With that, the Spaniard turned sharply. "Gentlemen, we have accomplished our goal."

He turned to leave, and Drummond and Silence followed him. Outside, the gypsy folk pressed in close, evidently having overheard the exchange with Maleva. Drummond's hand moved toward his revolver and he could feel the tension in Dr. Silence. It had grown dark while they were talking to the old witch, and the idea of fighting their way out in the shadows left even Drummond wary.

But Don Luis, hard as steel, full of a sort of dynamic energy, simply parted the crowd with the sheer force of his personality. Drummond and Silence followed in his wake.

When they were clear of the camp, and Drummond was sure they hadn't been followed, he stopped the other two.

"Say, what was that White Wolf business back there? The old girl turned white as a sheet when you mentioned it."

Don Luis ignored the question. He was eyeing the sky. A close fog was rolling in on the ground, and a chill was in the air. From between the trees, the rising moon could be made out. The full moon.

"Too late," Don Luis said. "Too late. Quick, gentlemen, we must hurry. All isn't lost yet."

Drummond couldn't say why, but instinctively he followed the Spaniard's lead, tabling his question, but they had not gone ten feet before something stopped them in their tracks.

It was an inhuman cry. A mournful, soul-chilling sound.

The howl of a wolf.

Drummond swore under his breath and drew his revolver. He saw Don Luis' hands turn white-knuckled gripping the wolfshead stick.

A black form loomed out of the darkness and Drummond would have fired if Silence hadn't laid a hand on his.

"Thank God, I've found you," Father Brown said, puffing slightly with the exertion. "Young Talbot has gone mad. He broke out of his room and ran off across the moors. Sir John has followed him. I fear for them both. Constable Montford and Dr. Lloyd have gathered some men to help look for them, but I came ahead to find you."

Don Luis grabbed the little priest by the forearm. "You go with Captain Drummond and Doctor Silence. I will go on alone. Captain Drummond, if you find anything, fire your revolver once."

He was gone before the others could protest.

Half-an-hour passed as they called out for Sir John and his son. Then, in the distance, they heard a commotion, shouts, and an inhuman scream that chilled them to the very bone.

Drummond swore and plunged in that direction, followed by the others.

Beneath a great tree, they found Sir John unconscious, his silver-headed walking stick caked with blood and hair, and beside him lay the hulking form of his son.

"He's dead," Silence said, after having checked the body of the younger Talbot.

It was an understatement. The young man's skull had been crushed with the silver-headed walking stick that lay beside the unconscious Sir John.

"But not Sir John," the little priest said.

Drummond, hearing shouting and movement in the trees, realized that it was the Chief Constable and the others. He shouted loudly, then discharged his revolver once in the still night air, as Don Luis had instructed.

Above them, the full moon illuminated the grim scene.

Colonel Montford, the County's Chief Constable, had gone, having taken everyone's statements. He had been on the phone with Colonel Nielson in London, and a raid on the gypsy camp was in progress even as they spoke.

Drummond had spoken to Nielson, and it struck him that he could not have organized a raid on such short notice. There was something going on he hadn't been told.

He joined Father Brown in the library to wait for news of Sir John, and poured himself a stiff whisky while the priest stood, watching the fire in the hearth. When Silence came down and joined them, Drummond presented him with a whisky as well.

"He'll live," the doctor told them. "But we won't get much out of him, I fear. He's in shock. I doubt he will ever be able to tell us much. Dr. Lloyd is staying with him for now."

"Not much to tell," Drummond said. "It's pretty obvious what happened. Sir John caught up with his son, who attacked him. Sir John defended himself. The inquest should be pretty cut and dried. Poor damned soul, your pardon, Padre, his mind twisted by all that gypsy nonsense about pentagrams and wolfsbane. He must have snapped. That Maleva has much to answer for, or I should say, Arsène Lupin has much to answer for."

Silence looked up from his whisky. "Lupin? What the devil has Arsène Lupin to do with this business?"

"As you know," Drummond said, "Colonel Nielson asked me to come down and poke around, but what you don't know is, it wasn't just because of his acquaintance with Sir John. For some time now, there have been rumors of a group of gypsies involved in a large criminal enterprise. They would move into an area, establish an encampment, and then engage in various criminal activity, not the usual petty theft associated with gypsies, but quite large crimes, jewel thefts, banks being held up—you probably read about the one in Cardiff being hit a week ago? Nielson had received intelligence from an unknown source that this camp of Maleva's was the front for all this, and rumor was that none other than Arsène Lupin was the mastermind behind it all.

"This werewolf business was part of it, but something went wrong, this time. That attack on young Talbot was supposed to convince locals that a werewolf was in the area, distracting them from what the gypsies were really up to, but Talbot accidentally killed their man and they were forced to come up with another werewolf—and that poor devil fell into their trap. As I said, Lupin, that devil, has much to answer for. All pretty cut and dried."

"Oh, yes," Father Brown said. "Cut and dried, I agree. And the three of us shall properly attest to what we saw tonight, and our statements, while not false by any means, will none the less leave out the truth."

Drummond looked annoyed. "If you mean that werewolf nonsense..."

"No, Captain Drummond. I do not mean the werewolf nonsense. I am not a superstitious man. Evil has many forms, most of them quite banal. Tonight, we have witnessed a tragedy, but only a part of it, and only the part we were supposed to see. The background is far more complex, as your story begins to reveal."

"I'm afraid you lost me there, Padre," Drummond said.

The little priest blinked and, with the poker, stirred the embers in the fireplace.

"I should perhaps begin with some knowledge which I possess that will change how you view this affair. It begins properly with our missing friend, Don Luis Perenna..."

"You know," Silence said, "I hadn't even thought of him. Where do you suppose he got to?"

"Don't suppose he's gotten himself lost," Drummond said. "Don't seem the type to get lost, but as mad as this night has been..."

"Don Luis is not lost, gentlemen," Father Brown said. "I assure you of that, though we won't be seeing him again, I would wager. He's accomplished his goal and departed."

"Well, whatever he's up to," Drummond said, "I bet that old witch, Maleva, got away too, Nielson's raid or not. That Lupin is a clever devil."

"No," Father Brown said. "I can assure you that neither *he* nor his faux Romany friends will escape this night. The White Wolf will see to that."

"He? You mean, Lupin? Faux Romany? And what's with this White Wolf business? Don Luis mentioned it, and old Maleva turned ghost-white. You're talking in riddles, Padre."

"That's right." Silence said. "I thought the old girl was going to faint when Don Luis mentioned a white wolf."

"Well, *he* might," the little priest said absently. "But let me explain, at least what I know, and what I think I know. We have been witnessing a drama these last days, but not the drama we thought we were witnessing. As you both conjectured, the whole business of gypsy curses and lycanthropy was a distraction. The truth is both more mundane, and, in its own way, fantastical, if only because of the fantastic nature of one of the protagonist, the one I refer to in this case as the White Wolf."

The little priest seemed to draw himself up and, in doing so, Drummond noted for the first time that there was considerably more to the little cleric than he had surmised.

"I should begin with how I come to have some special knowledge in this affair. I have a friend, a colleague of sorts, whose name may be familiar to you—Flambeau. He was once one of the most successful jewel thieves in Europe, before he reformed. Now, he offers his services as a sort of private detective, and he's quite effective. In any case, as you might imagine, he is well versed in the underworld of our continent, and it is he who first told me of the Black Wolf and the White Wolf."

"Just a minute, Padre. Black wolf? White wolf?" aid Drummond. "How many damned wolves are we talking about here?"

"Three. A black wolf, as malevolent a figure as you can imagine; a gray wolf, quite tragic and a victim of the first; and, a white wolf, who seeks to set everything straight again."

Drummond poured another whisky for himself and offered one to Silence who refused. "I have a feeling this is going to call for more than one drink," he said.

"It was from my friend Flambeau," the little priest began, "that I first learned of a criminal figure in Europe that I shall call, for lack of a better name, the Black Wolf. He first emerged, at least in any public eye, working for a man who called himself Gurn, who was also known by a more fantastic name, Fantomas. That was during the war, if you recall. Of course, you, Captain Drummond, may have been too occupied to take notice of it.

"This figure appeared again as part of a criminal organization known as the Vampires, a rather bizarrely costumed gang who plagued Paris for a while. After that, he was briefly involved with a man you are quite familiar with Captain, one Carl Peterson ..."

"This chap of yours gets around, don't he?" replied Drummond.

"He does indeed. His associations are a veritable who's who of crime, even the mysterious Mr. King of Limehouse. Most recently, he was in Berlin in Germany, involved in the underworld there, where he took on the rather colorful *nom de guerre* of Mack the Knife, a *mack* being underworld slang for a procurer of women. He was supposedly slain there, but in actuality, he escaped and, while he was in hiding, he came upon a band of the Romany folk and conceived his great plan.

"Taking the name of Arsène Lupin, he convinced the gypsies to follow him. He then organized them into an efficient criminal organization, traveling across Europe, building in strength and reputation before coming to these shores. Among his more successful ideas was the whole fantastic werewolf scheme, as Captain Drummond deduced. Nothing like superstition and fear to cloud men's minds from observing the real evil under their noses."

"So, that accounts for your Black Wolf," Silence said. "But what about this White one, and what was Maleva's role?"

"Ah, Maleva. I should point out that, while in Berlin, this Mack the Knife operated around a theatrical crowd and no doubt learned a great deal from them. His former masters, Fantomas, Peterson, Mr. King... they were all masters of disguise. Maleva *is* the Black Wolf. *Maleva was a man.* You remember that you never saw her in good light. She kept herself well hidden in shadows and behind that crystal ball. You must have seen her hands though. They were hardly the hands of an elderly woman, despite the long nails. There is nothing to keep a man from growing his nails long you know."

"Damn," Drummond said. "Makes sense. But you said there was a White Wolf, too. So far only a Black one and a Gray one have been accounted for."

"Yes," Father Brown said, blinking as he again turned to look into the embers of the fire, his face cast crimson by the lowering flames. "The White Wolf. We are all in his debt tonight, though he is long gone. The White Wolf, the mere mention of his name striking fear, as you noted, into Maleva,'s breast... He can only be one person..."

"Arsene Lupin," Silence said.

"Lupin," Drummond exclaimed. "Around here?"

"Not merely around here, Captain, but intimately involved. I draw your attention to the grotesque scene we found tonight when we came upon Sir John and poor young Lawrence. Did any of you happen to notice Sir John's stick?"

"The wolfshead," Silence said. "Ironic that young Talbot was killed by a silver-headed cane wielded by his own father, but..."

"But I ask you," Father Brown said, turning to the two men who were both now sitting forward in their chairs, "was that Sir John's stick that we found? Or didn't you notice that Don Luis carried one exactly like it in every way?"

"Of course," Drummond said. "Even makes sense—but why take off then? I don't..."

"I begin to see," Silence said. "The game was still in play."

"Yes, he had not counted on young Talbot escaping and running wild, or attacking Sir John, but once it happened, he sprang his trap. Colonel Nielson's men already had the gypsy camp surrounded. The signal to strike was..."

"A single gunshot," Drummond said. "And I fired it."

"Exactly. And in doing so, no doubt prompted Maleva to slip away during the confusion of the raid. Of course, our friend the White Wolf would have been prepared for that. I would imagine we will not see Maleva again. Justice, of a sort, has been arranged for poor young Talbot after all."

"So this Don Luis was in league with this Lupin chap?" Drummond asked.

Father Brown turned again to stir the embers of the fire then back. "In league, no. Don Luis, I conjecture, *is* Arsene Lupin."

Drummond barked with laughter. "I'll be...! You know, Padre, there was something about him... They way those gypsies just parted when we left Maleva's tent... I half think you may be right. Puts a whole new light on all this business, all the mumbo jumbo about werewolves, pentagrams, silver bullets, and wolfsbane... Silly superstitious *fol de rol*."

John Silence had stood up, and was standing by the window, looking out. The fog was dissipating and the first tinge of morning light was showing in the east.

"Superstition, yes. But such things are part and parcel of us, you know. And I can see from the look on Father Brown's face he sees the same irony I have, whether he wishes to embrace it or not."

"Irony... " Drummond began.

"Dr. Silence refers to the whole business of wolves and the like. Mundane as this all may seem exposed to the light of day, there are still undeniable facts."

"Such as the gypsy Bela and young Talbot both killed with a silver-headed cane," Silence said.

"Coincidence surely," Drummond said flatly.

"Perhaps," Father Brown said. "But I could not help but seize on one curiosity. As you know, one protection against the lycanthrope is the wild flower known as wolfsbane. It is fairly common here and in Europe, but not known by the same name in all countries obviously. As I said, here in England, we call it wolfsbane, but it has another name in France."

John Silence smiled enigmatically when Drummond turned to him questioningly.

"Wolfsbane, here," he said, "but in France it is known by another name..."

"*A lupin*," Father Brown said, solemnly. "Rather appropriate, don't you think, for the White Wolf?"

We end this year's collection of Shadowmen stories with a follow-up to last year's tale "The Piano Maidens," starring Eugenie Danglars and Louise d'Armilly, from The Count of Monte-Cristo. *Now in fear-filled Styria, our two lovers are about to encounter another Sapphic icon...*

Jared Welch: *Styrian Rhapsody*

September 29th, 1839

Eugenie Danglars and Louise d'Armilly were traveling through Styria on their way to Vienna. Passing through a small town in the shadow of an old Gothic looking Castle, they decided to stop at an inn.

Eugenie spoke to the inn keeper.

"Do you have any rooms to let?"

"Yes," he replied. "A few... Two beds?"

"No," Eugenie said. "One bed will be sufficient."

After settling into their room, they decided to go to the dining-room.

"What a coincidence to see you two here," a familiar voice said.

Eugenie recognized Father Rodin, whom they had met not long ago.

"These two young ladies were present for my victory in Naples," he proclaimed to the other members in his party.

"At least, what you called a victory," Eugenie said.

Rodin ignored the snide remark and came to sit down at their table. At that moment, Louise noticed a strangely pale, yet beautiful, girl with long, raven black hair, sitting alone in the corner of the room.

"We're traveling to Vienna," Eugenie told the Jesuit. "What brings you here?"

"I was sent to this dull backwater to investigate rumors of vampirism. I'd much rather deal with mortal heretics," Rodin answered.

"They sent you to investigate vampires?"

"Yes. I once encountered the Ténèbre Brothers once. That's when I obtained this book on the subject, *The Legend of the Ghoul Addhema and the Vampire of Szandor* by Professor Hans Spurzheim."

"Well, I can't say I've ever met a vampire, since I highly doubt that Monte-Cristo was actually Lord Ruthven, as some have claimed."

"Many strange men have been mistaken for Lord Ruthven," said a new voice entering the conversion. It was the mysterious dark-haired girl Louise had first observed a moment ago. "From Lord Byron to the Marquis de Rio-Santo to, most recently, the Count of Monte-Cristo. But none of them were real thing."

"It's a shame Rio Santo didn't succeed in his stated goal," Rodin mused. "The Anglican British Empire is the root of all modern evil,"

"If you're here to investigate vampires, Father, let me tell you about our local lore." The woman looked at Louise for a moment, then continued, "My name is Rimcalla, by the way." She smiled at the pretty blonde, and then sat down.

"The castle to the north of here is called Karnstein; it was home to the House of Karnstein, an ancient and noble family now extinct in the direct line. Their history begins actually in Anjou in the Dark Ages, contemporary with Clovis the Merovingian. Gandin, a descendant of Neroweg, was the ruler of Anjou; his heirs were his sons Galoes and Gahmuret, but he left Styria to his daughter, Lammire. She had an affair with a knight named Ither, and the son born of their liaison inherited the land of Karnstein, this land.

"It is said that in the 1540s, the then-Count of Karnstein sold his soul to Beelzebub and married the Countess Dolingen of Gratz, who also had Karnstein blood through her mother. They both became vampires and, for over 150 years, the Karnsteins were the source of all vampirism in Austria.

"In 1698, the heir of Karnstein was the beautiful 19 year-old Countess Mircalla Karnstein, who, through her father's mother, had Habsburg ancestry. Her favored lover was the beautiful Baron Vordenberg. Vordenberg is mostly remembered, even by her descendants, as a man, probably because of her anatomy, as she was technically the father of her children, but, she was in reality a very elegant and graceful woman.

"The vampires were becoming particularly active at that time. Mircalla herself was attacked by one at a ball. Then Vordenberg took it upon herself to kill all the fiends, and did so courageously. But when she realized Mircalla had been turned, she couldn't bring herself to kill her great love, so she hid her body, hoping it would not be able to do any harm.

"Vampiric activity has been quiet since then, until very recently. Why it started again, I can't speculate." Here, Rimcalla ended her story.

Father Rodin contemplated all this for a moment, then said:

"That's a little different from how I heard it from others, but that is to be expected, I suppose." He pondered some more. "Well, I must return to my party, so I bid you *au revoir*." Then he left.

"What are your names?" Rimcalla asked the two women.

"I'm Eugenie Danglars," said the one with short black hair who looked slightly boyish but feminine at the same time.

"And I'm Louise d'Armilly," said the radiant, fair-skinned beauty with golden blonde hair.

"Oh, so you are the Piano Maidens I've heard so much about? How exciting," Rimcalla responded.

"Yes, we're on our way to a performance in Vienna," said Louise. Then, she added, "This talk about vampires reminded me of when we were in Florence. We were told a story about a werewolf named Wagner."

"I have heard that legend as well," said Rimcalla, "but in Florence, I doubt they know that he had made a deal with Faust."

"That is interesting," Louise replied.

After continuing to chat with the stranger for half an hour, the Maidens got up.

"Well, I think I'm ready to retire," Eugenie said to Louise.

"Me too," Louise replied. "It was a pleasure to talk to you," she said to Rimcalla.

In their room, preparing for bed, Eugenie asked Louise:

"Has all this talk about vampires scared you?"

"Of course not," Louise responded. "After all, you still have the Russian dagger you bought in Venice?"

"Yes, it's right here." Eugenie pulled it out. "It's supposed to be real silver."

"Why did you name it Chekhov?" Louise asked.

"Honestly, I don't know. It just came to me."

After getting undressed and into bed, the two lovers kissed each other on the lips.

"You have nothing to be afraid of when I'm with you," Louise said softly as they began to make love.

After waking up in the morning, Eugenie noticed that Louise seemed on edge.

"Is something wrong?" she asked.

"I had a strange dream. At least, I think it was a dream," Louise responded.

"What happened in it?" Eugenie asked.

"I sensed someone making love to me. At first, I assumed it was you, for it certainly felt like a woman. She was kissing my chest and my bosom, and kept one hand between my thighs, the other exploring me. I became very excited, and as I approached climax, I called out your name, but then, she suddenly stopped. That's when I first suspected that it might not be you, but, for some reason, I still couldn't bring myself to open my eyes. Then, I felt a sharp pain on my right breast, followed by the sensation that all my strength was deserting me. I felt light-headed. However, the sensation stopped after a few moments. I finally opened my eyes and there was a large black cat on top of me. I wanted to scream, but I couldn't, and... That is all I remember."

After finishing the story, Louise put her hand on her right breast and felt something. Eugenie looked and exclaimed:

"Two bite marks—like a vampire's! No, that can't be. There is no way that could have happened without me waking up."

"Right" Louise said. "They must be from a mosquito or something."

After they got dressed, Eugenie said, "I'll go see if there is a shop where I can buy something to help treat that."

"That's a good idea," Louise responded.

After Eugenie had been gone for a while, the door opened

"Did you find any..." Louise stopped herself as she saw that it was Rimcalla, not Eugenie, who had come into their room. "What are you doing here?" she asked.

Rimcalla answered, "I heard you were alone up here and figured you might like some company."

She closed the door behind her. Louise felt strangely uncomfortable, but was too polite to ask the other woman to leave.

Rimcalla walked slowly towards Louise. "You're quite beautiful," she said with a smile as she approached the Maiden.

"Thank you," Louise replied nervously.

Rimcalla, now standing directly in front of Louise, ran her fingers through the other woman's hair. "Such wonderful, golden hair you have," she said. But Louise didn't reply.

"Did you enjoy last night?" Rimcalla asked.

"What do you mean?" Louise whispered, frightened.

"Oh, you're assuming it was a dream, aren't you?" Rimcalla said, her hand now caressing Louise face rather than her hair.

Louise's eyes widened in shock. "You mean... That was you?"

Rimcalla smiled at her.

"I don't usually seek prey who have already tasted of the Garden of Sappho, but always ones I could sense yearned for it. I was taken aback when you called out Eugenie's name in ecstasy last night. So far, no girl has ever called out a man's name while I'm savoring them."

"You shouldn't do that to someone," Louise said, feeling very afraid.

Rimcalla licked her lips. "You were quite enjoying it, too," she said matter of factly.

"That doesn't make it right. I thought you were Eugenie, and I was clearly half-dreaming since you became..."

"A large cat?" Rimcalla interjected.

"How did you know?" Louise's fear was building.

"I think you've already figured it out," Rimcalla replied. Then, she moved her head, leaning forward towards Louise's neck.

"Stop," Louise begged, but Rimcalla didn't. She licked Louise's neck. Stunned and frightened, the Maiden was unable to move.

"Do you *really* want me to stop?" Rimcalla asked seductively, as she pressed her lips against the other woman's neck.

"What is going on in here" suddenly said a new voice.

Eugenie had just walked in. '

Louise, finally able to move from the shock, backed away from Rimcalla and muttered, "She... she's a v...v...vam..."

Eugenie quickly pulled out a crucifix and held it out in front of her. She advanced towards Rimcalla and said, "Get away from her!"

"Silly mortals," Rimcalla said.

She met Eugenie half-way and placed her hand on the crucifix. "Such silly catholic superstitions don't affect true children of the night." She then crushed it in her hand and smiled, revealing her extended canines.

Eugenie's eyes widened. Her mind could barely comprehend what was happening to them.

"Why would a lover of her own sex put any faith in Adonai anyway? Didn't he have some very strong things to say about us?" Rimcalla added. "Shouldn't the worship of Nephthys, or the Great Goddess Diana, suit us better?"

"You speak of Heathen rituals done in the worship of Moloch. And they were entirely about men. The Puritan attitude towards sex comes from Augustine and Plato, not the Bible. Paul dedicated his Epistle to the Romans to refute the Platonic attitudes of Hellenistic Judaism," Eugenie said, as she tried to buy herself some time to think of a plan.

"That's an interesting theory," Rimcalla said.

Then, she grabbed Eugenie by the neck. "You are also quite stunning, but I'm partial to blondes so I'm not going to claim you," she added, with an evil grin. "I'm just going to..."

Suddenly, Rimcalla let out a sharp scream. Louise d'Armilly had snuck up behind her and plunged Chekhov into her back.

The vampire woman let go of Eugenie and backed away. She reached behind her and pulled the dagger out of her back. She then hissed like a cat and dropped the blood-stained blade on the floor.

"Beelzebub has a devil put aside for me," Rimcalla said, and then she jumped through the window, shattering it. In the blink of an eye, she was gone.

Eugenie and Louise looked at each, stunned and silent for a few moments, then embraced each other.

Jed Puma & Tashi
("*A Dollar's Worth of Fists*")

Credits

Galazi in the Enchanted City

Starring:	Created by:
Galazi the Wolf	H. Rider Haggard
Queen Touloumia	Eugene Hennebert
Nomma	based on Marcel Griaule
Co-Starring:	
People of the Axe	H. Rider Haggard
Umslopogaas	H. Rider Haggard
Loubari	Eugene Hennebert
Mgoussa	Eugene Hennebert
Mousammouria	Eugene Hennebert
Minruth the Mad	Philip José Farmer
Hadon	Philip José Farmer
Kwasin	Philip José Farmer
Kohr	Philip José Farmer
Pag	H. Rider Haggard
Sahhindar	Philip José Farmer
Solomon Kane	Robert E. Howard
Rezu	H. Rider Haggard
N'desi	Christopher Paul Carey
Hareton Ironcastle	J.H. Rosny Aîné
Doc Ardan	Guy d'Armen/Lester Dent
The Wandarobo	John Peter Drummond
And:	
Kisimbasimba	Eugene Hennebert
Kôr	H. Rider Haggard
Crystal Basin/Crystal Tree	H. Rider Haggard, Philip José Farmer & Christopher Paul Carey
Grey Stone Sphere	H. Rider Haggard
Watcher of the Fords/U-nothlola-mazibuko	Bishop Henry Callaway
Groan-Maker/Inkosikaas/Iron Chieftainess	Robert E. Howard
Staff of Solomon	Book of Exodus & Robert E. Howard

Jason Scott AIKEN is a fantasy and horror author. He enjoys penning weird fiction and sword & sorcery tales. He chronicles the adventures of his red-haired swordswoman, Nuja of Lomar, in a sword & mythos setting in various fantasy and horror anthologies. Jason can be found online at *http://jasonscottaiken.com* and he's @jasonscottaiken on Twitter. This is his second contribution to *Tales of the Shadowmen.*

A Dollar's Worth of Fists

Starring:	Created by:
Gio	William Tunberg
	& Fred Freiberger
Regis	Al C. Ward
Colonel Bozzo-Corona	Paul Féval
Marchef	Paul Féval
The Black Coats	Paul Féval
Ming	Henri Vernes
The Shin Tan	Henri Vernes
Tong of the Avenging Dragon	Robert Schlitt
Tong of the Black Scorpion	Robert Holmes
Jed Puma	Carlo Cedroni & Enzo Magni
Tashi	Carlo Cedroni & Enzo Magni
Baby Brother (Bambino)	Enzo Barbone
The Shaolin (Kwai Chang Caine)	Ed Spielman
Sammy Wong	John Tomerlin
Shanghai Joe	Carlo Alberto Alfieri
	Mario Caiano
	& Fabrizio Trifone Trecca
Tiger	Franco Lattanzi
El Caballero Enmascarado de Plata	Rafael García Travesi
	& Fernando Osés
Co-Starring:	
Robur	Jules Verne
The Wing Kongs	Gary Goldman
	David Z. Weinstein
	& W. D. Richter
Also Starring:	
Louis Vigneron	
Arpin the Terrible	

Matthew BAUGH lives and works in Albuquerque, NM. He is the pastor of a small church and an editor for Permuted Press. He is also the author of *The Vampire Count of Monte-Cristo*, a mash-up of the classic story of adventure and revenge with vampires, ghosts and Faustian bargains, the co-author, with Win Scott Eckert, of *A Girl and Her Cat*, which continues the adventures of classic TV heroes, Honey West and T.H.E. Cat, and a regular contributor to *Tales of the Shadowmen*.

Harry's Homecoming

Starring:	Created by:
Harry Dickson	Anonymous
Doctor Ox	Jules Verne
Ichabod Chang	Harry Stephen Keeler
O. Ming Lee	Harry Stephen Keeler
Doctor Meirschultz	Hildegard Stadie
Li Shoon	H. Irving Hancock
Tom Wills	Anonymous
Co-Starring:	
Donald Carrick	H. Irving Hancock
Doc Ardan	Guy d'Armen
Tinker	W.J. Lomax
Dr. Alfred Carroll	Lawrence Meade
	& Arthur Hoerl
The Grisson Gang	James Hadley Chase
Burma Roberts	Hildegard Stadie
Sherlock Holmes	Arthur Conan Doyle
Hatteras	Jules Verne
Professor Flax	Louis Forest
Lindenbrock	Jules Verne
Captain Nemo	Jules Verne
Si-Fan	Sax Rohmer
Professor Moriarty	Arthur Conan Doyle
Doctor Quartz	Anonymous
Malaglou	Sax Rohmer
Pelton	Harry Stephen Keeler
Don Maxwell	Hildegarde Stadie
Dr. Thorkel	Tom Kilpatrick
Dr. Vornoff	Ed Wood
Murder Legendre	Garness Weston
Li Chang Yen	Agatha Christie
Hanoi Shan	Harry Ashton Wolfe
Dr. Natas	Guy d'Armen

Sexton Blake	Harry Blyth
And:	
Litan	Patrick Granier,
	Jean-Pierre Mocky
	& Jean-Claude Romer
Quiquendone	Jules Verne
Herakelophorbia	H.G. Wells
Taduki	H. Rider Haggard
Super-adrenaline	Hildegard Stadie

Adam Mudman BEZECNY has been writing for twelve years now, and still the nightmares come. His publications include the online sci-fi story *Dieselworld*, the trash-pulp Ramble House novel *Tail of the Lizard King*, and a forthcoming volume of stories from Airship 27 Productions starring pulp hero Jim Anthony. He is also the editor of *Odd Tales of Wonder Magazine*, where he tells the tale of his supernatural heroine Bloody Mary. This is his second contributor to *Tales of the Shadowmen*.

The Aquila Curse

Starring:	**Created by:**
Renaud de Montauban	Huon de Vlleneuve[1]
Sir Wilfred of Ivanhoe	Walter Scott
Etienne de Navarre	Edward Khmara
Isabeau d'Anjou	Edward Khmara
Bishop of Aquila	Edward Khmara
Maugis	Huon de Villeneuve
Philippe the Mouse	Edward Khmara
Imperius	Edward Khmara
Robin of Locksley	English folklore

Nicholas BOVING lives in Toronto. He was formerly a mining engineer and traveled the world widely. He also worked from time to time as a docker, fruit inspector and forester. His books and screenplays draw on these experiences to provide characters, backgrounds and scenes. He is the author and publisher of the *Maxim Gunn* series of action/adventure books. He has also written some fifteen other novels and screenplays which follow the central character to countries and places where the forces of nature as much as people provide the conflict. He is a regular contributor to *Tales of the Shadowmen*.

---

[1] While the characters of Renaud de Montauban, Maugis, etc. were first introduced in earlier 12th century *chansons*, their more popular and definitive version is generally attributed to Huon (or Hugues) de Villeneuve.

From Paris With Hate

Starring:	Created by:
Fantomas	Pierre Souvestre & Marcel Allain, revised by André Hunebelle, Jean Halain & Pierre Foucaud
Hubert Bonisseur de la Bath (OSS 117)	Jean Bruce
Armand Lesignac	Michel Hazanavicius
Eva Kant	Angela & Luciana Giussani
Diabolik	Angela & Luciana Giussani
Anthony Logan (Kriminal)	Max Bunker & Magnus
Co-Starring:	
Lupin III	Monkey Punch based on Maurice Leblanc
Dick Malloy (077)	Sandro Continenza, Marcello Coscia & Leonardo Martín
Inspector Clouseau	Maurice Richlin & Blake Edwards
Satanik	Max Bunker & Magnus
Killing	Ponzoni & Pietro Granelli
And:	
The Pink Panther	Maurice Richlin & Blake Edwards
The Village	Patrick McGoohan & George Markstein

Nathan CABANISS lives and works in Atlanta, GA. His stories have been published in English and in French in various publications, including *Fictionvale Magazine, Cranial Leakage, Vol. 1, Darkness Abound* and *The Vampire Almanac* from Black Coat Press. His weekly newsletter *Notices From The Abyss* serializes his continuing novel *Alamud Ahab & The Great White Werewolf*, and he is also the creator of the webcomic *The Life and Times of Stickman*, both available at his blog, *Girls, Guns & Cigarettes*. He is a regular contributor to *Tales of the Shadowmen*.

A Purpose in Life

Starring:	Created by:
Michael Myers	John Carpenter & Debra Hill

Colonel Bozzo-Corona	Paul Féval
The Marchef	Paul Féval
Co-Starring:	
Laurie Strode	John Carpenter & Debra Hill

Matthew DENNION lives in South Jersey with his beautiful wife and daughters. He currently works as a teacher of students with autism at a Special Services School. Matthew writes giant monster stories for *G-Fan* magazine and he has recently published three giant monster novels, *Chimera: Scourge of the Gods*, *Operation R.O.C.: A Kaiju Thriller* and *Atomic Rex*. He is a regular contributor to *Tales of the Shadowmen*.

The Berlin Vampire

Starring:	**Created by:**
Boris Liatoukine	Marie Nizet
Countess Marcian Grigoryi	Paul Féval
Von Bork	Arthur Conan Doyle
Control	John Le Carré
David Harker	based on Bram Stoker
Baroness Phryne	Paul Féval
Co-Starring:	
Sherlock Holmes	Arthur Conan Doyle
Dracula	Bram Stoker
M	Ian Fleming
Hunter	James Mitchell
And:	
Selene, the Sepulchre	Paul Féval

Brian GALLAGHER has a BA in Politics and Society and lives in London. He works in the media and for many years has written on the politics, economics and many other aspects of Croatia and has been quoted in Croatian and international media. In relation to that he has written extensively on Croatian-related cases at the International Criminal Tribunal for the Former Yugoslavia. He has always been interested in science fiction, classic horror, comics and is proud to be a lifelong *Doctor Who* fan. He is a regular contributor to *Tales of the Shadowmen*.

Rouletabille Rides the Horror Express

Starring:	**Created by:**
Joseph Rouletabille	Gaston Leroux
Professor Sir Alexander	Arnaud d'Usseau

Saxton	& Julian Zimet
Dr. James Wells	Arnaud d'Usseau
	& Julian Zimet
Sean O'Hagan	Arnaud d'Usseau
	& Julian Zimet
Miss Jones	Arnaud d'Usseau
	& Julian Zimet
Grashinski	Arnaud d'Usseau
	& Julian Zimet
Father Pujardov	Arnaud d'Usseau
	& Julian Zimet
Inspector Mirov	Arnaud d'Usseau
	& Julian Zimet
Maletero	Arnaud d'Usseau
	& Julian Zimet
Countess Irina Petrovski	Arnaud d'Usseau
	& Julian Zimet
Oleg Yevtushenko	Arnaud d'Usseau
	& Julian Zimet
Natasha	Arnaud d'Usseau
	& Julian Zimet
Conductor Konev	Arnaud d'Usseau
	& Julian Zimet
Count Marion Petrovski	Arnaud d'Usseau
	& Julian Zimet
The Ice Creature	Arnaud d'Usseau
	& Julian Zimet
Captain Kazan	Arnaud d'Usseau
	& Julian Zimet

Co-Starring:

General Trebassof	Gaston Leroux
Sherlock Holmes	Arthur Conan Doyle
The Devil Doctor	Sax Rohmer

Also Starring:
Jack the Ripper

Martin GATELY is the author of the official prequel to Philip José Farmer's first novel, *The Green Odyssey* (*Samdroo and the Grassman* in *The Worlds of Philip José Farmer 4 – Voyages to Strange Days*). His writing career commenced in 1988 when he wrote for D C Thomson's legendary *Starblazer* comicbook. He is also a contributor to the UK's journal of strange phenomena *Fortean Times*. For Black Coat Press, he has provided stories for the following anthologies: *Night of the Nyctalope, Harry Dickson Vs. The Spider* and *The Vampire*

Almanac Vol. 1, as well as the "Rouletabille Nemo-Cycle" for Tales of the Shadowmen. His story, *The Roebuck Cabal,* which features Harry Dickson, appears in *The Mammoth Book of Jack the Ripper Stories* which was published by Little, Brown and Company. He is a regular contributor to *Tales of the Shadowmen.*

The Goat of Saint Elster

Starring:	Created by:
Quentin Moretus Cassave	Jean Ray
Brom Cromwell	Micah Harris
Frater John	Micah Harris
The Barbusquin Order	Jean Ray
The Blind Dead	Armando de Ossorio
The Oyarsa	C.S. Lewis
The Protective Force	William Hope Hodgson
The Great God Pan	Arthur Machen
The Hogge	William Hope Hodgson
The Ab-Human	William Hope Hodgson
Ubbo-Sathla	Clark Ashton Smith
The Dark Archon	C.S. Lewis
Co-Starring:	
Philarète	Jean Ray
Madame de Saint-Ange	Marquis de Sade
Sigsand	William Hope Hodgson
Natvilcius	C.S. Lewis

Micah S. HARRIS is the 2016 Pulp Ark Award winner in the category of best novel *for Ravenwood, the Stepson of Mystery: Return of the Dugpa.* He is also the author with artist Michael Gaydosof the graphic novel *Heaven's War*, a historical fantasy pitting the Oxford Inklings against Aleister Crowley. His most recent publications are the mystery novel *Murder in the Miracle Room* and an in-depth article, published in *Little Shoppe of Horrors*, on the "lost" sword and sorcery movie of the early 1980s, *Thongor in the Valley of Demons*. His out-of-print *The Eldritch New Adventures of Becky Sharp* recently became available again as an e-book. His other publications include *The Frequency of Fear* (also available as an electronic book), *Jim Anthony: the Hunters* (with Joshua Reynolds) the Image Comic book *Lorna, Relic Wrangler* (with artist Loston Wallace) and his short fiction collection, *Slouching Toward Camulodunum*. He is a regular contributor to *Tales of the Shadowmen.*

The Island of Exodus

Starring:	Created by:
Andoche	Albert Robida
Moderan	Albert Robida
Professor Cabrol	Albert Robida
Barlotin	Albert Robida
Melanie	Albert Robida
Babylas the cat	Albert Robida
Phanor the dog	Albert Robida
The People of the Pole	Charles Derennes
The Wandering Jew	Paul Féval
And:	
The Aerochalet	Albert Robida

Travis HILTZ started making up stories at a young age. Years later, he began writing them down. In high school, he discovered that some writers actually got paid and decided to give it a try. He has since gathered a modest collection of rejection letters and had a one-act play produced. Travis lives in the wilds of New Hampshire with his very loving and tolerant wife, two above average children and a staggering amount of comic books and *Doctor Who* novels. He is a regular contributor to *Tales of the Shadowmen*.

As Easy as 1, 2, 3...

Starring:	Created by:
Dejah Thoris	Edgar Rice Burroughs
John Carter	Edgar Rice Burroughs
Jean Saint-Clair	Jean de La Hire
Co-Starring:	
Tars Tarkas	Edgar Rice Burroughs
Jason Gridley	Edgar Rice Burroughs
Carthoris	Edgar Rice Burroughs
Tara	Edgar Rice Burroughs
Tardids	Edgar Rice Burroughs
Also Starring:	
Nikola Tesla	
Kolman Czito	

Paul HUGLI has a degree in Zoology, and has written for everything from *Cracked* magazine to general interest pamphlets, and for most of the first, second *and* third tier adult magazines. He is the author of three published "adult fantasy" novels, and the acclaimed *Traci Lords Companion*. He has also been employed as a science/math instructor, and as a "Floor Manager" at a local "Gentleman's Club." In addition, he once owned/managed Destiny Bookstore, which dealt in SciFi, comics and adult "fantasy" magazines, for 30 years. He now has three novels in the works. He is a regular contributor to *Tales of the Shadowmen*.

Eve of Perfection, Eve of Destruction

Starring:	Created by:
Paula Hest	Rick Lai
Wolfgang Krampft	Marcel Allain
Eva Bjelke	Rick Lai
The Deathless One	August Derleth,
(Khosatral Khel)	Mark Schorer
	& Robert E. Howard
The Black Coats	Paul Féval
Fantômas (The Pallid Mask)	Pierre Souvestre
	& Marcel Allain
Malbodius (Dr. Mabuse)	Norbert Jacques
Hugo Howey	Arthur Bernède
	& Louis Feuillade
Colonel Bozzo-Corona	Paul Féval
(The All-Father)	
Jacques Mabuse	Norbert Jacques
Madame Sara	L. T. Meade
	& Robert Eustace
Noel Moriarty	Arthur Conan Doyle

Co-Starring:	
Sherlock Holmes	Arthur Conan Doyle
Irene Adler	Arthur Conan Doyle
Chupin Detective Agency	Emile Gaboriau
Irina Putine	Rick Lai
Slumbering Kraken	Abraham Merritt
Odin (The Grey Man)	Robert E. Howard
The Elder Gods	August Derleth
Louis La Rothière	Arthur Conan Doyle
Rosita Bianchini	Arthur Bernède
	& Louis Feuillade
Countess Hermine	Maurice Leblanc
Phantom of Truth	Robert W. Chambers
Rambert	Pierre Souvestre
	& Marcel Allain

Secret Raiders	Arthur Bernède
	& Louis Feuillade
Sabine Balsamo	Rick Lai
Professor James Moriarty	Arthur Conan Doyle
Antonio Nikola	Guy Boothby
Lars Bjelke	Rick Lai
Professor Lindenbrock	Jules Verne
Professor Aronnax	Jules Verne
Cumal O'Brien	Robert E. Howard
Star-headed aliens	H.P. Lovecraft
Cthulhu	H.P. Lovecraft
Also Starring:	
Kaiser Wilhelm II	
Per Henrik Ling	
And:	
The Green Abyss	C. Hall Thompson
The King in Yellow	Robert W. Chambers
Rachë-Churân	Sax Rohmer
The Cult of the All-Father	Rick Lai
Eve of Perfection	Rick Lai
Elder Sign	August Derleth
Omidom	David C. Smith
Deminderon Scrolls	David C. Smith
Macedonia	Jack London
Bridewall Press	Robert E. Howard

Rick LAI is an authority on pulp fiction and the Wold Newton Universe concepts of Philip José Farmer. His speculative articles have been collected in *Rick Lai's Secret Histories: Daring Adventurers, Rick Lai's Secret Histories: Criminal Masterminds, Chronology of Shadows: A Timeline of The Shadow's Exploits* and *The Revised Complete Chronology of Bronze*. Rick's fiction has been collected in *Shadows of the Opera, Shadows of the Opera: Retribution in Blood* and *Sisters of the Shadows: The Cagliostro Curse* (the last two titles are available from Black Coat Press). He has also translated Arthur Bernède's *Judex* and *The Return of Judex* into English for Black Coat Press. Rick resides in Bethpage, New York, with his wife and children. He is a regular contributor to *Tales of the Shadowmen*.

Maximum Speed

Starring:	**Created by:**
Dr. John H. Watson	Arthur Conan Doyle
Monsieur Lecoq	Emile Gaboriau

Constable Japp	Agatha Christie
Inspector Lestrade	Arthur Conan Doyle
Bartholomew Daniels	Nigel Malcolm
Loveday Brooke	Catherine Louisa Pirkis
Albert Marple	Nigel Malcolm
Jane Marple	Agatha Christie
Josephine Balsamo	Maurice Leblanc
Simon Carne	Guy Boothby
Co-Starring:	
Sherlock Holmes	Arthur Conan Doyle
Professor Moriarty	Arthur Conan Doyle
Ebenezer Dyer	Catherine Louisa Pirkis

Nigel MALCOLM lives in Kent, England. He works as a teacher of English as a Foreign Language. He is a long-term *Doctor Who*, *Star Trek* and *Prisoner* fan—long before all the new-fangled versions came along. He is still working on that elusive steampunk novel and various short stories. He is a regular contributor to *Tales of the Shadowmen*.

Bad Alchemy

Starring:	**Created by:**
Ludwig von Frankenstein	Christofer Nigo
	based on Mary Shelley
Julianne von Frankenstein	Christofer Nigro
The Genie of the Black Rock	Charles Nodier,
	Antoine Béraud
	& Jean Toussaint-Merle
Zam	Charles Nodier,
	Antoine Béraud
	& Jean Toussaint-Merle
Charles	J. Searle Dawley
Co-Starring:	
Zametti	Charles Nodier,
	Antoine Béraud
	& Jean Toussaint-Merle
Charles Victor von Frankenstein	J. Searle Dawley
Septimus Pretorius	William Hurlbut
	& John L. Balderston
Victor von Frankenstein	Mary Shelley
Janskin	Charles Nodier,
	Antoine Béraud

	& Jean Toussaint-Merle
Cecilia	Charles Nodier,
	Antoine Béraud
	& Jean Toussaint-Merle
Lord George	August Nodnagel
The Dragon	August Nodnagel
Also Starring:	
Conrad Dippel	
Paracelsus	
Johann Ferdinand von Kufstein	
And:	
Black Sarcophagus	Charles Nodier,
	Antoine Béraud
	& Jean Toussaint-Merle

Christofer NIGRO is a writer of both fiction and non-fiction with a strong interest in pulps, comic books and fantastic cinema, and a regular contributor to *Tales of the Shadowmen*. He may be known to some by his websites *The Godzilla Saga* and *The Warrenverse*, as he is an authority on the subject of *dai kaiju eiga* (the sub-genre of cinema specializing in giant monsters), and the characters featured in the comic magazines published by Warren. He has recently revived and expanded Chuck Loridans' classic site MONSTAAH, and has since been published in the anthologies *Aliens Among Us* and *Carnage: After the Fall*. He is a regular contributor to *Tales of the Shadowmen*.

Time to Kill

Starring:	**Created by:**
Bob Morane	Henri Vernes
Bill Ballantine	Henri Vernes
André Durand-Mareuil	Jean Girault & Louis Sapin
Jules Maigret	Georges Simenon
The Carrigans	John Peel
Co-Starring:	
Janvier	Georges Simenon
Professor Hunter	Henri Vernes
And:	
Royale-les-Eaux	Ian Fleming

John PEEL was born in Nottingham, England, and started writing stories at age 10. John moved to the U.S. in 1981 to marry his pen-pal. He, his wife ("Mrs. Peel") and their 13 dogs now live on Long Island, New York. John has written just over 100 books to date, mostly for young adults. He is the only author to have written novels based on both *Doctor Who* and *Star Trek*. His most popular work is *Diadem*, a fantasy series; he has written ten volumes to date. He is a regular contributor to *Tales of the Shadowmen*.

The Taking of Frankenstein

Starring:	Created by:
Gouroull	Jean-Claude Carrière
	based on Mary Shelley
Wu Fang	Robert J. Hogan
Dr. Maurice Xavier	William J. Makin
Co-Starring:	
Victor Frankenstein	Mary Shelley
Dr. Yen Sin	Donald E. Keyhoe
Val Kildare	Robert J. Hogan
Michael Traile	Donald E. Keyhoe

Frank SCHILDINER has been a pulp fan since a friend gave him a gift of Philip Jose Farmer's *Tarzan Alive*. Since that time he has written his first novel with Black Coat Press, *The Quest of Frankenstein*, with a sequel, *The Triumph of Frankenstein*, due out next year. Frank has been published in *The New Adventures of Thunder Jim Wade*, *Secret Agent X* Volumes 3, 4, 5, *Ravenwood, Stepson of Mystery*, *The Black Bat Mystery*, *Pride of the Mohicans*, *The New Adventures of Richard Knight* and *The Avenger: The Justice Files*. Frank works as a martial arts instructor at Amorosi's Mixed Martial Arts. He resides in New Jersey with his wife Gail who is his top supporter. He is a regular contributor to *Tales of the Shadowmen*.

Bringer of the Outer Dark

Starring:	Created by:
Hareton Ironcastle	J.-H. Rosny *Aîné*
Francis Xavier Gordon (El Borak)	Robert E. Howard
Frank Chandler (Chandu)	Harry Earnshaw,
	& R. R. Morgan
	& Vera Oldham
Dracula	Bram Stoker
The Mi-Go	H.P. Lovecraft
Sâr Dubnotal	Norbert Sevestre
Annunciata Gianetti	Norbert Sevestre
Haz'El	based on Hazel Heald
	& H. P. Lovecraft

Aeon	based on Hazel Heald & H. P. Lovecraft
Co-Starring:	
Nadji	Harry Earnshaw, & R. R. Morgan & Vera Oldham
Muriel Ironcastle	J.-H. Rosny *Aîné*
Sydney Guthrie	J.-H. Rosny *Aîné*
Philippe de Maranges	J.-H. Rosny *Aîné*
Prof. William Channing Webb	H.P. Lovecraft
The Gun Club	Jules Verne
Yig	Zelia Bishop & H.P. Lovecraft
Shub-Niggurath	H.P. Lovecraft
T'Yog	Hazel Heald & H.P. Lovecraft
The Dark Outer Gods	H.P. Lovecraft & Robert E. Howard
The King in Yellow	Robert W. Chambers
Azathoth	H.P. Lovecraft
Yog-Sothoth	H.P. Lovecraft
The Lord of Spiders	Stephen King
The Crawling Chaos	H.P. Lovecraft
Set	Robert E. Howard
Professor Van Helsing	Bram Stoker
And:	
The Staff of Solomon	Robert E. Howard
Yuggoth	H.P. Lovecraft
Opar	Edgar Rice Burroughs
The Deplorable Word	C.S. Lewis

Sam SHOOK is a 21 year old university student majoring in creative writing, and he would not be caught dead without a nice outfit and a hat. An actor, fencer, singer, and panpipe player, he has always been a bit different from the rest of his friends in Oklahoma (though he prefers the term "eccentric" over "ridiculous"). From the days his parents would read to him, to now diving into *The Dark Tower* series, old pulps, classic literature, and, of course, *Tales of the Shadowmen*, he has always loved a good yarn. The only other thing he enjoys as much is telling tales. Having been creating stories from a young age for the entertainment of himself and others, he used those simple adventures to hone his skills, and he decided to make a career out of it. He is a regular contributor to *Tales of the Shadowmen*.

One Summer Night at Holy Cross

Starring:	Created by:
Bob Morane	Henri Vernes
Harry Callahan	Harry Julian
	& R.M. Fink

Co-Starring:	
Bill Ballantine	Henri Vernes
Fred	Michel Stéphan
Also Starring:	
Bela Lugosi	

Michel STEPHAN was born and lives in Brittany with his wife and two children. He has been a fan of science fiction, fantasy and horror since age 10. He loves Universal monster movies (especially the *Frankenstein* series), sci-fi serials and collects Aurora model kits. He has recently written new *Madame Atomos* novels for Black Coat Press's French sister imprint, Rivière Blanche, and is a regular contributor to *Tales of the Shadowmen*.

The Moon of the White Wolf

Starring:	Created by:
John Silence	Algernon Blackwood
Father Brown	G.K. Chesterton
Arsène Lupin (Don Luis Perenna)	Maurice Leblanc
Bulldog Drummond	H.C. McNeile
Sir John Talbot	Curt Siodmak
Lawrence Talbot	Curt Siodmak
Maleva	Curt Siodmak
Mack the Knife	Kurt Weill
	& Bertolt Brecht

Co-Starring:	
Colonel Nielson	M.C. McNeile
Gwen Conliffe	Curt Siodmak
Bela	Curt Siodmak
Jenny Williams	Curt Siodmak
Dr. Lloyd	Curt Siodmak
Colonel Montfort	Curt Siodmak
Dr. Jekyll	R.L. Stevenson
Flambeau	G.K. Chesterton
Fantômas	Pierre Souvestre
	& Marcel Allain

The Vampires	Louis Feuillade
Carl Peterson	H.C. McNeile
Mr. King of Limehouse	Sax Rohmer

David L. VINEYARD is a fifth generation Texan (named for his gunfighter/Texas Ranger great grand-father) currently living in Oklahoma City, OK, where the tornadoes come sweeping down the plains. He has useless degrees in history, politics, and economics, and is the author of several tales about Buenos Aires private eye Johnny Sleep, two novels, several short stories, some journalism, and various non-fiction. He is currently working on several ideas while battling with a three month old kitten for household dominance and the keyboard of his PC. He is a regular contributor to *Tales of the Shadowmen*.

Styrian Rhapsody

Starring:	**Created by:**
Eugenie Danglars	Alexandre Dumas
Louise d'Armilly	Alexandre Dumas
Father Rodin	Eugène Sue
Mircalla Karnstein (Rimcalla)	Sheridan Le Fanu
Co-Starring:	
Tenebre Brothers	Paul Féval
The Legend of the Ghoul Addhema and the Vampire of Szandor	Paul Féval
Hans Spurzheim	Paul Féval
Count of Monte-Cristo	Alexandre Dumas
Marquis of Rio Santo	Paul Féval
Lord Ruthven	J.W. Polidori
Gandin	Wolfram von Eschenbach
Galoes	Wolfram von Eschenbach
Gahmuret	Wolfram von Eschenbach
Lammire	Wolfram von Eschenbach
Ither	Wolfram von Eschenbach
Countess Dolingen of Gratz	Bram Stoker
Baron Vordenberg	Sheridan Le Fanu
Wagner the Werewolf	George Reynolds
Johann Faust	*Anonymous*
Also Starring:	
Lord Byron	
Clovis	

Jared WELCH lives in Racine, WI. He is a fan of *Pretty Little Liars*, DC Comics, Paul Féval, Alexandre Dumas, *Annie On My Mind* and *Good Moon Rising* by Nancy Garden, The Animes *Pokemon*, *Sailor Moon*, *Noir*, *Madlax*, *Code Geass*, *Death Note*, *Revolutionary Girl Utena*, *Rose of Versailles*, and the *Star Wars* prequels. He is currently working on a few plays, novels and has blogs online where he discusses various topics under the name JaredMithrandir. He is a regular contributor to *Tales of the Shadowmen*.

WATCH OUT FOR

TALES OF THE
SHADOWMEN
VOLUME 14: COUP DE GRACE
TO BE RELEASED DECEMBER 2017

Bob Morane & Bill Ballantine
("*Time to Kill*")

www.ingramcontent.com/pod-product-compliance
Lightning Source LLC
Chambersburg PA
CBHW060431030726
47495CB00003B/838